PARTY

Karen Swan is the *Sunday Times* top three bestselling author of sixteen books and her novels sell all over the world. She writes two books each year – one for the summer period and one for the Christmas season. Previous winter titles include *Christmas at Tiffany's*, *The Christmas Secret*, *The Christmas Lights*, and for summer, *The Rome Affair*, *The Greek Escape* and *The Spanish Promise*.

Her books are known for their evocative locations and Karen sees travel as vital research for each story. She loves to set deep, complicated love stories within twisty plots, sometimes telling two stories in the same book.

Previously a fashion editor, she lives in Sussex with her husband, three children and two dogs.

Visit Karen's author page on Facebook, follow her on Twitter @KarenSwan1, on Instagram @swannywrites, and her website www.karenswan.com.

Also by Karen Swan

Players
Prima Donna
Christmas at Tiffany's
The Perfect Present
Christmas at Claridge's
The Summer Without You
Christmas in the Snow
Summer at Tiffany's
Christmas on Primrose Hill
The Paris Secret
Christmas Under the Stars
The Rome Affair
The Christmas Secret
The Greek Escape
The Christmas Lights
The Spanish Promise

The CHRISTMAS PARTY

KAREN SWAN

PAN BOOKS

First published 2019 by Pan Books
an imprint of Pan Macmillan
The Smithson, 6 Briset Street, London EC1M 5NR
Associated companies throughout the world
www.panmacmillan.com

ISBN 978-1-5290-0606-3

1 3 5 7 9 8 6 4 2

A CIP catalogue record for this book is available from the British Library.

Typeset by Palimpsest Book Production Ltd, Falkirk, Stirlingshire
Printed and bound by CPI Group (UK) Ltd, Croydon, CR0 4YY

For Jo Nana
A donkey on the edge with me.

Prologue

The letter slipped from the book like a leaf falling from a tree, silent as a yacht peeling from its mooring and gliding out across the water. Defiantly free.

She stared at it. The writing was familiar and yet she couldn't place it. The uppermost edge of the envelope was jagged from where it had been ripped open in haste, the swirl of the 'e' at the end of the name bleeding softly into the vellum. A drip of champagne perhaps? Or a teardrop?

It was just a letter and yet the instinct quivered through her that there was weight in its tucked-away words. Like a doe in the grass, she sensed a threat she could not yet see. An innocuous moment had suddenly turned critical and now everything pivoted on what would come next. Breath held and still, she ran her eyes over the script, seeing at once that the game was already in play, understanding that she had already lost. Like the doe, she had only one viable choice.

Run.

Chapter One

Tuesday, 26 November 2019
Lorne Castle, Kilmally, Ireland

'Nobility is nothing but ancient riches!'

'Oh Christ, he's pissed,' Pip whispered in her ear as Ottie arched a sceptical eyebrow, their father's voice echoing around the galleried hall.

'Yes, you heard me right, to be sure you did,' Declan Lorne insisted. 'Devil be damned, it means no more to me than the socks on my feet.' As if to prove the point, he shook off one of his velvet slippers – embroidered with the family crest in gold thread – to reveal his pale big toe poking through the end of a red sock. A murmur of shocked amusement rippled through the crowd.

'Dec,' his wife quietly admonished him with a despairing, ladylike shake of her head. 'Those were new too.'

The murmur broke into a skitter of guffaws as he looked around delightedly at the gathering of friends and family who'd made the tricky and somewhat arduous trek to be here. Save for the villagers and those arriving by helicopter, it was an hour drive from Cork airport, with half of that spent on single-track lanes, navigating slow-moving dairy herds and bridging fords.

'It's important I make the point, my beloved,' he said, looking over at her with fiercely loving eyes. 'I don't want a single person in this room to leave here tonight thinking I give two hoots about the damned title stopping here with me. I don't. God gave us three wild, precociously talented, beautiful daughters and I wouldn't change a one of them for some name.'

'He definitely would have traded me in after that time I cleaned his gun with Vaseline,' Pip whispered, leaning in again and jogging her with an elbow.

'If he could have caught you,' Ottie replied, grinning at the memory. 'You slept in the boathouse for two nights, I seem to remember.'

Pip waggled her strong dark eyebrows, a mischievous glint in her green eyes. With her ragged auburn crop, constellation of freckles and rangy boyish frame, she looked like an overgrown leprechaun contemplating wreaking havoc. 'Aye, and by the time I skulked back, he was so relieved to see me, he'd forgotten why I ran in the first place.'

'You always could twist him round your little finger,' Ottie tutted.

'Ha!' Pip scoffed. 'That was one of my rare successes. *You* got away with murder.'

'Me?' Ottie hissed back, scandalized.

'Don't play the innocent,' Pip grinned. 'You've always been his favourite. The firstborn. Little Miss Perfect.'

The smile faded on Ottie's face. She knew exactly what she was and it wasn't that. The champagne-fuelled light in her eyes dimmed as she watched her father holding out his arm, their mother slipping into the crook of it like a silken fox. He kissed her on the cheek to a chorus of 'aaahs' – this was, after all, their thirtieth wedding anniversary party, and amongst their peers, theirs was *the* great love story: still in love after all these years.

'Be in no doubt that without Serena by my side, I would have ruined meself years ago. She has been both my guiding light and my anchor these past t'irty years. I'm not an easy man to be married to, I'll grant you that, but she's kept me on the straight and narrow, all the while bringing the castle back to life and making it a home for our three beautiful girls.'

He looked up, his gaze casting around the double-height great hall finding first her and then Pip. 'Jeesht, would you just look at them? The finest beauties in all the land,' he said proudly.

A cheer of agreement went up and Pip groaned loudly as Ottie rolled her eyes. 'Oh God, his cup always runneth over when his glass runneth over,' Pip muttered beneath a forced smile.

'Aye, I am the luckiest of men to have been blessed with the four women in my life. But—' He paused dramatically, scanning the audience. He always had been able to work the crowd. 'But I'll put my hand up to it, I didn't always know that.' Ottie looked up, startled by the frank admission, and found he was looking directly at her; to her amazement, the usual merry dance in his eyes was now but a tiptoe. 'But I do now. By Jove, I know it now.'

She felt the thick walls of the castle fall away, the colourful party fading to white as he held her gaze, his eyes saying more than his words . . .

'And many of you I know have noticed that our wee Willow couldn't make it here tonight.' His voice faltered fractionally, losing its customary skip and bounce. 'It goes without saying that she is missed. More than she'll ever know.'

Beside her, Pip stiffened, drawing in a deep breath. What was this – a confessional? But after another moment, he looked away from the two of them again, reconnecting with his guests and bringing that familiar jig back into his eyes. This was a party after all!

'But she's got commitments that must come first,' he said, airily hopping over their sea of secrets like it was a puddle. '. . . Work. The *big* social life in Dublin. After all, let's be honest, why the hell would she want to come all the way back here to make small talk with a bunch of old farts like us?'

A roar of laughter met his words.

'Face it, my friends, we are over the hill! *But* at least we're all still on this hill together.'

'Hear! Hear!' Several cries went up.

Declan laughed, his ruddy cheeks flushed brighter than ever. 'So I want to thank you all for making the no-doubt epic trip to join us here tonight, and I'll finish by raising several toasts to the women in my life. To my *darling* wife, Serena –'

'To Serena!' cried the raucous room as her mother gave one of her most enigmatic smiles. She had kept her figure and her looks and was used to being the centre of attention.

'To my beloved girls who are here: Ottie and Pip.'

'To Ottie and Pip!'

'And though she be not here, she is not forgotten – to my little bird who has flown the nest, Willow.'

'To Willow!'

Ottie arched an eyebrow and clinked her glass against Pip's, their eyes meeting in rueful silence. 'To Willow.'

The same night, Croke Park, Dublin

Willow closed her eyes, feeling the deep vibrations thrum through her chest, making even her ribs buzz. She had her arms in the air, her head tipped back as she joined the rest of the crowd in singing at the tops of their voices. She swore that if the sky was a lid upon the earth, it would have been blown off by the sheer energy radiating from this stadium: laser strobes criss-crossed the night sky, the white dots of tens of thousands of phone cameras swaying in unison. On stage, graphics flashed on three-storey screens, and though the band were but pinpricks from her distant spot up in the gods, the state-of-the-art acoustics brought Bono's voice to her ear as clearly as if he'd been standing beside her.

But it wasn't these accoutrements of a slick, multimillion-euro roadshow that was making the hairs stand upright on her arms – it was the intensity of being completely in sync with eighty thousand other people; sharing in one moment being multiplied and amplified eighty thousand times over. *This* was what it was to be alive, to belong. It was the high she was constantly chasing. Her drug.

Beside her, Caz was jumping up and down on the spot, one arm punching the cold November night air as she sang – shouted, really – as loudly as she could. She was wearing just a T-shirt with her jeans but somehow temperature became irrelevant when the lights flashed on and the first strum of bass guitar reverberated through the amps. Caz's long blonde hair swung from side to side, the small swallow tattoo at the base of her neck playing peek-a-boo, the multiple hoops in her left ear flashing in the lights. She stopped jumping up and down mid-lyric to take another greedy gulp of her beer, and

Willow chuckled at her friend's astonished and then outraged look as she found that her glass was nigh-on empty, completely oblivious that most of the pint was now on her boots and on the ground. She looked across at Willow with surprise.

'I'll go get us some more!' Willow hollered in her ear, taking the glass from her hand.

'No! It's my turn!' Caz shouted back.

'I know, but I need the loo anyway,' she shrugged.

Caz beamed delightedly and gave her the thumbs-up. 'Well, okay then!' She was an uncomplicated soul, not given to false modesty or tricksy politics. What you saw was what you got with Caz and it was what made their flat-share so fun and easy: there were never any arguments about who'd finished the houmous or forgotten to buy milk, no passive-aggressive comments about the mismatched shoes strewn over the floors or jeans left wet in the machine for days. Caz had a 'shoot from the hip' frankness to her that Willow not just admired, but needed: Be real. Be authentic. Be fucking honest.

Taking both their plastic glasses, Willow skipped down the steps towards the exit, past the stewards and into the pits encircling the stadium. It was still busy down there – people dashing to the toilets, the bars, queuing for the merchandise stalls. Willow took one weary look at the stationary line filing out of the Ladies and decided she could wait till she got home.

She headed to the nearest bar instead. It was still three deep, although that was better than the twenty-strong depth before the band had come on. Well used to the drill, she scanned the crowd for signs of weakness, looking for the loose link in the chain, and slipped into a gap that suddenly opened up on the far right side. Only one back from the front.

She felt the impatient mass jostle and immediately close behind her as the breach was discovered a moment too late. She stood firm and pushed her elbows out slightly, trying to take up more space. The guy in front of her was being served and she stood patiently, trying to catch the barman's eye as he went to and fro, pulling pints. Willow wondered how the guy was going to carry them all back without a tray; there had to be at least six.

The back of the bar was mirrored and as she waited, she caught sight of her own reflection. There was a momentary time lag before recognition. It was odd – startling even – to suddenly glimpse herself in the crowd, to see herself as a stranger did – the thick, shaggy, almost-black hair which had always made her stand apart now roughly cut to her shoulders, eyeliner like a tattoo around her glacial blue eyes, her pale narrow face and full mouth, multiple earrings in her left ear, black 'hot lips' T-shirt from last year's Rolling Stones summer tour here. Even without being able to see the buckled boots and tight black jeans, she looked pleasingly 'rock chick', which was the whole idea. No one would ever guess she was a knight's daughter.

The guy in front, having paid up, splayed his fingers wide, precariously clutching three pints in each hand, and everyone immediately around him took a half-step back, not wanting his beers to be spilled down their fronts as he slowly turned.

Willow dipped slightly, turning herself sideways around him so that he could move into her space, and she his. Immediately the crowd shifted and swelled forwards towards the gap again, like hot oil spreading in a pan, but she was nimble and slim and well practised in the art of getting served.

'Hi,' she grinned, lunging into the spot and making immediate and direct eye contact with the barman, leaning both her elbows on the bar so that she was on tiptoes. The counter was sticky and wet but she didn't care.

'Hey, what can I do you for?' he asked with an interested tone, angling himself in towards her to hear over the rabble.

'Four pints, please,' she said to his ear. She wasn't going to queue again.

He nodded, turning to make eye contact again. 'Coming right up.'

Willow gave a pleased grin as she looked up and down the bar. It was an unfair fact of life, but pretty girls always got served first, legions of burly, grumpy men standing behind her with arms outstretched on the bar – trying to physically claim a place – tenners stuffed in their fists.

She looked in the mirror again, checking her reflection, and saw someone further along was watching her – a guy with a buzz-cut, a razor slash through his right eyebrow. He looked edgy. A little dangerous. She immediately smiled at him and his chin lifted fractionally in return. Acknowledgement of the moment. Confirmation of the attraction.

Willow looked away again but she couldn't stop the grin from stretching across her lips. This would be interesting. He was two back from the front of the queue, a couple of guys now jostling behind him. Would he forsake his place to catch her on the way past? Was he interested enough? Was she?

Her phone buzzed in her jeans pocket and she reached back for it. Caz wanting her to get some crisps? She always got the munchies after beer.

'Yeah?' she shouted, her eyes returning to the barman as he came back with the pints.

'Willow?'

She hesitated at the voice: unheard for so long, and yet so familiar too. '*Ottie?*'

'Jeesht, where are you?' her sister asked, raising her voice to be heard.

'Out,' Willow said, more snappishly than she'd intended.

But it was a shock having her past suddenly step back into her present like this. 'What is it?'

'You need to get back here.'

'Twelve euros,' the barman said to her. She looked at him blankly. Suddenly, there was too much happening at once. 'I . . .' She patted her jeans, remembering the twenty in her pocket. The barman had his hand out waiting, all the other outstretched and bunched fists tapping impatiently, waiting for their turn. Even pretty girls could only get away with so much at a bar this busy. She handed over the note with a frown. 'No.' Her response was simple and brutal because it was brutally simple: she would never go back.

'Willow, please, it's urgent.' Ottie's voice sounded strained, like a length of yarn that had been untwisted and stripped apart. 'You need to get home as soon as you can.'

'Otts, I'm sorry, but I've said no.' She held out her hand as the barman handed her back the change, his gaze already on the next punter, her temporary hold on him gone again. 'That's my answer. I'm not going to—'

'It's Dad!' Ottie burst out. 'He's dying.'

What?

The music switched to silence, the press of the crowd suddenly falling away, gravity loosening its hold upon her. She felt light, spectral.

Down the other end of the line, 180 miles away in Cork, Ottie burst into tears, her sobs wretched. 'He's not going to last the night,' she gasped, struggling to speak, to push words past the tears. 'Please, Willow. You've got to come home.'

Her fingers tightened around the wheel as she tore passed the sign that signified she was officially back on home turf: *Welcome to Lorne. Please drive slowly through our village.*

No chance.

It was the middle of the night now, the populous stars studding the sky like a wedding tent threaded with tea lights, drawing the eye ever upwards. Her car's main beam was the only light to be had: the street lamps were off at this witching hour and there wasn't a light on in a single house as she sped past in her battered, albeit trusty black Golf. Her gaze swept over the village green and the silhouetted low-slung cottages that fringed it, the blue and white awning of the Stores now rolled back in, the fruit and veg crates carried in from the pavement for the night.

Nothing ever changed here – well, only by single degrees. The Hare might debut a new pub sign, or a flag might fly from the short stubby tower of the church in the far corner on a saint's day, but that was the extent of it. She could point to exactly which oaks would be circled by snowdrops in January and primroses in April; she could recall word for word the dedication on the brass plaque on the bench by the pond; no doubt the gum she had stuck to the underside of the slide in the playground aged thirteen was still in situ too.

She looked left as she raced past the church and the graveyard, where so many of her ancestors now slept in eternal peace. Her eye caught sight of the large mossed stone angel on the central tomb, head bowed and hands pressed together in prayer. But instead of reassuring her of God's grace, as it was supposed to, its unseeing eyes had always given Willow nightmares as a girl and she could never pass it without a shiver. Perhaps she had just never believed *enough*. Perhaps she had always been a cynic.

She bombed out of the village and along the narrow lane where the plane trees reached towards one another and touched fingers overhead. She had used to love cycling beneath them on the way home, her bike wheeling through the pools of golden evening light that somehow managed to penetrate the dense canopies, pigeons and chaffinches calling from the branches. Whenever she thought of home, which wasn't often these days, this arched view through the tree tunnel was one of the most wistful – and certainly one of the better ones – that came to mind.

Home.

She could see it already now: the grand stone pillars topped with the flying eagles, the ornate black ironwork gates pinned back as though in readiness for her arrival, though in truth they were rarely closed. Her heart beat harder as she turned in sharply and felt the scale of the place mushroom – the drive grew wider than the road, sweeping down a gentle slope and planted on both sides with fastigiate hornbeams. The sky opened up like a thrown-out tablecloth, the parkland rising and falling with careless grace, acres of frost-stippled grass interrupted only by ancient yews with thick boughs so heavy they grew along the ground. In the distance, looping around the promontory of the sprawling estate, the dark ribbon of sleeping sea gleamed like an oil slick.

A lone stag nibbling on a rowan tree lifted its head as her headlights grazed the ground, steadily bringing into view the colossal mass of honey limestone that had been quarried and first set in place here seven hundred years ago. Even as a very young girl, she had instinctively understood her home was special, extraordinary even, but seeing it again after a three-year absence . . . her heart contracted at the sight of it: the battlemented square towers on either flank, the canted bay in the centre, the ornamental doorway at the top of a flight of balustraded steps . . . Lorne Castle stood as proud and magnificent as ever.

But this was no sentimental homecoming and unlike the dark sleeping village, the lights blazed from within as though there was a fire raging. Not a room was left unlit as though light itself was all that was needed to drive away the darkness that was threatening to claim her father.

She parked with trembling hands, noticing how her sisters' cars – Pip's muddy Land Cruiser, Ottie's old-school yellow Mini – were parked at odd angles at the bottom of the steps, suggesting haste, hurry. Panic.

She felt her anxiety spike again. All the way here, as she had driven through the night and along the width of the country, she had told herself it was a false alarm, maybe even her family's way of forcing a reunion, bringing her back into the fold when she had refused point-blank every request. But there was real crisis here, she could feel it, a metallic tang in the night air. She shot from the car, oblivious now to the owl hooting for its mate in a nearby tree as she ran up the limestone steps two at a time, feeling suddenly dislocated and anomalous in her hard-edged concert clothes.

She ran through the giant arched door that was as thick as her forearm and into the great hall, stopping as suddenly as if she'd run into a wall. Her eyes scanned the double-height space, tripping over the ornate, dark – almost-black – wooden panelling and split staircase. Great bunches of holly and eucalyptus had been tied at intervals to the bannisters, urns filled with elegant flower arrangements on every surface, a silver banner that read 'Happy Anniversary' strung up along the gallery. Some ashtrays were filled with cigarette butts and an overlooked bottle of whiskey was tucked half out of sight at the bottom of the stairs. She knew it had been her parents' thirtieth wedding anniversary today because she had worked very hard at making sure she didn't think about it all. But it wasn't the remnants of a party that she saw but instead the bloody-minded constancy of the place: nothing had changed in her absence, not a single thing. The harp was in its usual place on the half-landing, Rusty – her father's prized suit of armour, belonging to the 1st Knight of Lorne – still standing stiffly between the dining room and yellow drawing room doors. The Qing vase was still set on the guéridon table in the middle of the space, the grandfather clock still four minutes behind time. In three years, she was the only thing to have stepped out of position here.

A sound – muffled, alarming – came to her ear from upstairs and she ran again, feeling the panic course. Fists pumping, she tore up the stairs, resolving to say 'sorry' first. They were beyond recriminations now. She had let the past dictate the present for too long.

She got to the landing but on the top step she tripped, her foot catching on one of the many threadbare rugs that criss-crossed over each other like patchwork. She staggered forwards, arms outstretched to break her fall just as a door opened and a pair of socked feet came into sight, a twig of straw caught in a trouser crease.

'Willow,' Pip gasped, catching her and staggering backwards.

'I'm here,' she panted. 'I made it. Where is he?'

'Willow.'

'Pip, get out of the way,' she said urgently. Because in that one word, she had heard a tone. 'In there?'

Pip's fingers squeezed harder around her arms, forcing her to stop, to look up. To understand—

'Willow,' she whispered.

Willow shook her head, feeling an icy hand clutch her heart. 'No . . . No.'

'I'm so sorry.'

The world tipped onto its side, the ground falling away beneath her feet as she felt herself begin to slide. To fall. She couldn't be too late. She couldn't. She'd driven through the night, across the country. There had been no faster way to get here—

'He passed a few minutes ago.'

Her legs buckled beneath her, taking Pip down too as she fell. And kept falling.

There had been no faster way to get here. Nothing she could have done to have seen her father one last time.

Unless—

The realization was devastating. Unless, of course, she had never left him at all.

Chapter Two

'Eat this.' Ottie set down the bowls of porridge, the drizzle of honey a translucent vein swirled across the top, steam twisting up to the high ceilings.

Nobody moved.

'I said *eat*,' she said in her best bossy Eldest's voice. 'You're no good to anyone with low blood sugar and I for one did not pack my smelling salts today.'

Still, nothing.

Ottie sighed and sank down into the nearest empty chair at the long refectory table, looking down at her own bowl with a look of disdain. She wasn't sure she could force it down either. 'Look, we've got to try to hold it together. We've got to be strong. Mam's not . . . well, this isn't going to be an easy road. So, eat.'

There was another long pause, as though she'd been talking behind a wall and no one could hear her, but after a moment, Pip picked up her spoon and did as she was told; the motion was mechanical, almost robotic, and Ottie knew she might just as well be eating dog food – she wasn't tasting any of it. Willow lifted the spoon from the table too but it lay cradled in her hand, hovering across the bowl as she stared into space again, the fingers of her other hand automatically rubbing on the grooves inflicted by knives and knocks over tens of generations. Their father had grown up at this table and his father before him, and his . . .

The clatter of Pip's spoon on the bowl made them all startle. Pip was staring into the abyss of porridge, shoulders hunched. 'I'm going to throw up,' she whispered.

Ottie reached over to her, rubbing her arm. 'It's the shock, Pip. Digestion is always the first thing to shut down.'

Willow let her spoon drop too, as though Pip's nausea released her from the obligation to eat.

Ottie sighed, feeling defeated, feeling their despair. 'I know it all feels impossible – eating, sleeping . . . going on without Dad . . .' Her voice broke as she looked at her exhausted sisters. 'But somehow we have to just keep putting one foot in front of the other and make the best of things.'

Pip's swollen eyes swivelled to meet hers. 'How do we "make the best" of Dad being gone?' There was no sarcasm in the question for once, only bleak despair.

At her words, Willow dropped her head, elbows splayed wide on the table as she wound her fingers through her hair, as though trying to literally hold herself together. She was eerily quiet, having said barely a word since she'd arrived last night. The news that she was too late to say goodbye seemed to have knocked the breath from her body and her silent scream and mute sobs in the hall had been as heart-wrenching as anything Ottie had ever seen. Her little sister had seemed furious and devastated all at once, and whilst Ottie and Pip had spent the night in their mother's room, Willow had fled to her old bedroom and bolted the door – present, and yet still absent.

A knock at the back door made them all turn and they loosened in unison at the sight of Mrs Mac's face peering through the glass. She was wearing her usual patched tweed overcoat and gloves, her grey hair pulled up in a bun, her reading glasses perched as ever on the end of her nose and magnifying her shrewd, kindly eyes.

She came in without ceremony, pulling off her gloves and regarding them all with a 'tut' in her expression. Ottie knew that meant they all looked wretched, purplish crescent moons hanging below their eyes like bruises, complexions wan and drawn. Obviously they hadn't slept, as they'd taken it in turns to sit beside their mother's bed, helpless as she had howled and wailed like a wounded animal.

'You poor, poor chicks,' she said in her distinctive low voice. 'Where's your mam?' she asked, setting down a basket and hugging them briskly but warmly in turn, lingering longest with Willow. They had always been close, Willow, the baby of the family, and Mrs Mac, wanting to hold on to her the longest. Willow's sudden break from home three years earlier had hit Mrs Mac just as hard as the rest of them.

'Upstairs,' Ottie murmured. 'Dr Fitz came back this morning and gave her a sedative.'

Mrs Mac paused, then nodded. 'Aye. Probably best.'

They all stared at one another for a moment, the tragedy sitting between them like a lumpen mattress: unavoidable. Painful. This time yesterday they had been getting ready for the anniversary party in their respective homes, laying out clothes and taking long baths in readiness of an afternoon spent sipping champagne and telling lively stories; the anticipation in the village had been palpable – the Lornes' parties were always extravagant, exuberant and drawn-out affairs, and Ottie had been flabbergasted to see their former housekeeper in make-up and a velvet dress; she wasn't sure she'd ever seen her out of a pinny before.

'Tea?' Ottie asked, moving to get up from the table. 'I just made some. The water's boiled.'

Mrs Mac placed a hand on her shoulder, keeping her firmly in place. 'I'll see to myself. You sit there. You look like you need the rest.'

She regarded them all critically again, but there was love in her eyes. Although she had stopped working for them five years ago, she had been part headmistress, part nanny, part spy, during her twenty-four-year tenure here, making sure the girls ate well and were 'nourished', keeping up with their homework, and providing an inside scoop on what all their crushes were up to in the village. Many was the time the Lorne girls had bemoaned their 'bad luck' at being effectively imprisoned in eight hundred acres of land, away from so much as a streetlamp, much less a pavement or bus stop. 'You need to keep your strength up, for your mam's sake. She's not as strong as you lasses. She needs you to help her get through this.'

'And we will,' Ottie said, nodding and looking determinedly at her sisters. If they wouldn't listen to her, at least Mrs Mac's word was regarded as law.

'Everyone sends their love. I've nigh-on thirty meals in the car for you. You'll be eating pies till May, I should wager.'

'That's very kind of them,' Pip murmured, still looking green about the gills.

'Well, they see it as the very least they can do for you,' Mrs Mac said, bringing her tea over to the large table and sitting down heavily in the rush chair, one hand falling idly to pet the lurchers Mabel and Dot, who were greeting her with a mournful head on each thigh. 'What a shock it is for the whole village. Everyone's numb. O'Malley closed the shop when he heard, even though he was due a delivery from the abattoir.'

Shock. It was such a tangible thing. Ottie felt like she could reach out and bite down on it. She glanced across at Willow again – here but not here, staring into the grain of the wood as though there was something written there, just for her.

'Do they know what it was that took him yet?' Mrs Mac asked, her eyes full of concern.

Ottie flinched, hating the very word, not wanting to give it shape or sound. 'Aneurysm.'

'Oh—' Mrs Mac pressed the back of her hand to her mouth and squeezed her eyes shut as though the word itself had been a slap. 'So then it was quick,' she murmured, nodding over and over, almost as though soothing herself. 'That's a mercy at least.'

'Actually no,' Ottie said quietly, not wanting to think about it again, to remember those horrific dragging moments . . . 'He survived for nearly four hours.'

Mrs Mac frowned. 'But . . . I thought they took you quick, like.'

'Doctor Fitz said only forty per cent of people die immediately, three in five die within two weeks.' She shrugged, hating that these statistics had stuck in her brain, facts she had never known she never wanted to know. 'He said Dad had been diagnosed with it last Easter but because of where it was on the carotid artery, they couldn't operate to remove it.'

'He *knew?*'

Ottie nodded, swallowing down her own shock. Anger. Sense of betrayal. 'The consultant had told him that although it could go at any time, there was every reason to think he could live with it for years if he was careful. Most aneurysms don't rupture. Only one in a hundred burst each year, so . . .' She stopped herself, hearing the robotic note in her voice. Knowing the facts didn't alter the outcome. Her father couldn't be saved by statistics.

'Jeesht, the poor man,' Mrs Mac whispered. 'And he never told anyone?'

'Mam, but she said he didn't want to worry us.' She looked away. 'Typical Dad, always looking on the bright side – he assumed he'd be the one who got away from it.'

'Well, of course he would. He always had the best of luck, your dad.'

Ottie's eyes darted to her sisters, but for once, they didn't react to the assertion. Whatever other privileges their father might have enjoyed, good luck had not been one of them.

'So what happened? He was . . .' Mrs Mac didn't finish but Ottie knew what she'd been going to say: that he'd been fine when they'd left, hailing hearty cheerios from the castle steps, his cheeks flushed on wine and happiness.

'He and Mam went upstairs to change when Mam says he suddenly complained of a blinding headache. She ran to ring for an ambulance but by the time she came back, he was already unconscious.'

'Oh jeesht, the poor thing. What a shock it must have been for her.'

Ottie was quiet for a moment. Part of her mother's anguish – torment, even – was the fact that in his final conscious moments, he had been left alone. 'Yes. Dr Fitz was here within minutes but . . .' Ottie swallowed and shook her head. 'He said there was nothing could be done. It was a severe subarachnoid haemorrhage. There was no hope.'

The housekeeper's fingers interlaced around the mug and Ottie noticed her hands had begun trembling. Their old housekeeper may not be given to scenes of high emotion but she had a tender heart. ''Tis a terrible thing, so it is . . . and so close to Christmas too,' she murmured, lapsing into devastated silence with them.

The flicker and pop of the flame from the old yellow Aga was the only sound in the room and Ottie knew that meant there was a northerly wind today. It felt oddly appropriate, as though it was Death's chariot: biting and merciless, whipping around the stone walls and waiting for them in the bitter November chill. But in here . . . Ottie's eyes skimmed the kitchen. Out of all the heavily buttressed rooms in the castle, this one had always felt the safest. It was her favourite, possibly because it always felt so cosy, the tall, narrow, leaded windows with stone sills allowing the sunlight to fall into the room in long shafts. The floor was terracotta-tiled, worn to a pale peach from generations of foot traffic; long free-standing preparation tables were pushed against the walls and laden with cook-books and food processors, vases and Victorian banded creamware: giant milk jugs, butter dishes and cheese plates named with bold black lettering lest their purpose should be forgotten. Quantities of mismatched plates, many chipped, stood side-on to the room in racks and open shelves; copper pans dangled from the old rack in the ceiling. Nothing bad could ever happen in this room, much less Death stroll in.

'Well, I should be getting on,' Mrs Mac said finally into the silence, rising from the table with effort.

'You're not going already, are you?' Pip pleaded, the desperation sounding in her voice. She was always so convincingly strong but there was no such bluff today; like her, her sister felt hollowed out and frightened now their father was gone. He had been the family's anchor, its leader. Their mother, though beautiful, serene, loving and capable in various ways – if anyone wanted a colour scheme for the bedroom, she was the go-to expert – was fundamentally a fragile creature, spoilt by their father's love as he sheltered her from the worst of the world's betrayals and disappointments. Mrs Mac was the only functioning adult here.

The housekeeper patted her hand warmly. 'Of course I'm

not going, child. I only just got here. I'm going to make a start on the bedrooms. The beds'll need changing and none of you are in a fit state to see to it.'

'Oh, but . . .' Pip blustered, feeling a hot blush spread across her cheeks. Ottie met her gaze, knowing exactly what she was going to say.

'We can't afford to pay you, Mrs Mac,' Ottie said. It had been the first of the hard decisions Ottie had had to take when she'd stepped up to help their father with the estate. Having to be the one to break the harsh truth that they couldn't afford to keep on their beloved housekeeper had been heartbreaking for her and she'd carried the guilt with her ever since.

'Jeesht, as if I'd take your money,' Mrs Mac scolded. 'Do ya think it was the wages that kept me here all these years?' She tutted, reaching a hand out to stroke Willow's head tenderly – and enquiringly, for Willow had never been a quiet child and her silence now – another form of absence – had not gone unnoticed. Ottie saw Willow relax at the touch. 'I'll keep popping in to stay on top of things for you, till I'm sure you're all back on your feet again.'

As though her words were balm, Willow turned and rested her head against the old housekeeper's hip, tears streaming in silence down her cheeks again. 'There, there, pet, it'll get better, you'll see.'

But the way her sister's tears flowed – silent and endless, bitterness in the anguished pull of her lips – Ottie wasn't so sure.

'– Hello?'

The high voice carried through the great hall, echoing and travelling down the oak-panelled corridor to the old kitchen. Ottie felt herself tense as she heard the clip of heels on the floorboards and, a moment later, the blow-dried head of her mother's best friend appeared around the door. Her eyes were so red and puffy as to be almost swollen shut. Briefly it occurred to Ottie that it was poor taste for her to be more visibly – showily – upset than the deceased's own family, but she forced a smile as she always did.

'Hey,' she said quietly.

'Oh my goodness, here you all are,' Shula Flanagan cried, bursting into tears with a violent sob and pressing a handkerchief to her nose. Her husband Bertie came in and stood behind her with a nod. His eyes looked watery too, though he didn't break down, simply standing stiffly as his wife wept for them both. An ex-military man, like her father, he didn't do displays of emotion either but Ottie could tell from the high set of his shoulders and the way his chin was raised just a little too high to be natural that his true feelings were only just below the surface.

Mrs Mac slipped discreetly from the room with pursed lips. She had never been a fan of the Flanagans, even though living on the next great estate, Rockhurst, just past Dunmorgan, twelve miles away, meant they were frequent visitors to Lorne. They were regularly to be found around the dining table of a weekend and very often at the breakfast table the next morning too, when they and her parents had decided to dip deeper into the brandy.

Ottie closed her eyes and submitted as Shula clutched her in a hard, perfume-drenched embrace.

'You all look wretched,' she cried, sobbing harder. 'You poor, poor things.'

No one said anything. Pip, Ottie knew, couldn't trust herself not to come back with some withering riposte; she never did well with the fragrant, high-maintenance types of which

Shula was a cheerleader, and Willow – well, she just wasn't speaking at all, of course.

'Mam's in bed, I'm afraid,' Ottie offered as Shula pulled out a chair at the table and sat down. 'The doctor's just been to give her a sedative.'

'I bet she didn't sleep a wink last night,' Shula said, trying to frown as much as her top-up would allow. Always an attractive woman, she had recently succumbed to the temptations of 'a little help' as she put it – facials morphing into chemical peels, weight-loss retreats segueing to a chin tuck . . .

'No.'

'No, *of course* she didn't. She must be beside herself. I mean, the *shock* of it . . .' She pressed a hand to her heart. 'I honestly thought Bertie was going to pass out when he took the call this morning. He was so white!'

Ottie looked across at him. He didn't look like most fifty-eight-year-olds. An avid fitness fanatic, he regularly ran marathons around the world and could easily have passed for being in his mid-forties. Where her father had 'grown' a paunch, Bertie had a six-pack and pecs, and her father's whiskery jowls could never pull off the designer stubble Bertie got away with. In fact, it was Bertie's obsession with fitness – fostered in the army – that was now earning him his second fortune. A canny businessman, he'd already built and sold a business importing teak furniture from Asia in the 1980s, but latterly, he'd tapped into the burgeoning market for extreme-endurance races: thirty-six-hour marathons run over hostile terrain in punishing seasons. Her father had laughed and scoffed over his brandy when Bertie had first floated the idea but he'd been on to something because now his Ultra brand was looking set to eclipse his first fortune. The man just couldn't seem to stop making money, it seemed. Unlike her father, who always complained he was 'born with holes in his pockets'.

'Is there anything we can do?' Bertie asked, looking back at her. As the eldest and her father's right-hand on the estate, everyone always automatically deferred to her; besides, Pip was too fiery and unpredictable; most people knew to stay away. But the sincerity in his words stirred up the emotions she had been trying to keep lying still in her heart – at least until she got back to her bedroom – his question like footsteps through a pond, muddying the water. Because this was it – the beginning. After the shock had to come the action. The *doingness* of death. Funerals needed to be arranged. Affairs sorted. Phone calls made.

She looked away, unable to hold his gaze. She didn't want to cry in front of everyone. 'Actually, yes,' she said after a moment, talking to the floor. 'Could you contact Dad's old army friends, work contacts – let them know what's happened and pass on the funeral arrangements once we've got them?'

He nodded sombrely. 'Of course.'

'Thanks.' She bit her lip, hardly able to believe she had just mentioned her father and funeral in the same sentence, the memory of him waggling his big toe in front of everyone just yesterday still fresh.

'Would you like me to draft something for the obituary too?'

She looked up at him. 'The obituary?'

'For the *Irish Times*,' he nodded. 'They'll want to run something on him, for sure.'

Ottie flinched. Of course they would. Her father had been no ordinary man. He had been the 29th Knight of Lorne and the last surviving knight in all of Ireland. Of the three historic

Old English knighthoods to have survived since Norman times, Declan Lorne had been the last man standing. It wasn't just a husband, father and best friend who had died last night; a legacy had been extinguished with him too. Seven hundred years of uninterrupted lineage, which had seen off three revolutions, a siege, two fires and numerous bankruptcies, hadn't been able to survive the simple genetic bad luck of producing three daughters and no son.

Ottie bit her lip, trying to hold her emotions down as she nodded. The day she – and her father – had spent her whole life dreading was finally here, for she was no heir. She was the firstborn, yes. And the first disappointment.

Chapter Three

Pip had never noticed how colourful her home was until it was filled with people wearing black. The sunflower silk-lined walls of the drawing room, exuberant oils of faraway landscapes, blue and white Chinese lamps, threadbare rugs of indiscriminate provenance and size overlapping each other so that scarcely a patch of floorboard remained . . . But today, with mourners drifting the halls like black poppies, it was hard to feel the verve that had been carefully nurtured and cultivated within the castle.

Leaning against the wall in the shady recess beside the heavy curtains, she watched the proceedings with detached disinterest. Grief was like a cloak that everyone shared, faces that she had grown up with – locals who'd worked at the estate, old babysitters, secret crushes when they'd been teen-agers – transformed today as frown lines were deeply embedded into brows. She looked down at herself, changed too, for she was wearing a dress – a dress for Chrissakes! – and a dab of blusher on her cheeks, which Mrs Mac had forcibly dusted on her as she went to leave for the church. Her hand self-consciously reached up to her bright auburn hair – always cropped short over kitchen sink, it was in sore need of a trim, tufty bits curling at her ears and neck. Her hand dropped down again, her ill ease as evident upon her as a scarf. She was so rarely ever out of her jodhpurs and boots that this strange uniform of 'civilian dress' made her feel even more exposed and vulnerable – really not what she needed today of all days. She personally had felt her father would have approved of her standing grave-side in her riding kit. It was who she was; who he had loved.

Ottie was circulating the room with her usual poise, a black velvet ribbon tied in her long strawberry-blonde hair, a tray of canapés in her hands and a forced smile on her face, nodding politely as sympathetic hands were placed on her shoulder and condolences ladled upon her like gravy.

She could see her mother sitting on the George II settle, Shula beside her, untouched cups of tea in their hands resting on their laps, as friends clustered around them with pale faces. Even in the throes of despair, her mother was the most beautiful woman in the room, doll-like in her petite proportions but with sharp, refined features: angled green eyes, button mouth, planed cheekbones, thick wavy russet hair which these days was kept in a bob. She had always been able to command a room with just a slip of her smile and her father had been no exception. Declan Lorne's famous heritage as the 29th Knight of Lorne had fostered a notoriously wild and riotous bachelorhood which came to a distinct and final stop the very moment he laid eyes on the elegant Serena O'Shaughnessy. It was a coup de foudre for him, although her mother had taken rather more convincing to agree to dinner – but by the night's end, she had known she would never meet a man more dangerously exciting than this modern knight and they had fallen madly in love.

Theirs had been the aspirational love story, and back in the day they had been quite the 'It' couple, always in the pages of *Tatler* and friends with everyone from Prince Charles to

Bryan Ferry. Life had always just seemed to fall in place for her mother, so to suffer the bad fortune of becoming a widow so relatively young . . . Pip half assumed that was what most people found shocking, that this tragedy should have happened to *them*.

Mrs Mac was moving around the room too, with the teapot, refreshing cups and pointing the way to the toilets. She had worked tirelessly the past few days, getting the castle ready for this, polishing the woodwork, vacuuming the rugs and tapestries, arranging flowers in all the vases – of which there were many – changing the sheets in all twenty-four bedrooms 'in case of guests'. Pip sincerely hoped there wouldn't be. All of them seemed to share an obsessive need to be alone. Only Mrs Mac was allowed free movement in their inner sanctum.

Willow wandered, blank-faced, back into the room and Pip realized she had been absent. Again. She had a glass of wine in her hand and seemed ever so slightly unsteady on her feet. Pip moved over to her quickly.

'You okay?' she asked, looking directly into her sister's bright-blue eyes; though glassy and unfocussed now, they were the reason she and Ottie had catcalled her 'gypsy' during their fights growing up, both of them so jealous of how the colour seemed to 'pop' against Willow's dark hair.

'Fine. Ab-so-lutely fine.' Willow held her arms out as if to prove the point, a bead of Merlot flying from the glass and landing on the rug. Pip watched it sink into the fibres, disappearing almost immediately in the melange of red, orange and green tones.

'How much have you had to drink?' she asked in a quiet voice.

'Enough to make this *bear*able,' Willow sighed, a look of desolation washing over her face like a wave.

Pip put a hand lightly on her arm. 'We're nearly through it, okay? Just . . . hold on. They'll be gone within the hour. And then we can put our pyjamas on and, if we're lucky, Mrs Mac might let us have supper in front of the fire.'

'And then what?' Willow asked her simply.

Pip stared at her, knowing her baby sister wasn't asking what they would be watching on telly later. 'And then we . . . carry on carrying on. It's what Dad would have wanted.'

Willow gave a small scoff and took another angry glug of wine.

'What?'

'Well, poor Dad – he never had much luck getting what he wanted, did he?' she mocked.

Pip scowled, though she couldn't deny it.

'I'm worried about you,' Pip whispered, but so quietly she wasn't sure her sister had even heard.

'It all just seems so . . . empty now,' Willow murmured, her gaze casting around and over the drawing room, every possible surface filled with some trinket or photograph or portrait. But Pip knew exactly what she meant – like staying at a wedding after the newlyweds had left, their ancestral home lacked purpose suddenly.

They stood in silence, watching as the room buzzed with sympathy, knowing that at some – possibly subconscious – level, many of the mourners were also delighting in the chance to sip tea and make conversation in the grand old castle, like it was a birthday outing for an aged aunt.

'Devil on horseback?' Ottie asked, stopping in front of them with the tray.

'Ah, so is that what we're calling Pip these days?' a bemused voice enquired.

They turned to find Taigh O'Mahoney approaching; the

Lorne postmaster-slash-firefighter-slash-paramedic, he was the closest thing the village had to a hero. He kept a defibrillator in the back of his car as well as in the post office, and had made the cover of the *Lorne Echo* in the summer when he'd 'brought back' old Joanie Fitzgerald after she'd collapsed collecting her pension.

'Taigh, just the man,' Ottie said, turning and offering him a canapé as well. He took two.

Pip watched as he winked his thanks, his dark curly hair flopping as he ate. He had a face she wanted to slap – it was covered with freckles, like hers, but his hazel eyes were perpetually laughing as though he was in on some ongoing joke.

'I was going to come and find you.' Ottie frowned. 'Is it true they're not going to rebuild the village hall in Agmor?' she asked.

Taigh's smile faded. 'Aye. The rebuild cost the insurance company is quoting is too low. Won't cover getting the roof on, last I heard.'

'But that's awful. It's pretty much the only meeting place in the village besides the pub, isn't it?'

'Aye, 'tis.'

'What's happened?' Willow asked flatly, out of the loop of all the local news.

'The village hall in Agmor burned down a few weeks ago,' Taigh said sombrely.

'Isn't there something they can do?' Ottie pressed. 'Appeal to the insurers? Get a fund going?'

'Well, given the church roof fund has been stuck at seventy per cent of its target for three years straight now, there's not much appetite for more do-gooding. People are strapped enough as it is.'

'Do they know how it started?' Willow asked, sounding underwhelmed, almost bored, by the provincial drama. She lived a bigger life these days.

'Arson, for sure. We found a rag stuffed in a bottle just in by the door.'

'No!' Ottie gasped. 'But who would do such a thing?'

'Kids.' He said it so matter-of-factly.

'But . . . why would they . . . I mean, they have nowhere else to go *but* there. I can't believe that!' Ottie spluttered, sounding almost angry about it. 'It doesn't make sense.'

'Boredom,' he shrugged. 'Fire's exciting.'

'I guess it must have been exciting for you too, having a real fire to go to for once,' Pip said tartly. 'Beats rescuing cats, surely?'

Pip saw Ottie flinch and even Willow seemed taken aback as a stiff silence opened up at her words. She wasn't entirely sure herself why she'd said it. Her feisty attitude often had a kamikaze element to it and this was no exception, for there was no love lost between her and Taigh. They had dated briefly as teenagers – she had loved what she thought was the scandalousness of the Knight's daughter snogging the butcher's son, but it had all gone wrong when their fathers merely shrugged at the news and Taigh promptly broke it off with her, saying he wasn't ready to be in a relationship – only for her to catch him steaming up the bus stop with Lizzie Galloway that same night. Try as she might, she had never quite been able to forgive him that humiliation.

Taigh gave a small sigh and forced a smile, well used to Pip's ongoing hostilities, though he always appeared prepared to give her the benefit of the doubt any time they met. 'And with that, I will bid you adieu, ladies. I just came over to offer you my condolences. Not that you need any more of those, I'm sure, but I'm sorry all the same. It's a terrible loss. You know how highly I thought of your da.'

'Oh, Taigh, no, wait—' Ottie protested as he turned to leave.

'And it's good seeing *you* back here, Li'l Will,' he said to Willow, using another of her childhood pet names. 'I can't remember the last time I saw you. Don't be a stranger now. Come by to say hi before you go back. It'd be nice to catch up.'

Willow nodded as they all watched him walk away.

'What on earth is wrong with you?' Ottie hissed, slapping Pip lightly across the stomach. 'That was just plain rude.'

'Actually, he was the rude one for interrupting us.'

'He came over to offer his condolences.'

'He called me a devil on horseback!' Pip said indignantly.

There was a surprised pause, but then she saw the first hints of grins flicker on both her sisters' faces. 'Well . . .' Ottie mused wryly. 'It's not an *in*accurate description of you.'

Willow gave a giggle, the sound escaping like a bubble through water. It was such a surprise to hear anything at all from her that Ottie cracked a grin too and even Pip allowed herself to feel a ripple of amusement at the riposte. She supposed it was reasonably droll. *Devil on horseback.*

The moment simmered, steadily bubbling up to a boil as their gazes locked, until Willow burst out laughing first, helped along by the copious amount of wine she had drunk. Pip couldn't help herself – she chuckled too. And Ottie. And Pip felt that thing happen that had always used to happen to them as little girls, as they laughed when they shouldn't, the giggles coming on like a rash, covering them, unstoppable . . .

People turned to look, heads swivelling as the three daughters of the last Knight stood in a huddle, laughing as one, tears streaming down their cheeks. Pip wasn't sure if she was laughing or crying. Maybe both, for she didn't think they were just laughing about the wisecrack now: grief, shock, childhood mischief, togetherness, amusement, hysteria – pick one. But she knew their father would have approved. He had always laughed at funerals, and they were their father's daughters after all.

Chapter Four

Wednesday, 4 December

The library fire crackled drowsily, spitting out stray embers every now and again and making Mabel startle; she was stretched out on the rug, oblivious to the leaden mood that permeated the room. They were all gathered together, the three of them and their mother, who had been coaxed from her bed, having retreated there again for days after the funeral.

Willow cast an agitated eye around the room trying not to think about the last time she had been in here, that fateful afternoon three years ago. Like the rest of the castle, it looked exactly the same: loden velvet curtains, mahogany panelling, three-metre-high bookshelves laden with antique leather-bound books interspersed with her father's orange-spined collections of first-edition P. G. Wodehouse and Ian Fleming paperbacks.

She kept expecting him to burst through the doors at any moment. This had been his domain and although the room had never been off-limits per se, she had rarely come in here as a child. It was where the adult things happened: paper-work, the difficult conversations, hushed or harried phone calls. It was where secrets were kept – and sometimes revealed. It was where their father had kept his desk and liked to take his morning tea, as well as his early evening dram. Routine was king in this space – the newspaper would always be left by Mrs Mac on the small table beside the orange leather reading chair; the crystal decanter kept forever half-full on the butler's tray; his pair of ox-blood leather slippers set beside the fire even in the summer. Looking at them now, they were tokens of a life interrupted.

A quick rap at the door announced the family lawyer's arrival and she looked up to see Mrs Mac leading him through with her usual comfortingly brisk efficiency; though she returned to her own cottage in the village every night, she was always in the kitchen by the time they came down in the mornings, porridge already in the simmering oven, and didn't leave again till they'd all been fed at night.

Thomas O'Leary, bespectacled and as tall and lean as a punting pole, entered with a quick stride and impassive expression, and they all struggled to their feet. Willow wasn't sure she had ever seen him in anything other than a dark suit; she had known him her entire life but it was almost impossible to imagine him in chinos or jeans or swimming shorts. Dark tailoring defined him – strict, precise, formal, a stickler for the small details.

'Serena, how are you bearing up?' he asked, clasping their mother's hand in his own, as though holding her upright. Willow thought that was rather self-evident. Her mother's hair was unwashed and unbrushed and she wore no make-up; she easily looked a decade older than the stylish woman who had nuzzled in the crook of her adoring husband's arm only last week.

Serena nodded rather than replied, her eyes swimming with yet more tears and O'Leary's face became even more sombre. 'I know,' he said gravely. 'Come. Sit.'

They all sat again, as though this was his office and not their home. Even though they had arranged the chairs to fan around the far side of the desk, as he set his briefcase down and sat in their father's chair, Willow saw Pip wince. She caught Ottie's startled gaze too – they had never seen anyone sit there but her father, and it felt now like catching someone wearing his pyjamas.

They watched in suspended silence as he pulled out files and papers, before setting his case on the floor, inhaling deeply and pressing his palms down on the green leather desktop. 'Let me begin by saying how terribly sorry I am for your loss. Declan was an absolute tour de force of a man and it was a great privilege to have worked so closely with him for all these years. Everyone in the firm wishes to extend to you their sincere condolences. He shall be deeply and sorely missed.'

His clearly rehearsed words sank into the air like a lap dog on a velvet cushion. 'That's so very kind,' their mother said after a moment with one of her gracious nods.

'Yes, thank you,' Ottie murmured, stepping up as the second-in-command.

Willow said nothing. She just wanted to get the hell out of here – not just out of this room, not just out of the castle, but Lorne itself. She wanted to be back in Dublin in her tiny flat with Caz where the most she had to think about was what scent of candle to burn that day and the most she had to feel was the pounding of her hangover. She wanted to be back to pretending again. It was easier than this. She stared at her hands, feeling sick.

O'Leary allowed for another beat of respectful silence – or perhaps dramatic licence – and then it was down to business. 'Well, I know, Serena, you were bewildered that I've called you all together for the reading of the will. It's not standard practice in this day and age but you don't need me to tell you, nothing about Lorne is standard. The estate is an unwieldy beast, its sheer age meaning there are numerous arcane laws to navigate. I'm happy to report, however, that Declan took his responsibilities as the 29th Knight very seriously and was thorough to the point of meticulous in managing his affairs. As an executor, I have rarely come across such thorough forward planning.' He took a deep breath. 'However, not everything can be planned for in life, and there has been a development since my last meeting with him that was unanticipated.'

Willow frowned, glancing up. What development?

'But before I get to that, I must first give you some context for Declan's actions. As you're no doubt all aware –' Willow watched his gaze sweep straight over to her, having been three years absent – 'the estate has been struggling for a while. Your income streams derive from four sources: Declan's army pension, the rents paid to you by the tenant farmers, the takings from the campsite, and the pony-trekking business. These are modest income flows, however, and in the latter two instances, also largely seasonal.'

Both Ottie and Pip – whose businesses they were – bristled slightly, shifting in their chairs.

'The problem is, that income will largely be swallowed up by the inheritance tax, income tax and capital gains tax now due, not to mention the need to settle up with any outstanding creditors. In fact, breaking even would be a very good result.'

They were effectively broke? Willow looked at the others: Pip, as ever, looked furious. Her mother just looked numb. But Ottie – she looked like she was about to burst into tears, her cheeks flushed and eyes burning brightly, hands blanched white in her lap; Willow knew just how hard she'd thrown herself into trying to get the estate to turn a profit.

'But . . . my trust,' Serena stammered after a pause, trying to draw herself straighter, as though deportment alone would get them out of this hole. 'When we were married, I had a trust. Several million.'

O'Leary gave her both an apologetic grimace and a concerned look. 'You may recall the tax problem several years ago now, Serena? Declan had to access it to satisfy Revenue's demands. You signed a consent form at the time.'

'Oh . . . yes. Yes,' she murmured vaguely, sinking back and looking bewildered. Defeated.

'Declan was only too aware of the scale of the problems facing the estate upon his death. Everything I'm telling you now, he already knew and he tried his best to safeguard your interests. He did everything he could to boost profitability, streamline the estate and trim running costs, but I'm afraid it was a losing battle. We met frequently in Dublin and managed to establish the subsistence-level business model that has kept the estate ticking over – allowing you to keep some of the ground staff and set up the smaller peripheral estate businesses. But he knew it was just treading water and that there would be inescapable problems when he died – that the death duties and taxes would eat up what capital you had left. So when he got his diagnosis back in April, he set about investigating several options he thought might reduce the burden upon you as his beneficiaries – one of them including selling the estate.'

Pip gasped. 'He did not!'

'Dad? Sell Lorne?' Ottie gasped harder.

Willow felt her heart rate accelerate into a gallop. In spite of everything she felt about this place now – her own desperate need to get as far away from it as she could – it was impossible to imagine the Lornes without . . . Lorne.

'There was an interested party earlier in the year and negotiations were quite far advanced when the deal fell through,' O'Leary said calmly.

'It was never a viable option,' her mother said, rallying to a withering tone. 'He was a quite disgusting individual, trying to rob us with his underhand tactics. What was the term, Thomas?'

'Gazundering.'

'Yes, that. He tried to slash the sale price the day we were due to sign contracts. Your father was having none of it, of course. This man tried to back-pedal when he realized he'd overplayed his hand but, by then, your father wouldn't sell to him on principle. Quite rightly.'

O'Leary, checking Serena had finished talking – it was the most determined she had sounded all week – took another of the deep breaths that Willow was beginning to recognize as the herald of yet more bad news for them. 'Serena's right. Declan was disillusioned by the experience of trying to sell, so he made another decision and approached An Taisce.'

Willow frowned. The National Trust for Ireland?

'In light of the negative sale experience and given all the different pressures, he felt gifting Lorne Castle and the estate to them instead was the most viable option available – and the most desirable outcome for all of you.'

'How? By robbing us of our home?' Pip exploded, jumping up from her chair. Willow watched Ottie place a hand on her arm, silently imporing her to sit back down again.

'Well, that's the point,' O'Leary said calmly. 'If the estate is gifted to An Taisce, conditions can be attached so that you can all continue to live here, rent-free, for the rest of your lives, and your children too. Your grandchildren and successive generations could also live at the castle but they would be subject to a market rent.' He paused, taking in their stunned expressions. 'At the time of his passing, Declan was adamant this was the best solution – it would keep the family with the estate but without any of the burdens and financial pressures that come with running it.'

'But we wouldn't own it? It wouldn't be ours?' Pip cried, her bottom lifting an inch off the seat again and Ottie's arm restraining her.

He shook his head. 'No.'

'But Lorne has always belonged to our family – seven hundred years of us,' Ottie said in a split voice, trying to reason with him.

'I know.'

'Mam, did you know about this?' Ottie asked.

Their mother nodded, looking broken. 'He told me just the other week. I can't say I like it, but given the other options facing us –'

'So we just *give* them the castle, is that it?' Pip demanded, glowering back at O'Leary again.

'Well, actually—'

'No.' Pip folded her arms. 'We won't do it.'

'Pip, darling . . .' her mother said, sounding tired.

'Mam, there's another way. I know there is. Dad tried dealing with this all on his own but he shouldn't have. We're adults now. We could have helped him. Ottie *was* helping him. Did you know about this, Otts?'

But one glance at her face was all the answer required.

'Pip, you've all got your own lives. You're busy with the stables, Ottie's got the camping business as well as helping your dad with things, Willow's off in Dublin. He didn't want to burden you with these troubles.'

'Really? I bet he would've bothered if we'd been boys,' Pip said bitterly. 'He'd have told us then. If he'd thought there was any chance of keeping the knighthood going, he'd have tried to keep the castle too. But because we're just girls, we were useless to him; he was losing the lot anyway, so he gave up on us.'

'Philippa, no!' her mother said, suddenly fierce, almost herself again. 'That is not true. You girls were everything to him.'

Willow noticed how she wasn't the only one to recoil at those words. Ottie had flinched too. None of them believed it.

'If I could just—' O'Leary said apologetically, trying to butt in.

'Loving us and believing in us are two different things, Mam. And he didn't believe in us. He couldn't do it so he didn't think we could either. He wants us just to give up, give this place away . . .'

'If I might interrupt,' O'Leary said in a firmer voice. 'This was the unexpected development I wanted to discuss with you today. I'm afraid it's not quite as straightforward a matter as simply giving the estate to An Taisce.'

'Whatever do you mean? Why not?' Serena frowned, looking shocked.

'To give you some background, the Trust was originally set up to preserve important country homes that were being demolished after the wars. People couldn't afford to run them any more, lifestyles were changing and so forth . . . But as the Trustees soon discovered, these properties needed vast funds of money to restore and maintain them. The coffers can only run so deep and the government rarely dips into its pockets to help out, unless the asset is of national historical importance – which, I'm afraid, Lorne Castle wouldn't be. In recent years, their focus has been on acquiring land, and specifically the coastline, in order to protect the landscape from development, so on the rare occasions they do acquire a landed asset, it's with stipulations of their own.'

'Stipulations?' Pip echoed suspiciously, like it was a dirty word.

'The estate must either come as a going concern with proven profitability or else be transferred along with a significant endowment.'

'How significant?'

'Five or six million euros.'

'But we don't have anything like that!' Serena cried, clutching the arms of her chair and looking ashen.

'I know.' He took another – yet another – deep breath. Willow wanted to scream, even though she knew she could barely manage a squeak. 'Which is why, I'm afraid,' he said, speaking at half speed, 'they have regretfully declined your husband's very kind offer.'

Silence exploded like a fireball in the room, singeing them all.

'Declined it?' Serena whispered.

O'Leary interlaced his fingers and nodded.

'You mean to say we can't even *give* this place away?' Pip cried, indignant from the other side of the fence now.

'Not as things stand, no.'

'What did Declan say?' her mother whispered. 'I can't begin to imagine . . .'

'He never knew. The letter arrived the day after he died.'

Her mother gave a small sob, pressing her hand to her lips and shaking her head in distress. 'That was a mercy then – it would have devastated him. This place was everything to him. For them to just . . . throw it back in his face like this . . .' She began to weep.

'He would have been more devastated by what it meant for you,' O'Leary said gently. 'He was very, very concerned with trying to ease the burden on you. I don't think it occurred to him they might reject the offer.'

'But surely you'd advised him that might be an outcome?' Pip demanded.

'Actually he never consulted me on it at all. He went ahead and made the approach on the spur of the moment; apparently he met the Secretary at some golfing tournament soon after that sale went sour.'

Willow stared at the lawyer in disbelief. Her father had decided to give away his castle after a round and drinks at the nineteenth hole?

'I only found out after the event. He felt it was the answer to all your problems.'

No one knew what to say. What could they say? They couldn't afford to keep the castle but they couldn't afford to give it away either? What kind of double bind was this?

'So what are our options now then?' Ottie asked finally, drawing herself up and trying to forge a way forward as she always did.

'You could go back to trying to sell. That would be the most straightforward option.'

'But then we wouldn't . . . we wouldn't be here at all. It would leave the Lornes for ever. There must be another alternative,' Ottie insisted.

'Well, if you can find an endowment—'

'Sure,' Pip said sarcastically. 'We'll all go marry the next rich blokes we see and we'll all be saved. That's what daughters of knights are good for, right? Marrying well?'

'This isn't Mr O'Leary's fault, Philippa,' her mother said in a tremulous voice.

Ottie shot her a warning look not to upset their mother further and Pip sat back chastened, trying to button her lip.

'You could also examine alternative business propositions. I appreciate that is easier said than done but the economy is much improved since you tried the B&B business. Tourism is flourishing again. You could reconsider that?'

Ottie shook her head. 'The castle isn't what it was. It would need so much money spending on it if we were to take public bookings again. The roof is leaking almost everywhere but the quote we had to repair it was half a million!' She gave an appalled, brittle laugh. 'We don't have anything like that. And it's not like that was the only renovation project we had to let slide. There's so much to do . . .' A tremble in her voice made them all look over. Ottie never broke. She was the eldest, the strong one. She always knew what to do. 'I just wouldn't know where to begin tackling it all.'

Willow blinked, feeling a flush of panic.

'I understand,' O'Leary nodded. 'That was just a suggestion. I'm sure there are other business ideas that might come to mind.'

If there were, they weren't presenting themselves to anyone in a hurry.

'I know this is a lot to take in, and it all seems like bad news, but there is some relief in the form of the specific bequests, which I'll go on to now, and then we can come back to the over-arching plan afterwards,' O'Leary said, moving on and clearly uncomfortable with the high degree of feminine emotions at play. 'Serena, in the event of An Taisce not accepting Declan's gift, the bequest clearly cannot stand, so the will reverts to the preceding version which Declan drew up three years ago.'

Willow watched as her mother straightened her back as though bracing for the next onslaught.

'Ottilie, as the eldest child, your father wanted me to start with you. He has bequeathed you the land currently used for the campsite, referred to in the deeds as Sawday's Patch. This includes the private beach at the southern end and the boat-house where you currently reside.' Ottie bit her lip hard but nodded frantically, indicating she understood, one hand pressed to her chest. 'Had the bequest to An Taisce been accepted, he had stipulated this land would have been deemed inalienable, meaning it was separate from the rest of the estate. As it is, it is yours, regardless. He also gives you his mother's ruby and diamond earrings and necklace, and the Singer Sargent landscape in the yellow drawing room, which you always admired so much.'

'The Sargent?' Ottie echoed, tears beginning to track her cheeks. Their mother reached over to clasp her hand, pressing it to her lips.

He looked at Pip. 'Philippa, the stables – the land, animals and all contents – are bequeathed to you. In his proposed plans to the Trust, your father had ring-fenced off the land from Coppers Beech in the north, down to Finnegan's Gallop in the south, and stretching from Broad Oaks in the east to Clover Field in the west. Again, had the bequest to An Taisce been accepted, this land would have been deemed inalienable, meaning it was separate to the rest of the estate. As it is, it is yours, regardless. You father also wanted you to have his mother's emeralds, and the Lorne Cup.'

'The Lorne Cup?' Pip echoed, looking stunned. It was a relic that had belonged to the 1st Knight of Lorne, back in the thirteenth century, made from pure gold and studded with rubies. But that wasn't what made it priceless – as a little girl she had loved to run around the castle with it on her head, pretending to be a Viking. Their father had remembered that?

'Wil—'

'*Don't* call her Wilhelmina,' Pip said quickly, a friendly warning look in her eyes.

O'Leary smiled and nodded, but not before glancing at their mother. He took a deep breath and Willow felt her body brace. 'Willow, with the exception of the specific bequests previously mentioned, the contents of the castle and the Dower House, your father has bequeathed you the entirety of the estate.'

There was a long confounded silence as everyone relayed his words in their heads. *Your father has bequeathed you the entirety of the estate.*

Her mother laughed, a shrill hysterical sound as her hand fluttered to her throat, fear winging through her eyes. 'What?'

'*What?*' Ottie demanded too, unusual thunder in her voice. 'Willow's getting the castle? Not Mam?'

Nor her?

'Serena, Declan has bequeathed to you the Dower House and contents of the castle,' O'Leary said quickly.

Serena blinked back at him, a film of tears shimmering in front of her eyes. '. . . No,' she whispered, smiling weakly, beseeching him for signs that this was a joke. 'No, that . . . It makes no sense. He wouldn't . . . he wouldn't do that . . . Thomas? '

Willow stared over at her mother in dismay, seeing how ashen she looked – even her lips were pale – and knowing she looked the same. Her mother was right, this couldn't be what he'd meant. It was a mistake. Some perverse joke. How could her father have left effectively everything to her and not his wife? She wasn't even the eldest child, or his favourite. She had walked out of here three years ago and not looked back. She had abandoned them. Rejected them. Him. He wouldn't just *give* her the very home she had turned her back on.

'I appreciate this comes as a shock,' O'Leary said, looking between her and Serena. 'Please bear in mind Declan had thought that gifting the estate to An Taisce would override this version of the will and circumvent the problem altogether. These were *not* his final wishes. It didn't sit well with him at all – he was concerned you might construe it as being evicted from your own home – but in the absence of any other alternative he was also adamant he did not want the burden of the upkeep of the castle falling to you—'

But it's okay for it to fall to me? Willow thought, seeing the shock on Pip's face too. She was white and open-mouthed, not blinking. None of them thought she was deserving, not even her.

Serena was shaking her head, looking distressed. 'But . . . but poor Willow, my baby. What can she do with it that we couldn't? She can't be expected to take on that burden. What was he *thinking*?'

'I'm fine, Mam,' Willow said into the void as everyone turned to look at her. 'Really. I'll be fine.' Her voice felt scratchy and foreign, her throat still raw from the silent screams the night her father had died.

'You live 150 miles away, darling. You've made a life for yourself in Dublin. What are you going to do with this old place and eight hundred acres?'

'Actually, taking into account the land apportioned in the specific bequests, the estate's inalienable acreage now stands at four hundred and thirty-five acres,' O'Leary corrected.

Oh, *much* more manageable, Willow thought to herself bitterly.

'This can't be it, Thomas,' her mother said pleadingly. 'Declan wasn't in his right mind when he wrote this. He can't have been! He never would have done this to his youngest child!'

Willow stiffened.

'I'm so sorry, Serena, I know it's hard. But although this wasn't Declan's first choice, it was his second and any judge would rule this will stands.'

A tense silence expanded and hovered in the room like an unwelcome rain cloud on a summer's day.

'Mam, we'll work it out,' Ottie replied in an uncertain voice, but shot a sharp look towards her, as though Willow had wilfully betrayed her in some way.

'So Willow's expected to abandon her life in Dublin to take on all the stresses of running this place and I'm to move to the Dower House?' Serena asked, beginning to cry, her fingers rubbing over her string of pearls frantically. 'That's what you're telling me? Declan wanted me to move to that dingy, dark, depressing place?'

'Serena—'

'No, I don't believe you. Declan wouldn't do this to me *or* Willow. He wouldn't. He loved us. He adored me.'

O'Leary leaned forwards on the desk, trying to appease her. 'Declan did indeed adore you, Serena, but he was a good man forced into making hard choices. His aim was to reduce the burden upon you; he wasn't trying to punish you.'

Willow stared at the solicitor, her heart hammering. The man in the suit was right. This wasn't about punishing his wife. It was about punishing *her.*

Chapter Five

Ottie sat by the boathouse window, staring out into the blackness and letting the tears fall. On her own at last, they just kept coming and she felt powerless to stop them. Mrs Mac had urged her to stay at the castle again tonight but she hadn't been able to spend another minute up there, not even to swallow down the stew the housekeeper had lovingly made them all. Pip had felt it too, she knew, escaping back to the stables on the pretext of feeding horses that had been looked after perfectly well for the past week by one of the village girls, Kirsty.

There were so many memories tightly packed in the castle walls, it was as though the air itself was Lorne-tinted and she couldn't breathe there, she had needed space. Their father's will had changed things, shifting the molecular structure of their family dynamic and they each needed time to process it. Willow's new status as the official heir of Lorne, the legal owner of the castle, had dumbfounded them all. Nothing about it made sense: this was their mother's home – where she had raised her family, fought to keep the place going by her husband's side. For him not even to have told his own wife he was pulling the castle rugs out from beneath her . . . ? It was eviction, no matter how much O'Leary tried to sugar-coat it. How could her father have kept such a major decision from his wife?

His daughter?

She closed her eyes, easily conjuring the image of him walking across the field towards her, one hand planted on the top of his head to keep his flat cap on, cheeks ruddied, bright-green cords tucked into wellies. Every day for the past five years she'd worked with him shoulder to shoulder, helping to free a sheep tangled in barbed wire, or cutting up a fallen tree. They'd have their packed lunches together, sitting on moss-covered rocks, or making sandwiches at her cottage and eating them on the beach, looking out to sea. If he was going to leave the estate to anyone *but* her mother, surely it should have been her? Even if she wasn't the oldest, which she was, she was also his estate manager! His right hand. What did Willow know about maintaining the coastal footpaths on the Wild Atlantic Way that wended over their land? What clue did her baby sister have about coordinating signage for dog walkers to keep their pets on leads during lambing season? She, if her Instagram feed was anything to go by, just drank matcha lattes and held the tree pose and went to parties and concerts and took laughing selfies with good-looking but anonymous men who never cropped up on the grid more than twice.

But then, Willow hadn't exactly looked thrilled by the revelation either. She didn't want this, Ottie knew, and she certainly hadn't had any inkling it was coming. Apart from one feeble protest that she would be fine, she had fallen deeper into the same stunned silence that had gripped her since their father's death: a second shock; a second grief.

Ottie dropped her head again, silky sheets of long strawberry-blonde hair falling forwards, her hands pulling into fists. She didn't want to hate her sister for this. It wasn't her fault, and yet . . .

Who else could she be angry with? There was no one to rail against. Not her mother, not O'Leary, for he was just the messenger. As for her father, the architect of all this mess, he wasn't here. It wasn't like the Holland poem; he wasn't in the next room at all – he had departed for another time and place altogether, leaving them with stone walls and sheep and trinkets and each other. And all of it counted for naught.

Her head was spinning, anger and bewilderment making her blood rush, and the rocking chair creaked as she rocked herself faster, trying to self-soothe, her dressing gown pulled tightly around her skinny frame.

The phone screen had gone dark again but it was still open on the latest text she had sent: *Emergency. Leaky valve. Water pouring down the walls. Please hurry.*

How many had she sent? She had no idea. She didn't even know how long she'd been sitting there. The sun had seemingly set a while ago now but she hadn't noticed, the staggering view over the curved bay to the purple hills beyond steadily slipping into the dark folds of the night. But what she could not see, she could hear – the heavy crash of the sea booming through the thick, double-height plate-glass window that filled the gable end wall of her beloved beach cottage. Her father had arranged the installation of the picture window as her twenty-first birthday present; while all her friends had received cars or strings of pearls or deposits on a flat, he had given her the gift of light. It had been the best present she had ever received.

The knock at the door made her jump. The campsite was currently deserted, the expected onslaught for the weekend not due before tomorrow at the earliest so she wasn't expecting visitors. But that was no ordinary knock, and that meant this was no ordinary visitor. With a sob of relief, she flung off the blanket and flew across the old blackened elm floor, flinging the door open. 'You came,' she gasped.

'Of course I did,' he said in his melodic low voice, his eyes taking in her pale face and tear-streaked cheeks, red eyes, shivering slight frame. 'I came as soon as I could get away. I've been so worried about you. Come here.'

Like a gazelle, she leapt up and into his arms, her legs clasped around his waist, her face pressed into his neck, the sobs coming faster now. He was her release, her safety. He always had been.

'My darling,' he murmured as she wept, stepping into the little house as though she weighed nothing more than a bag of shopping and kicking the door shut with his foot behind him. 'You've been so strong. So brave. It's killed me not being able to get over here.'

She cried even harder as he carried her through the cottage and sat down on the sofa opposite the little woodburner, Ottie straddling his lap. He pulled back to see her better, pushing her hair away from her wet face, his thumbs sweeping over her skin, drying away the tears and smoothing out the sorrow lines that felt embedded in her forehead. She knew she must look wretched but he always looked at her with such awe and tenderness, making her feel she was enough. More than enough . . .

He kissed her slowly, his lips gentle against hers. She pulled away and looked at the face of the man she loved – the only man she had ever loved. There was none of the stomach-skipping glint in his eyes today, only sadness.

'You look wrecked, my darling,' he said, concerned.

Another sob escaped her. 'It's been so terrible, I can't tell you how awful it's been. Mam's such a wreck and Pip's so angry and Willow's so . . . fucking *quiet*. Everyone's on the edge and I don't know how to keep them okay. I feel like if I turn to one, the others will fall.'

He slid his hands inside her dressing gown, feeling the chill of her skin, and gave her a disapproving look; he knew she always became cold when she didn't eat. His hand felt warm against her and he ran his touch up her torso, cupping her breasts and feeling the weight of them in his hands. 'It isn't your responsibility to look after everyone.'

'But how can I not?' she cried. 'They're not coping.'

'That's just the shock, the suddenness of your father's passing, no warning . . . But every day, it will get a little bit better, a bit easier, I promise.' He swept her long hair off her shoulder, reaching up to kiss the nook between her neck and shoulder, sliding down her bra strap.

She shook her head. 'No. It won't. You don't understand. It's just getting worse and worse.'

He frowned at her words, popping out one breast from its bra cup, that familiar look of awe spreading over his face every time he saw her naked body. It was a moment before he remembered to answer.

'How is it getting worse? You got through the funeral, which is always the hardest part. Your reading was superb, darling.'

She put her hands over his, stopping his caresses. 'We had the reading of Dad's will today.'

'Oh?' He arched an eyebrow interestedly although whether that was the sight of her nipple or the topic in hand she wasn't sure.

'He's gone mad! He's given the estate to Willow.'

'What?' He looked away from her bare breast to read her expression.

'Exactly! Willow! Willow, our millennial snowflake who

knows everything about social media branding and jack all about estate management.'

He frowned, looking baffled. 'What did she say about it?'

'Nothing! Didn't you know? Willow barely speaks these days. She's taken a vow of silen—' She swallowed, feeling instantly guilty for the bitchy remark. 'She looked traumatized actually,' she said in a quieter voice.

'I bet she did.'

She looked at him imploringly, as though he held all the answers. 'What the hell did Dad think she's going to do with it that he couldn't?'

'It's very strange, I agree,' he frowned. 'And what does it mean for—'

'Mam?' She rolled her eyes. 'Dad wants her to live in the *Dower House.*'

'The Dower House? Where's that?'

'On the furthest side of the estate, hidden by trees. It was built by some vindictive ancestor wanting revenge on his mother-in-law or something and he put it in the darkest, coldest, shadiest spot he could find.'

He frowned. 'Ah.'

'Exactly. And Dad's basically evicted her to go and live there!'

'. . . I can't believe he'd do that to your mother.'

'Well, he did!' She realized she was almost shrieking, her body tense and rigid. She forced herself to breathe deeply and she closed her eyes, trying to relax as he shushed her comfortingly, his hands sweeping over her hair and skin, staunching her fear with kisses. He always knew exactly how to calm and soothe her, to bring down those flighty, fluttering feelings of anxiety that left her breathless and unrooted. She pulled back again, too distracted by her mind to lose herself in her body.

'That wasn't the only thing. Apparently he tried to give Lorne away.'

'What?'

She was pleased to see he was as shocked as she. 'Offered it to An Taisce. It would have meant we could continue to live here – only they refused! Apparently you can't give things away for free these days, you have to pay through the nose for the privilege.' Sarcasm dripped from the words like treacle.

He nodded slowly. 'Ah, yes: endowment or proven profitability, I did know that.'

Of course he did. He knew everything. 'Anyway, that was his actual last wish but because it got knocked back, the preceding version of the will stands and Willow gets the lot.'

He frowned. 'Surely he left something for you?'

She gave a small groan knowing she was being unfair, flagging only the headlines. 'Ugh, yes . . . I don't mean to suggest he disinherited the rest of us. Dad would never do that. He loved us.' She sighed. 'I've got this place and some land. Some jewellery and a painting I always loved.' She stared at a spot on the wall beyond his ear. 'In every other regard, it was all so . . . well chosen. Perfect, really.' She stared into space, not seeing the hairline crack in the wall, a spider tiptoeing across towards the corner. 'It wasn't too much, just everything he knew I truly loved or admired. He knew what this place means to me and why: that view, the light here, being *in* the elements.'

He gave a wry smile. 'Your father was always very indulgent of you.'

Indulgent? Was that the word, she wondered? It grated, feeling somehow sharp.

'And Pip? What did she get?'

'Similar: she got the stables and contents, which was all she ever wanted too. As well as Granny's emeralds, which, I mean . . .' She tutted. 'Lost on her. She'll *never* wear them.' She frowned, looking into his arctic-blue eyes again. 'But don't you see? That's why it's so odd, him doing what he did to Mam and Willow. It's like he got it all the wrong way round – a typo or something. It'd have made much more sense for Willow to get the Dower House; after all, it's not like she's ever even here any more.'

'So why did he do it then?'

'O'Leary thinks he was trying to save Mam from the burden of the pressures of the estate.'

'By placing them on his youngest child instead?' He frowned. 'Odd call.'

'Exactly what I thought.'

He was quiet for a moment. 'Well, perhaps he felt difficult choices will have to be made in the future and your mother isn't the one to make them,' he suggested tactfully. 'When you've lived somewhere for a long time, sentiment and nostalgia can be hard to push past – though it seems hellish hard on Willow, putting all the burden onto her.'

He thought about it for another moment more, then gave a shrug as though discarding the topic and bent his head to kiss her neck, her shoulders, her breasts. She felt him stir against her but she pulled away. 'I'm really not feeling in the mood tonight,' she murmured, rubbing the backs of her hands apologetically up his cheeks, feeling the stubble against her skin. 'Can't you hold me?' she whispered. 'I just want to be held.'

His lips kissed her hair, his stubbly chin nuzzling her neck. 'I always want to hold you. I just don't know when I can get away again, that's all. It's been hard enough getting here tonight.' He looked up at her with doleful eyes. 'God, you know how much I miss you, Ottie. Being apart is like a form of torture. Having to pretend . . . Some days I think I'm going mad with longing for you.'

'I know. Me too. But—'

He put his hands under her arms and lifted her up slightly, just enough to hoist her off his lap and lower her down onto her back on the sofa. 'It breaks my heart to see you so upset like this. Let me make you feel better. Please, darling, let me . . .'

His lips grazed her shoulder, her gown completely splayed open beneath her now as he travelled down, fluttering kisses on her bare skin. She scrunched her eyes shut, feeling confused, not wanting to want this. It wasn't the right time; she was upset. But then again, this was the story of their life together – there was *never* enough time. They couldn't keep Shula waiting.

It was the dead of night but the room was bright, the full moon climbing past her window and throwing shadows on the old rose-printed walls. The leaded bars on the windows created grids on the carpet, a faint crackle on the panes betraying a frost that was being worked up outside.

Willow tucked her knees up and pulled the eiderdown higher over her shoulder as another shiver rippled down her body; it was always a shock adjusting to Lorne's signature chill after months in the capital's centrally heated embrace, but she knew this freeze had nothing to do with single-loop heating systems. It was coming from inside her. She was frozen from the inside out, the fire that had first raged inside her as she stood in the study three years earlier cooling over time like magma, into something immovable and permanent. A new landscape.

The worst of the afternoon's shock had passed – that tight-chested constriction, the dizzying black swirl of her mind – and now the revelation was beginning to settle and become simple fact: Lorne was hers.

It was a poisoned chalice, she knew that. Contained within the 'gift' of almost five hundred acres and a thirty-thousand-square-foot castle was not just debt – far more than she could ever hope to pay – but the termination of a legacy and dismantling of a heritage. The buck had had to stop somewhere and it was going to finish at *her* feet. Her father could easily have left the estate to his wife to dispose of – though she had lived here almost her entire adult life and raised her family here, she wasn't Lorne by blood; the guilt for dismantling the estate would be dramatically less than if he'd had to do it. Or he could have passed it to Ottie, the eldest child and traditionally, rationally, the heir. Or to Pip, his favourite child, the tomboy, the son he'd never had. But no, he'd chosen her and she knew why. She knew why exactly. It was as devastating and comprehensive a rejection as he could ever have wanted to deliver and the force of it had felt physical, knocking the breath from her all over again, robbing her of words, protest, voice, presence.

But now, as the minutes ticked and the hours slid by, the other dimension to her father's bequest was beginning to present itself. Her family couldn't turn back the clock and unlearn what they all knew or undo what they'd all done; the die had been thrown and this was where their lives had landed: together but apart; divided by Lorne, the very thing that had once united them.

And if she was going to have to be the one history recorded as breaking up and selling the estate – and really, O'Leary had presented her with no other viable alternatives – then wasn't there also a silver lining? If she sold Lorne, she'd be rich. She could go anywhere, do anything, be anyone. Wasn't that worth the shame and the guilt that had been placed at her door? After all, her life had already changed anyway, the horrors of three years earlier, forcing her to move away from here and everything she had ever known and loved. It was simple enough – she had turned her back on this place once before. Now all she had to do was do it again.

Chapter Six

'A beer, thanks, Joe.' Pip nodded to the barman, sagging against the counter and dropping her head wearily.

'You're back in the saddle then?' Joe asked, reaching for a pint glass, one eyebrow arched bemusedly at the sight of her, rain dripping from her onto the bar. She was still in her kit and boots: her long Driza-Bone mac almost down to her ankles, fleece and face flecked with mud, the tough suede rancher hat soaked from its usual conker colour to a dark chocolaty shade.

'Yep,' she sighed. It had been her first day out with clients since her father's death and it had been a mistake. It had been in the diary for months and Kirsty had offered to take it for her but she had declined, thinking 'getting back to normal' would be good for her; she had thought it would be easier than trying to busy herself around the yard. What was she waiting around for anyway? Her father was buried, his last wishes made known – they couldn't just keep moping around the estate with pale, teary faces. Life had to resume sooner or later, although in her mother's case, it was clearly going to be later. She had been stunned enough by losing her husband so suddenly, but the reading of the will seemed to have hit her even harder.

'Long day?'

'You could say that. I've just finished a trek over to Americas Point with a family from Sligo.'

'In this weather?' he chuckled, casting a lazy glance out the window at the driving rain. 'Still, it's nice that way,' he said mildly, pulling on the tap.

'Aye, 'tis. But it wasn't the view that was spoilt,' she said, reaching for the nearest bar stool, her 'usual spot'. It was still early and there was no one else in yet, apart from Stan Burr sitting in his usual place by the fire, checking up on the day's races.

'No?'

She shot him one of her unimpressed looks. 'One of the kids was so terrified, it took a half hour just to get him to put his foot in the stirrup. I practically had to strap him on with webbing in the end.'

Joe frowned. 'Why'd they book a pony trek if the poor kid's terrified of the animals?'

'They thought it'd help if he "confronted his fears",' she said, putting quotation marks in the air. 'Anyway, his brother was entirely the other way, a cocky wee thing wanting to jump all the hedges – to the point where I had to grab the bridle at one point, to stop him from taking a run at one and almost going over the cliffs on the other side.'

'Jeesht.' Joe grinned.

'And as for the mother, turned out she's highly allergic to horses and spent the whole trek back with her eyes swollen shut.'

'Oh, sweet Mary,' Joe chuckled. 'You copped a bad lot today then.'

'The absolute worst. Honestly, I must be mad,' she said, taking off the hat and running her face through her hands. A piece of straw fell from her hair onto the bar and she picked it up absently, running it through her fingers.

'Still, look on the bright side – you're out in the air with your animals. That's all you ever wanted, right?'

Her eyes flickered up to him and down again. 'I guess,' she sighed. 'Thanks,' she said as he set down her pint and she handed over the cash. She watched as he walked over to the till.

'Why the hesitation?' Joe asked, handing back her change. 'Thought you loved working with horses?'

'Not all working with horses can be considered equal.' She took a deep slug of the drink, not caring about the little foamy moustache it left her with as she lowered the glass. Taking her time, she dabbed it off. 'I don't think Sheikh Mohammad's stable staff ever had to deal with traumatized kids and anaphylactic mothers in a day's work.'

'So that's what you wanna do, is it? Get into racing?'

'No, not racing.'

'What then?'

She gave a deep weary sigh, running one finger around the rim of the glass. She couldn't bring herself to say it out loud: *Bloodstocks. Breeding. Running her own stud.* It always sounded so . . . implausible. Impossible. A rich man's game. 'I dunno. Just . . . not quite this.'

Joe picked up a glass and began polishing it. 'I heard your da left you the stables.'

She gave him an arch look. 'Did you now? And how'd you hear that then?' The gossip in this village was ferocious. There was no such thing as a kept secret in Lorne.

He cracked a grin. 'Oh, you know, the usual. People chattin'.'

Yes, she knew. She gave a shrug. She didn't care if people knew one way or the other, although she wondered what the response had been when they'd heard it was Willow, and not Serena or Ottie, who was now the lady of the manor.

'So you can do what you like with it then, can't you?'

'With what?' she frowned, tuning back into him. 'You've lost me.'

'The business. If it's legally yours now. I thought it was your da who always wanted it to be a trekking business.'

'Well, sure, he said there's no point in living on the Wild Way and not making a penny from it.' It was the same thinking that had seen him establish the camping business too, providing jobs and homes for two of his daughters and keeping them close. Not the third one though. She'd bolted like a horse spooked by a mouse.

The door to the pub opened and Pip looked around to the sound of laughter spilling in. A small group was stamping the mud from their boots, each of them sheltering beneath a copy of the local paper, which had a photo of her father's face on the front of it.

'Evenin' all,' Joe nodded, taking in their excitable moods.

Pip felt her day take another turn for the worse. 'Great,' she muttered under her breath, turning back again.

'Hey, Joe. Pip.'

'Taigh,' she muttered, taking a sip of her beer.

'Four beers and a G and T, please, mate. Don't s'pose you've got any of that fancy rhubarb stuff left, have you?'

'That's an expensive date you've got tonight, Taigh,' Joe quipped, reaching for the bottle of Arrowsmiths.

Pip rolled her eyes and stared down into her drink. It would be just like Taigh to confuse expensive with classy.

'And I'll just grab some –' Taigh went to reach past her and she leaned way back, well out of the way – 'menus. Thanks.' He looked back at Joe. 'What're the specials tonight, Joe?'

It was another of Taigh's jokes. The Hare famously didn't

do specials. The punters ate whatever was in season and had been delivered by the farms that week.

'Pheasant stew or steak pie,' Joe said by rote.

Pip tapped her finger slowly on the bar as Taigh pretended to procrastinate.

'I'll bring your drinks over,' Joe said, sensing her ill-concealed irritation. 'It's quiet at the moment.'

'Thanks. Weather's keeping everyone in, I guess. Only nutters would go out in this.'

'Ha!' Joe barked amusedly. 'Hear that, Pip?'

'Oh, I heard,' she replied in her best bored voice.

Taigh went to turn away, then stopped and faced back to her again. 'Pip, uh, how're you doing? You holding up okay?'

She swivelled round on her stool to face him directly. 'Me? Oh, I'm just peachy,' she said sarcastically. 'It's been a cracking week.'

His mouth opened to say something in reply but he appeared to think the better of it and merely nodded instead, glancing at Joe, who was regarding him with a sympathetic look. He went to join the others at the table by the fire.

Pip wouldn't give him the satisfaction of watching after him, but she'd already spied his latest date anyway – a dirty-blonde in tight jeans with too much eyeliner who lived over in Dunmorgan. Pip knew this because the girl – Laura? Lorna? Yes Lorna Delaney – occasionally ran the local stores for her parents, where Pip would quite often take a detour with clients if they wanted a drink or ice cream on the trek home. She had what Mrs Mac would call a 'reputation'.

'Another?' Joe asked as she finished the beer.

She hesitated. She really fancied another one. Today had left her feeling flat and frustrated. Yesterday had left her feeling confused. (What the *hell* had her dad been thinking, leaving the estate to Willow? She still couldn't get her head around it.) The week generally, devastated. But she wasn't sure she wanted to go back, yet, to her small, quiet digs above the stable block. On the other hand, she had no desire to listen in to that lot's preludes to seductions either. 'No, I'd better not,' she sighed, picking up her hat. There was a bottle of Pinot Noir at home. 'Got paperwork and stuff to deal with.'

'Ah,' Joe nodded, not prying further. Death always involved paperwork. 'Good luck with that.'

She shrugged her eyebrows in reply and turned away.

'Oh, hey, Pip, before you go – I meant to ask: will we see ya at the Mullanes' party on Friday?' Joe called after her.

She looked back at him blankly. 'The Mullanes?'

'Remember they said they'd throw a bash to celebrate their win at Aintree? It's this weekend. Terry came in himself here just a coupl' a days ago, wondering.' She walked slowly back towards the bar again and he lowered his voice a little. 'He was in Dubai when your da passed, so he's only just heard the news. He feels hellish bad for missing the funeral.'

'He wasn't to know,' she said stiffly, hating how her throat seemed to close up with every mention of her father, how – for someone who hated tears – they felt permanently poised at her eyes, ready to fall.

'He talked about cancelling the party altogether, you know, as a mark of respect 'n' all.'

'Jeesht, no, he mustn't do that,' she said quickly. This party had been in the calendar for months. Practically every local in a ten-mile radius had been invited to celebrate the 'great stock' that was bred and raised on this very soil. 'Dad would have hated any party to stop on his account.'

'That's what I said to him. Still, he's in two minds.'

'Tell him I said not to be.' Her voice sounded thick. Her father had been so looking forward to the party himself.

'Will yis go then? Terry's really hoping you'll make it.'

Pip looked up at him, realizing too late that her eyes had filled up with tears again and were shining in the lights. '. . . Maybe . . . I'm not sure.'

Joe reached over the bar and squeezed her hand comfortingly. Her tears – unlike her scorn – always seemed to alarm people. 'Hey, no pressure. It's early days. See how ya feel nearer the time.'

'Thanks, Joe,' she said in a croaky voice, pulling her hand away quickly and putting on her hat. She turned away, dipping her head to hide behind the brim as she rushed over to the door, eager for the camouflage of rain upon her face. Some people she would never let see her cry.

Back home, she watched the ready-meal for one going round and round on the microwave plate. Is there anything more pathetic than this? she thought to herself, as the bell went and her stomach growled appreciatively.

Slinki, her cat and chief mouse-catcher, wound herself in figures of eight through her legs as she tried to pull off the plastic cover without scalding herself on the steam. 'Oh, Slinki,' she tutted exasperatedly, almost falling over her as she turned to put her dinner on the tray. 'You've already eaten. I haven't.'

She picked up the tray and took it over to the small sofa, sinking down into the cushions with a sigh and picking up the remote. Slinki jumped up onto the arm of the chair and mewed plaintively. 'No, listen to me – chicken tikka masala is not what your intestines want, no matter what you think your stomach is telling you. Believe me.' Pip groaned at the thought. 'Urgh, it really doesn't bear thinking about.'

'Are you talking to your cat again?'

'Wha—?' Pip almost dropped the tray all over her lap as she looked up to find a disembodied head peering around the doorway at the top of the stairs. 'Jeesht, Willow! What in hell's name?'

'Knock knock,' Willow said, walking into the flat.

'There's no point in knock-knocking *after* you've frightened the life out of me!' Pip cried. 'I nearly die—'

The word faded on her lips.

'I thought you'd have heard the car,' Willow said after a beat. She set down a box of teabags on the worktop. 'Mrs Mac said you were nearly out.'

Pip looked over at them in surprise. Mrs Mac had been in here, looking after her? 'Well, you know what a stealth machine that car is,' Pip said instead, referring to the lumbering airforce-blue 1958 II Series Landy their father had bought their mother for their tenth wedding anniversary – Tin.

'Wine?' she asked, holding up the bottle of cheap red and watching as her little sister sloped across the tiny flat and collapsed heavily into the armchair opposite, dropping her head back and letting her arms and legs go scarecrow-limp.

'No. Too tired.'

'Just as well. It tastes like soap,' Pip said with a grimace as she took a sip. She began tucking in to her dinner. 'So, you look like hell.'

'Thanks. You too.'

'I've got a good reason,' Pip said with her mouth full, stabbing at the air with her fork. 'I've just spent the day trekking *frickin'* miles in the *pissin'* rain with a family that should *never* have left the mall.' Willow gave a wry half smile, her eyes still closed, head still tipped back. 'What's your excuse?'

'Oh, you know, just the small matter of deciding what to do with a seven-hundred-year-old castle that needs half a million spending on it just to make it watertight when we've fifty-eight cents in the bank.'

'Hmm, fun,' Pip said brusquely as she forked a piece of chicken. If it was sympathy her sister wanted, she wouldn't find it here. She felt irrationally angry at her baby sister, even though she knew Willow's inheritance was a golden bullet, one she'd been very glad to dodge. But it was Ottie and their mother she felt sorry for. It was the two of them that had been robbed. 'How's Mam?'

Willow was quiet for a moment. '. . . Avoiding me, I think.'

'Oh.' Pip swallowed, instantly feeling bad. The rational part of her knew this wasn't Willow's fault. 'Well, give her time,' she mumbled. 'She'll come round. It's just the shock.'

'Yeah. There's been a lot of that about lately.'

Pip glanced up at her. 'Any idea what you're going to do?'

Willow shrugged carelessly. 'Sell it, of course.'

Pip's fork froze mid-air. 'Just like that?'

'No. Not just "like that",' Willow said defensively. 'But what other course of action is there? Dad exhausted every angle: we can't make the place work without a massive cash injection, which we don't have; we can't give it away without a bloody dowry. The place is falling into disrepair. Maybe you don't see it because you're here all the time, but it's shocking how run-down it's become.' She gave another shrug. 'If we can't afford to look after it, then the most responsible thing to do is sell it to someone who can.'

'Well, when you put it like that . . . It's so pragmatic of you, Will. So rational,' Pip said with her utmost sarcasm.

'Alternatively, you could at least try to *think* of some ideas for making it work before you cash in! You only got the bloody deeds yesterday!'

'Well, what would you suggest? The luxury B & B didn't work –' Willow said, holding up her fingers and beginning to count.

'Only cos of the recession, though. Things were going great before that.'

'Dad got a two hundred thousand loan for trying to update the place for that and he never recouped it.' She held up another finger. 'The partridge shoot didn't work.'

'Only cos the foxes got the chicks cos some towny idiot left the hatches open.'

'The food festival didn't work.'

'That jam was bloody overpriced! I said that at the time.'

Willow shot her sister a look. 'You know as well as I do they tried a hundred other different ventures and nothing worked – not on the scale that's needed. We're on the Wild Atlantic Way but the clue's in the location: we're too remote, too rural. Camping? Great. Pony trekking? Great. Small-scale, inexpensive ventures work, but there's not enough money in them to keep the castle itself going. If people want to stay in a castle, they want the 'Cinderella at the ball' experience, not the girl sweeping ashes in rags.'

Pip tutted as hard as she could but, actually, she couldn't refute the truth in her little sister's words. What was it O'Leary had said yesterday? They were getting by at a 'subsistence' level?

Willow sank back into the cushions again, closing her eyes. 'I've contacted my friend Hels –Helena Talbot. She's a client liaison at Christie's in Dublin. We've got a lot of mutual friends. She went to school with my flatmate.'

'Shaz.'

'Caz.'

'Ooh,' Pip said, in her snootiest voice, unimpressed.

Willow sighed, looking exasperated. 'I've asked her to come down and look over everything. Mam's inherited all the castle contents but there's far too much to take down to the Dower House, so she should probably look into having an estate sale.'

'Don't you think *she* should arrange that then, seeing as that's just about all Dad left her?' The accusation rang out in her voice again.

Willow's eyes narrowed, reading her position on this clearly. 'I'd suggest that if there's anything you particularly want from the castle, you get it sooner rather than later.'

'Jeesht,' Pip muttered, feeling more bad-tempered by the minute. 'It's not enough to lose the house but we have to lose all the things that made it a home too? Don't let the grass grow under your feet now, will you?' she quipped angrily.

Willow looked away and said nothing – her default position now, it seemed – as Pip continued to eat. The silence between them lengthened and Pip felt the walls come down around her sister again. There was an edge between them these days that she didn't understand. They'd been so close growing up, Willow always looking up to her as the naughty big sister, giggling behind her hand as Pip dared to do what she did not. But then Willow had upped sticks for Dublin and everything had changed. *What happened to you?* It was the question that was always on the tip of her tongue now, the only answer she wanted to get. It wasn't so much her sister's departure itself which had been so hurtful – Willow had never had the same physical ties to this place as her and Ottie, she didn't need the land like they did – but the way she had almost deliberately dropped contact with them, not returning calls or texts, forgetting birthdays, not even coming back for Christmas because she was always on some retreat in Goa or Acapulco or Tulum. The family had taken it in turns going up to see her in Dublin every few months – although it was hardest for Pip to get away on account of leaving the horses – but none had come back feeling reconnected to her and the distance between her and them had just seemed to grow and grow.

Several times over the years, she'd tried bringing up the subject – she wasn't slow to speak her mind, everyone knew that – but something in Willow's eyes always stopped her, a warning that there were landmines beneath her feet if she tried to cover that ground.

'Well, you'll have a bastard of a time selling it, I'll tell you that now,' Pip muttered, taking another sip of her wine with a mouthful. 'You heard what O'Leary said about that shyster who tried to pull the fast one. And Mam told me that before that they'd been looking for a buyer for most of last year. No interest.'

'Well, who had he put it on with? McGinty's in Cork is hardly going to have the international reach Lorne needs.' Willow's lip curled and Pip knew her sister's head had been turned by Dublin's bigger, flashier scene. No doubt Lorne was just a provincial backwater to her now.

Pip hoped her gaze was shooting arrows. 'You'll see. It's dead out there.'

'I don't believe there was no interest in the place,' Willow snipped back.

Pip shrugged. 'Only the gazunder fella and that was always doomed to fail.'

'Why? They couldn't have known he'd try to slash the price.'

'Not that.'

'What then?'

Pip furrowed her eyebrows, as she always did when she wanted to look her most imposing. 'Mam told me he was English.'

'*So?* What's that got . . . ?' Willow's eyes widened. 'Oh my god, are you joking?'

'Are *you*?' Pip almost choked on her dinner. 'How could Dad sell his castle to an Englishman? You've got to be kidding me! Don't you care anything about our history? It was built in the first place as a reward for defeating the English!'

'Yes. Seven hundred years ago!' Willow scoffed. 'Time to let go of that particular grudge, don't you think?'

Pip shook her head firmly. 'Nup. Never gonna happen. Mam said Dad accepted he may not be able to keep the knighthood going, nor even keep us living there, but selling it to a double-crossing Englishman would be over his dead body!'

Willow didn't reply, a look of horror crossing her features at her big sister's clumsy choice of words. 'I've got to go,' she said tersely, getting up from the sofa, tears shining in her eyes.

'Will . . .' Pip stared at her, feeing at a loss. Why did every conversation seem to end in an argument now? What had happened to them? They couldn't be fighting at a time like this – even if it was their father who had set them at odds with each other. 'Look, wait up.'

'What is it?' Willow snapped from the doorway. She looked pinched and hollow-cheeked.

Pip racked her brain looking for neutral ground. '. . . D'you want to come to a party?'

'*Now?*'

'No, not *now*, jeesht, what do you take me for?' Pip tutted.

'Actually, don't answer that . . .' she muttered. 'It's at the weekend. Terry Mullane's place in Wickling. His horse Midnight Feast won—'

'The Grand National. I remember,' she said flatly. Horses didn't quicken Willow's pulse.

'Right. Well, they're having a belated party to celebrate – they've spent most of the season in Dubai. It should be big. Vintage champagne, dancing all night, I reckon. Your kind of scene.'

Willow stared down at her, looking unwittingly statuesque and lean in her leggings and baggy jumper, and Pip thought for the hundredth time how much her little sister had changed – grown up, she supposed. Still she could never quite get used it – sleek muscles where there'd once been teenage podge, green elixirs in the fridge instead of Coke, sports leggings and trainers replacing jeans and wellies; tight boxer braids replacing her dark swinging ponytail. It felt not so much like an evolution as a revolution, a rejection of the naive country girl she'd once been for something entirely new: slicker, sleeker, better. '. . . I don't think so. It doesn't seem like the right time for a party.'

'Yeah, I know, you're right. I was thinking the same,' Pip sighed, her shoulders slumping. Everything felt against them.

There was a pause and Willow shifted her weight, getting ready to go again. '. . . Then again,' Pip murmured to her back, 'I suppose if the past fortnight's proved anything, it's that the only time is *now*.' She bit her lip and waited as her sister turned back to her again. 'Don't you think?'

Chapter Seven

Friday, 6 December

Ottie pulled her anorak tighter around her as she walked forlornly around the tent pitches, her clipboard pressed flat against her chest. It was blowing a hoolie today, a storm barrelling its way across the Atlantic straight towards them, and her wet hair kept pinging against her cheeks like a violin's plucked bow.

'Hello, everything okay for you?' she asked a couple of women coming out of the toilet and shower blocks, towels flung over their shoulders. They were dressed much the same as everyone else who had descended here over the past day and a half – tracksuits, polar fleeces, windcheaters and industrial-looking trainers. Most of them were spending the time resting in their tents and cooking up pasta on their camping stoves, a lot of pasta. Bertie's now-famous Kilmally Ultra event was kicking off at daybreak tomorrow, with pre-race briefings in the Gallaloe village hall tonight, and a sense of anticipation already hung in the air.

'One of the cubicles is out of loo roll,' one of them said as she walked past.

Ottie nodded, sensing the boundless energy and stamina of the woman; she was going to run for miles and through nights, *willingly*, while it was all Ottie could do to get around this field; her father's absence was glaring everywhere she turned. She understood suddenly that they were living, she was merely alive. 'Okay, I'll see to that, thanks.'

She watched the women walk away, the two of them falling straight back into conversation, arms almost brushing as they walked, and she felt another stab of jealousy. She'd never had a best friend like that; she'd never needed one. She and Pip and Willow had always been as tight as a fist – as children anyway; but growing up seemed to have meant growing apart: Willow had moved away, of course, but although Pip was still close by, although they could still predict what the other was going to say, or insult each other as merrily as drunken pirates, it wasn't the same now, because always in the background was her big fat secret. It sat over her like a shadow at all times, whether she was in the pub or at the kitchen table, and there wasn't a soul she could tell: not her sisters, certainly not her parents, not even Mrs Mac. She was a woman in love but no one could ever know it.

She walked into the wash block. As these things went, it was an attractive building, a converted black house – old stone walls, thatched roof – with the packed earth floor latterly flagged with local slate. Keeping its eco-credentials up had been important to her and her dad when they'd decided to develop the campsite behind the beach, so they'd installed a water storage and recycling system in which the loos flushed with grey water and the showers ran off captured rainwater (of which, this being Ireland, there was plenty).

She unlocked the cleaners' supplies cupboard and restocked the loo rolls in the cubicles, checking everything was clean and running clear, that all the showers had been turned off properly. She found a towel still hanging on one of the shower hooks, a Columbia microfibre muffler on the floor behind a door and an Adidas plastic slide under the sink units. She put them all in the Lost Property wicker basket in the corner – the owners would have until next Saturday to reclaim them before they were either binned or sent to the charity shop in Agmor. With one final look-see, she signed the inspection chart and hung it back on the wall for the day. The cleaners would be in again first thing in the morning.

Heading back out into the elements, she dipped her head and braced herself against the wind and sleet. Though it was only mid-afternoon it was already growing dark, and the temperatures felt raw thanks to the bitter wind as she did a final walk around the site, checking the condition of the pitches and that no litter was being left. In the space of a few hours, the site had filled up almost to capacity, and she moved past the countless orange, sky-blue, olive-green tents, keeping an eye out for stray pitch lines. In some, she could hear people chatting, someone else snoring, music being played quietly, the rustle of books or maps, and as she headed back to the wind-proofed warmth of her office, she wondered for the umpteenth time what it was that made camping out in these conditions so attractive to these people. Why would anyone willingly choose to sleep on a hard floor, shivering with cold and with nylon sheets flapping over their heads all night? Then again, that was feather-filled luxury compared to what they put themselves through actually competing in the Ultra course: running for hours and hours and hours through the days and nights, barely stopping to eat or drink or sleep or even go to the toilet.

As a steward for the race – it was manned entirely by volunteers – she saw what it did to the body, with runners collapsing, vomiting, suffering hypothermia and injury. What drove someone to put themselves through that? Modern-day asceticism? A greater pain? A spiritual calling?

Then again, Bertie not only belonged to this tribe – he was their pack leader. She saw at first hand his drive, his need to push harder, be more than most humans . . . It was entrepreneurial and dynamic, an engaged consciousness, a more visibly focused and directed way of being alive. It was one of the reasons why she loved him, his energy directly feeding hers. He made her feel luminescent and tingling with life. Who wouldn't feel special – safe – around a man like that?

She got back to her office, closing the door on the wind with relief, and went straight to put the kettle on. She shrugged off the wet coat and hung it on the hook behind the door, rubbing her hands and blowing on them in front of the small electric heater.

The space was tiny, converted and built up from an old sheep pen, and only big enough for a desk and chair. But the drystone walls were double-skinned and on bitter, windswept days like these, the meagre proportions at least meant it warmed up quickly. It had two windows, one to the east overlooking the entrance to the camping field and to which people came for booking in, the other diametrically opposite, looking west towards her cottage and, immediately beyond it, the Lorne estate private beach, open only to family and campers. She stood there now, waiting for the kettle to boil and watching a pair of buffeted terns wheeling through the sky, riding the wind like surfers. The tide was going out, leaving long ropes of kelp on the golden sand, a few bright-blue twists of old fishing nets and half a yellow bucket visible all the way back here. She gave a sigh at the sad familiarity of it. She'd already done her daily clean-up, picking out the plastic bottles, odd shoes, carrier bags and such, but with every tide came fresh debris.

The water boiled and she poured herself an instant coffee, looking out with some satisfaction at the sight of the fully booked field; her father had always called this event their 'Glastonbury'. It was a gaudy patchwork of colours, noisy too, the way the tents were battered by the wind, and she knew it would take her and the grass at least a week to recover when they'd all gone again. But it was the last booking of the year; come Tuesday, she'd be closed until the end of February and she wasn't sure if she was excited about it or dreading it. Was time on her hands really what she needed right now?

She leaned against the desk and checked the diary. There was only one more booking due to be checked in – a Ben Gilmore, flying in from Heathrow – then she could clock off for the day. She stared out of the window, impatient for him to show; she couldn't leave till she'd booked him in, given him a key to the wash block and the temporary code that would release power to his pitch: even campers wanted charging stations these days. The booking said he'd be here at 4 p.m. but it was half after that now and she was desperate to get away. Bertie was holding the official briefing for tomorrow's race at six this evening and she needed to be there. He'd be expecting her. It had been forty-eight hours since he'd surprised her – sneaking away by telling Shula he was going to check on some of the race signs that were being put up – and her longing was building again. She missed him desperately. It was always hard having to wait for their snatched moments but now that her father had gone, her loneliness, her feeling of being completely alone in this world, had multiplied exponentially. Her mother had officially retreated to her room since the reading of the will, Mrs Mac even having to bring her meals up there to her now, and Willow had been nowhere to be found either last time she'd popped in to the castle. Pip was straight back into the swing of things, of course: working all day and then hitting the pub in the evenings . . .

Distractedly, she played a game of solitaire on the computer. Lost. Tried again. Lost again.

'Come on, come on, Gilmore, where are you?' she murmured impatiently as the minutes passed, walking to the window and staring out of it till the windows fogged. She began to pace. Made another coffee. Paced some more.

She watched it grow dark outside, the athletes beginning to stream past the office in a steady file now, all making their way to Gallaloe's village hall for the safety talk and briefing. Bertie had laid on coaches at all the main campsites out of town, given the woeful lack of public transport services.

Half five came and went, her patience with it. Five to six. Ten past. She felt demented. Enraged. Furious. Helpless.

It was quarter past when she had a brainwave. Without a car of one's own, there was only one way in and out of this village. Quickly, she made a call and waited impatiently as it rang three times.

'Seamus, hi, it's Ottie.' she said in a rush, the second he picked up.

'Ottie, hello dere,' the village taxi driver called back, a leisurely smile in his voice, static on the line. 'How are ya?'

'Yes, good, thanks.'

'You're busy down dere den. I've been op and down dat road a yours like a rat op a drainpipe today.'

'Ha, yes . . . Seamus, listen, that's what I was calling about actually – you didn't happen to do an airport run earlier this afternoon, did you? I've got a booking that's gone AWOL.'

'Woy, yes, I'm jost back, in fact.'

'It wasn't a chap called Ben Gilmore, was it?'

'Gilmore . . . Gilmore . . . Me memory's not what it was,

like. He was an American fella though, I can tell you that. Quiet sort. Didn't have moch to say for hisself.'

'American? Oh, I don't know if that's him.' Ottie bit her lip. 'I've just got he was flying in from Heathrow.'

'Aye, from Heathrow, that's right.'

Her ears pricked up hopefully. 'Did he look like an elite runner?'

'Looked damned hungry from where I wos sitting. Not a pick on him. These fellas would do well to make acquaintance with a good pie now and den.'

'Sports kit? Trainers? Wind burn?' They were easy to spot.

'Nup. He was in a suit.'

Ottie heaved a sigh of despair. No one in a suit would have booked into a campsite. 'No, that can't be him.' She bit her lip. Where the hell was her client? Had he seen the wild forecast and booked in to a B&B instead? She couldn't imagine where though; everywhere with rooms in a five-mile radius had been booked for months now. Perhaps he'd missed the plane? Or just come to his senses about the madness of running a hundred-plus miles in a day and night? Maybe he was injured and hadn't bothered to cancel? He better not have done, she thought darkly – she'd turned away six people already today.

'He did ask me to drop him straight at the village hall.'

'*What?*' She felt something inside her snap.

'Aye. Said he'd call me later to take him on to you. I'm going backs there in an hour, after I've had me tea.'

He was at the briefing? He'd gone straight there? Ottie felt her rage bloom. All this time she'd been sitting here, waiting to book him in and he hadn't had the decency to ring ahead and let her know? 'The bloody idiot!' she exploded.

'Did I do somet'ing wrong?' Seamus asked, sounding alarmed.

Oh God. She dropped her head, pinching her temples between her fingers as she tried to gather herself. 'No, Seamus, I'm sorry, no. You didn't. I . . . I'm just furious with *him.* I'm supposed to be at the meeting too, that's all. I'm stewarding tomorrow.'

'Pah, what d'you want to be troubling yeself with dat meetin' for? Yus been doing it long enough to know the score. Dese tings are for ole Bertie Moneyboots to puff up his chest and make he'self sound important to the newcomers. It's an ego trip. He always says the same thing every year anyways: proper shoes, no gom, follow the flags, spare batteries for dem headtorches, bivvy packs, whistles and maps. Blah blah blah.'

Ottie closed her eyes, knowing he was right. She didn't need to be there for the technical details – but he couldn't possibly know why she really wanted to be at that meeting, and she could never tell. It was always the same, having to pretend that it meant nothing if she saw him in the street, or that it didn't hurt if his wife reached over to muss up his hair during a drunken dinner with her folks. Everything had to be a secret, her entire life run as a charade, and most of the time she could just about do it; she could bear it well enough. But this wasn't most of the time. This was the worst of times and she needed him, the man she loved.

She checked the clock on the wall, feeling desperate. Six twenty. It'd take her twenty minutes to get there from here; the track was bumpy and rough even mid-summer but this time of year, in this weather, it'd be like a slip-slide. If she was lucky, she'd be arriving just as everyone was leaving. No, it was already too late. Tonight's precious opportunity to see him in plain sight – the race meeting an alibi for them both – had slipped from her grasp.

'You're right, Seamus,' she said in a tight voice, reasserting self-control again. 'I'm overreacting. Sorry. I just don't want to let anyone down is all.'

'As if ye could. Jost you put your feet up. I'll finish me dinner then pick 'im op and drop him down to ya in a bit. Don't worry about a ting, pet.'

'Thanks, Seamus.'

She hung up and dropped her head forwards, giving a small scream of frustration. Was the entire world against her? She had wanted only to glimpse him tonight, to maybe find a moment together in the loos or in his car. Was it really so much to ask? She had just needed to look into his eyes, to feel his hands in her hair. Something to keep her going, to keep the loneliness at bay. He was competing in the race tomorrow so she knew there'd be no midnight visits tonight and as pride made it a necessity for him to run his own course, she knew exactly how depleted he'd be for days afterwards too, Shula no doubt chomping at the bit to whisk him off to the Bahamas for a 'proper rest' and 'a little winter sun before the Christmas rush'.

She flung herself back in the chair, agitated and upset, bitter tears sliding down her face again as she thought of Shula carelessly opening another bottle of wine, not even noticing her husband across the kitchen, turning away from him in bed each night, oblivious to what she had in him. It wasn't fair. She didn't even want him, she just wanted what he could give her: the lifestyle, the cachet, the jewels, the horses, the holidays . . .

And what did Ottie get? She didn't care about *things* or *stuff*. She just wanted him and she couldn't even have that.

She stared around her tiny office, seeing it as if for the first time – a converted animal pen set in a windswept field beside a remote beach. Was this really everything life had to offer her? It was a question that she kept trying to push away: she was in love, that alone made her one of the lucky ones, and yet she couldn't help but notice that she was as trapped by it as she was freed. There were rarely impromptu nights at the Hare for her, in case Bertie called while she was out; and she never took up the offers for dinner that she sometimes got from the guys that camped here – adventurers, walkers, runners – for she had no interest in making Bertie jealous. It wasn't like he'd chosen this love either – it had surprised and overtaken them both. How could either one of them have known that the offhand offer to repair a broken lock when her parents had been away would prove to be the cataclysmic event in both their lives? She'd never even thought about him in that way till he'd caught her mid-trip over her shoelace and they'd found themselves eye to eye, nose to nose, mouth to mouth . . . It made her shiver to remember it as they'd crossed that invisible line, their bodies tingling with the frisson of illicit attraction.

But if their love had started out as an accident, it had become a very deliberate secret and she, for one, was exhausted keeping it. Life was short, her father's death at fifty-eight proved that. Surely they had to live for today and grab their tomorrows with both hands?

'Hello?' A voice outside, followed by a knock at the door, made her startle momentarily and she peered out of the window, just able to make out a couple in blue cagoules with a Yorkie shivering at the end of a lead. Ultra runners they weren't. Hurriedly she brushed her tears away.

Yes, things had to change, she thought, as she opened the

door and they looked up at her with hopeful eyes – and she would personally make sure they did.

* * *

Ottie had only just climbed out of the shower and wrapped a towel around her hair when she heard the knock at the door. Her heart gave a little leap – he must have been driving fast! – and she quickly checked her appearance in the mirror; his concerned text – where had she been? – had transformed her mood and evening. Picking up her glass of red wine, she skittered out of the bedroom, making a dash to the front door and only slowing to a sashay as her hand reached for the handle.

'Hey . . .' she said seductively, the smile dying on her lips as she caught sight first of a pair of leather shoes. Bertie only ever wore suede brogues out here.

'Hi. Are you Ottie Lorne?'

At the sound of the accent, her expression set harder than concrete.

'Who's asking?' she asked, already knowing perfectly well who he was.

'Ben Gilmore.'

'Ben Gilmore,' she repeated, making no move to say anything further. He didn't look like a Ben Gilmore. She supposed she'd been expecting a wholesome smile and dark, swept-back hair, round eyes and a look of contented suburbia about him. A Netflix jock. Instead he was tall but rangy, with light-brown close-cropped hair and a lean, angled face. His eyes were sharp too, in shape but also, she sensed, perception for he had a quiet intensity about him. He looked exactly like the sort of person who'd consider running a hundred miles in the middle of winter a 'good time'.

'I've got a booking for four nights.' And when she didn't reply, he added: 'At the campsite.'

She waited for a few seconds and then gave a look of surprise. 'Oh yes, Mr Gilmore. We were expecting you.'

'I went to the office but no one was there. Someone told me to try you over here.'

'Someone told you to find me here?' she echoed in surprise.

'Yes. Couple with a dog.'

'Ah yes, the Packards. Lovely couple. Cute dog.'

His brow puckered slightly, as though baffled to be given back these details. 'Yes.'

'Crackers, I think they said his name was.'

'. . . Right. Well, anyway, if I could just get the paperwork sorted and whatever I need from you, I'll pitch the tent. It's going to be tricky enough getting it up in the dark with this wind.'

'Yes.' She crossed her arms over her chest. 'It's a real shame you didn't get here in the daylight.'

'Yeah.' He shifted his weight and she noticed the large red North Face duffel bag on the ground behind him, which belied the Brooks Brothers tailoring and revealed the true him. 'Heathrow air traffic control was against me on that one.'

'Well, I'm sorry to have to tell you this, Mr Gilmore, but I was obliged to release your booking and I'm afraid we're fully booked.'

He looked confused, no doubt because she'd delivered the bad news with a smile. '. . . I'm sorry, what?'

'Yes. Check-in is by six o'clock latest at this time of year. As I'm sure you can appreciate, it's a safety hazard to have people pitching tents in the dark.'

'But I had a booking. I booked my pitch months ago,' he insisted. 'You can't just give it away.'

'Well, in accordance with our t and c's,' she said with infuriating politeness, 'check-in must be completed by 6 p.m. or the reservation is null and void.'

He stared at her with an expression that flitted between outrage and disbelief. 'This has to be a joke, right?'

'I'm afraid not. We Irish aren't that funny.'

'But I'm competing in the race tomorrow. I can't just—'

'You could try Maureen's place, three miles up the road from here. It's out of season for her so I don't know if she's put the cows in the field now but you could always ask her.'

'No,' he said firmly. 'It is dark and freezing out here. I have no car—'

'Well, how'd you get here?'

'Some maniac cab driver who drove ninety-five all the way from the airport.'

'Ah, Seamus. Yes, he's a poppet,' she smiled, going to close the door on him. 'Anyway, I'm sorry I can't help. Good luck tomorrow.'

'Wait!' His command was so forceful and panicked it could have made the fish breach the water. 'You can't just . . . you can't just leave me out here.'

'Mr Gilmore, I don't see what more I can do. You forfeited your reservation here.'

'But my flight was delayed! And then I had to go straight to the briefing for the kit checks and bag drops. I got here as soon as I could.'

'Of course. Of course. I understand that, Mr Gilmore,' she said, tutting sympathetically. 'And if you'd only rung ahead and explained, I could have held your pitch for you.'

'But I . . . I didn't realize.'

'No. People don't. They think we'll just sit around in a field for hours, waiting for them to turn up.' She gave a shrug of her shoulders. 'The Packards turned up just as I was locking up so they got it instead. Last pitch this side of Cork, I shouldn't imagine. I told them they were lucky, especially in this weather.'

She watched him stand there in the rain, his suit getting soaked through, tidemarks beginning to seep up the leather shoes. She took a sip of her wine, feeling only a little bit bad for him. Yes, it was mean to give away his pitch, but had he given any regard whatsoever to his actions inconveniencing her earlier? Of course not. He had no idea of what the consequences of his selfishness meant for her.

'Look, I'm sorry I didn't call ahead, okay? It was . . . it was selfish and you have every right to be pissed at me. But surely I can set up my tent in a corner somewhere?'

'I wish I could oblige you, but that would infringe our health and safety guidelines, not to mention invalidate our insurance.'

'But it would just be for tonight. It's imperative I get a decent night's sleep before the race. I won't even be sleeping in the tent tomorrow night – I'll be running straight through and be done by dawn on Sunday morning.'

She suppressed a knowing smirk. Before dawn on Sunday? He fancied himself, clearly. There was a reason the race finished at six that evening.

'Mr Gilmore, please,' she said, giving a tight smile. 'You're putting me in a very awkward position. I wish I could help but my hands are tied. Good night now—'

'This is bullshit!' he cried as she went to shut the door on him, her eyes suddenly fastening on a beam of light behind the hedgerows, coming down the lane.

'What—?' Ben Gilmore turned to see what she was looking

at, just as the Range Rover turned around the bend and pulled into her short, rutted drive.

She looked back at him, realizing she had to get this man off her doorstep before Bertie got out of the car. 'Okay, look, you can uh . . .' She glanced around frantically. 'You can set up in the garden.'

'Really?' he asked, surprised. He looked around at the small patch of lawn, ring-fenced by a low mossy-topped stone wall. It was a surprisingly effectively windbreak for those rare days when she wanted to attempt a tan. Annoyingly, he'd sleep better there tonight than he would have done in the field, but she was over her earlier anger with him now. Bertie was here and that was all that really mattered.

'Yes, really.'

'Anywhere in particular?'

'No, no,' she said hurriedly. 'Just, away from the house. Over there somewhere,' she said, practically shooing him towards the far uppermost corner.

But Bertie was already out of the car and coming through the pedestrian gate. Too late, he saw her visitor on the door-step, visibly misstepping as his brain tried to calculate the benefits of a swift about-turn.

'Mr Flanagan,' Gilmore said, a note of surprise in his voice.

'Ah! Our American friend,' Bertie said, drawing closer and clearly recognizing him from the meeting too. 'Checking in, are you?'

'Trying to.'

Gilmore looked back at Ottie, before looking back expect-antly at Bertie again, as though awaiting *his* explanation for being here.

'Yes, I, uh, I came to check on Miss Lorne here, as she

missed the briefing just now and she is one of our stewards tomorrow.'

'I'm afraid I was waiting for Mr Gilmore to check in,' she said. 'His plane was delayed but unfortunately he didn't communicate that to me, so I was just explaining how I had to give his pitch to another couple.'

'Ah.' Bertie gave a suitably pained look but Ottie could see how he relaxed now her absence had been explained. 'How unfortunate.'

Ottie looked at Ben, wanting him to squirm some more but he seemed to be done for now. He had a very candid manner, she noticed. Was it an American thing? She gave a sigh. Who cared? 'Anyway, given the race is starting in less than twelve hours, and he's highly unlikely to find anything at all at this late stage, I've said he can pitch his tent in the garden overnight instead.'

'In the garden? Yes, I see,' Bertie said. 'Well, that's very generous of you.'

'It's only for tonight,' she shrugged. 'He'll be running through tomorrow night and then will move it by first thing on Sunday. Won't you, Mr Gilmore?'

He nodded back, but was regarding her with a look that she didn't appreciate – as though he knew this was all a charade. But there was no way he possibly could. It was her paranoia getting the better of her, that was all. Bertie's alibi was highly plausible, especially as it had been prompted by Gilmore's own actions.

She looked back at Bertie, eager to get this stranger off her doorstep and out of the way. The clock was always ticking . . . 'You said you wanted to discuss the stewarding, Bertie?' she asked disingenuously as he began to shuffle slightly, trying to dodge the rain.

He looked straight at her, the dance already in his eyes. 'I did.'

'Well, if you'll excuse us then, Mr Gilmore,' she said, stepping back to allow her lover in.

Gilmore looked at them both, before slowly reaching down to pick up his bag. 'There's just one more thing,' he said as she had almost closed the door.

She sighed. 'Yes?' she asked impatiently, peering her head back through the crack.

'Where do I get a key for the toilet and shower blocks?'

For pity's sake. Suppressing another sigh, she reached for her own key on the hook. 'Use mine and put it through the letterbox in the morning,' she said with a tight smile.

And before he could say another word, she closed the door, shutting out the wind, the rain and his damnable all-knowing stare.

Chapter Eight

Saturday, 7 December

'Toast?'

Her mother didn't reply, her legs curled up on the blue gingham window seat as she looked out over the gardens. She was still wearing her dressing gown, even though it was almost lunchtime, and she hadn't washed her hair since the funeral, faint smudges of mascara below her eyes. It was as though she had held herself together till that, but after the reading of the will, had allowed herself to slide into gentle ruin.

Still, at least Mrs Mac had talked her into leaving her room.

'Mam?' Willow tried again.

'Huh? What?' Her mother turned to face her. She had visibly lost weight over the past week and a half, her cheeks hollowing, the skin pulling down at the corners of her eyes.

'I asked if you were hungry. I'm making some toast.' It was all she could do not to snap the words.

'Oh. No. Not hungry.' She turned and looked out of the window again.

Willow put the bread in the toaster anyway and rummaged in the larder for the marmalade. She poured a fresh pot of tea and brought it over, carefully setting a mug in her mother's cold hands. 'Drink up. You're freezing sitting by the window. Why don't you sit by the Aga?'

'I like having the view,' she said quietly, resting her head against the wall.

Willow sighed, leaning against the Aga rail herself as she waited for the toast to pop up. She gazed around the room, wondering for how many years – generations even – this very scene had been playing. Mabel and Dot were in their usual places on the rugs, muzzles nestled between muddy paws after their morning bound around the grounds, eyelids drooping heavily. The kitchen had never been decorated in her lifetime, the cream wooden units and oak worktops were unfashionable and dull, but not offensive in any way, crackle-glazed farmyard tiles around the wall. She couldn't remember a time when those banded creamware jugs hadn't been sitting on the shelf above the ancient yellow solid-fuel Aga, and she had no idea how the crack in the bottom windowpane beside the herb pots had happened – an exuberant child or an oblivious robin? There were pails of seasoned logs and the old yellowing newspapers heaped in a basket, ready to be used to set the many fires, must surely date back years at the very bottom, for they only ever took from the top; the 1950s cookbooks with cloth covers and turned-down pages dealt in imperial measures. It was like a time capsule in here, she thought to herself, the only recent addition being a small enamel bucket newly placed on the floor in the corner by the pantry; she looked up at the ceiling above it and the bloom of damp spreading along the plaster. There were other buckets in the billiards room and many of the bedrooms too.

She looked at her mother again, slight and still against the window. If there was history caught and captured within these battlemented walls, it was also a living history – her mother's own story. This had been the beating heart of her home when her family had been gathered all around her, children playing quite literally at her knee as she devised menus for the dinner party that weekend and Mrs Mac cooked and ironed – those halcyon days of childhood and golden family time before they had all treacherously grown up, before Willow had left for city life, before her husband had died. Everyone abandoning her.

The toast popped up – the signature scent of the kitchen, Willow always thought; even in Dublin it made her pause, dragging her mind and heart back here. She sparingly spread the marmalade across the top, the way she knew her mother liked it.

'Eat up,' she said, taking the tea from her mother's hands and replacing it with the plate instead. 'You must keep your strength up, Mam.'

'But I'm not hungry.'

'Eat anyway.' Willow clambered onto the other end of the window seat with her own tea and sat opposite, making sure their feet didn't touch. She felt a silent spike of anger as she watched her mother dispassionately chew, realizing she was doing precisely what her father had always done – looking after her, protecting her. She looked so vulnerable there, as soft as pillows, small as a pocket – it seemed barely believable that she could have been the architect of so much pain and suffering. Willow supposed she was finding out first-hand now, what it felt like to have her destiny determined by another, her future ripped out of her own hands. She was treading in the very same footsteps she had forced her own daughter to make but she wasn't making a decent fist of it. Her mother was falling where Willow had risen. Willow supposed there had to be some satisfaction in that. Somewhere.

It was the first time they had been alone together since that day in the library when her father's will had been read and despite the indisputable fact that her mother was disabled by grief, Willow was also convinced her mother was avoiding her. Everyone was. They had all blown to their separate corners of the estate like petals in a storm. Ottie hadn't come up to the castle once in the past few days, and Pip was edgy around her too, blowing hot and cold, her words telling her one thing, her eyes quite another. Mrs Mac kept saying they all just needed time to adjust. But what about her? Who was helping her to adjust?

Besides, time – like money – was something else they didn't have. Like those buckets catching drips, the estate problems would soon start mounting up and multiplying. Heavy weather was forecast for this weekend and they were only just coming into the depths of winter. Nothing was going to get better any time soon and existing problems were going to feel magnified – heating costs, leaks . . .

Willow took a deep breath, steeling herself to say what had to be said. 'So you remember we've got the team from Christie's coming this morning?'

Only the vaguest surprise registered on her mother's face. 'Christie's?'

'Yes. Mrs Mac said she told you when she brought in your breakfast yesterday.'

'Oh. Yes.' She gave a sigh. 'If you say so.'

As if on cue, Mrs Mac came through with the water jug for the iron. She filled it up wordlessly, but glanced over at Serena with a concerned look, arching an eyebrow at Willow as she passed on her way back out again.

'It's very informal, just an exploratory chat at this stage. If we don't like what they have to say, then we don't have to go any further with it. No pressure. They'll just want to get a sense of what we might include in an auction. Have you had a think about what you would want to keep?'

Her mother didn't reply, her eyes following a starling hopping on the ground. Was she even listening?

Willow bit back the spear of fury that lanced through her. 'Well anyway, if there's enough to justify it, then they'll arrange an estate sale, probably on site, and if not, then they'll enlist the bits and bobs for various specialist sales.'

Still nothing.

'At the same time, the realty expert will be looking around the estate, assessing the land and buildings to give us an indication for asking price and marketing strategy.'

Her mother leaned her head back against the wall again as though supporting herself was too much; she had forgotten to keep chewing and for several moments she sat motionless as she stared out at the glistening band of sea.

'Mam?' Willow prompted.

'Hmm?' she asked, beginning to chew automatically again as she was brought back into the moment.

'It's going to be my friend Helena Talbot coming to talk to us.'

'What is?'

Oh dear God. 'The Christie's representative. She's a friend from ho—' She stopped herself just in time but her mother's eyes were suddenly, reflexively, upon her; she'd heard the slip. *That* she'd heard and for a moment, the dark truth that had never been spoken came and sat between them, filling the space like a fat purring cat. Would her mother say something now? Would she acknowledge it? Say she knew why she'd run? The moment swelled, tautened –

Popped.

Her mother's eyes swivelled down and Willow swallowed, feeling the rejection of so much more than a conversation.

'She's from Dublin. She went to school with Caz, my flat-mate.'

'That's nice.'

'Yes.' It was like talking to the wall. More silence, but this time it held nothing. 'And then I thought, later, you and I could go over to the Dower House and take a look around together. I popped by yesterday. I hadn't seen the place in years.'

'No. No, I don't think I'd want to do that.'

'But, Mam—'

'I don't care what O'Leary says. Your father did not intend for me to end up in that dark, dingy house,' her mother snapped.

Willow felt herself fall back into the numbness that had become the best course for dealing with her mother. 'It's not dingy, though, that's the thing. It's actually very pretty. Of course it's overgrown at the moment, but I had a good look around and I think if we got Ted Flaherty to take down some of the trees, it'd make a big difference. The house is only dark because it was built in the middle of the copse, but you could cut down a swathe or even remove the whole lot. The lawn's level there and with the trees gone, you'd get a view of the headland. Plus it's close to the village over there. You'd be able to walk in, no problem.'

'No.'

Willow stared at her mother. This was the conversation her father had tried to avoid, the one he'd left her to have instead. She was to be Bad Cop? Fine. 'Mam, we've gone over this. We have to sell.'

'No.'

'*Yes*, there's no other choice. We cannot afford to stay. We have to sell it, get a good price, take our memories and move on. It's time.'

She knew her mother – pampered, spoilt, indulged, too-loved – had no idea of the reality facing the estate. The castle – now that the decay had begun – was beginning to deteriorate rapidly; they had to sell before it got any worse. Had her mother ever left her room she would have known that each day since the reading of the will, Willow had met up with O'Leary to go through the probate in more detail. Her father had left the paperwork in good shape, but it was clear her mother didn't have the first idea of how precarious their financial position really was; her father had protected her from everything. 'What about the original buyer – do you think he might still be interested?'

Her mother looked back at her blankly, before a seed of recognition dawned. 'You mean the Englishman?'

Jeesht. Not again. 'Does it matter what nationality he is?'

'It mattered to your father. Very much.'

'Well . . .' Willow wondered how to phrase this. Bluntly? 'We might have to overlook the unfortunate fact of his place of birth. Beggars can't afford to be choosers. There's not many people who want, much less can afford, an Irish castle at the best of times – and we all know these are not the best of times.'

Her mother shook her head, engaged now at least. Indignation was seemingly the only thing to rouse her from her torpor. 'He wouldn't be interested. He and your father parted on very unsavoury terms.'

Willow wasn't interested in making new friends. 'Do you remember his name?'

'No, but even if I did, you're not to call him. He was awful. Your father died hating him: arrogant, cocky, r—'

'Rich?'

'I was going to say rash.'

'Well, rich is all that matters. We don't need to like the guy. We just need him to buy this place and take it off our hands.'

Her mother looked back at her with the focus that had been missing for the past week and a half. 'Is it really that straightforward for you? Something simply to be dealt with?'

'I've had the meetings with O'Leary, you haven't. It's a burden, Mam.'

'No, it's our home. Your home.'

Her mother flinched as Willow gave a bitter laugh and the fat cat stretched and purred between them again; it was always there, even if sometimes it was out of sight.

They stared at one another, Willow feeling a pressure rise in her chest, the anger like a heat and warming her up. She felt her breath become shallow, the pertinent question her mother wouldn't ask shimmering in front of them both like a knife, ready to cut and wound. Just waiting . . .

Mrs Mac walked back into the kitchen, carrying the ironing board under one arm and tutting about the spitting rain wetting her sheets.

The bubble popped again and this time it was Willow who looked away first. She tried to recover herself, forcing her breathing to become slow and steady again before looking back at her mother like she was the child. 'You should get dressed now, Mam.'

Willow shut the door to the library and quietly crossed over to the desk, her breathing still coming quickly, the torrent of adrenaline from dealing with her mother still pumping in her bloodstream. It had become *her* room in the intervening days since the will had been read, towers of files and paperwork arranged in piles on the desk and on the floor, neon Post-its fluttering on top like road signs telling her where to go.

She sat in the chair and cast an impassive gaze around the room from the hallowed spot. This wasn't just where her father would conduct his business affairs, but where he 'couldn't be interrupted', where all the difficult phone conversations had happened, where her own life had fallen apart.

Her eyes fell to the desk and the A4 black mock-croc, leather-bound diary positioned to one side, the tip of a ribbon peeking through the gilt-ended pages like a snake's tongue; her father always used to buy the same model every year from Smythson, his initials stamped in the bottom-right corner. Perhaps she would do the same. That, at least, might be a family tradition they could keep to.

With a grim determination she began to flick through, working backwards and trying not to be pained by the very sight of his handwriting. What would her father have written to record the meeting with the man who wanted to buy his castle, she mused as she turned over the pages. She didn't suppose he'd have explicitly written *Buyer* to help her in posterity.

Still, an appointments diary, she saw, was a surprisingly intimate record of a person's life, and she felt her heart begin to beat a little faster as she scanned over the noted meetings, lunches and dinners that had shaped his final days: 2 November, dentist; 26 October, golf, Bertie; 23 October, Rotary Club dinner; 18 October, Mr Hopwood, Mercy University Hospital; 17 October, MRI; 15 October, Cycle, Bertie; 14 October, GP; 2 October, shooting, Dunmorgan estate . . .

She paused suddenly.

Wait. Hadn't O'Leary said when it first came up that the sale had been negotiated around Easter time? She flicked straight back to March and thumbed forwards instead . . .

stopping eventually on 15 April, *C. Shaye, 11 a.m.* There was nothing to illuminate her on C. Shaye's business with her father but the telephone number beside it had a London dial code.

She stared at it. Worth a punt, surely?

So her father had hated him. So what? So he was an Englishman. So what? What did it matter if he was a rich Englishman coming over here to do what his ancestors had not – take what he wanted, not with force but the silent exchange of cash. Was that worse, a victory seven hundred years in the making?

She grabbed her mobile and dialled.

He answered on the first ring. 'Yep.' The voice was brisk, distracted.

It took her a second to find her own voice. '. . . Hello, Mr Shaye?'

'Who is this?' She could almost hear the frown in his voice, everything in it her father hated: imperiousness, arrogance, superiority . . . Immediately she knew why he'd hated him.

'You don't know me but I believe you met my father, Declan Lorne.'

There was a pause – thankfully – and when he spoke next, she heard the focus in his voice. She had his attention. 'As if I could forget.'

She took a deep breath, hoping to sound as direct and forceful as him. 'Am I right in thinking you were interested in buying Lorne?'

There was a pause. 'I *was*.' His stress on the past tense wasn't encouraging.

'Might you be interested again?'

She heard his scoff down the line. 'Your father told me Lorne would never be available to the "likes of" me.'

Willow rolled her eyes. She could imagine how plain her

father had made his feelings about him. He'd never been one to disguise his emotions and he prided himself on calling a spade a shovel. But what could she say to this man? She didn't want to tell him too much about their changed circumstances; the news of her father's death wasn't some throwaway line to pop into conversation with a stranger.

'Things have changed and we're putting Lorne on the market again. Given your previous interest, we thought we'd make contact in case you wanted to look at it off-book.'

'Who's we?'

'. . . The family.'

There was another long pause and she could almost hear the deductions clicking in his brain – the out-of-the-blue call, the evasive daughter . . .

'Well, I appreciate the call, Ms Lorne, but my portfolio's closed at the moment. I'm not looking to make any further investments at this time.'

'Oh.' She couldn't hide the disappointment in her voice. She swallowed. 'I see. Well, if you—'

She heard a click.

'Hello? Mr Shaye? Are you still there?'

'We're all missing you desperately!' Hels said as they walked through the parterre, her mother's favourite part of the garden. 'The studio's not the same without you there. I went to the Go Slo Flow class this week and they've got this interim manager in. Apparently she's decided to *economize* by spraying Glade around, instead of your wonderful meditation mist.'

'She has not!' Willow said, horrified. Pyro Tink was the pyrotechnic gym with a cult following, the high-octane antidote to the yoga revolution and with waiting lists that the city's members' clubs could only dream of. When she had first arrived in Dublin, it had been the only way to calm her down, to beat back her anger, and she had spent almost all the money she made from waitressing taking slavish daily classes and drinking protein smoothies in the juice bar every day. She'd been a devotee before she'd been an employee and when the manager's job had come up, she'd jumped at it. She'd never been in better shape and she was instantly everyone's new best friend at parties whenever they found out where she worked. But her Aussie boss ran the Dublin branch to the tried-and-tested formula that had made his business a $22m success story back home and he didn't like to deviate from the plan; every tiny initiative she'd implemented had been hard-won and getting the organic meditation mist approved for the wind-downs, although expensive, had been one of her great wins. All the clients loved it, plus they made a 46 per cent profit on every tube they sold, and she'd been on the brink of proposing they develop their own branded line of products when she'd taken the call about her father. So to hear she'd not yet been out of the city two weeks, and already her legacy was being eroded . . . ?

At their backs, the castle stood noble and impenetrable; before them, an ancient yew appeared almost to curtsey as one bough swept to the ground. It was one of those days when the very light seemed tinted, warming up the world with a rosy blush. Willow knew it was the calm before the storm, like the intake of breath the sea always took before a tsunami, or before a scream took a girl's voice. Gale-force winds and lashing rain were forecast for tomorrow, as much as a month's worth in three hours.

'I've missed you too, Hels. It's been –' She swallowed. *My father died six minutes before I arrived home. My family won't talk to me*. 'Intense.'

'Oh, I'm so sorry, babe.' Helena squeezed her arm consolingly. She looked freshly tanned from her recent safari break in Kenya with her new boyfriend. 'You've been *so* much in our minds.'

'Thanks.'

'Oh my god, look at that!' Hels laughed delightedly as a peacock strutted across the lawn.

Willow just smiled. There had always been peacocks at Lorne, certainly throughout her lifetime, and once they'd even had a pure-white one; Pip had called it Midnight, just to be contrary.

Helena inhaled deeply and stopped walking, throwing her arms out and her head back. 'God, it's so unbelievably quiet here.'

'I know,' Willow murmured, wondering if it was a good thing. She was all for noise and distraction herself. 'It's so heavy and dense, sometimes I think you could bite down on it.'

'I'll be sure to put that in the particulars – edible peace,' Hels laughed. Always chic, even in a sweaty pyro class, today she looked especially smart – or perhaps that was just because Willow felt like a bumpkin in her old jeans and jumper, a mud splatter up the backs of her calves; her urban gloss was already getting gritty. She had left Dublin in such a rush, there'd been no time to pack and she was getting by in the old clothes left in her wardrobe from three years ago.

Hels, by contrast, wearing a pleated navy dress and Tabitha Simmons Mary Janes, looked like a chess piece from the city chequerboard, groomed and sophisticated, and everything this gently crumbling, leaking, battered and windswept estate wasn't. Just the sight of her was a stinging reminder of everything Willow had left behind by coming back here and she felt even more desperate now to get away again as soon as she possibly could. Every day that passed, she could feel the city slipping its bonds and moving further away from her. Leaving her behind.

'It really is incredible, Willow. I had no idea this was your home. You never made any reference to who your father was. I mean, what a heritage! You're a knight's daughter. How could you never mention that?'

Willow looked away quickly. 'Yeah, well . . . it's not something to be particularly proud of,' she shrugged. 'Besides, what was I supposed to say? "Hi, Willow Lorne, general manager at Pyro Tink and knight's daughter"? It's not like it's anything to do with me. It's just a title – and a male one at that.'

Hels' smile faded. 'It is so sad – having to sell *and* the title dying out . . .'

Willow could feel her body stiffening. 'Well, you know what they say – all good things must come to an end sooner or later, and we had a good run here: seven hundred and twelve years is a good innings by anyone's standards. Besides, it would never be the same here without Dad. He *was* Lorne.'

'And there was no way to get the knighthood transferred to you or your sisters?'

Willow shook her head, feeling a wave of heat, anger, rise up inside her. 'He did try but there was no budging on it. Had to be a "sir".'

'Honestly in this day and age . . .' Hels sighed wearily.

'I know.'

Hels turned to face her squarely. 'So then you're absolutely sure this is what you want to do? Sell the lot?'

'Depends what you think we can get for it,' Willow said non-committally, even though 'anything at all' could only be an improvement on their current financial predicament.

Hels laughed as though she'd cracked a joke. 'It'll be an

enormous upheaval for you – emotionally as well as physically.'

'I'm bang out of other options,' Willow shrugged. 'Can't give it away, can't afford to keep it and can't think of a great business idea with which to make my millions.'

Hels turned on the spot again, taking in the projecting bow windows on this facade, the many leaded windows, corbelled chimney stacks . . . 'Well, something of this calibre deserves to find a sensitive buyer, someone who knows how to do what needs doing, sympathetically. As you said, there's a fair of amount of restoration work that'll have to be done by the new owner. It's not for the faint of heart – the scale of it would frighten a lot of people – but the right buyer is out there, that's for sure.' She looked back at Willow again. 'At this level though, it's a matter of waiting for them. You know that, right? There's not that many of them around.'

'And what level are we talking about, roughly?'

Hels blew out slowly through her cheeks, making even *that* look elegant. 'The team thinks five and a half, maybe even six million—'

'Holy shit!' Willow exclaimed. 'Seriously?'

'*If* we had the right buyer on the right day. And *if* there was a following wind.' Hels grinned. 'A lot of ifs. And it could take a long time – months, definitely, but maybe even a year or two . . .'

Willow blinked, feeling her euphoria dissipate. A year or two? She didn't have that kind of time; certainly not that kind of patience. She couldn't be saddled with this place – and everything it had done to her – for anything like that long.

Hels saw her expression and rubbed her arm sympathetically. 'Listen, market conditions are challenging. Which is corporate speak for shite,' she smiled. '*Everything*'s sticking at the moment. It's a buyers' market. But you could always sell it for less if you wanted a quick sale. People act fast when they think they're getting a bargain.'

'Right,' Willow murmured, but it was hard to get six million out of her head now it had been planted there. 'And what about the contents sale – when could that happen? Assuming my mother goes for it, I mean.'

'Well, there's a hell of a lot to get through. Your family's collected a lot over the years! We'll need to get a team onto it. Inventorying it all will take weeks, if not months.'

'But when could we go to auction, do you think?' she pressed.

Hels considered. 'I'm thinking probably around Easter.'

Damn. 'Really?' Willow bit her lip. Even that felt too long to wait. She wanted to get back to Dublin and her proper life. Her temporary replacement was spraying Glade around in her absence for Chrissakes while she was losing her edge out here, she could feel it – the ever-present threat of lapsing back into who she'd once been here: sweet, pliable, gullible Willow. The baby. The idiot. The—

'Well, an estate of this scale and importance, we need to get it right. And, listen, you've had a huge amount to deal with lately. You've been through so much. It's important you take time to really think about what's right for you and especially your poor mother—'

'I don't need time to think,' she said sharply. Decisively. Her mother wasn't the victim here. 'Let's do it.'

Hels looked astonished. '*Really?*'

'Yes,' Willow said, looking up at the ancient castle that had once been her home, her safety, her refuge and was now none of those things. Her father had left her this place specifically to get rid of it and her mother would just have to deal with it. 'I need to be shot of this place once and for all. Let's sell.'

Chapter Nine

The same day

Ottie stood in the rain, shivering violently, clipboard in her arms again as she waited to mark off the runners as they passed by, writing down the time and the numbers pinned on their chest and backs. The race had started at 6 a.m., weaving a looping course from the Flanagan estate along the coastline, and although she'd been at her post for over an hour now, clocking on at 7 a.m., it would take even the fastest runners two hours to get here as the course wended along the jagged coastline.

Every so often, one of the race marshals would drive up on a quad bike, a walkie-talkie clipped to his belt, checking up on the pit stop stations and stewards and handing out bottles of water. It wasn't water she wanted though – coffee, tea, hot chocolate, anything warm. Weather conditions were a lot harsher than had been hoped and exactly as had been predicted – driving rain, and a strong offshore wind that kept a permanent chill in her fingertips and toes. Ottie was certain it was harder going for the stewards than for the competitors, at least they got to move around and generate heat; she on the other hand was stuck on her watch, an especially narrow stretch of the Way with a steep drop on one side straight down to the sea and nowhere to shelter in either direction for several miles. Her particular station was positioned on, if not quite a promontory, a small belly, meaning the wind and rain caught her from all sides. In vain, she had dragged the little striped canopy and table and chairs slightly further round the bend, trying to get at least some protection from the severe conditions, but the towering blackened clouds stacking in the sky promised little respite.

Most of the race along the Wild Atlantic Way was run along the top of the cliffs, exposed to the wind but wide and firm underfoot at least, but here the path dropped fifty feet below the summit and was dug into the side of the cliffs, rendering it both narrow and prone to erosion. That heavy rain was not going to help anyone here. It was one of the most perilous sections of the course – far too dangerous to attempt at night, which was why the course was run this way round, so that it was always tackled first thing in the morning light. Bertie had given it to her, knowing she knew it better than anyone, for it was on Lorne land after all; she and Pip and Willow had spent their childhoods racing up and down this trail, their parents walking hand in hand behind them.

She stepped side to side, squinting into the rain and looking hopefully up and down the track for signs of another runner or anyone bringing coffee – she didn't care which. She was bored and cold and just wanted something to break the monotony, for there wasn't even a visible horizon to watch. Only the prospect of fleetingly seeing Bertie cheered her; supporting him was the sole reason she volunteered to help with this, hidden in plain sight. They'd shared a magical hour together last night and he'd made a promise to try and throw off any neighbouring competitors as he neared her post, to share a quick kiss as he passed. He could afford to slow up if required; in spite of his still-formidable fitness, at two years shy of sixty, even he no longer harboured any hopes of running the race in a competitive time – Ottie just wanted him to get round safely – but as the competition owner, and a once notable participant, he was at least afforded the courtesy of setting off ahead of the predicted race leaders, as an official 'hare'. Going by Ottie's chart, he'd already been overtaken by three runners who'd passed by her just a few minutes ago and she kept eagerly putting up her binoculars in the hope of seeing him coming along the track. It should be any minute now. According to last year's race stats, he'd already passed this point two minutes ago.

But no one appeared on the horizon the abysmal weather slowing the race down. That was the drawback to this event. The qualifying standard was far beyond the reach of mere mortals: just to take part required fiendish levels of fitness, stamina and mental grit that bordered on SAS-levels, but the gap between the race leaders and the stragglers could be immense, sometimes as wide as fifteen to twenty hours between first and last place. She could be waiting here for a while before she saw anyone else at all.

She paced, trying to stay warm, trying to ignore the growing sense of urgency in her bladder. She had quickly got through her thermos of tea in an effort to wake up, warm up, and stave off boredom but now it was beginning to tell. She carried on stepping from side to side, trying not to think about it, but the cold and the lack of anything else to do made that difficult.

Pulling the toggles of her hood tightly, she jogged a little way down the track, back towards the direction of the start line and away from the exposed bend, trying to get out of the wind just a little. A few boats faint on the horizon sailed past, the heave and trough of the stormy grey seas tossing them like soap suds.

She got to the small fork in the track where the path divided, the outermost branch splitting into an even narrower tributary and winding down the sharply angled bank for a short distance before disappearing into the grass like smoke into air. Devil's Fork it was known as, for good reason, and she had never been allowed down there as a child; they even used to walk the dogs on leads on that section.

She checked the time again, beginning to feel desperate to pee. The marshal had only just gone past her twenty minutes ago and wouldn't be back again for a while. Should she radio for cover? But it'd be a couple of miles to the next station on a quad bike – plus she'd have to wait for that to get here first.

'Jeesht, great weekend, Otts,' she muttered to herself as a particularly strong gust almost knocked her backwards and whipped off her hood. Righting herself, she checked the path's horizon again. *Still* no one. What were they all doing back there? Hopping?

Sod it. She couldn't wait any longer. Her bladder was crying out for mercy. She looked left and right uncertainly. The track might be clear, but it was also completely exposed: the moment someone appeared, she would be in their direct line of sight. Reports of one of the stewards relieving herself path-side was not the kind of PR Bertie wanted. She looked around apprehensively. Unless . . . She looked back at the bend behind her. If she was to lean in against the steep hill-side just around the far side of that corner, she might be hidden from view for just long enough . . . ?

Jeesht, what else was she to do? There really was nowhere else to go.

Jogging back to the shallow blind spot behind the bend, she undid her jeans as quickly as she could, her fingers fumbling in the cold and struggling with her long raincoat and all the many layers she put on to get through today. Quickly, she relieved herself, closing her eyes happily as her bladder released, and mere minutes later she was straightening up again and rearranging her clothes. No one would ever know.

She looked left and right again. Not a soul—

No, wait. Someone *was* coming.

She frowned. That would have been Sod's Law, she tutted to herself, jogging back to the little hut and grabbing her clipboard, preparing to record their times. A few moments earlier and she'd have been hard-pressed to protect either her modesty or dignity.

'Well done,' she cried heartily as the runner approached, pen poised above her clipboard ready to record his time. 'You're doing great! Keep it up, number . . .' She squinted to see as he drew closer. 'Well, hello, number 69,' she laughed. 'Did you get that number especially?'

Bertie pulled to a stop and looped his arm around her waist. 'What do you think?' he panted. He was sweating heavily, his face pale rather than flushed. He reached in to kiss her. 'Did I time it well?' he asked, indicating how no one else was around to see them.

Ottie laughed as he swooped in to kiss her neck. 'Oh, you have no idea!' she giggled. 'You timed it perfectly.'

Willow stared at the text, her hands feeling quivery as she reread the words over and over.

On consideration, I would be prepared to resubmit my previous offer of 2.75m euros. Please reply by return if interested. C. Shaye.

Two point seven five? It was far below the six million Hels had indicated to her. Far, far below. Out of sight below. He was having a laugh. No wonder her father had kicked him into touch. A low-ball offer was one thing but this was frankly insulting.

Offensive.

Ridiculous.

And what was it he had done – *gazundered*? Reduced his offer on the point of sale? Clearly he couldn't be trusted. She threw the phone onto the bed and crossed the room, finger-tousling her dark hair angrily in the mirror. It shone in a way it never did in the city – the water was softer down here. She had some colour in her cheeks too – the onshore breeze always saw to that.

Her hand paused, mid-tease.

On the other hand, O'Leary had told her fixing the roof was going to cost half a million alone.

And the property market was dead.

And Brexit was a disaster.

And Hels had said six was 'top whack', 'if they were lucky', 'with a following wind', found 'the right buyer on the right day . . .'

Probably five was the realistic number, four and a half if they wanted a quick sale.

'Willow!' Pip's voice was loud, even with three-foot walls to penetrate. She typed quickly with her thumbs: *Market list will be five but could be flexible on that if you can proceed immediately.*

Before she could allow herself to hesitate, she pressed send, watching the screen to make sure the message went – then instantly regretting it when it did. She gave a nervous wince. She'd basically asked for almost double his offer when everyone knew what a bird in the hand was worth. She stared at the screen for another moment, feeling conflicted – angry, impetuous, reckless, defiant on the one hand; wary, hesitant, rueful on the other. She was out of her depth, that much was clear.

The minutes dragged and still the screen stayed dark. No doubt he'd shrugged at her crazy counter-offer and put his phone away. Whatever.

She bit her lip and tried to do the same, telling herself there wouldn't be a quick fix to this. Seven-hundred-year-old castle estates didn't get sold off the back of a single phone call and a couple of texts. This was business. They were discussing millions of euros. Like it or not, she was simply going to have to do this Hels' way and be patient.

She grabbed her coat off the bed and was at the door when her phone pinged again.

If you can agree four, we have a deal.

Her mouth opened in amazement. He'd pay four million? Just like that? It was a third less than Hels had said she might get, but over a million more than his original offer. And for a speedy sale . . . She needed a quick, clean break, but this was almost surgical.

Her heart was pounding but she forced herself to slow down and take a breath. He was pushing hard, wanting to close on a deal without going through any of the usual preliminaries with her. Yes, he'd been here before with her father – he'd have had the particulars first time round, he'd know the intricacies of the estate and its relative merits and failings, they didn't need to break new ground here. But . . . if he was this desperate to get it agreed remotely and quickly, then there must still be a little room for manoeuvre. Possibly?

She typed slowly. Was this greed or good business? *Can't agree four but can agree we're close. Suggest we meet to discuss further.*

She waited for his response, biting on her thumbnail anxiously. Come on, come on. Bite, man.

'Willow!' Pip hollered again.

'Ugh,' Willow groaned, doing a jig on the spot as she restlessly waited for his reply, knowing her sister was going to barge in here at any moment . . .

Fine, on the condition it stays off market and can proceed quickly. I'll contact you next week. CS.

She squealed, slapping her hand over her mouth in delight. He'd tacitly agreed to four-*something*? Just like that, she'd made all their troubles go away? Pip had been sarcastic when she'd levelled the accusation at her the other night, but *pragmatism* had done what her father's sentimentality could not: she had forged a path into the future. He had refused to sell on medieval principle to an Englishman who'd tried to undercut a deal, but she'd just kept it simple: Sell. To a Buyer.

'Willow!'

Willow sighed.

'Are you ready or what?' she yelled.

'What,' Willow said with a sarcastic smile a moment later as she stepped out of her old bedroom and peered over the balustrades to find her sister lying sprawled on the bottom step, as though she'd been there for *days*.

'Finally!' Pip said dramatically at the sight of her.

'How long have you been waiting for?' Willow asked as she came down the stairs. She felt lighter than she had in weeks. No, years. She felt free.

'Ages!'

'Five minutes? Three of which you spent chatting to Mam?'

Pip rolled her eyes as Willow reached her. 'Hmm. Not sure I'd call it a chat. She told me to drink responsibly and not stay out late – like I'm fifteen or something.'

Willow frowned as she looked properly at her sister's outfit. 'Is that what you're wearing or are we stopping by the stables first?' she asked with a wrinkle of her nose as she pinched the fabric of Pip's shirt – it was one of their father's old tattersalls, far too big on the shoulders and rolled up at the cuffs.

'Is that what *you're* wearing?' Pip demanded back, pinching her leather trousers and making them squeak. They had been in the 'emergency' bag which Caz had packed for her – and which Hels had brought down – along with a sachet of her favourite whey powder and a surreptitious bottle of vodka with a Post-it note across the front saying 'in case it's all getting too much'. Pip laughed – her point made – shoving her little sister lightly as they wandered through the hall. 'Bye, Mam!' she hollered again. 'We're off now!'

They both waited a moment for a return shout but there was nothing. They looked at each other, flickers of concern in both their faces, before Pip shrugged and they walked out into the night. After the wild weather earlier, things had settled somewhat. It was still bitingly cold but the driving rain had ceased, at least for a while, and the gale-force winds had subsided into bad-tempered gusts. They climbed into Pip's Land Cruiser and pulled away, the headlights shining up the grand formal drive, occasional rabbits pausing from their twitchy foraging under bushes to stare as they drove past.

'You look chipper,' Pip said, glancing over at her as they got to the gates and she checked for traffic.

'Do I?' Willow looked in the mirror and fussed with her hair for distraction. She wanted to tell her sister the good news, she really did – but would she see it as good news? Willow suspected not. Pip was only just getting her head wrapped around the notion of Lorne being put on the market. To hear it was almost a done deal already, that she had acted so decisively and swiftly . . . No, it was too soon. 'I guess I'm just looking forward to having a bit of a blowout,' she said instead. 'Tough few weeks.'

Pip reached over and squeezed her affectionately on the knee. 'Sure has been, kiddo.' She pulled right onto the leafy lane, away from the village. 'So how's the Ultra been, do we know?'

'The leaders are expected to finish about three in the morning, I think.'

'Jeesht, mad nutters,' Pip winced. 'Who'd put themselves through that, running through the night?'

'Search me,' Willow muttered, searching her phone for her Spotify play list. 'What d'you fancy? Indie list, Walk Like A Badass – hmm – or 90s dance?'

'Dance, definitely. Let's get some good tunes in while we can; God only knows what music Marie Mullane's going to have lined up for us – Daniel O'Donnell on repeat?'

Willow groaned. It was true. Terry and Marie Mullane were their parents' ages and though they might be amongst the richest people in the area, they were by no means the coolest. 'Are we scooping up Otts too?' she asked, hoping her voice didn't sound odd. It had been days since she'd last seen her biggest sister. Since they'd learned their new fates, in fact.

'Nope, she's been stewarding the race all day. Started at crack of sparrows she said, and now she's soaked and frozen and intending to binge *Game of Thrones* for the rest of the weekend.'

'Has she still not seen that?' Willow tutted. 'My God, it's like she's living in the dark ages.'

'Listen, you forget about our broadband out here,' Pip said defensively. 'It's taken her almost a year just to download the damn thing.'

'If you say so.'

Pip glanced across, as though detecting something in her tone. 'Have you seen her lately?'

'Nope.'

'Yeah, not a surprise I guess. She's been pretty flat out with all the race preparations. I saw Seamus earlier and he said it looks like Glastonbury for teetotallers over there.'

'Sounds grim,' Willow said, staring out into the darkness and feeling her momentary buzz begin to fade, ancient stone walls and skeletal trees rushing past the windscreen in a blur. Bunting had been strung up at the bus stop and laminated race arrows were fastened to tree trunks every fifty metres. A hand-painted sign pointing out Christmas trees for sale had blown over in the winds.

'The clean-up will be, that's for sure. It was a nightmare last year. As I said to her, Bertie Flanagan can't keep just letting the event get bigger and bigger just to boost his profits,' Pip tutted. Willow fidgeted on her seat at the mention of Bertie Flanagan. She hated the man. She knew exactly what he was. A liar and a cheat. 'At a certain point he's going to have to restrict numbers. The infrastructure can't take it and, frankly, nor can the land. Can you imagine what that footpath's going to look like after two and a half thousand ascetic maniacs have pounded along it in this weather?'

'Nope.'

Pip glanced at her. 'Well, you'd best have a look for yourself on Monday. You might be shocked – and it's your problem now you're the boss. You're the one who's got to find the cash to make the repairs.'

Only, she hadn't. If there had been a dig in Pip's words, she didn't feel it, and a tiny smile flickered at the edges of her mouth again. 'Okay then, I will,' she replied lightly, resting her arm along the ledge and staring out of the window. She had just all but sold a castle. Was it real?

Pip gave a crafty wink. 'Tell you what you should do – tell

Bertie he'll have to pay if he wants to use Lorne land in future. Dad thought about it often enough, but Ottie always talked him out of it.'

Willow felt another stab of jealousy at the casual way Pip talked about their father, her and Ottie's daily discussions with him about the running of the place building a bond between the three of them she had never been able to forge. Willow may have inherited the estate, but it was Ottie and Pip who had come away with most – memories that could never now be replicated.

'She told Dad it would affect their friendship,' Pip continued, giving a scoffing bark. 'As if that would stop Bertie if the roles were reversed!'

Willow glanced at her sister. Did Pip know what she knew? Did she know just how unscrupulous that man really was?

Pip gave a despairing sigh. 'Yeah, Dad said, when push came to shove, he valued their friendship more than an opportunity to make a fast buck.'

'Even though that buck was badly needed?'

'You know Dad,' Pip shrugged. 'Always a softie.'

Willow looked out of the window, not trusting herself to hold her tongue. It was almost more than she could stand to hear her father had refused to take his slice from the friend who was not just profiting from his goodwill, but had betrayed him in the most terrible way possible. She hated that his secret was now somehow her's. It burned her up.

They passed through sleepy villages and sped past dormant fields, the wind whipping through bare hedgerows, occasional badgers scuttling through the roadside undergrowth. Pip sang loudly – and badly – most of the way, trying to pitch herself into the party spirit (Willow knew her sister was a great believer in the 'fake it till you make it' principle), until eventually she heaved the car round sharply to the right and they turned into a drive marked by a pair of eight-foot-high red-brick pillars with scrolled ironwork gates. 'Trelannon Manor' was inscribed in gilt on a stone plaque set in one of the pillars.

Pip tapped the wheel in time to the music, head bopping to the beat as the electric gates automatically sailed open with a low whirr. They rolled slowly forwards, low lights either side of the drive lighting up like a Mexican wave as they approached, immediately dimming again as they passed by.

'That's mad, it's like an airport runway,' Willow murmured as they passed the post and rail fences, the paddocks behind them manicured and empty.

But Pip was quiet for once. Her chin was almost on the wheel as they drew closer to the house, a look of awe in her usually defiant eyes as they passed by the smart American barns where the horses were stabled. 'Jeesht, would you look at that,' she whispered, gaze on the spotless cobbles of the courtyard, the Mullanes' logo picked out in a mosaic in the centre. 'That's when you know you've made it.'

'Get you, fangirl,' Willow said, wrinkling her nose. As far as she was concerned, a mosaicked logo in the stables was in the same bracket as a mosaicked dolphin in the swimming pool – but she thought better of saying it out loud. Mullane's was arguably the most successful and prestigious stables in the whole of Ireland, and the pedigree of the horses kept here second to none. This was Pip's dream and suddenly Willow understood why she'd been so keen to come along tonight.

They parked, the muddy, battered Land Cruiser standing out amongst the rows of gleaming Mercedes and Range Rovers, even a couple of Bentleys. Willow sent up a little prayer of thanks that she'd dressed up after all; seeing Pip looking dressed for a night at the pub had given her second thoughts back home, but her big sister didn't break stride as she walked up to the house, eyes gleaming with bright ambition.

They knocked at the door, Willow looking around her as they waited for someone to open up. Would this be the sort of thing four-something million could buy her? It wasn't to her taste, the perfectly cubed building dressed in a neo-Georgian style. It was all too neat and tidy; too shiny. Lead planters stood before decorative pillars by the front door, conifers clipped into smart twists and fairy lights threaded through the trees. Lights spilled from every single one of the floor-to-ceiling sash windows, as though sheer wattage alone could indicate the occupants' wealth and power. But then again, maybe it could, given the level of high spirits coming from inside.

Pip rang again impatiently, just as the door was opened and Terry Mullane stood there wearing raspberry cords and a yellow cashmere sweater.

'Oh good God,' Pip muttered under her breath. 'Terry, hi!'

Terry's ready smile faltered as he registered them both: the recently bereaved Lorne girls. 'Willow, Pip,' he said, stepping out and placing a hand on each of their arms and squeezing them sympathetically. 'You made it.'

'We did,' Pip said brightly, and Willow knew her sister was trying to ignore the pity in his eyes. 'Thank you for inviting us.'

'Nonsense. We were truly hoping you would make it.' He peered over her shoulder. 'Your mam?'

'I'm afraid it's still too early for her,' she said quickly.

'Of course, of course,' he said looking pained. 'Twas never expected.'

'And Ottie would've come but she's been working at the Ultra all day so she's soaked through,' Pip added.

'Such hard-working girls, the lot of you. No wonder your dad was always so proud of you.'

Willow felt her smile freeze in place.

'Listen, before we go in, I want you to know we were all set to cancel tonight, out of respect to Declan. He was a good friend.'

'Joe told me,' Pip said briskly. 'And we're glad you didn't. Dad would have wanted it this way. You know how he loved a party.'

'That he did! He was always the life and soul. It was such a terrible shock finding out he'd passed. We were in Dubai at the time.'

'A successful trip, I heard,' Pip said, and Willow could tell from the tone of her voice that she desperately wanted to move the conversation on. Pip and sympathy went together like orange juice and toothpaste 'It's been a helluva year for Mullane's. We're so pleased for you.'

'Thanks, Pip, that's kind of you,' he nodded, seeming to get the point. 'But come, you must come in. It's freezing out here and there's a party in there waiting to get started.'

'It sounds like it's already in full swing,' Willow said politely as the door was opened again and the dulcet tones of Daniel O'Donnell drifted out. She swallowed her dread, wishing they hadn't come. This was a mistake.

They walked into a marbled entrance hall, the black and white floor polished to a shine, an immense crystal chandelier glittering ferociously. A giant LED-lit blue Christmas tree stood in one corner, bedecked with silver and blue baubles.

Willow felt her heart sink further as she shrugged off her jacket. Daniel O'Donnell and V-neck jumpers did not make for a party in her opinion, and her leather trousers were suddenly feeling very risqué. No one batted an eye in Dublin, but glances were sliding her way like curling stones now. The black, nearly sheer blouse probably wasn't helping either.

'Perhaps this has been a mistake,' she muttered under her breath as Terry immediately rushed off to bring them some drinks.

'You've got to be joking,' Pip murmured back, her eyes on the lavish equine oil portraits on the walls. 'I'm in heaven!'

'Have you switched your hearing aid on? They're playing "Danny Boy". Actually playing it. Like, not for a joke.'

'Don't care. This place is heaving with equestrians. I may never leave. D'you think they'd adopt me?'

'Pip . . .'

Terry Mullane came back with two suspiciously pink drinks, which he placed in each of their hands. 'Drink up. These were designed especially for tonight – Midnight Feasts,' he grinned.

'What's in them?' Willow asked, looking sceptical. This drink would not dare show its face in any of the bars she frequented in Dublin.

'Absolutely no idea,' he laughed. 'But I asked for them not to be *too* strong. You know what cocktails are like: everyone's slaughtered after two drinks otherwise.'

Willow smiled. Cocktails she supposed she *could* do – for one night anyway. She was soon to be four million euros up and that was something to celebrate, even if it was in secret. 'Well, congratulations,' she said, toasting him. 'And may your success continue for many years to come.'

'Thank you.'

Pip furrowed her brow and immediately looked shifty. 'Actually, Terry, while I've got you . . .'

Willow took another sip of the pink drink – it was predictably sweet, but highly quaffable – picking up on her sister's unusually earnest tone too.

'There's something I'd love to discuss with you in more detail: how exactly *did* you start out?' Pip being polite always made Willow nervous. 'It's always been my dream to get into bloodstocks.'

'Has it really?' Terry asked interestedly. 'I thought you were more involved in the . . . family experiences side of things.'

'Oh no, no, no,' Pip said quickly, her cheeks flaming at his tact. 'I mean, yes, we are currently running a trekking business but only because it . . . you know, tied in with our location on the Wild Way. What I'd *really* love to do is what you've managed—'

'Terry!' An excitable woman in an ill-advised dress rushed over, clasping his face in two hands and kissing him on the lips. 'We made it!'

'So you did!' he replied with a faintly horrified expression, the woman's blazered husband bearing down on them with an even wider smile.

Willow watched on, bemused. It was one thing to be the manager of oh-so-trendy Pyro Tink but she could only imagine what it must be like as the owner of the Grand National winner.

Pip sidestepped around her, trying to get closer to her target again. 'Anyway, Terry, I bought this lovely mare last summer, Shalimar. Anglo-Arab. Beautiful, she is. I had to sell my trailer and I would've sold a kidney too if I'd had to. But anyway, I almost bankrupted myself to get her and—'

'What an absolutely terrific party, Ter darling!' the woman said, angling her head so that Pip's view to him was blocked.

'Everyone's here! Now, where can we get one of those delicious-looking drinks?'

Terry looked at Pip with a frozen expression. 'If it's all right with you, Pip, can we pick this up later? I'd better get Nancy and Bob here some drinks.'

Pip looked crestfallen. 'Sure.'

'But I'll come and find you, okay, and we'll pick this up? I'd love to hear more.'

'Sure you will,' Pip murmured under her breath as Terry was almost wheeled off.

'Come on,' Willow said, seeing how her sister's face fell, jogging her elbow and beginning to move through the crowd. 'I feel like Spock waiting to be beamed up under that thing.'

Pip glanced up at the waterfall chandelier as they moved out of the spotlight. They found a pillar to stand by, providing a good vantage over the party. A lot of the guests seemed to have received a memo about wearing tinsel as a decorative accessory and there were one or two Christmas jumpers on the men which Willow wasn't convinced were being worn ironically. They stood in silence for several moments, both of them feeling out of place and wishing they'd stayed at home.

'Oh my God,' Pip gasped, suddenly paling.

Willow felt a burst of fright. 'What?'

'Over there.'

She looked over to where her sister was staring: a magnificent gold trophy was positioned against the back wall of the hall, locked in a glass cabinet and set upon an ebonized pedestal. A painting of a black stallion hung above it.

'Jeesht, you don't think—' Pip whispered, her eyes almost on stalks.

'It can't be,' Willow frowned, just as she noticed the thick-set men in dark suits standing either side of it, hands crossed in front of them, legs widely planted. 'Can it?'

'It's so beautiful and . . . goldy.'

Willow glanced at her. 'That's not a word.'

'D'you reckon the glass is bulletproof?' Pip asked, gulping down her drink.

But Willow didn't hear her. Her gaze had fastened upon something even more transfixing than the trophy. He was in jeans, a white shirt and navy velvet blazer, listening impassively to something his companion – a man in his forties – was saying.

'Oh my God, I just can't believe the Grand National cup is here. At a party. We've got to go and see that thing,' she hissed urgently. If Pip had been fangirling in the car, she was quickly approaching stalker level in here.

'No,' Willow said quickly, shooting out a hand to stop her sister from bolting off.

Pip's eyebrows shot up. 'Huh? Why not?'

Willow glanced back at the man again. Even just his profile made her heart catch.

'Will? Let's go see it,' Pip said desperately.

Willow looked back at her equally desperately. She couldn't go over there. He was barely a metre from the cabinet, and he was for looking at, not talking to. 'It's . . . tacky to go and make a fuss about it.'

'*Tacky?*' Pip spat, looking outraged. 'Why do you think they've put it there? They want people making a fuss about it!'

'Well, you go then,' she said stubbornly, taking a step back.

Pip frowned, watching her with an incredulous expression before looking back at the cup – and then slightly left. '. . . Ohhhh.'

'What do you mean "ohhhh"?' she asked defensively.

Pip shrugged. 'Got it.'

'Got what?'

Pip looked back across the room straight at the stranger and gave a low whistle. 'He is a hottie.'

'Pip—'

'Funny – I thought you were pretty upfront with guys. There's enough of them on your Instathingy. You don't come across as shy there.'

'I'm not being shy,' Willow protested, even though her sister had a point. Why *didn't* she want to go over there? She usually made a beeline for the guys who caught her eye, notorious amongst her Dublin crowd for her love-them-and-leave-them approach.

'What d'you think his name is?'

'How would I know?' Willow rolled her eyes, even as her mind was racing through options: *James? Chris? Paul?*

'I wonder who he is. He looks very . . . urbane,' Pip mused. 'Bet he goes to museums and then on to brunch.'

'Stop staring at him!' Willow hissed, nudging her to turn away from him, quickly looking at the man herself to check he wasn't looking. He wasn't. Why wasn't he looking?

She downed her drink nervously and they both nabbed fresh ones from a passing waitress.

'Has he seen you yet?' Pip asked like a bad spy, her glass poised at her lips as though she was smelling it.

'No.'

'Course he has,' Pip said confidently after a moment. 'He definitely would've seen us come in from where he's standing.'

Willow looked back to the centre of the room and realized that point was actually true. It had felt like standing in a prison spotlight as Pip had yabbered on to Terry. 'Well, if he did see us, he's not looking bothered about it.'

'He's just playing it cool.'

Willow frowned. 'Since when did you become the expert on men?'

'No one needs to be an expert on men, little sis; they're simple creatures, never forget that. Dick and stomach. Sorted.'

Willow tutted. 'I can't believe you just said that.' She rolled her eyes. 'You know, this explains a lot about why you're still single.'

'Some of us aren't looking for love,' Pip shrugged.

'I'm not either.'

'That's not what your Instathingy says.'

'That's not love. There's a difference.'

Pip's eyes narrowed. 'Hmm, well that's a sea-change in your thinking for starters. You were forever playing weddings with the tablecloths when you were little.'

'When I was little. Yes.'

'You've decided true love's not for you then, is that what you're telling me?'

'Exactly.'

'Not gonna get married.'

'Definitely not.'

'Because . . . ?'

'Because it's hormones and convenience wrapped up in commercial-grade sentimentality.'

'Ouch!' Pip winced, as though she'd been burnt. 'Savage condemnation.'

'Says you. What's your excuse for confirmed spinsterhood?'

Pip gave a breezy sigh. 'Haven't met a bloke I like more than my horses.' She sounded perfectly happy about it.

Willow gave a groan, knowing there was no winning this particular argument, just as Pip suddenly, suspiciously, straightened up. 'Oh, shit. Incoming,' she murmured between stilled lips.

'Huh?' A shadow fell over her.

'Hi.'

Pip gave a tiny squeak. *Actually* a squeak.

Willow turned and looked around. Up. The hot guy had crossed the room and was standing beside them. He wasn't smiling, and yet – he'd crossed the room. 'I'm Connor.'

Connor. Not James or Chris or . . . whatever. Connor. Good name. Good face. All round . . . good. Excellent even. She swallowed hard. Up close, he was even more attractive – wavy dark hair worn in a side parting, full dark lips, 'cat and mouse' blue eyes that made it clear he was the cat. 'Hi, I'm Willow,' she said in a voice that amazingly did not wobble. 'And this is my sister Pip.'

'Pip and Willow. Interesting names.'

'Mine's short for Philippa,' Pip said quickly, a signature gleam in her eye. 'And hers is short for—'

'Don't even . . .' Willow said quickly, one finger held up warningly.

Connor hitched an eyebrow as Pip broke into laughter.

'It's just Willow,' she said, turning back to him.

'Well, pleased to meet you, Pip and Just Willow.'

Pip cracked up laughing again. 'Just Willow! I like that! I like *him*!' she guffawed, before suddenly noticing her glass was empty again. 'Oh no! Huh, would you look at that? I need a drink.' And with a smile and not remotely subtle wink, she sauntered off.

They watched her go.

'Shy and retiring then, your sister?'

'It's a burden.'

A smile hovered at his eyes. 'Is she older or younger?'

'Older by two years.'

'Any others?'

'Another sister, a year older than Pip.'

'Ah, so you're the baby?'

Her stomach did a little flip. The most beautiful man she had ever seen had crossed the room and was actually flirting with her. 'I'm afraid so. How about you? Any siblings to torture you throughout your life?'

'Hell, yes. Also two sisters who still talk about dressing me up as their doll and practising make-up on me.' Oh God, she could only imagine him with mascara on. Even more beautiful. His eyes were positively dancing now but still no smile curved his mouth – from a distance, it might look as though they were discussing Brexit or the going at Cheltenham – and she wondered what it took to make this man smile.

'The scars must run deep,' she teased.

He shrugged his beautifully straight, dark eyebrows. 'So how do you know the Mullanes?' he asked, stepping to the side slightly as a brunette in a silver wrap-jumpsuit squeezed between them, her eyes flicking ever so slightly in his direction as she passed. He looked at her briefly, his gaze coming back to Willow again.

She forced a smile, even though she felt her insecurity rise. He must have women hitting on him all the time. 'Family friends.'

'Oh. You live locally?'

'My family do. About half an hour from here – or twenty minutes if Pip's driving.' She took another sip of her drink, her eyes watching the woman cut a swathe through the crowd. Almost every male head turned.

'But not you?'

'I'm in Dublin now.'

'Ah. City girl.' His eyes swept over her. 'That explains the trousers.' She felt a deep blush stain her cheeks. 'I thought they were going to need to open the windows when you came in, the temperature went up so high.'

Oh. Dear. God. He was saying she looked hot? She swallowed, willing herself to remain calm. 'How about you?' she asked, deliberately ignoring the compliment. 'Where are you from?'

'London, although I've got a place in Dublin too.'

Too. There was suggestion right there, in that one word. 'And how do you know the Mullanes?' she asked.

'I'm part of the consortium that owns Midnight Feast.'

Her eyes widened. 'Wow! How exciting.'

'Yes, it is.'

A horse man. She wouldn't have guessed that. She'd have said banker or something. 'So what's it like winning the National?'

He considered for a moment. 'Bruising.'

'Bruising?' she asked quizzically.

'Yes, it appears that when your horse wins a race, you must submit to the birthday bumps. I've never been hoisted up onto so many shoulders.'

'Oh,' she chuckled. But her smile faded as their eyes met again and she felt all the words leave her head. No more silky chit-chat. No more witty repartee. No more mercurial brunette even. He was distracting, overwhelming, the chemistry between them . . .

'Your glass is empty,' he said after a moment, tearing his gaze from her eyes to her glass. Wretched glass, distracting him. 'Would you like another drink?'

And just like that, the bubble popped. She knew exactly what that question signified: cue his speedy exit on the pretext of finding a waitress. She did it all the time in bars when she wanted to ditch someone. How could she have read this so wrong?

'Sure,' she shrugged, feeling her confidence, and buoyant mood, nosedive. Had she said something wrong? Been too flirty? Not flirty enough?

She looked away, bracing for his departure. The party was already slipping from its polite bonds, the pink cocktails and blue Christmas tree beginning to sprinkle a little magic over the crowd: heads were being thrown back in laughter, mannerisms becoming more expansive, voices raising . . . At first glance, she had noticed only her parents' friends, but now she saw the younger contingent too, skulking in the corners and shadows, coming out of side rooms. The ambient noise level was growing rapidly.

Pip, she saw, was in the middle of a group of guys, all laughing uproariously about something, and doing shots. Willow watched – her sister may have been dressed like 'one of the lads' in her tattersall shirt and scruffy hair, no make-up on, but she didn't look like them with her fine bones and bright eyes. Willow supposed Pip had no idea at all she was beautiful; she might even be mortified by the thought.

'Excuse me!' She looked up to see Connor with his hand in the air, his chin up to get someone's attention. 'Thanks,' he murmured as a waiter dashed over and he took Willow's empty glass from her hand, replacing it with a fresh one.

Her gaze fluttered up to his in surprise.

'What?' he asked, sipping some champagne; no pink stuff for him.

'Nothing, I . . .'

His eyes pinned her down, sensing her evasion. 'Say.'

She shrugged. 'I had assumed you were going to make a discreet exit.'

He frowned. 'Why would I do that?'

Her eyes found the silver-clad brunette, still glancing their way. ' . . . It's nothing. Ignore me.' She looked away again.

There was a small pause. 'Well, unfortunately, that seems to be just about the one thing I can't do.'

Her gaze snapped back to his, the flirtatious smile that had been in his eyes before, now replaced with definite heat.

'Ignore the prettiest girl in this room, I mean.'

She felt her heart tear into a gallop, the room begin to spin. Was that him – or the pink drinks? She didn't even care that they were playing Daniel O'Donnell any more. Was this really happening? Could there be this much luck in one day? She felt overloaded with it. Drunk on it.

'You look flushed.'

'Do I?' Her hand flew to her cheek.

'. . . Would you like to get some air?'

She stared back at him. She had never wanted air more desperately in her life. 'Lead on.'

Chapter Ten

The French doors burst open, bodies streaming through ahead of her, past a couple getting hot and heavy on the chairs, everyone cheering as they ran out into the night. A hard frost was already forming, the garden draped in a bluish tint, trees spreading like hard corals against the inky sky, the lake down in the dip at the bottom of the lawns a foxed-glass mirror.

They ran like warriors, arms aloft as they roared and Pip was glad the shirt she was wearing was too big – it only made it all the easier to pull over her head in one fell swoop. She raced over the grass, their leader in this, her arms pumping, eyes fixed on the end point – the pontoon floating in the middle of the lake. It wasn't like the ramshackle pontoon her father had built and tethered off their private beach when she was little: a few old oil drums cleaned out and tied together with baling twine. This was a smart purpose-built floating deck with a pagoda above it – for romantic sunset suppers, she supposed. She couldn't imagine ever being someone who would choose – or even think – to have her dinner in a floating glorified shed at the bottom of the garden but who was she to judge? She was the nutter who bet she could swim up to it in the middle of winter.

'Pip?' The voice was faraway and shocked, but familiar. So familiar. Willow?

Pip tried to flash a smile in her general direction as she dared a glance over her bare shoulder. She was definitely drunk, she knew that – those shots had wiped the floor with her – but it was sheer desperation that was propelling her, not the booze. She could do this. She *had* to do it. Everything depended upon it.

Sean, her portly, out-of-shape rival, was barely two strides behind, struggling with removing his shirt and having to rip it open to shrug it off. She stopped running abruptly and tucked down unsteadily, trying to pull off her jodhpur boots; it meant Sean overtook her and he laughed, waving his arms congratulatorily over his head as he sped past, but, like F1 cars couldn't avoid pit-stops, she knew he'd need to take off his shoes too.

The socks came off with her boots – her pet hate at any other time – but she was grateful for the efficiency now and she began sprinting immediately again, the soles of her bare feet almost tickled by the stiff blades of grass. The lake was a football-pitch length away and she pumped her arms as hard as she could, chasing Sean's bulky silhouette down the lawn, oblivious to the freezing temperatures. He was bigger and stronger than her, but he was also heavier and out of shape. She had the edge on him fitness-wise, she knew it.

She caught up with him at the water's edge and she slipped off her jeans without even having to undo the zip, while he had to first take off his trainers – which were inconveniently double-knotted.

'Pip!'

Somewhere, far behind her, she could still hear her sister's shouts but there was no time to stop and explain now. Too much was at stake. Her entire future was on the line.

Without hesitation, she ran into the water first, her entire body immediately clenching with the utter shock of the freezing temperatures. It whipped the breath from her, the ground underwater stony and uneven and she stumbled, falling headlong into the lake.

Everyone was cheering when she resurfaced again but she was splashing and spluttering so much herself, she couldn't tell whether Sean was in the water now too. The cold was of a level she had never experienced before, her breath reflexively coming urgently, faster than she could count as her brain struggled to make sense of the immense physical shock.

She could hardly see, much less think straight, but somehow she fixed her eyes upon the pontoon and began to move: the sooner she got to it, the sooner she could get out of here. Behind her, the cacophony only grew. Word must have spread through the party, a number of guests swelling the onlookers on the banks and raising the noise levels. She could hear her name being called, but Sean's too. She swam with all her might, all her desperation, but was that even enough?

She felt a slip of skin underwater on the sole of her foot and she realized he was right behind her again. He was a big unit, six-one at least, and she willed her arms to keep going to wheel faster, her legs to kick harder – perhaps she could splash him into retreat?

Only, her limbs didn't appear to be obeying the commands her brain was sending out. Faster. Faster, she was urging, but she was going slower and slower. It was becoming hard even to lift her arm out of the water, her legs not so much kicking now as fluttering.

She felt a spike of panic. The bank had to be fifty metres or so behind her, Sean beginning to overtake in a flurry of thrashing white water. The pontoon was only another ten, maybe fifteen metres away but her breath was coming so quickly and her body wouldn't obey . . . Her arms weren't breaking the surface at all now, the cold feeling like a frozen iron stake that was tracking its way through her veins stiffening her into a spike.

Sean pulled ahead, too hidden in his own splashes to even see her, and she felt another bullet, not just of panic but of fear now too. Her legs were dropping beneath her body; she was beginning to sink.

She had to move. Why couldn't she move? She was panting desperately, hyperventilating, trying not to swallow water, coughing. She couldn't hear the crowd on the banks any more. Couldn't see the pontoon. The waterline was beginning to creep over her jaw, up her face . . .

Her brain screamed at her limbs to flail, strike, whip, wheel but she couldn't even feel her hands now, the sensation blocked below her elbows and creeping upwards. Her legs hung below her like ribbons.

Jesus, no. She couldn't die. She couldn't die just after they'd buried her father. Her poor mother. Willow. Ottie . . . Swim! But she couldn't move, her body utterly inert and useless as the cold began to make her drop like a stone. The hyperventilation would drown her as the hypothermia kept her still, her body spasming for breath as, slowly, she slipped under the water . . .

The last thing she saw before she dropped below the surface was the moon – dazzlingly bright and lusciously round, rising into the sky like a giant pearl. It was her last glimpse of light, the enveloping darkness complete under the water, all sound becoming muffled and indistinct.

She blinked into the murk but there was nothing to see in the depths. No fish. No reeds. No Sean. No sound. No colour. Everything was closing down. She was losing her grip. Reality skewering into fantasy in the dimming of her consciousness, as she fought to hold her final breath against a frantically panicking heart.

She couldn't. She couldn't. Her lungs were screaming. Her brain telling her to do it: breathe. Open your mouth and take the breath. Open your mouth. Open your mouth.

It was too much to deny. She opened her mouth, feeling the water flood her, claim her, rushing at her, explosions of colour in her mind as her screams found no purchase and the blackness grew deeper . . .

Pain – sharp and excoriating – intruded on the fog, flooding her body. Her scalp felt like it was being torn, water rushing over her skin and then, suddenly, the whacking slap of air on her face. She surfaced but couldn't gasp, her body limp as something grabbed at her, desperate and merciless, bruising her skin.

Distantly, numbly, she felt herself leave the lake's icy embrace and fall heavily onto a solid surface, moons crowding around her, crevices moving but no sound reaching her ear. Weight was applied to her useless form, the wind moving across her skin, the first twiggy tips of trees beginning to inch into her field of view. Her fixed gaze found the moon again but even that bright pearl could not win against the inexorable pull coming from deep within her body as she slid down, down, down again, into the dark.

Warmth is a colour – the colour of fruits: peach, growing into nectarine, into blood oranges . . . She saw it blooming against her eyelids, spreading over her cheeks, around the back of her head, down her neck, over her shoulders . . .

Sensation was growing, her block-of-ice hands and feet beginning to throb painfully, blood flow returning. Her body was stiff and stretched flat, like Gulliver pinned down by the

Lilliputians, spasms wracking through her like electric currents she could neither control nor stop.

Sound was returning too: the murmur of voices talking in urgent tones. Monitors beeping. A rushing depression of air. A rustling close to her ear.

Heat was building fast, wrapping around her and making her stir. She turned her head but her eyes wouldn't open. She was trapped inside her body, as clutched close to the heat as she had been the cold.

A sound vibrated through her. Came from her.

'Pip? Pip, can you hear me? . . .' Pressure upon her shoulders, a squeeze of her hand.

The voice was distant. Distorted.

'. . . She's coming round.'

'Make sure that strap's secure.' Another voice. '. . . tremors are getting worse. We don't want her striking out.'

'She's in deep hypothermia. How long till we get there?'

'Three minutes. They're on standby for us.'

'Have they got venovenous haemofiltration available?'

'I'll page through and ask.'

'Tell them she's hypoxic. Oxygen saturation's at fifty two. Acidosis is a risk.'

'Okay.'

Another sound came that vibrated through her bones. 'Pip? Can you hear me?'

'Get another blanket on her.'

Her body felt rigid and brittle. Uncontrollable. Detached from her own self, like Peter Pan's shadow. She tried to open her eyes but the heat, the light . . .

She sank back down into the darkness. The heaviness. The silence.

*

'We've got to call Mam.' Ottie's voice was fearful. It had that shake in it, like jelly being wobbled.

Willow looked up at her from her position on the other side of the bed. 'No. Not yet. Give it a little longer. Let her sleep.'

'But she needs to know!' Ottie insisted.

'And she will. But there's nothing to be done right now.' Her voice was flat and toneless. 'Pip's stable and being monitored; there's no point in worrying Mam when the worst is passed and there's nothing she can do here. It's not yet six. Let her rest while she can; she's going to need all her strength when she's told what's happened.' Willow dropped her head wearily. She'd been awake all night.

Ottie bit her lip, knowing all too well that another broken night wasn't going to help their mother. '. . . Fine,' she murmured, wondering how strange it was that she and her little sister seemed to have somehow switched roles again: Willow no longer the baby but the heir. And now the protector? It was the first time they'd seen each other since the reading of the will. Ottie had been avoiding her, not quite sure she could successfully mask her feelings about what had gone down that day. 'Another hour then. For Mam's sake.'

'Another hour.'

They both looked back at Pip, inert and pale in the bed, each of them holding her hands. It was a perverse sight, going against the natural order of things. No one had ever seen Pip knocked down before. She was always such a fighter – ferocious, indomitable . . . Reckless.

'Why did she do it?' Ottie whispered. 'Who runs into a freezing-cold lake in the middle of the night three weeks before Christmas?'

'She was off her head, knocking back shots with Sean Cuneen and all his mates.'

'But surely . . . I mean, how drunk would you have to be to lose all sense of danger?'

Willow gave a heavy sigh. 'Well, apparently there was also a bet.'

Ottie frowned. 'What kind of bet?'

'Not sure. I just heard some people in the crowd.'

Ottie blinked at her. 'She almost drowned herself on account of winning a bet?'

Willow shrugged her shoulders.

'But this'll . . . this'll break Mam's heart – how could she have been so *stupid*? Putting us all through, after everything that's just happened . . .' Her rapidly rising voice split in half.

'I know.' Willow's tired eyes rose to meet hers. 'And we'll kill her once she's strong enough.'

Ottie felt a small unexpected smile come in place of a sob as their father's sense of humour came to the fore again – laughing at funerals, hospital beds . . . nowhere was safe, the more sacrosanct the better. 'Exactly, yeah.' She dabbed her eyes with her free hand. 'Hear that, Pip? We're going to kill you once you're recovered from this.'

A nurse came in and Ottie and Willow immediately stiffened. They watched as the nurse checked the monitors, and they both fell into obedient, apprehensive silence.

'Is everything okay?' Willow asked, as the nurse fiddled with some of the intravenous tubes, before clicking her heel down smartly on the bed leg brake and making to leave with their sister.

'Pip is stable but I'm going to have to ask you to leave now. We're taking her up for another bath to stabilize her temperature, then she'll need to have some X-rays.'

'*X-rays?* But she's not broken anything, has she?' Willow asked, surprised.

'It's standard procedure in cases like these. If she's aspirated any water it could lead to a pulmonary oedema, which in turn could lead to respiratory distress, and even collapse.'

'You mean, secondary drowning?' Ottie said sharply. She had completed a lifeguarding course as a precaution, when they had first opened the campsite. Though she had no legal obligation to monitor the beach, it had seemed only prudent to know something of what to do should an emergency ever develop outside her window.

'Yes. But she's in good hands,' the nurse simply said, noticing the exhaustion on both their faces. Ottie was still in her pyjamas, a coat thrown over the top and her feet in the rubber clogs she wore for traipsing the field, her strawberry-blonde hair hanging in straggly fronds. Compared to Willow – all in black, leather-clad, body-con silhouette, smoky make-up – they made quite the mismatched pair. 'But we'll be a while. Why don't you try to get some rest?'

Willow looked at her elder sister. 'We could go get Mam now? With any luck, we can be back here by the time Pip's down again.'

Ottie nodded, allowing herself to be led away. She turned back once, flinching at the sight of her sister being wheeled out of the ward and down the corridor, tubes coming out of her, blankets atop her. She looked so pale, so quiet, fragile as a little bird. With her tufty, cropped hair and wild crop of freckles, she could have easily passed for a twelve-year-old boy.

'Come on,' Willow said, marching at a clip, no longer the baby. 'This way.'

Ottie glanced over at Willow as she drove them both back. Beneath the expertly applied make-up, her little sister looked pale and drawn. She had lost weight recently but, then, perhaps they all had. In spite of Mrs Mac's best efforts, no one had much appetite.

'So did you see it happen?' she asked in a quiet voice, her fingers tightening around the wheel as she peered out into the darkness. The sun hadn't yet risen and it could have as likely been midnight as six.

Willow hesitated. '. . . Yes.' She nodded and looked out of the window, her profile stoic but, in the reflection, Willow could see the tears shining in her eyes. 'I was already outside when she ran past.'

'You were outside?' Ottie frowned. 'But it was *freezing*. What were you . . . ?'

'I met a guy.'

'Oh.' The fact was presented with straightforward simplicity. Willow was nothing if not forthright about her love life these days: she liked guys, they liked her.

Willow shook her head. 'I should've been with her. I should have known she'd do some crazy thing.'

Ottie glanced over again. 'Don't be crazy, you're not her keeper. She's twenty-four years old. You were at a party. It's not your job to look out for her placing stupid bets and running into lakes.'

'But I saw her doing the shots. I should've known she'd go too far.'

'Willow, Pip's an adult. She makes her own choices – bad though they may be.'

Willow didn't reply but looked out of the window again, her expression still riddled with guilt, and Ottie knew it didn't matter what she said, she wouldn't be able to persuade her otherwise.

'So what was his name?' Ottie asked, trying to change the

subject instead. Dwelling on the disaster helped nobody. 'This guy.'

'Huh? Oh . . . Connor.'

'Connor what?'

'I don't know. We didn't get that far,' Willow mumbled, looking harder out the window.

Ottie grinned. '. . . Good-looking?'

A little involuntary groan escaped Willow in reply.

Ottie's fingers gripped the wheel tighter. 'Tell me *more*.'

Willow hesitated, as though trying to resist falling back into the memories, as though it was better to hold on to the misery than the light. '. . . He's about thirty, I'd say. English—'

'With a name like Connor?'

Willow frowned, as though trying to remember. 'I think he might have mentioned an Irish grandfather?'

'Passable then. And what does he do?'

Willow squinted, trying to peer back into the pink-tinted shards of the night before. 'He's part of a consortium . . . I think?' She shrugged. 'I dunno, we weren't really doing much talking.'

'You're outrageous,' Ottie tutted.

'Why am I? I'm twenty-two years old. I'm supposed to kiss strange men at parties.'

Ottie shrugged her eyebrows, feeling prudish. She was the elder sister but she'd never kissed a strange man at a party. Bertie was her one and only. 'So are you going to see him again?'

Willow's face fell. 'I didn't get his number. With everything that happened with Pip . . . I just left. One of Terry's friends drove me to the hospital and I didn't even think about it.' She put up her elbow on the sill and bit down on her finger. '. . . It didn't even cross my mind.'

'Well, it wouldn't, let's face it,' Ottie said, trying not to imagine the scene Willow had been privy to: her sister almost drowning in the lake.

They were both quiet for a moment, shaken by the image, the memory. 'Yeah, but I never even thanked him. He was the one that pulled her out, you know.'

'Huh?'

'When I saw everyone running down the lawn after Pip and that fella, I realized what she was going to do. Connor helped me get the boat in the water and rowed us over to her.'

'Oh!'

'Yeah. Fine thanks he got for all his trouble.'

'He'll understand, Will. Anyway, if you like him that much, just ask the Mullanes for his number. They invited him, right?'

'Yeah, right, can you imagine? "I know my sister nearly drowned in your lake, but what's the name of the hot guy I was snogging in the back garden?"' She wrinkled her nose. 'I don't think so.'

Ottie was quiet for a moment. It did seem inappropriate. '*Did* you like him?'

Willow shifted in her seat. ' . . . No, it's fine. He was just a guy. A very pretty guy,' she added ruefully. 'But there's thousands others out there.' She looked out of the window again, her arm along the sill, biting on her index finger. 'Pip's okay, that's the only thing that matters.'

They diverted to the Mullanes' place on the way past so they could collect Pip's car. Willow hadn't wanted to revisit the scene of the accident so soon, but she'd also known there'd be no better time to do it – it was early enough that none of the Mullanes would yet be awake and they could come and go unnoticed and not have to answer the litany of questions that would no doubt soon be coming their way.

Ottie had stared down at the lake, just visible from the

drive, while Willow got Pip's car started, and she'd tried not to imagine the horror of last night. But in the headlights, she could see the pontoon bobbing on the crystalline surface, the water still and dangerously dark. It was the sight of the lawn that had appalled her most, its blanket of frost trashed with the hundreds of booted footsteps like smashed glass, as though bearing witness to the mob, the crush, the panic . . .

Ottie followed behind her sister's car all the rest of the way back home, their headlights bouncing off hedges and stone walls, occasionally glancing off the cataracts of old sheep. They passed the Lorne village sign and a staggering runner wearing all the layers he must have packed in the pre-dawn chill, his backpack all but empty. Willow slowed down so as not to crowd him on the dark, narrow lane. Ottie waved politely at the steward on duty for this stretch of the Ultra. How long had he been on shift for – all night, or had he just come on? It wasn't yet seven in the morning but the race had carried on throughout the night, the competitors having run through all day yesterday and last night, with as little as three hours' sleep to sustain them.

Vaguely, she wondered how Bertie was doing as she hooked a left just before the main castle gates, down the lane that led to her campsite. She didn't know how he could do it, especially at his age. She'd been so relieved to have her done her duty when she'd clocked off last evening; one day of volunteering was quite enough for her, and she still felt chilled from standing on the Way in the wind and rain all day yesterday.

Her little car bumped along the rough track, the rolling fields either side rising up like puddings as the land gently dropped away and down. It was still too dark to see the glistening sea, to gauge its mood and know whether today it would pound or caress her little curved stretch of beach. Not that it mattered either way, she wouldn't be around to see it. Today would be spent under strip lights, listening to beeping machines and smelling antiseptic.

As she rounded the bend, her headlights swung over the patchwork of tents in the field, before homing in on her cottage as she approached the narrow parking spaces. She felt her heart give a flutter at the sight of it. Her little home. It was opposite to the castle in every way: long, low and narrow, it was white-washed and opened to the rafters inside. It stood side-on to the lane, the pink front door set in the gable end wall. The cottage was dug into the gentle slope, and from here, it was impossible to see the little room tucked below the ground-floor level on the far side that had once been a store for the boats. The garden was almost ridiculously small given the acres of free space and fields that surrounded it, but the coastal winds and salty air made it all but impossible to grow anything and she was just grateful the stone wall provided something of a windbreak when she was lying on a towel in the summer.

She cut the ignition and jumped out. She needed a shower and a desperate change of clothes – she'd literally grabbed her keys and run from the house when she'd received Willow's call – but there wasn't much time; Willow was simply going to collect their mother from home, then scoop her up from here on the way back to the hospital again.

She set the flashlight on her phone and pushed open the squeaky gate, walking up the narrow path and noticing with a flash of instant annoyance the red tent still pitched in the topmost corner of the garden. She frowned, remembering the American and the trouble he'd caused her, his silent insolence, the way he seemed to judge her without saying a word. She'd pretty much forgotten all about him. It had been such a full-on weekend. What was his name again? Gilman? . . . Gilmore?

He was supposed to have gone by now; she'd explicitly said he could stay for the one night only: sleep there Friday night, run through Saturday, be gone by Sunday. It was now Sunday.

Well used to campers trying to push their luck by overstaying their bookings, she crossed onto the grass and cleared her throat. She waited a moment and then did it again. When there was no response, she scratched her nails against the nylon. 'Mr Gilmore?'

Nothing.

'Mr Gilmore, I'm afraid you're going to have to move this pitch now. We agreed it was for one night only.'

She waited for the apology, sign of life even, but nothing came. Was he asleep?

'Mr Gilmore,' she said tetchily, not in the mood for this as she crouched down and tugged up the zip. She was in the middle of a family crisis. She did not need inconsiderate tourists impinging upon her goodwill or hospitality right now.

She peered into the tent.

It was empty. Or at least, *he* was not in it. But there was a sleeping bag and mat, a camping pillow and, lying neatly atop it all, in a zipped-up Ermenegildo Zegna hanging bag, the suit he had travelled in, she presumed.

She came back out with a sigh, zipping up the tent again. The crafty sod was clearly still running, having oversold his ability to her by saying he could complete the course and be out of her way within twenty-four hours. With a curse, she strode up to her front door and let herself in with a kick. She needed her privacy and, frankly, a little respect. They had made a deal and he was reneging on it. If that bloody tent was still there when she got back here later, she resolved she would cut it up with scissors and stuff it in the bins herself – suit and all.

Chapter Eleven

Willow stood by the door, feeling time not just standing still, but shifting into reverse. She felt like a child again, the familiar smell of her parents' room as comforting as a blanket and just as soft. Her mother was sleeping, curled up on Dad's side of the bed and wearing one of his cashmere jumpers, the framed wedding photograph just beyond the reach of her curled fingers on the bedspread.

Willow felt her courage fail her as she saw the peace in her mother's face as she slept and she let go, just for a moment, of all her anger, all her bitterness. Standing there, it was easy to believe she was as she seemed: the passive and gentle mother she remembered of her childhood; the mother who had delightedly celebrated the onset of every weekend with a freshly baked 'Friday Cake', who had made their Sunday-best dresses with cottons bought from Liberty of London, who had read them stories lying on the sofa together on rainy afternoons and made lawn picnics on the sunny ones. It was easy to remember, in that quiet and still moment, the sheer simplicity of the love she had once had for her. Before she had known better . . . But she knew that when those green eyes opened, that purity of emotion would fall away. They were broken, the two of them, and her mother either didn't know it or didn't care.

Neither option seemed viable. Could she really not care? But then, could she really not know? Did she honestly accept at face value all the lies Willow had told about wanting a 'bigger life' and big city excitement – cover stories that had never fully washed with her sisters or father? Had her mother really never once asked herself, what if . . . what if . . . ?

But standing there – caught between two worlds – there was a dark and uncomfortable question hovering at the furthermost reaches of Willow's own mind: what if it *hadn't* been kindness that had motivated her to let her mother sleep through Pip's crisis this morning? What if, at heart, she had wanted to punish her, to cast her out of the loop in the way Willow had been? Was she a monster now, too? Was she capable of such conscious cruelty?

She wasn't even sure she knew. Grief could be a twisted mistress without anger in the mix as well, and they were all messed up, one way or another; living under the Lorne curse had taken a toll on them all.

Willow crossed the room, hearing the floorboards creak underfoot, the heels of her boots muffled on the layered rugs. She sank onto the soft mattress and let a hand cup her mother's shoulder; she was warm, her slight body heavy on the sheets. Her eyelids fluttered, dazed, but as her green eyes met Willow's blue ones, time clicked back into its gallop again, pushing out the past. There was only now. Only this. Only them.

'What is it?' her mother gasped, waking instantly, her sleepy blush already in retreat as she was alerted by her daughter's foreign intrusion into this room.

Willow blinked. '. . . It's Pip.'

Ottie was waiting for them by her garden gate when they stopped at her house – she'd showered and changed too – and in tense silence, they sped through the sleeping county. Briefly Ottie tried to keep a conversation going from the back seat, but her mother wouldn't be reassured until she had seen her child with her own eyes, and the silence became easier to sink into, all of them staring out of the windows with glassy stares.

In spite of Willow and Ottie's endless activity through the night, it was not yet eight on Sunday morning and apart from a few Ultra race stragglers, some early-bird cyclists and the milkman, they had the roads to themselves. It was just over half an hour to the hospital and Willow pulled into the car park an hour and fifteen minutes after they'd left it, just as the sun peeped over the horizon. The morning was dawning clear after yesterday's storm and a growing red blush would soon tint the sky. Willow took it as a hopeful sign, a token of a bright, new, beautiful, glad-to-be-alive day.

'You two jump out while I park,' she said to her mother and Ottie, dropping them at the entrance doors.

Her mother hurried out without seeming to acknowledge what she'd said; Ottie shot her a worried look. 'Don't be long,' she murmured.

There was no hope of that, no chance of even a few minutes' respite driving around in circles, looking for a space. Instead, the car park was almost empty and Willow parked quickly, finding herself back in the building and back on the ward where Pip was being monitored, only moments after the others.

'– if I'd lost you too.'

Willow stopped in the doorway at the scene. Her mother was reaching over the bed, heaving with sobs, Pip somewhere engulfed in her arms.

'I'm so sorry.' Pip's voice was muffled, but even when their mother moved away, drawing back to take a better, disbelieving look at her, her voice remained weak and thin. 'I never meant to put you through—'

'I can't believe this has happened to us. Why is this happening to us? My baby girl!'

Pip kept her gaze down. Willow noticed the first hints of colour were returning to her cheeks, that she looked marginally better than she had when they'd left. She was still covered in the heavy blankets; the doctors had treated her with warming fluids all night but now she'd had the special hot bath too. She was out of danger but she still looked like someone who had teetered on the precipice.

A nurse orderly edged past her and Willow stepped out of the way of the door. The orderly was carrying a small neat pile of clothes and she set them down carefully on the table at the end of her bed. Everyone's eyes came to rest upon them – they were the clothes Pip had been wearing last night: tattersall, jeans, underwear, already washed and ironed. Willow saw that something was missing though – her boots – and she realized they must still be sitting on the lawn where her sister had torn them off, tiny monuments to an act of gross stupidity.

'Thank you,' her mother said gratefully as the orderly nodded and left again. She stared at the folded laundry as though it was toxic, responsible for global warming and suicide bombs. '. . . What made you do it?' She looked back at her middle daughter – the defiant, strong one, the tomboy, nobody's victim.

Pip kept her eyes downcast, nibbling on her lip nervously. Willow was amazed – she hadn't seen that particular little tic since childhood. 'We had a bet.'

'A *bet*?' Their mother's voice sounded suddenly faint.

'Shalimar for Sean Cuneen's best horse. First to the pontoon.'

It was a long time before their mother spoke. 'I see,' she said quietly, staring at the spot behind Pip's head for a long, drawn-out moment, before pressing her palms against the mattress and slowly getting up from the bed. Her eyes were becoming red-rimmed, the colour draining from her as it returned to her daughter.

'Mam, I'm sorry. I know it was an eejit thing to do,' Pip said urgently, reaching a hand towards her. 'I'd been drinking. I wasn't thinking straight.'

Her mother looked down at her, suddenly cold. 'Your life means so little to you, you'd gamble it on a horse?'

'No! I was trying to make my life better. And it wasn't just any horse. I was going after my dream, Mam.' A single tear rolled down Pip's pale cheek.

'No dream is worth dying for, Philippa.' Her voice was calm and measured, but as she walked to the doorway, Willow saw she was visibly trembling.

'Where are you going?' Pip called.

'I'm sorry but I can't . . . I can't look at you right now. I need to get some air.'

'Mam!' Pip cried as she brushed past Willow, out into the corridor, and bumping unseeingly into a doctor as the tears began to flow.

'Fuck,' Pip whispered.

'I'll go after her,' Willow said, but Ottie shook her head.

'No, let me. It's probably better if I go.'

Willow heard the rebuke in the words and she felt herself recoil. Become smaller.

'Why's Mam upset with *you*?' Pip asked weakly as Ottie dashed from the room.

There was a small silence. Willow felt sick. 'Probably because I didn't call her immediately to say you were here.'

Pip's shocked look made her feel worse. 'Why not?'

Willow swallowed. 'I was trying to save her from unnecessary worry. You were coming round, the paramedics said your signs were good for a full recovery.' She winced at the memory. It certainly hadn't *looked* good as they'd wheeled her off the ambulance – tubes, foil blankets, blue lips, paper-white skin.

'Right,' Pip murmured, looking ashamed and sinking deeper into her pillows.

'Obviously if things had been worse, I wouldn't have hesitated,' she said quickly. That much was true, she knew it was. She had wanted her mother to know what it felt like to lose control of her own life, her own family – just for a moment. 'But the doctors said you were stable and I thought it was better for her to rest. I knew it'd be so worrying for her when she was finally told and what was the point in her sitting up through the night when you weren't even conscious? After everything she's gone through with Dad—'

'Oh, Will, what have I done?' Pip sobbed, huge tears beginning to roll down her cheeks.

Willow dashed across the room and hugged her; Pip's grip was weak but her sorrow and regret palpably fierce. 'We're all just so relieved you're okay.'

'I hate myself, I can't believe I've done this to you all.'

Willow pulled back and sank onto the side of the bed, taking Pip's hands in her own. They felt warmer now. 'No hating allowed,' she said simply, squeezing them. 'But this bet – you have to explain it to me. Why did you take it? How could it have been so important?'

'I didn't take it, Sis, I was the one who extended it.'

'You wanted another horse that badly?'

'No, not just any horse. The *right* horse. All my life I've wanted to breed my own stock. It's my dream.'

'But you've never said,' Willow frowned.

'What was the point? It takes serious money – money we don't remotely have and never will.' She sighed. 'I know I'm lucky getting to work with horses. It's great; I'd go mad without them . . .'

'And none of us would ever want to see that,' Willow teased.

Pip cracked a weak half-grin. 'But trekking tourists along the Way isn't enough. And with Dad dying, so suddenly, so young, it's made me realize – I can't keep putting off how I really want to be living my life. I've got to make it happen somehow. Take a chance. When I bought Shalimar, it was always with a wing and a prayer that I could use her as my brood mare. She's got such a great bloodline.'

'How did you afford her then?'

'Because of a ligament injury. The previous owner was going to have her put down. I had to beg him to let me have her and even the vet thought it was a long shot. It took seven months of bloody intense, daily physio to get her back on her feet again. She'll never be rideable but that's fine, I've got plenty of other horses for that. She's by far the best horse I've ever had.'

Willow watched her sister's eyes shine. 'So who would you mate her with?'

'That's the big question,' Pip said wistfully, staring into space. Her eyes slid back to Willow again. 'You know Shula Flanagan's horse, Dark Star?'

Willow wrinkled her nose and shook her head. 'Uh . . . no, sorry. I just about know the names of your lot.'

'Well, he was a below-the-radar novice. Tall, dark, oh my God, so handsome. Longest eyelashes. Soulful eyes.'

Willow swallowed. Was she describing a horse? Or Connor? '. . . *Was?*'

Pip's brow furrowed. 'Until his father won the Grand National.'

Willow gasped. 'Dark Star is Midnight Feast's son?'

Pip nodded. 'And no one gave a damn about it until Midnight went and won that bloody race and then, suddenly, his value sky-rocketed.' She weakly swept her arm upwards.

'But could you have afforded him even before that?'

'Yes! He was so nearly mine, Will. We were that close.' Pip pinched her fingers together.

'We?'

'Me and Dad. He approached Bertie for me.'

'Bertie?' Willow echoed, feeling that familiar tension set in her bones at the mention of that man's name.

'On one of their golf days. Shula hardly ever rides him anyway; they're never bloody here, always off in Barbados or Gstaad or something. Dad had pretty much got him to agree a price when Midnight went and won the biggest bloody race in the world and all of a sudden, the deal was off and they wanted seven figures for him. They had *no* idea what quality they had in him before then,' Pip said, stabbing the air viciously. 'They're just philistines. They needed to see a flashy trophy before they believed he had any value.'

'Pip, I'm sorry.'

She pursed her lips, disappointment set deep in her bones. 'Dark Star was the perfect horse to get me started. He and Shalimar . . .' Pip looked over at her. 'And before you say it, don't tell me there'll be other horses like him, because there won't. Not at my level.'

'So that's why you went all or nothing for Sean Cuneen's horse.'

Pip shrugged disconsolately. 'He's not Dark Star's quality, nothing like, but he would have been a halfway decent start block from which to jump off.' She looked away, the corners of her mouth pulling ever so slightly downwards, a single tear rolling slowly down her pale cheek. 'I figured the bet was the only avenue open to me: an all-or-nothing punt. Because, let's face it, I'm never going to have the money to do it the usual way.'

Willow couldn't disagree with that. The top horses were crazy money. Connor had told her what it had cost him to buy into the syndicate and she'd almost dropped her drink down her front.

There was a rap at the door and they both looked up.

'Oh, hey, Taigh!' Willow said, getting up and greeting him with a hug as Pip hurriedly rubbed out the tear staining her cheek. He was wearing his uniform and looked every bit as shattered as she; he'd been up all night too. 'Are you clocking off now?'

'I am. We just came back in with another patient so I thought I'd look in. How's she doing?' he asked, stepping tentatively into the room, his eyes going straight to the monitors and checking the numbers for himself, before looking at Pip, tiny and bundled-up beneath the covers.

'*She* can answer for herself and is doing just fine. What are *you* doing here?' Pip asked shortly.

Taigh looked taken aback. 'Uh . . . I just wanted to check you're okay.'

'Take the gossip back to the village, you mean.'

'Pip!' Willow said exasperatedly. 'It was Taigh who brought you in last night.'

'What?' Pip's expression changed. She looked shocked, but also something else . . . Angry? Embarrassed? Ashamed? Willow couldn't tell.

'I was on duty when the call came in,' he shrugged, almost as if apologizing to her. 'We were just finishing up a call-out in Repley so we were the nearest responders. Got to you in four minutes, which, under the circumstances . . .'

Pip looked dumbstruck, her mouth hanging open in dismay. Were the memories from last night rushing back at her, Willow wondered? It was hard enough for her to think back over them, seeing Pip's bright hair floating below the water's surface; she couldn't imagine what it must be like for her sister when she closed her eyes or tried to sleep. Was the darkness something to be feared now? Would she suffer nightmares? Flashbacks? Was she going to need counselling?

He gave an uncertain smile as her silence lengthened – no thanks forthcoming; even at a time like this, he was still not welcome. 'Anyway, I can see you're busy, I won't intrude any further. I just wanted to check you were . . . good. And you are. Y'are, so I'll head off now.'

Pip made no move to stop him but Willow followed him out into the corridor. 'Taigh,' she said, touching his elbow. He turned around. 'I'm sorry, she's . . . she's still very shaken. She's not herself.'

But they both knew that was a lie. She was entirely herself – Pip's ongoing hostility towards him was the one constant it seemed they could rely on. 'Just keep an eye on her, the shock's going to likely catch up with her soon,' he simply said.

'We can never thank you enough for what you did. Mam will want to see you too, to thank you in person.'

'I just did what I'm trained for,' he shrugged. 'Besides, it was you as did most of the work. If you and that fella hadn't 'a got to her when you did . . .' He shook his head, looking almost bewildered as he too sank back into the drama of last night. 'Funny, but it never occurred to me she might actually be mortal. She's always so damned tough. I think I actually did believe she was titanium-plated or something.'

'Yes, I think we all did.' Willow gave a snort of agreement that came out more like another sob. Her emotions were scratch-and-sniff ready. 'It was a close call.'

He held her arms, looking at her kindly. 'But she got through it. I've just spoken to the nurses and they're minded to discharge her tonight.'

'Tonight? But isn't that a little soon?'

'They'll monitor her through the day but her body temp's back up in normal range, chest is looking clear, although she'll need regular checking on – you'll need to be vigilant for a cough, chest pain, sleepiness, difficulty breathing—'

'Oh my God.' Willow frowned, feeling panicked. 'How can they discharge her if there's still all that to go wrong?'

'Don't worry, those are just things to watch out for. If the doctors thought she was at risk of any of them happening, they wouldn't discharge her yet. They'll explain all this to you in further detail when they come to—'

'No.' Willow shook her head, alarmed. 'It's not fair to put that level of responsibility upon us.'

He hesitated. 'They need the beds, Willow.'

But she simply shook her head and clasped her arms over her chest. 'Mam's been through enough. You know she has. We can't ask her to look out for signs of her daughter suddenly dying too.'

Taigh stared at her. Could he see the pain on her face? 'Yes, you're right . . .' His brow furrowed as he searched for a solution. 'Okay, look, why don't I check in on her for the next few days? Billy's off this week – he's got county football trials in Cork – so I'm doing the newspaper rounds m'self anyway. I can look in, make sure she's doing all right.'

'Oh, would you? Thank you,' Willow gasped, throwing her arms around him. 'Thank you.'

'It's only for a few days anyway. We all know your sister. She'll not stand for being molly-coddled for long.'

Willow winced. 'I know. She's going to be a *terrible* patient. I apologize in advance.'

'She's going to be even more terrible when she knows it's me as looking after her,' he said with a roll of his eyes.

Willow couldn't deny it. If Pip could manage to remain frosty to the man who'd brought her out of hypothermia, she wasn't going to be tolerant of his community care visits. 'Tell you what, if *you* survive it, I'll buy you a drink to say thanks,' she called after him as he walked down the corridor, heading for the exit.

'A drink?' he scoffed. 'You'll owe me the whole damn pub by the time she's done.'

'*Ottie, where are you?*'

She frowned at her lover's unexpectedly snappish tone of voice, changing gear as she turned right and pulled away from the castle gates. It was dark again, her main beam sweeping over the sturdy trunks of ancient elms and oaks, and she realized she'd not seen daylight today. 'I've got you on Bluetooth. I'm in the car. I've just dropped Mam and Pip and Willow back from the hospital.'

'. . . The *hospital*? What were they doing there?'

Ottie felt a jolt of surprise to realize he didn't yet know about the crisis she'd just lived through. It hadn't occurred to her to call him – partly because he was uncontactable, competing in the race, but also because it hadn't crossed her mind. Family was all she'd been able to think about, comforting her mother as she sobbed in the hospital cafe.

'I'll . . . I'll tell you when I see you,' she said instead, not wanting to go into it over the phone. If she had to recount the horror of nearly losing her sister ten days after their father, she wanted to do it with his arms around her. 'What's wrong? You sound stressed.'

'You could say that. Look, I need you to get over here.'

'What, *now*?' Rockhurst, his estate, was a twenty-five-minute drive from here and after a day spent being pummelled by the weather yesterday, almost no sleep last night and hanging around the hospital all day today, she wanted nothing more than her pyjamas, a vat of tea and to watch TV in bed. Even he couldn't tempt her out.

'Right away. We've got an unfolding situation and I need everyone back on site.'

'Uh . . . okay.' He was speaking to her like she was an employee, his voice distant and distracted. What was happening over there? 'But—'

'Come straight to the main tent.' And he hung up.

Ottie pulled into the bus stop and stared at the Call Ended sign. What was going on? With an exhausted sigh, she turned the car round in a three-point turn and headed back into town instead, past the church and the village green, past the butcher's and the Stores and the post office. The race bunting was still threaded up between the lamp-posts but it was past six now and that meant the Kilmally Ultramarathon was officially over for another year.

She exited the village and headed deeper into the narrow lanes, her main beam bouncing off hedgerows, glancing across an owl sitting on a low branch. By the time she crossed onto Flanagan land twenty minutes later, the first stars were already beginning to stud the night sky. She drove down the farm track away from the main house – a neo-classical stuccoed mansion Shula's father had owned – towards the staging camp for the Ultra event. It was set up in a large field, a marquee and two bell tents set inside the gate.

She parked where she could on the hard standing – there was only so much mud her Mini could take – and got out. There were dozens of people milling around. Surprisingly many, in fact. She knew she'd have just missed the prize-giving ceremony, it was always held around now – the winners fully rested after several hours' rest, the stragglers only just over the line – but it was unusual for so many to have stayed gathered here. Most of them needed help getting in and out of cars, or on and off chairs, their bodies were so wrecked. Staying to party or celebrate seemed unlikely.

She wove through them to the marquee; the ground was rough and uneven underfoot, but nightlights had been set up on posts so that people could move about clearly – a twisted ankle on the way back from the registration tent was not what any of these competitors needed.

She lifted the flap of the tent and ducked in, stopping in surprise at the sight of all the race marshals and stewards in their yellow high-vis vests, Bertie standing on an apple crate at the front and holding a microphone. His eyes grazed over her but he did nothing to acknowledge her summoned presence. He gave no sign that she was extraordinary or special to him, that he was pleased to see her. He gave no sign in fact that he'd even noticed her at all, but then they were both well practised at hiding an elephant in a room.

'– all to check your records and write down on the map here, the time he passed you. When we've been able to establish the last stop he was recorded as passing, then we'll know where to start looking. Please, hurry now.'

He stepped down from the box, wincing as he did, his own body clearly battered. She watched him as he made his way through the crowd towards her. He was limping slightly, his gaunt cheeks covered in a greying stubble. Several people stopped him, wanting directions or clarification or leadership, and he pointed in the direction of the far corner, where the other stewards were now huddling like a herd of sheep in the snow.

'Hey,' he murmured. He looked exhausted, utterly spent, and all she wanted was to throw her arms around him, to tell him about the horrors of her day and hear about his. Instead, she stood by impassively, not able even to extend a hand towards him in public.

'What's going on? Has something happened?'

'We're a man down.'

'Sorry?'

'We're a racer short. He is recorded as having set off but he hasn't finished and the marshals have checked the course three times on the quads – there's no one still running out there.'

Ottie frowned. 'So, he's lost?'

'Looks that way,' he sighed. 'It's a pain in the arse but clearly we've got to find the guy.'

'Right,' she said, rubbing her hands over her face. This was the absolute last thing she needed.

He looked down at her properly then, seeing the tense set of her bones. 'You said you were at the hospital earlier. What's happened with you? It's not Serena, is it?'

Her mother? Why would he think that? She frowned. 'No, she's fine. It was Pip.'

'Pip?' he echoed, as though nothing could ever be wrong with her.

'She was at a party last night and got drunk and –' The recklessness, the sheer stupidity of the act twisted itself around her again like a wind. 'And she ran into a freezing cold lake. Very nearly drowned.'

'Jesus God!' Bertie exclaimed loudly, looking horrified. Several people turned around to stare. 'But she's okay?'

'Yes, she's going to be. Luckily there was a row boat and they managed to get her out in time. But she's been in hospital under observation all last night and today.'

'Jeesht, poor Serena.' He ran his hands down his face. 'It's true what they say – it doesn't rain but it pours. Christ.'

Ottie stood silently. It hadn't somehow been the unburdening she'd expected.

He placed a hand on her arm, an avuncular gesture of sympathy should anyone be watching. 'Well, listen, I'm sorry to have called you up here. If I'd known . . . But I just need to see your records from yesterday. Have you got them?'

'Sure.' She'd remembered to bring her backpack out from the car, knowing she needed to give back her pass and clipboard anyway.

She pulled it out and handed it to him. Immediately, he began scanning down the sheets, one finger sliding down the paper, top to bottom. He went through all eight pages and then double-checked again.

'Nope. He never got as far as you.' His frown deepened. He looked genuinely concerned.

'What's wrong?'

'Well, it'd be one thing if he lost his way during the night stretch, but you were in one of the first stages of the race. Even with the storm, light and visibility were still fair at that point.' He turned and started heading towards the large course map on the board in the corner. 'Who was manning Kinaughton Point?' he called.

Ottie followed after him as they pushed into the crowd. Kinaughton Point was the preceding steward station eight miles before hers.

A hand went up. 'Me!'

Bertie went and stood in front of the man, his blue eyes piercing in their intensity. 'Did 271 pass you?'

'Aye, at . . .' The steward checked his notes. It was on the first page, right at the top. 'Seven forty-seven.'

'And the next runner after him was . . . ?'

'069 at seven fifty.'

'06 . . . ? That was me,' Bertie exclaimed. His gaze met hers. They both remembered perfectly well him arriving at her station, his hands up her shirt. He quickly looked down again, scrutinizing her notes. 'And I got to the next stop at eight thirty-six.'

But runner 271 hadn't. Somewhere between the preceding station and hers, he'd disappeared. Early in the morning, early on in the race . . .

'Could he have just given up? Walked off the course without telling anyone?' she asked.

Bertie gave a scoffing laugh and the crowd around them broke up into a buzz of chat and speculation. 'No. Absolutely no way,' Bertie said. 'He's got way too much invested in this to just do a disappearing act. Not only is 271 one of the race leaders, he's also the Ultra Patagonia Champion and the Ultra Atlas Champion. He doesn't need to do this race to qualify for the Mont Blanc next month – he's just using it as a training run.'

This was a *training* run? So he hadn't been boasting then? Ottie's eyes widened. The Ultra Mont Blanc was the Olympics of the extreme endurance world: 106 miles run up a 10,000-metre elevation. The winner of that race held the World Title. Not only that, she had spent enough hours lying in bed next to this man – obsessive, competitive, driven – to know he had offered a one-million-euro pot to anyone who could pull off the hat-trick of holding all three Ultra titles at once. Bertie figured his money was safe. In the seven years that the offer had been set on the table, no one had managed it yet.

He addressed the crowd directly. 'Number 271 has not – excuse the pun – done a runner. And it isn't viable to think he got lost on a clearly tracked course in broad daylight. So we have to conclude he's injured,' Bertie said solemnly. 'Most likely badly. He must have slipped and fallen somewhere or he'd have been seen by the marshals or other runners. It's the only thing that makes sense.'

He walked over to the map and drew two large red circles around Kinaughton Point and Devil's Fork, where she'd been working. She could imagine him in the army, commanding his men, issuing orders. 'From what we can gather, it appears he's disappeared between these two stations. An eight-mile stretch. Now, for much of that, the track there is below the ridgeline and cut into the cliffs, which means the search area will be commensurately narrow – he couldn't and wouldn't have gone up. This is both a good and bad thing as it means he can only be below.'

A grave hush fell over the room. Everyone knew what that meant. The land was steep there; a fall could very well have meant an unstoppable slide down the slopes, over the cliffs and into the sea.

'But let's not get ahead of ourselves,' Bertie said authoritatively. 'We have several advantages here to work with – a narrow search area within a known stretch, and . . .' His voice failed as he realized that was it; the only positive to be had. 'So let's get out there and find him.'

Ottie looked around at the sea of worried, unfooled faces. This runner had been missing for thirty-four hours now, last sighted and recorded at 7.47 a.m. yesterday. That was thirty-four hours in which no one had noticed and no one had looked for him. The weather conditions had been harsh all day yesterday and temperatures had plummeted overnight beneath the clear skies so he had to be presumed injured *and* exposed? It wasn't called the Wild Atlantic Way for nothing.

'Now!' Bertie snapped.

The room sprang into action, the volunteers shrugging on their waterproof coats and putting on headtorches as they headed for the door like a herd of bison crossing a river.

'Wait!' someone cried from the back. 'What's this fella's name? Who are we even shouting for?'

'Gilmore,' Bertie said. 'Ben Gilmore.'

Chapter Twelve

The wind was punishing, pushing them back as they rode headlong into it on the quads. Ottie felt her eyes stream, her heart pounding fast as she tried to keep up. Bertie, driving just ahead, was like a man possessed. No matter that he'd completed the course himself in twenty-six hours, that he hadn't slept, that his body was wrecked, here he was out in the deathly December temperatures when he should have been recovering himself. But his reputation was on the line. He knew that if this man, Gilmore, was – God help them – dead, that would be the end of Ultra.

And it'd be all her fault, for hadn't she seen with her own eyes this morning that he wasn't back? She'd seen it and she'd done nothing about it. She'd opened his empty tent, knowing he'd said he would be back and gone by this morning, but instead of checking he was still competing and that everything was okay, she'd let another twelve hours slip by.

By definition, this was an extreme event. It was supposed to be tough – but not hazardous. It was why there were so many checks and marshals along the route. It was why only people with a proven completion track record of endurance events were allowed to qualify and participate. To have been so cavalier about his continuing absence, to have assumed he had simply lied and overstated his ability, rather than think something had happened . . .

Bertie cut the throttle and jumped off his bike as they reached the Kinaughton Point station. The small blue and white striped waterproof tented canopy with the desk and metal chair inside was still there, the chair collapsed and set on its side, ready to be dismantled and collected tomorrow.

The peloton of marshals following him stopped in line and they all stood together in a huddle, braced against the winds that felt gale-force as they buffeted straight into the cliffs, fresh from a four thousand-mile surf from the American coast.

'The coastguard's been notified,' he shouted, straining to be heard. 'They're going to do a sweep of the area below,' he cried, waving his arms around to indicate the treacherous and rocky cliffs. 'You are *not* to attempt to go down there yourselves. I repeat – do not go down onto the cliffs yourselves! I want you to break up into small groups of two or three and concentrate on hundred-yard stretches of the ground immediately around the track. Do not go beyond your own search zone. There's enough of us here to cover the area quickly if we work thoroughly and methodically.'

A sudden gust of wind rammed at his back, almost sending him sprawling to the ground and he widened his stance, his waterproofs flapping loudly. 'Use the bikes to travel to your designated search zone. I'll go up front, Ottie can come with me. She worked the Devil's Fork station yesterday and knows this stretch better than anyone. The rest of you, get into groups between here and there and let's get on with it.'

Everyone did as they were told, even her, following meekly after Bertie as he indicated for her to get on the quad bike with him. Without a word, they pulled off again, the small convoy behind them steadily dropping away, two by two, over the eight-mile stretch, until eventually it was just them.

Bertie didn't speak. His jaw was set to thrust, his whole body primed and tense. Ottie thought he looked like a safari tracker, his eyes darting intently into the dark, his head twitching as his ears strained to pick up any stray sounds over the wind.

'You go up to your station and work your way back to me. We'll meet in the middle.' His voice was hard and emotionless and Ottie nodded, knowing he was only doing the right thing – a man's life was at stake. Still, she felt that tightness in her chest that she sometimes got when she sensed – feared – she was losing him, that perhaps his interest was waning . . .

She ran in a half-crouch along the stony track, the beam of light from her headtorch bouncing up and down as she desperately scanned the dark for signs of a body. What if they were already too late? It would be on her. Unless he had fallen and been killed outright, death by hypothermia or exposure would be her responsibility.

'Of course, he's not dead,' she told herself as she ran, her breath coming hard, her feet stumbling over the rough ground. But the facts suggested otherwise; people died all the time – her father, so nearly Pip too. Didn't things come in threes?

The wind howled. A couple of miles inland in the village, protected by the bluffs and the trees, no one would particularly notice the gusts tonight; but out here, exposed on the very edge of the Atlantic, it was merciless and bitter.

Ottie saw the fork on the path and gave a groan of relief as she jogged past. She was within metres now of her station. She could . . .

Wait.

She stopped and looked back. She walked over and shone her beam onto the fork. The lower path couldn't be called a track as such; it was so narrow, only goats and surer-footed animals would attempt to get down it. Her father had always warned them about it as girls – it led to nowhere, the faint trail segueing into a grass pitch that was too steep and slippery even to stand on. *They* knew that, the Lornes. This was their land, ordinarily this stretch for private use only, except for this one event in which her father opened up access for his old friend. He never took any money for it but made only a single demand: that this section was properly signposted.

The thought of someone taking the wrong fork – and subsequently suing him – had worried him so much he had made it the condition of his agreement that an arrow needed to be placed here on the course, to be on the safe side.

But there was nothing here now.

'Gilmore?'

She could hear Bertie hollering into the wind, his voice faint from here but the desperation clear. It was the sort of tone reserved for mothers seeing their child drop a ball on the road, for soldiers running into a barricaded house.

'Ben!' she joined in, turning her back to the wind and shouting as powerfully as she could, hoping her voice would carry too. 'Ben Gilmore!'

She scanned everywhere she could see, looking behind rocks where he might have hidden for shelter – they were all far too small to be effective, but something had to be better than nothing out here, surely. She peered over the sides of the path where the ground fell away sharply, but it was just a dark void. Surely not . . . ? Please no.

But there was nowhere else he could be: he was either on this track or in the sea. She felt a hollow whistle through her bones as sheer logic closed down the options. According to the charts, he had been sighted and recorded at Kinaughton Point but had never made it over to her. Here. And she had just driven the eight-mile length of this section with Bertie; thousands of other competitors had followed after him too. Marshals had double-checked it. If he was on the track there, someone *would* have seen him. Which meant . . .

It meant . . .

Far, far below, she could just hear the heavy rise and fall of the ocean. It sounded immense and almost corporeal, a great mass shifting. If he was down there, they'd never find him tonight. If they waited till morning, he would definitely be a dead man.

'Gilmore! Ben Gilmore!' she screamed into the night. Her voice felt as ragged and torn as the rest of her.

Bertie's shouts intersected with hers; he was close now and drawing nearer quickly. 'Anything?' she asked breathlessly as he reached her. It was a pointless question, of course; they'd all know if there was something to know.

He shook his head, looking wretched. This would be the end of his Ultra empire, he knew it. People couldn't be dying on these events. They were supposed to be about endurance, not survival.

'Bertie, you don't think . . . ?' She stared down at the lower track on the fork.

'Don't be ridiculous. He wouldn't have gone down there. It's clearly impassable.'

'. . . But where's the sign?'

He looked over to where the sign should have been. A strong silence pulsed. 'Well, obviously it's been cleared away.'

But her gaze fell to the ground, followed by his. There was no sign of any hole in the ground to indicate a sign had been positioned there recently. And none of the rest of the signs or huts had been cleared yet.

He turned to face her, paler now. 'Well, you were the steward on duty for this stretch, surely you remember? Did you see the sign here?'

She stared at him, trying to think back. Had she? 'I . . .' She squinted against the wind. 'I can't remember. I don't recall noticing it.'

'But it was your job to notice it, Ottie! That's *why* you're stationed here – for the competitors' safety.'

His words were brutal but they were right. She felt her breathing come faster, a lump swell in her throat as tears began to press against the backs of her eyes. 'I don't think I did see it.' She had failed in her one duty, knowing better than anyone this spot was hazardous. How could she not have noticed the sign hadn't been put up?

'Oh Jesus,' he suddenly whispered, putting a hand over his mouth as he remembered something. 'You're absolutely right. The sign never did go up, I remember now.'

'Bertie, why not?' she cried, looking up at him desperately. 'You know it was Dad's one demand. The only one.'

'Yes. But it was because of you, Ottie. The other night – when I came to see you, remember? You'd been texting me all day, saying how bad you were feeling . . . I was *supposed* to be putting the sign out but I came over to your place instead. I was worried about you.'

Ottie felt her panic gather. Her texts. Her tears. Her anger with Willow. Her father. 'So then, it's . . . it's because of us that he's . . . down there?'

'Us. Me. You.' He shrugged. 'Who knows how the authorities will view it.' He looked down the fork path again, seeing how it led to nowhere. 'The priority has to be find—'

Another memory made him startle and Ottie flinched as she watched him, feeling her panic gather again. 'Christ, there *was* someone ahead of me along this stretch, I remember it now.' He scrunched his eyes shut as though that would make the memory brighter. 'He was a few minutes ahead – sometimes he was in sight and sometimes not.'

'You think it was Gilmore?'

'I've no idea, he was just a shape from where I was.' He frowned, looking at her again quizzically. 'But *you* must have seen him coming if he was just ahead of me. And he must have seen you too. How could he not have? Your station is on the nose of the bend for that very reason.'

Ottie felt the blood pool at her feet. No, it couldn't be. That moment, that one minute when she'd deliberately hidden herself from view . . . That was when he'd come along? Spending a penny had cost a life? 'Oh God, Bertie, it's all my fault,' she whispered. 'I had to pee. I ducked out of sight around the corner. Only for a minute. Not even!'

His eyes widened. 'Fuck!'

She felt like she was going to faint – shock, horror, panic, exhaustion . . . She swayed, eyes closed, sinking down onto her heels in a controlled swoop and dropping her head in her hands. This couldn't be happening. She opened her eyes, needing comfort, reassurance, but Bertie had already set off again, shouting orders frantically into his radio and heading down the fork.

'Bertie, no!' she screamed, forcing herself after him.

He was already on the lower path, and she angled herself into the lee of the cliff as she followed after, her father's warnings – 'Never, *ever*, go down this path! You will die!' – reverberating through her head.

She couldn't see Bertie clearly, only the bouncing beam from his headtorch as he scrambled down on his haunches, his hands behind him to keep his weight back and to counter-balance the forward momentum that wanted to hurl them both from this cliff into the frothing waters below. She had no idea where the trail petered out, when what little grip they had would suddenly stop and the slide would begin . . .

Suddenly, the headbeam stopped bouncing. 'Gilmore! Ben Gilmore!' Bertie's voice was a warrior's cry, splitting the sky like an arrow. 'Gilmore! Jesus!'

He turned back, his expression changing in an instant as he saw her twenty metres behind him. 'Ottie, get back!' She stopped obediently, sinking onto her bottom and trembling violently. 'Get back up onto the path. I can see him!'

'Is he alive?' she screamed. Oh please, God, let him be alive.

There was a long pause. 'I don't know, he's not moving! I can't get any closer! Get back onto the fork and call mountain rescue! We're going to need a stretcher and ropes!'

Pip stared out of the window, biting her nails frustratedly as she watched Willow struggle with the buckets of feed across the yard. She was carrying them all wrong and she'd put far too many oats in the feed.

Willow glanced up, as though sensing her sister's disapproving stare, and – in the absence of having any free hands – nodded her head by way of reply. Pip nodded back, biting hard on her lip. It was like torture, being forced to watch and not 'do'.

It was also ridiculous. She was perfectly capable of feeding her own horses. She was *fine*. She had slept well last night in her old bed at the castle, she'd eaten all the breakfast Mrs Mac could put in front of her; she'd even put on a vest to 'keep her core warm'. But a deal was a deal. Her mother had only allowed her back here – 'out of sight' – if she agreed to rest and let Willow muck out and feed the horses for the rest of the week. What choice had she had? It wasn't like Willow had looked thrilled by the prospect either. The sooner they could all get back to normal, the better.

She moved away from the window. It was better all round just not to look; she'd never been a good delegator. The television was on – some property show she remembered from a sick day back when she'd been a student – but she couldn't bring herself to watch it. She wasn't sick, just stupid. And selfish.

She put the kettle on again – the third time since getting back twenty minutes ago but she kept forgetting to pour the tea. She was so used to always being on the go, she didn't usually step indoors between the hours of seven and seven. What was she going to do all day?

The dishes on the draining board stared back at her as if in reply. She supposed she could make a start by putting them away . . .

'I timed it well, I see.'

The sudden male voice in the room made her scream in fright and she spun round, an omelette pan outstretched threateningly in her hand.

Taigh put his hands up in a sign of surrender, a small smile playing on his lips at the sight of her weapon. 'I'm definitely not taking you on with that thing in yer hand. You'd beat me to a pulp.'

'I'd beat you in an arm wrestle,' Pip muttered, knowing it

was blatantly untrue but trying to cover the fact that she'd just screamed like a little girl. 'What the hell are you doing here, anyway?'

Confusingly, he was wearing his postal kit but was holding his paramedic's bag. 'I saw Willow downstairs. She told me to come straight up.'

She rolled her eyes. 'No, I mean, what are you doing *here*?'

'Didn't they tell you?' he frowned. 'I'm here to check up on you.'

'What? I don't need any checking up on!' she protested vociferously. 'The doctors discharged me. I am absolutely fine.'

'You're fine enough for someone who almost accidentally killed themselves two days ago, but there's still checks need to be done. I know they'd have mentioned there's a bit a shadow on your chest that they're wanting to keep an eye on. Last thing you need is pneumonia. That really would stuff up your Christmas plans.'

Pip glared at him. The doctor had indeed said exactly that, but she'd expected a community nurse or her GP at least. Wasn't it bad enough to have been saved by him? Now he had to carry on looking after her too? 'Surely there's someone else who could do it.'

'Thanks!' he replied with a sarcastic smile, before crouching down and opening the bag, slinging a stethoscope around his neck and rummaging for something else too. 'But I was passing on the newspaper round anyway and I'm sure you're aware resources are tight enough, without people having to make duplicate visits.' The kettle boiled, switching off with a distinct click. 'Ah, just the milk and two for me, thanks for asking.'

With a groan, Pip turned away and reached for the cups. The nerve of the guy.

'So I like what you've done with the place,' he said to her back.

She glanced back over her shoulder. 'Very funny,' she snapped, but as he chuckled to himself, she sneaked a surreptitious fresh look at her little flat. It was true she had never touched it; the walls had been left with the original rough lime plaster, and the only things on them were flyers for hunt meets, yard sales, horses for sale. A newspaper cut-out of Midnight Feast winning the Grand National had been sellotaped, in lieu of something more formal or framed, above the brown cord sofa that sagged in the middle. Much like at the castle, the floor was covered with dozens of small overlapping threadbare rugs she had found rolled up in the attic there, and she'd come away with several blue and white lamps too – not because she liked or prized them, but because she desperately needed the light. Her flat was in the eaves above one of the stable blocks and aside from rudimentary electrics, any heating she had came from the coal-burning stove set in the middle of the wall (which also provided her hot water); her bed was set behind a slightly moth-nibbled silk screen, also taken from the castle attic, and her clothes (what few of them she had) hung from a washing line tied up between hooks on the walls. 'It serves a purpose,' she said defensively.

'Like everything in your life, right? Nothing superfluous to needs. Nothing hanging around simply because you like it, or it happens to make you happy?'

She frowned – it sounded like a pointed comment – and handed him a weak cup of tea, hoping he liked it strong. 'I don't have any sugar.'

'But there's some cubes right there,' he said, pointing to the pot on the counter.

'They're for the horses.'

He looked astounded, then burst out laughing. 'Well, that's me told,' he chortled, taking a slurp of tea and openly grimacing.

Pip gave a wide smile.

He swallowed, smacked his lips together and gave a dramatic shudder, before pinning her with his bright eyes. 'Could be worse I s'pose.'

Pip looked away and, for a few seconds, silence filled the tiny room. She could feel his gaze upon her and she felt a self-conscious blush rise up her neck. She liked having short hair – she'd never been the sort of girl to want ribbons or plaits or 'styles' – but right now, she'd gladly take a mane to hide behind.

'All right then,' he said finally as she offered up belligerent silence in lieu of small talk . 'Well, why don't you sit on the sofa and I'll give you the once-over?'

She gave a sigh of annoyance but obeyed – the sooner he was done, the sooner he'd be gone, right? No doubt he'd be reporting straight back to her mother and if she wanted to stay alone down here . . .

'I'm going to need to listen to your chest so if you could just undo the top buttons of your shirt.'

Eyes down, she did as she was told, turning her head to look out of the window as he placed the stethoscope – warming it first – on her sternum.

'Take a few breaths,' he murmured.

She glanced at the top of his head, the dark curls flopped on their sides like overturned liquorice wheels.

'– Pip, I'm off.'

She looked up to find Willow peering around the door. She frowned. How did everyone manage to climb her stairs without her ever hearing them?

'Did you add the molasses to Fudge's feed?' she demanded.

'Yes.'

'And you checked for mould?'

'Just as you told me.'

'Did Whippy seem okay?'

Willow shrugged. 'Seemed horsey enough to me. I did ask why the long face when I left him though.'

Taigh chortled, appreciating the joke, pulling away from her and rocking back on his heels. 'Nice one.'

'Ta,' Willow grinned, seemingly happy to have her sense of humour appreciated for once. 'How's the patient?'

'Impatient for me to get the hell outta here,' he said, shooting Pip a sly look.

'Don't take it personally. She can't wait to see the back of me either,' Willow groaned, before looking back at her. 'Unfortunately for you, I'll pop back this evening to feed the nags their dinner and bring down some supper for you too. I've put Mrs Mac's soup in the fridge for you for lunch. *Eat* it,' she said sternly. 'Don't think I won't be checking later.'

'Ugh,' Pip groaned, noticing Willow and Taigh share another conspiratorial look before her sister dipped from sight again.

He glanced up at her, as though silently requesting permission to approach again, and replaced the stethoscope on the other side of her chest. Willow's light-hearted mood had left the premises with her.

'Okay.' He pulled back after another minute. 'Now, I need to listen to your chest. If you can just gather your shirt up and lean forward.'

She felt the metal disc move across her back in slow-motion bunny hops and after a minute or so, she wondered what was taking him so long – did she have a disco going on in there?

He got up and sat on the sofa beside her. He pulled a thermometer from his shirt pocket. 'Just pop that under your tongue,' he murmured. 'While we read your blood pressure. If you can just roll up your sleeve.'

Jeesht, this would all be a lot easier in a T-shirt, she huffed to herself, rolling it up. He placed the cuff on her upper arm and began squeezing the pump rapidly several times until she felt the band pinch against her skin. 'Just straighten your arm out,' he said, taking her hand and placing it gently, upturned, on his knee, his eyes on the digital screen.

She watched him watch it, his usual laughing expression replaced by something far more serious and grown-up. She'd never noticed how long his eyelashes were before; nor the little scar on the outer edge of his eyebrow. She wondered how he'd come by it, though she knew she'd never ask; showing any interest in him, no matter how small, was something her pride would never allow.

The cuff released and he pulled away the Velcro bindings. He reached over and took the thermometer from her too. 'Hmm.'

'What does "hmm" mean?' she asked in her best bored voice, rolling her shirt sleeve back down again.

'Your temperature is slightly elevated.'

'That's a good thing, isn't it, given how low it was yesterday?' She was being flippant, she knew, but she couldn't seem to help herself. He brought out the worst in her.

'It could be a sign of infection. Do you remember swallowing any water?'

She flinched, looking away quickly as the memories suddenly came unbidden at the question. She didn't *want* to remember any of it, wasn't that obvious?

'Hey. It's okay,' he said quickly, reaching a hand to her arm. 'You're safe now.'

'I know that,' she snapped. 'I'm not an idiot.'

'No,' he sighed, letting his hand drop again. 'You're not – but you would be if you pushed yourself right now. Your body's in deep recovery and you need to take it easy. We need to keep an eye on that crackle still in your chest: stay warm, don't go outside, rest. If it's not gone by end of play tomorrow, you'll have to go on antibiotics. It's not worth taking any chances.' He looked straight at her. 'You don't want to give your family another fright.'

There was blame in his voice. Anger, even.

She watched as he got up and replaced his equipment in the bag, just as the beeping sound of a truck reversing started up outside. He glanced out of the window.

'Expecting a delivery?' he murmured.

'Who from?'

'Cuneen Livery?'

'*What?*' She darted to the window, feeling her panic flood and her colour rise as the horse truck was carefully parked up. She couldn't believe it, she didn't want to, but there was no doubting it – Sean bloody Cuneen had come to collect his winnings. She felt the floor drop beneath her, her body run cold again, the memory of the water closing over her head . . . 'That *bastard,*' she whispered. At the very least he could have given her more time! Picked up the phone and made a courtesy call to let her know he was coming over to cash in his winnings. She was barely home from the hospital, for Chrissakes.

'What's wrong?' Taigh asked, both of them watching as Sean's vast bulk emerged from the truck, his trousers hanging low on his hips and revealing beneath his caught shirt, a deep bum crack.

Could her life get any worse?

Taigh looked at her, his curiosity morphing into concern. 'Why's he here, Pip?'

She took a slow, deep inhale at the question. He was here because he had a right to be: he had won and she had lost, plain and simple. She swallowed and drew herself up, determined to bring her feelings under control. She wouldn't let Taigh see her upset. 'Just finishing up some . . . admin.' She walked across the room and grabbed her coat off the hook.

'Where are you going?' he called after her. 'You shouldn't be outside in these temperatures. It's bitter out there at the moment.'

'This won't take long,' she said, stuffing her feet into her yard boots.

'Hang on a second!' His voice changed, stopping her. 'Is that Cuneen as in . . . Sean Cuneen?'

She already had one foot on the stairs. She leaned back through the doorway impatiently. 'So what if it is?'

He looked at her in disbelief. 'That's the guy you were racing in the water?'

'So what if it is?' she repeated coolly, but her heart was pounding wildly, her emotions raging just below the surface. She felt the tears pressing against the backs of her eyes, her heart pounding like a jackhammer. She'd not said goodbye to Shalimar yet, not even mentioned what she'd done, the terrible risk she had taken and how it had backfired. How everything was now in ruins . . .

He gawped at her in disbelief. 'Don't tell me . . . do not tell me he's come to claim his prize? You're not honouring that stupid bet?'

She stared at him, seeing how his horror matched her own. In truth, the entire wager hadn't even crossed her mind since that night. She'd forgotten all about the fact that she had lost and he had won; she'd been too busy trying to survive. 'A deal's a deal,' was all she said flatly.

'A deal's a—?' Taigh cried, looking suddenly furious, his happy-go-lucky demeanour completely gone. 'Does nearly drowning not count for anything here? You didn't lose a race, Pip; you nearly lost your life! I'd say all bets are off, wouldn't you?'

She didn't reply – couldn't, her tears were close to falling – just simply turned away and went down the stairs. He caught up with her at the bottom, grabbing her by the elbow.

'Look, are you scared of him, is that it? I can understand that, he's a big fella. But I can make him go away, Pip. You don't need to do this. It isn't right.'

'We had a verbal contract,' she said simply.

'Bollocks to that! No court in the land would honour his so-called claim.'

'But honour's precisely what it comes down to. We made a deal in good faith and I lost. I don't suppose he'd be here if I *had* died – he's not that much of a shit – but I didn't. I'm perfectly fine apart from this supposed crackle that's getting your knickers in a twist.'

Taigh ignored the slight. 'The bet should be null and void.'

'I'll admit he could've given me a few day's grace; it's . . . tacky, turning up here so soon.' Her voice tremored slightly at the thought of saying goodbye so prematurely. If she'd only stopped to think . . . 'But I'll be damned if I'll give him the satisfaction of saying I sticked him on a deal. Our family may not have much left these days, but we've got our bloody pride.'

Taigh stared at her, disbelief and frustration running across his features, and she could see she was an enigma to him – inexplicable and confounding.

'So I'll be needing my arm back,' she said, glancing down pointedly at her elbow which was still held firm in his grip.

'Oh.' He released her. 'Jeesht. Well, do you at least want me to come out there with you and help?'

'You?' she scoffed. 'I wouldn't ask for your help if my—' She stopped short.

'Life depended on it?' His green eyes flashed with rare anger as they squared up in the narrow stairway. She felt he wanted something from her, but what? An apology? A thank-you? She'd never asked for his help that night, and she didn't need it now. Without another word, she turned away and strode out into the yard, to do what had to be done.

Chapter Thirteen

Willow pulled into the drive, coming to a stop in her usual place in front of the low purple rhododendron. But she didn't get out. She didn't want to go into the house yet and check up on her mother's mental state this morning, or help Mrs Mac with the beds. She didn't want to move a muscle. She just wanted to sit here and be quiet, still, invisible, forgotten.

She looked out over the undulating lawns to the silver strip of sea glittering in the morning sun and leaned forward against the wheel. The view sat before her, comforting and familiar, as unchanged during her twenty-two years as it had been the previous hundred, give or take a garden bench here or a felled tree there. This was home, a part of her as solid as any bone. She had taken it for granted growing up, believing it would somehow always be hers, that like the landscape of her childhood it would remain untouched and absolute. But that dream had come to an end long before her father had died, and now too so would this.

It was hard though – harder than she'd expected. Hels had acted with impressive efficiency after their meeting last week and the first Christie's team was due to arrive later today to begin the daunting task of counting, listing and appraising every item they owned. Willow had yet to deliver the news to her mother and had no idea how to go about it. The timing could hardly have been worse, given that Pip had only just been allowed home for the night – near-drowning to house move in one weekend. This conversation wasn't going to go well.

She tried to think of ways she could spin it: the estate was being chopped and parcelled up anyway, her sisters officially keeping the bits that chimed with their hearts – for Ottie, the beach; Pip, the gallops. Willow had never had that, one part that felt exclusively hers; to her, Lorne had always been the sum of its parts and her family had assumed that somehow meant she loved it less. It never seemed to occur to them that perhaps she had loved it more than anyone else? On those quiet, boring Sundays in the flat in Dublin, hung-over and lying on the sofa, watching the television unseeingly, her mind would wander back to here like a homing instinct or a factory settings button, remembering the 'sticky mud' game they used to play on the staircase landing when their feet couldn't touch the floor, sledging over the sloping lawns, hide and seek through the secret doors, timed races through the hidden passage between the kitchen and the library. She had missed her sisters . . . She remembered lying on the window seat of her bedroom as a teenager, legs up the wall, trying to imagine the exciting, glamorous life that must exist for her beyond these ancient stone walls and never once thinking it would include lying on a sofa thinking back on this. She remembered the Christmases with always preposterously giant trees – one year, they expected squirrels to jump out of the enormous bushy tree her father had cut down and dragged back in his annual show of knightly pride; she remembered him too putting on Rusty, his beloved suit of armour, for the costume party for her mother's fortieth – he hadn't been able to sit down all night nor go to the loo, had had to eat dinner standing up, couldn't climb the stairs and he'd been left bruised and stiff for four days afterwards. Her mother had called it their best party ever—

Her mother. Everything always came back to her somehow, but where once she had been the light in the centre of her life, now she was a shadow on Willow's heart. A black spot in a pristine landscape, ruining something pure and perfect.

She dropped her head on the steering wheel. She knew she couldn't put this off. She had to go in there and get it over with – tell her mother about the sale, show her she had done what her father had charged her to do, the one thing he could not.

She wasn't sure which was going to be received more badly – the identity of the buyer or that she'd tacitly accepted an offer which proposed taking almost a million euros off its potential value. In truth, she had barely given it a second thought all weekend: meeting Connor that evening, then staying at the hospital with Pip all night and all day on Sunday had meant she'd crashed into bed early last night, sleeping dreamlessly and awaking in the same position she'd fallen asleep in. But now, on a cold, bright, blustery Monday morning, when the world felt fresh and hopeful again . . . had she done the right thing? Or in her haste to be done with it, had she confused selling up for selling out?

A sudden hard rap at her window made her jump.

'Mam!' she said, through the glass. 'Are you all right?'

She didn't look it. Her usually serene mother was still wearing the pyjamas with Dad's cashmere jumper which she'd been wearing when Willow had left to take Pip back to the stables two hours earlier. The look wasn't complemented by her pair of short wellies; her hair was badly in need of its daily blow-dry and her reddened cheeks suggested either a quick run around the vegetable garden or a glass of wine. She looked flustered and very, very angry.

'Where have you been?' she demanded as Willow clambered out of the car.

'You know where – I took Pip back to hers and then I did the horses for her.'

Her mother looked wrong-footed and bewildered. 'Oh . . .'

'And then I said I'd get some bread on the way home.' Willow held up the loaf in her hand by way of proof.

Her mother raised a hand to her cheek and turned away slightly. 'Oh yes. You did.'

Willow watched her with concern. Had she taken another sleeping pill? Was she drowsy? 'Come on,' she said. 'Let's go inside and I'll make you a cup of tea and some toast. I imagine you haven't eaten yet?' Weariness inflected in her voice like sunlight off water.

'No! I don't want to go in there,' her mother cried, as though suddenly remembering her anger again.

'Why not?'

'Because *he's* coming back!'

Willow felt a spike of concern. Her mother was hardly making sense. 'Who is?'

'That ghastly man,' her mother snapped, a rare glimpse of true fury in her eyes, and Willow understood that she was angry at her for so many reasons: this (whatever it was); not calling her earlier about Pip; inheriting Lorne; failing at the one thing she had been born to do . . . Take a pick. And it was always there that anger, festering just below the surface of their every interaction. 'How *could* you have called him, after everything I said?'

'Mam, I don't know who you're . . .' Her voice faded as

suddenly she did. 'Wait! Shaye came *here*?' He said he'd be in touch next week, not on the doorstep!

'He said you'd made him an offer. He'd said you offered him first option to buy the place and that you've struck a deal.'

'No. We're *negotiating* a deal. Nothing's signed yet.'

But merely contacting him was betrayal enough. Her mother stared at her, reddened eyes swimming with tears. 'How could you, Willow? I told you your father had discounted him and why – pulling that stunt the way he did, right at the last gasp . . . It was dishonourable. Disgusting. And a shitty thing to do.'

Willow was shocked. Her mother never swore.

'I told you your father had said he would sell to that man over his dead body. Is that what you're intending to do?'

'Mam, I—'

'You're going to sell Lorne over his dead body?'

Willow swallowed, feeling sick. She couldn't reply.

'He turned up here acting like he already owned the place,' her mother sobbed. 'Wanting to know where you were and when you'd be back. You weren't answering your phone.'

Willow groaned. Oh God – what were the chances? 'Ugh, no. I left it upstairs charging. I figured I was only going down to the stables. I've only been gone a few hours.'

'Do you know what he even asked me?'

She shook her head, already dreading hearing it.

'He asked whether the title came with the estate!'

'*What?*' Willow rubbed her face in her hands. 'Oh God, Mam, I'm sorry. What an arse. I can't believe he said that.'

'– Like we're some sort of nasty, tacky, buy-a-title *arrivistes*.'

'Mam, the only person he embarrassed asking that was himself,' she said, instinctively moving to put her arms around her and hug her close, before remembering; she pulled back, patting her arm awkwardly instead. 'And I'm sorry I wasn't here to deal with him. I can't believe he just turned up here like that – no bloody warning, no courtesy call.'

Her mother watched her, still wary. 'He said he was in the area.'

'Yeah, right,' Willow snorted, not believing that for a second. He just wanted to pin down his bargain. He'd smelled there was blood in the water and he'd swum over here quickly. 'How did you get rid of him?'

'I didn't!'

'So where is he now? Is he still here?' Willow looked in through the open arched door, feeling a spike of rage that he might be brazenly occupying their home, staking his claim prematurely.

'No. He said he would drive around the area and come back shortly.'

'And when was this?'

'An hour ago? I've been ringing and ringing you.'

Willow gave another sigh. When did she ever go anywhere without her phone? Ever? 'Okay, well look, don't worry about this. I'll deal with him.'

'But he's coming back.'

'I know and I'll . . . I'll get him to apologize to you. He was out of order behaving like that.'

'No, I mean, he's coming back. Look!' And she raised her arm and pointed at a navy E-Type coming down the drive. It was pristine, classic, priceless. The sort of car she supposed that ought to be coming down this drive – not battered old Land Cruisers and yellow-striped Minis. And yet it was too . . . flash. Too self-conscious.

'Oh jeesht,' Willow muttered below her breath. What had

she done? She remembered his dismissive tone on the phone – '*my portfolio's closed right now*' – the way he'd hung up on her, texting her that lo-ball offer without any preamble, no meet, no discussions . . . And now she'd led him to believe they almost had a deal. She was going to sell her family's heritage to a man who thought titles came with the deeds, like job-lot boxes at a car boot sale?

The sun bounced off the windscreen, only adding to the glamorous allure, as though this was the south of France and not a blustery corner of south-west Ireland; she half expected to see the fluttering silk scarf of a lady companion billowing through the window too.

'You go in, Mam, I'll deal with this,' she said grimly, turning away and trying to push her mother indoors.

'I don't want him coming into our home, Willow,' her mother warned, beginning to walk back to the castle.

'He won't, Mam.'

She watched her mother beat a hasty retreat back inside as he pulled up on the opposite side of the drive, the car's engine guttural and throaty, then she strode towards the inky bullet with some ammunition of her own, hands pulled into fists and fire blazing in her eyes. It was clear she had made a giant mistake. She had to act decisively, and fast.

The car door opened and she raised a hand to stop him. 'Don't bother, Mr Shaye. You should have rung f—' The word dropped from her lips, falling soundlessly to the ground.

There was a stunned silence.

'Well, I would have, Just Willow,' he replied finally. 'Only you left without giving me your number.'

She felt her heart engorge and race, then contract and twist. It couldn't be. No. No, no, no. Not him. '*Connor?*'

*

'Otts?'

Ottie groaned, wanting to ignore the voice, block it out. She was warm, heavy, drifting . . .

'Oi, Otts,' the voice came again and this time a hand on her shoulder too, shaking her not-so-gently. 'You're supposed to be working. Have you seen the state of the place out there?'

'Lemme sleep,' she moaned, refusing to open her eyes. How long had they been closed for – two hours? Three? Twenty minutes?

'Don't make me get a jug of water and throw it on you.'

Her eyes flew open. 'You wouldn't dare!' she gasped but Pip just laughed; they both remembered perfectly well when she had. She groaned and flopped an arm over her face again, trying to block out the offensively bright sunlight. Where had that been when she'd needed it all day Saturday? 'What are you doing here?'

'Thought I'd exercise Dolly. She gets nippy if she can't get out.' Pip lifted Ottie's legs up and sank onto the sofa herself, laying her feet back in her lap.

'Dolly?' Ottie frowned. 'Not Shalimar?'

'No, I thought I'd take Dolly out today.'

Something in her sister's voice made Ottie look over. 'You okay?'

'Sure.' She laced her hands behind her head and stared out of the giant window. Her body was stiff and unrelaxed, but then again that was Pip; she didn't do languid. Or sitting down. 'There's a coffee there for you, by the way.'

Ottie turned her head and saw the steaming mug on the small copper-legged coffee table beside her. Really? She'd slept through the kettle boiling and everything? '. . . Thanks.' She reached over for it with effort and took a long grateful sip, enjoying the feel of the steam on her face. She looked over at

Pip again, something occurring to her. 'Should you be out riding yet? I thought you were supposed to be resting?'

'Oh, please, hacking a pony across a few fields is hardly overdoing it,' Pip said with a roll of her eyes. 'Anyway, why are *you* so tired? You didn't run into a freezing lake too, did you?'

'May as well have done,' Ottie mumbled. 'All I've done is walk around in the freezing wind and rain all weekend. I think I'm getting a cold.'

But Pip had her inquisitive face on; she was like a bloodhound – always able to pick up the scent of a story. 'Tell.'

Ottie sighed. 'After I dropped you last night, Bertie called.'

'Flanagan?' Pip asked, clarifying, and Ottie remembered his name didn't trip off her tongue as easily, or frequently. It was a constant exercise to have to remember not to use his name so familiarly.

'Yes, exactly. One of the runners went missing during the race. It was only flagged up when the time was officially called and someone saw he hadn't been checked off the finish line.'

'Ugh, don't tell me he got lost,' Pip said dismissively, yawning. 'How is that even possible? There are flags and stewards everywhere.'

'Well, he managed it,' Ottie said in a small voice. 'And fell sixty feet onto rocks.'

'Oh jeesht,' Pip winced, looking instantly concerned. 'He's not dead, is he?'

'I don't know *how* he's not,' Ottie said quietly. 'He was unconscious when we found him. He's got a broken arm, three fractured ribs, concussion, and he's snapped the cruciate ligament in his right knee.'

'Bloody hell!'

'Plus, he's suffering from exposure. He'd been out there for thirty-four hours by the time he was found. No one could see him from the track where he fell, and we didn't know to even look for him till the finishing whistle went.'

'Surely someone must have heard him, though?'

'Not over the wind.'

'Oh Christ, poor sod.'

'Yeah.' And it was all her fault. Ottie gave another shiver as she stared into her coffee, warming her hands against it. She *had* caught a chill but that wasn't what was making her feel cold: she'd stood at her station for hours on Saturday – bored, frozen, wet, tired – and all that time, a man had been lying broken, slowly dying, a stone's throw away from where she had stood. 'What time is it, anyway?' she asked flatly.

'Twelve forty-five.'

She blanched. Four and a quarter hours' sleep then. She'd got home from the hospital – again! The nurses had looked astounded to see her coming through the doors with another casualty – at eight thirty this morning, just as they would have been wheeling Ben Gilmore into theatre. Suddenly she remembered – 'Oh, shit! Everyone's checking out.'

She went to scramble off the sofa but Pip merely tightened her grip around her legs. 'I wouldn't bother, you're too late. They've all gone. Left a godawful mess, I'm afraid, but there's not a tent left out there – except that red one in your garden.' Pip sipped her coffee. 'What's that all about? You camping out in sympathy or something?'

'Hardly. That's the injured guy's pitch.'

'In your *garden*?'

'He arrived late,' she shrugged. 'I'd already given his site to some walk-ups.'

'Still, you didn't need to give up your garden, Otts.'

'He was a runner,' she said numbly, remembering her petty

revenge. 'He wasn't going to find anywhere else to stay at that point.'

'Tch, you're too soft, you are.' Pip gave a little cough and looked out of the window. A sound that approached a sigh of relaxation escaped her. '. . . That really is the best view.'

'Yeah,' Ottie agreed. The beach – and her little house just off-centre to the back of it – sat nestled in a cosy dip, the shaggy fields hugging the golden crescent tightly, before rising up and away at each end. With the Atlantic storm finally passed over, the colours were blooming again – the pale washed-out greys and misty tints over the weekend restored to their authentic bold, dramatic shades of pine green, granite black, liquid silver and powder blue. After its dramatic toss and hurl in the high winds all weekend, today the sea moved like a lung, breathing in and out, up and down, gulls flocking around the mouth of the cave just by the headland as the fishermen on a small boat pulled up the lobster pots.

She felt her fingers twitch, the urge to capture the moment as physical as a thirst or an itch.

Pip coughed again. 'I'm starving. Have you got anything for lunch?'

'There's some four-day-old pasta we could reheat,' Ottie offered after a moment's consideration. Had she even opened her fridge all weekend? 'Or I might be able to do a sandwich if we toast the bread.'

'Let's go with the pasta,' Pip said, getting up. 'Then we'd better go and tidy up your campsite. Dad'll go nuts if he—'

She fell stock still, they both did, before Ottie reached over to squeeze her arm. 'Hey –'

'Yeah I know,' Pip said brusquely, pulling herself up and away. She walked across the old timbered floor and into the bright, open-plan kitchen. 'So when you say pasta, are we talking twists or shells? How excited should I be?'

'You can't come in.' Willow had folded her arms across her chest, hoping it reinforced her steadfast demeanour. She needed something in her armoury. Him, getting out of that car, looking like that, the memories of Saturday night still warm on her lips . . . 'I mean it.'

'Really?' Connor looked sceptical. 'Even just to talk?'

Of course just to talk, she thought to herself in alarm. What else did he think was going to happen – that they'd pick up where they'd left off on the garden chairs?

'You're not welcome here. You've upset my mother. She doesn't want you in her house.'

His eyes flickered over the castle. 'I thought she said it was your house?'

'Only legally. It's hers in every way that counts.'

He paused for a moment, his sharp blue eyes landing on her like blades, piercing the skin. 'Look, Willow, I had no idea you were Dec's daughter—'

'Ditto.' And when he frowned, she spluttered: 'You know what I mean.'

'And before we go any further, I want to say how sorry I am to hear that he . . . y'know.'

'Died?' she said bullishly, using the word like a stick with which to beat him back.

He looked uncomfortable. 'Yeah. He seemed like a good bloke.'

'Don't speak about my father like you knew him. You didn't. And he certainly didn't die thinking highly of you.'

He didn't reply, her words doing a good job of what she needed them to – repel him. He pulled his gaze off her after a moment and stared out over the lawns instead, trying to take stock.

Immediately she wished he didn't have such a glorious profile. Why him? Why did Shaye have to be him?

'You told me you were part of the consortium that owns Midnight Feast,' she said accusingly, hearing the note of despair in her own voice.

He looked back at her again with a frown. 'And I am. But that's not my day job. It's not what I *do*. I just got lucky enough to be invited to buy in.'

She sighed. If they'd only done a little more talking and a lot less kissing, she might have found this out on Saturday night and saved themselves this. 'Look, I'm sorry, this is a mess. But my father's principles meant he wouldn't sell to you, and as his daughter I won't either. I should never have called you.'

His eyes narrowed, flashing like sapphires. 'So, then, why did you?'

What could she say? Revenge? Defiance? Sheer spite? It wasn't a story she would tell him, or anyone.

'It was a mistake,' she said simply. 'My mother and I had had an argument and I acted rashly in the heat of the moment. I'm sorry you got caught up in it.'

He blinked, his eyes growing colder by the moment. 'So that's *it*? You're not going to sell to me after all?'

She nodded. 'I'm sorry for your wasted trip.' She turned abruptly and began heading back to the castle, his look of disbelief burning her back, her heart burning inside her ribs.

'. . . How's your sister?' he called as she was halfway to the door.

What? She turned back and he gave a small shrug.

'I tried calling the hospital but they wouldn't tell me anything. Only relatives. Can you just tell me – is she okay?'

She swallowed, remembering how powerfully he'd rowed across the water, getting to Pip in under ten strokes, the tips of her hair just breaking the surface of the water; she remembered how he'd thrown down the oars and reached over, pulling her up and out in one fluid swoop, as though she weighed nothing, the adrenaline pumping through him as much as her. He'd gone through it too, seen someone almost drown.

'She's recovering. Thanks.'

He took a step back, as though relieved. 'Good. That's really good to hear.'

Their eyes had locked again, holding her on the spot. It happened every single time. 'Thank you for what you did,' she said, feeling the emotion colour her voice again, as it did any time she thought back to that night. He may have betrayed her father but he'd also saved her sister. Which had been the greater – the slight or the rescue?

'It was nothing.'

'It wasn't nothing. You got her out of the water.'

He winced. 'And left her half bald in the process, I fear.'

Willow couldn't help a smile. 'Least of her worries. I doubt she's even noticed.'

She saw the way his eyes roamed over her face as she smiled and he instinctively took several steps forward. 'Look, Willow, can we just . . . take a step back for a moment and regroup? There's been a lot of misunderstandings. I dealt with things badly with your father, I know that. And to say it's a surprise seeing you here . . .'

She arched an eyebrow, felt her stomach flip at the way he was looking at her. 'Tell me about it.'

'If I'd had any idea on Saturday who you were, then obviously I wouldn't have—'

'Me neither.'

He stared at her, memories of their instinctive kisses in the garden playing through both their minds. They hadn't felt the cold once out there; hadn't even noticed it. She shivered now though. Everything was different in the bright morning light.

'But, look, you want to sell and I want to buy. We're already on the same page.' He took another step towards her. 'Can't we just start again? Pretend I never met your father. Pretend *we* never . . .' He stopped short, the memory of their kisses – urgent, in the moonlight – running on a virtual loop between them. 'Met.'

She swallowed. She wasn't sure pretending was going to cut it; an induced coma, perhaps?

'If we simplify this and take "us" out of it . . . ? Saturday night never happened, okay?' He shrugged. 'I've already forgotten it. Gone.'

He closed the gap between them, marching up to her with a directness that made her breath fail. 'Hi, I'm Connor Shaye.' His hand was outstretched and after a hesitation, she put hers in it to shake; but even that . . . she felt the electricity leap between their palms.

He felt it too. There was another pause before he squeezed her hand and looked her in the eye. 'I'm Connor Shaye and I'd like to buy your castle, please.'

'Hello, Connor Shaye, I'm Willow Lorne and that will be four and a half million euros, please.'

He tipped his head fractionally, the smile freezing on his mouth. '. . . I thought we'd agreed four was close.'

'Close but no cigar. Christie's have advised us to list it at six. Four and a half would be a steal and only on the table if you can move fast.'

'The roof needs redoing.'

'It does, yes.'

'That's got to be half a million at least.'

'Which is why I'm not asking for five,' she countered.

His eyes narrowed slightly, but they were glittering. The hunt was on. 'I'll give you four point one.'

'Four four,' she countered. 'You upset both my parents.'

'Four two and I will apologize to your mother.'

She smiled. 'Four point three five because she's never going to forgive you.'

He smiled back. 'Four point two five and I will make your mother love me.'

'Four point three because that's *never* gonna happen.'

'Four point three and she will and so will—' And so will what? He didn't finish.

She realized he was still holding her hand, their bodies connected. He must have noticed it too because he squeezed hers lightly. 'It seems we have a deal and we're shaking on it,' he said, his eyes probing hers again.

'So it does,' she murmured, squeezing him back before reluctantly pulling her hand away, because no matter what the chemistry between them said, he was right – they couldn't do business *and* be anything more. Lust clouded things. It made the simple, oblique.

He shoved his hands in his pockets as he looked down at her, and she wished she wasn't standing before him in jeans and muck boots, an ancient fleece and with hay in her hair. Saturday night's glamour-puss had well and truly left the building. 'So can I come in and see my new castle?'

She shook her head. 'Nope.'

'No?'

'You'll have to come back.'

The smile fell off. '*Again?* But this is already my second visit.'

'Yes, but you've upset my mother and that is not to be underestimated. I'll need to talk to her. This is a difficult time for us and, trust me, she will pick up my father's fights where he left off.'

'I see.' He shifted his weight and stuffed his hands into his chino pockets. 'So when were you thinking for this meeting?'

She thought for a second. 'Tomorrow. At eleven fifteen.'

'That's specific. Why eleven fifteen?'

'Because Mam's teaching her floristry class in the village hall for two hours then. And it'll give me enough time to get the horses done first.'

'You've got horses?' His eyes travelled up and down her in the way that had made her knees buckle at the party. 'You didn't look the horsey type on Saturday night in those leather trousers.'

'They're Pip's.'

'The trousers?'

'The horses,' she grinned.

'Ah.' He watched her. 'So I guess I'll see you at eleven fifteen tomorrow then.'

She nodded, feeling herself wilt under his gaze, like a daisy under a heat lamp. 'Bye then.' She turned and started walking away, hoping to God her backside looked as decent in the jeans as in the leather trousers.

'That's a ruthless negotiating technique you've got, by the way,' he called after her.

She turned and smiled. 'Did you think I'd be a soft touch just because I went soft at your touch?'

His lips parted in surprise at the provocative question. She walked up the castle steps.

'You went soft at my touch?'

Chapter Fourteen

'Hello again.'

'Hi,' Ottie smiled shyly as she passed by Reception. The staff were actually beginning to know her here now. They must think she was some sort of ambulance-chaser.

It was visiting time and the hospital was busy, well-wishers bustling through the corridors with flowers and chocolates, some balloons. There was a surprisingly optimistic buzz about the place; she always thought of hospitals as places to be feared, as the fulcrum of death and despair, but, of course, babies were born here, people saved, put back together, given other chances . . . That was finding the bright side, though. There were many pensive faces like hers too, people coming empty-handed, not sure of what they were going to find.

She walked along to the ward where he'd been taken earlier, stopping at the nurses' station outside.

'Hi.'

'You're back,' the nurse smiled in surprise.

'Yeah . . . Just thought I'd come and see how he's getting on. Did the operation all go okay?'

'That all went smoothly. He was in ITU for a couple of hours just as standard before coming back here. He's beginning to come round from the anaesthetic now. He's pretty woozy.'

'Yeah. Well, that's good to hear . . . that it went smoothly, I mean. I was worried about him.' But she knew she wasn't here for him; this man didn't know her, he didn't care about her hospital visits. No, this was for her – balm for a guilty conscience. She may never get an official pardon, or forgiveness, but she needed to know he was going to be okay at least.

The nurse looked bemused. 'Seeing as you're here, why don't you look in on him? He's in the last bed on the left.'

She felt a surge of panic. 'Oh, but – you said he's still coming round.'

'Yep. But having a visitor will be a nice thing for him to wake up to. I understand he's American?'

'Yes.'

'It can't be nice waking up in a foreign hospital with no one you know around you.'

'No, I guess not,' Ottie murmured, her guilt spiking this time. Slowly, she made her way over. Several of the beds had their curtains pulled around them, the low hum of urgent conversations drifting about like airborne feathers. His didn't though, and Ottie was stopped by the sight of him, sleeping half-upright – his left arm strapped across his body in a sling, his right leg suspended on a pulley. She barely recognized him as the sharp-suited, sharp-eyed, world-weary businessman who'd so enraged her on Friday night. He didn't look anything like an elite athlete either, lying there in a green-printed hospital gown. He was pale and haggard-looking, practically no fat on him, his stubble having come in thicker and darker over the weekend.

She approached the bed tentatively, standing by it and not daring to touch him. She couldn't hold his hand or stroke his cheek. He was a stranger. And yet, she owed him more than he would ever know. She might not be able to say the words out loud – it wasn't just Bertie's business that would come under threat if it became known he'd forgotten to put up the signs on account of their clandestine tryst – he might never get to know about the full, awful string of coincidences and accidents that had come together to leave him clinging to a cliff and now strapped up in this bed, but *she* knew. This was all her fault.

Her eyes flickered over the monitors. The numbers meant little to her, but even she knew 56 was low for a resting heartbeat, that 92/58 was low for blood pressure. Was it a sign of how sick he was? Or fit?

She brought her gaze back to him and gave a little jolt of surprise to find his eyes open – and on her.

'M-Mr Gilmore.'

There was a long pause, his gaze blank, his focus seemingly unfixed. She knew he had no idea who she was. 'B-b-ben . . .'

She gave a nervous smile. 'Ben, yes. How are you feeling?'

'. . . Excellent.' The word was so slurred it was practically sitting on its side.

She shifted under his gaze. Drugged-up, it had none of the directness or sardonic undercurrents she remembered as she'd kept him on her doorstep in the rain; instead he looked . . . boyish. Vulnerable, even. A small, half-cocked lopsided smile dragged up drunkenly on one side of his lips. 'So b-b-beauful.'

'I'm sorry, what?' she asked, but he didn't reply, his eyes fluttering shut and then opening again, his gaze landing on her every time like butterflies. She didn't know what to say. '. . . So the nurse said your operation went well.'

'Ex . . . cellent.' He didn't move, just continued staring. The usual social etiquette didn't apply to post-op patients.

She gave an embarrassed smile. 'Mr Gilmore—'

'Bbben.'

'Ben, yes. Is there anyone I can call for you? Your wife? Girlfriend? . . . Any family? Friends? . . . Colleagues?' There just had to be some way she could be helpful and make this up to him.

There was another long pause, before he shook his head fractionally. 'Nnno.'

No to all of them? 'Really? No one at all?'

'Nnno.'

She supposed they were all in the States, his colleagues – whatever it was he did – possibly in London? He'd arrived in a suit and that was where he'd flown in from.

His eyes had closed again; she could hear the exhaustion in his breathing, as though just to inhale and exhale was an effort. 'Well, I should leave you to rest,' she said quietly. His face had slackened again, his body sinking into unconsciousness once more. 'I just wanted to check you were okay.' Her voice dropped to a whisper. 'And to say I'm sorry. It was an accident. Please believe me.'

She felt a touch on her hand and saw his index finger twitch, as though reaching for her. Jeesht, was he awake? She felt a jolt of panic, but the next moment his hand dropped inert on the mattress again, oblivion claiming him swiftly and deeply, and before she could cause any more damage, she turned and hurried away, the secret still her own.

Pip stared into the flames. Her heart actually felt bruised. She had done her best to outrun the fact all day – riding over to Ottie's, helping with the post-race clear-up, mucking out the stables – but the second she stopped, it was up in her face again: she had given away her beloved Shalimar. Just given her away like that. She had gambled her for an idea of a future that could never be hers. She'd dared to think that she could reach her dreams if only she was prepared to leap. But life didn't work like that. It couldn't be reduced to an Instagram epithet or a T-shirt slogan. People fell short every day – good people, hard-working people. Desire wasn't enough, nor even determination, she was proof of that. But she'd risked it anyway – all or nothing, that was her. 'Binary', her father always used to say. 'You're on or off, black and white, Pip. You don't deal with the shades of grey, where most of us live.'

It was certainly where Taigh O'Mahoney lived. She'd seen his look of disbelief – verging on disgust – earlier, as she'd forced herself to honour the bet. To her, she'd simply lost, but to him, she was a victim; he felt playing the 'nearly died' angle was her Get Out of Jail Free card for a tricky situation, but where was the honour? How could she look in the mirror knowing she was the worm that had squirmed her way off the hook?

Slinki, her chief mouse-catcher, padded into the room, stopping to assess her misery for a few moments, before effortlessly leaping onto the windowsill and curling up tightly for a nap. Pip threw her head back against the sofa and let a few bitter tears fall, but she didn't feel any the better for it. It was unfair. She could have stood it if she'd lost because she'd deserved to but he wasn't the better swimmer or the faster runner or the fitter one out of the two of them. If she hadn't been drinking shots, she'd have known she couldn't win that bet purely because he was seventeen stone to her nine; logic dictated he could last longer in those temperatures than her. If she hadn't been drunk, she'd have had her wits about her and chosen something far more balanced – a race to the trees and back, a planking competition, a squat challenge . . .

She sighed, trying to imagine her beloved girl in her new home, and then banishing the thought just as quickly. She knew she'd be well looked after, that wasn't the concern – if anything, it'd be a step up from the digs here. Cuneen's stables were – if not quite in the Mullane super-league – certainly several notches higher than her flaky black-painted, wobbly-cobbled eighteenth-century stable block. Hers didn't have the super-deluxe manège facilities and top-of-the-range solariums, but she loved that the hoof marks left by horses two hundred years ago were still imprinted in the boxes, that they could nod to each other over the walls, that they could see and speak to one another, all gathered in one room, with her living above them, her footsteps above their heads at night, the closest she could reasonably get.

The other five horses had been restless without Shalimar all day, sensing the loss. Though Kirsty had come up to put them all out in the field for a few hours – having heard the news about her weekend; it was all around the village now – they kept nipping and kicking at each other, as though waiting for her to come in and get them back into line. Shalimar had been the boss, but who would lead them now?

Slinki suddenly jumped down from the window ledge, just as a sound outside on the drive came to her ear. She stiffened, immediately rubbing out the tears. Finally, she'd heard someone before they miraculously appeared in the middle of her flat! Was it Taigh coming to make a nuisance of himself again?

'It's only me,' she heard Willow say a few moments later, puffing as she came up the narrow staircase, emerging carrying a plate covered with tin foil. 'Careful, this is very hot.' She set the plate down and started blowing on her fingers. '*Very* hot.'

She looked up at Pip with a smile – the smile fading in a flash. 'Ohmigod, what's wrong?'

'Nothing,' she replied in alarm. 'What do you mean?'

'Your cheeks are all flushed.'

Jeesht. Was there no hiding? Pip shrugged. 'I've just come inside.' It wasn't quite true. She'd been in for at least forty minutes now.

'You were told to rest and stay indoors,' Willow said sternly.

'Oh yes, Dr O'Mahoney's instructions,' Pip said sarcastically. 'Ha, forgive me if I don't give a damn about what *he's* got to say.'

'Look, you don't have to like the guy but he knows what he's talking about, Pip.'

'Yeah, right, one first aid course and suddenly he's Meredith Grey.'

'It's rather more than that,' Willow said, fetching a tray from the cupboard and setting the covered plate on it. Pip watched as she filled her a glass of water and found some cutlery stuffed into the jam jar by the kettle. 'Now, eat that. Mrs Mac's finest lamb. She said she did the cutlets for you just the way you like them.'

'Special treatment? Perhaps I should try near-death experiences more often.'

'Pip!' Willow looked so shocked, Pip felt a stab of shame at her words as she peeled off the foil cover, steam escaping everywhere. It was a crass thing to have said; perhaps their father's dark humour had a time and a place after all – and an audience; her little sister clearly wasn't ready to joke about it yet.

Willow lingered restlessly as she began to eat, one hand drumming absently on the counter.

'Wassup?' Pip asked, her mouth full.

'Nothing.'

'You're all fidgety.'

'No I'm not,' Willow said, putting down a point-to-point brochure and sighing.

Pip frowned as her sister came over and sank onto the sofa beside her, grabbing the remote and flicking over the channels. The TV was set to mute.

'Make yourself at home,' Pip quipped.

'Mrs Mac says she wants the plate back,' Willow said, ignoring her sarcasm.

'Yeah, right. That's her way of spying on me from afar. She's checking to make sure I'm eating properly.'

'Course she is,' Willow muttered. 'I swear to God she's got spies in Dublin too.'

Pip laughed, which turned into a cough and she reached for the water. 'How's Mam been today, anyway? I kept expecting her to turn up with a suitcase and say she was never letting me out of her sights again.'

'Erm . . . she was okay I guess. I think she realizes you're happier in your own space.'

Pip glanced across at her sister. 'What was the "erm" for?'

'I didn't "erm".'

'Yes you did. You always "erm" when there's a problem. And you're restless as hell. What's happened now?' She saw Willow's shoulders slump and knew she was right. There was never any getting past what she called her 'bullshit detector'.

'. . . Okay, fine, she *did* get upset again today – but not because of you. Remember that prospective buyer she mentioned?'

'Mmhmm,' Pip mumbled, shovelling in another forkful of food. She felt ravenously hungry, she realized.

'Well, he turned up.'

Pip's eyes narrowed into dangerous slits. 'The one Dad sent packing last time?'

'Yeah.'

Pip's fork stopped mid-air. 'Oh my God, the bloody nerve! D'you think he heard Dad had died and he thought he'd just—'

'No,' Willow said quickly, looking sheepish. She cleared her throat. 'Actually, *I* had rung him. Last week.'

'What?' Pip almost shouted. 'Willow!'

'I know, I'm sorry. I hadn't realized—'

'What a knob he is?'

Willow shot her a look. 'I'd been going to say I hadn't realized quite how ugly things had got between him and Dad.'

'But I told you! Mam said Dad ruined his best nine-iron whacking it on the lawn after they got the call saying he'd dropped the offer by a million.'

'A *million*?'

'Oh yeah; he wanted a cool one mill off or he was gonna walk.' Pip stabbed her fork in the air viciously. 'Two-faced bastard. Mam said Dad was so gutted that was what got him thinking about gifting the place to An Taisce instead. I don't think he could bear the thought of Lorne ever being lived in by complete tossers like that.'

'You're such a potty-mouth,' Willow muttered. She'd never liked Pip's colourful language. 'Look, I get the point, I do, but on the other hand, it was just . . . a business tactic. It wasn't personal.'

'It was personal to Dad, Will! And this wasn't just a bit of a discount he was after. He wanted a million – a million! – off.'

Willow sighed. He was getting more than a million off, buying from her. 'Yeah.'

'Whose side are you on anyway?' Pip scowled. 'Dad thought he was the absolute worst. Scum of the earth. End of.' She speared a carrot into her mouth. 'What?'

Willow didn't speak for a moment. She looked like she was holding her breath. 'What if I told you he was the one who dragged you onto the boat?'

Pip felt herself pale. She could actually feel the blood draining from her hitherto flushed cheeks. 'Please tell me you're joking.' But Willow's face did no such thing. 'The guy Dad went to his grave hating is the guy who saved my life?'

Willow shrugged.

Pip felt her fork drop from her grasp. 'Christ, I couldn't have a run-of-the-mill hero, could I? No, I had to get the shithead our family hates.'

'Nobody's all bad, Pip.'

But Pip wasn't listening. 'Oh jeesht, isn't there some Chinese proverb about this? He saved my life so now I'll be forever in his debt till I can save his? Something like that?'

'I'm afraid it gets worse.'

'How?' Pip laughed bitterly. 'How does it get worse than that?'

'. . . I kissed him. Remember the guy who'd come over to us?'

The knife dropped from her hand too and clattered onto the plate as the mocking laughter turned instead to another coughing fit. '*Him*? Pretty boy?'

Willow reached over and smacked her on the back. 'It was

how I came to see you going into the lake in the first place. We'd gone outside together.'

'Oh my God!' Pip gasped and wheezed, trying to get her breath back. 'You snogged Dad's *mortal* enemy?'

Willow looked at her. 'I'm not sure I'd put it quite like that. I didn't know who he was at the time, and he didn't know who I was either. We only found out when he turned up today. He was every bit as shocked as me.'

'Oh, I sincerely doubt that. I bet he thought all his ships had come in at once. Jeesht, this is a right sodding mess: you snogged him and he saved my life. What is this – some perverse love-death triangle-thingy?'

'No.'

Pip looked at her. 'Have you told Mam?'

'Which bit?'

'Any of it? All of it?'

'No. That's what the "erm" was for. She got into a real state when he turned up earlier and I was over here mucking out. She's adamant that he can't even come into the house, much less buy it.'

'Because she associates him with betraying Dad right before he died? Yeah, fair enough! Come on Willow – wake up and smell the whiskey! Dad had his diagnosis, he was trying to get his affairs in order, to provide for Mam and all of us, and that tosser – sorry, *life-saving* tosser – came along and put a bomb under all his plans. ' She pinned Willow with a hard stare. 'I don't care how good a kisser he was, what he did was unforgiveable.' She picked up her knife and fork again and jabbed them in the air. 'There was no honour in his behaviour. Believe you me, he showed his true colours in how he dealt with Dad so don't you be fooled by a single word he says.'

Willow felt her chest tighten just a little bit at her sister's words. Was she right? Pip, for all her rash, reckless, impetuousness, was an excellent judge of character.

'Mark my words, anything he brought to you now would be about one thing and one thing only.'

'I know. Buying Lorne.'

Pip shook her head. 'Nup. Getting inside your pants.'

Chapter Fifteen

'Do you run a loyalty points scheme?' Ottie joked as she walked up to the nurses' station again.

'You'd be a gold member for sure,' the nurse smiled. 'The consultant's just in with him at the moment.'

Ottie glanced over towards Ben Gilmore's ward and saw the curtain was pulled around his bed. She felt a shiver of relief as she rested her arms on the counter. 'That's fine. I don't actually need to see him. I was just passing anyway so thought I'd drop by to see how he's getting on today.' That was a lie. The hospital was a half-hour drive away but she needed to know he was recovering according to plan. She had slept fitfully, her dreams filled with storms and cliffs, while she was always turning her back as a hand reached out to her . . . If his condition deteriorated, on her head be it.

'Well, he had a restful night and slept through, although that'll mainly be the chemicals still in his system. It'll be several days before he's fully clear of them. But everything's looking pleasingly unremarkable so far. No complications. His strength and fitness has definitely helped.'

'Really? Oh that's so great.'

The nurse smiled again. 'We rarely see a pulse in the low fifties. It's usually when someone starts crashing!'

'Ha, well, that's good.' She felt another little weight lift off her. He was going to be okay. He was through the worst now, surely?

'Could you contact Broad Oak again for me, please, Nurse Wilson, and see what they've got for Mr Gilmore.'

Mr Gilmore? Ottie turned to find a doctor in a white coat standing beside her and entering something into an iPad.

'Certainly, Ms Cunningham. For how long?' the nurse asked, picking up the phone.

'Let's advise up to three weeks but could be out in two.' She glanced back towards the ward. 'Probably will be. I don't think he's going to be a problem for doing the physio. Clearly driven.'

'Is this . . . is this for Ben Gilmore?' Ottie asked – but really, how many Gilmores could there be on one ward? – twisting to see that the curtain had been pulled back again. She could just see his exposed, elevated toes from where she was standing.

'And you are?' the consultant asked.

'Just . . . a friend?' she suggested hesitantly.

'I'm afraid I can't discuss Mr Gilmore's care with anyone except immediate family.'

'This lady is the one who found him,' the nurse said kindly.

The consultant looked at her again – not in an unfriendly way, but not impressed either. 'Then well done. You saved his life,' she said briskly. 'He wouldn't have survived much longer in those conditions.'

Ottie swallowed. There it was again, the crushing guilt; she might have helped save him but that didn't count when she was the one who'd nearly killed him too – ignoring it when he wasn't back on time, her being the reason the sign hadn't been put out, hiding herself from sight as he'd come along the track . . .

The consultant looked at her more closely, seeming to consider something. 'If you're a friend of Mr Gilmore's, why don't you have a chat with him? See if you can help in any way.'

'Help?'

'I'm afraid I can't get involved; he'll have to talk to you about it.' The consultant looked at the nurse. 'Just hold off making that call for a minute.' She jerked her chin in the direction of the ward. 'Go on, he's perfectly lucid.'

Ottie gave a faltering smile as she reluctantly headed over to the bed. Again. She really hadn't wanted to see him, she had just wanted to be sure he hadn't died in the night. Frankly, just the thought of him being lucid was an intimidating one. She clearly remembered his perceptive gaze. Would he be able to read the guilt all over her face? Would he know it was her fault he was in here, like this?

His head was turned away as she approached. He was staring out of the window but there was nothing of note to see from this second floor – just the odd stray pigeon flying by. Yesterday's clear skies were a distant memory already, thick clouds like cotton wool almost snagging on the treetops.

'Hello.' She stopped, still out in the corridor, not daring to get closer.

He looked over and frowned as he struggled to place her, his eyes clear but cold, a far cry from yesterday's limpid curiosity.

'Ottie Lorne. From the campsite.'

'Oh.' His expression became even more distant. 'Yes.'

It was clear he didn't remember yesterday's visit. 'I just came to see how you were.'

'As you can see . . .' he said tersely, trying to wiggle the fingers of his broken arm. 'Not so clever.'

'I'm so sorry.'

'Why? It's not your fault.' He turned his head and looked out of the window again. His face was impassive but his mouth was turned down fractionally at the corners, the sinews pulling on his neck.

'Is there anything I can . . . do for you? Anyone I can call?'

'No . . . Thanks.' He kept his gaze on the window.

'But there must be people who are worried about you?'

He turned to look back at her with an inscrutable expression. 'No.'

It was a firm rebuff, only just bordering on the right side of polite.

She looked down at her hands, not sure what to say next. She couldn't blame him for his curt replies. The last time they'd met – *compos mentis* – she'd treated him with scorn, kept him standing in the rain, forced him to pitch a tent in her garden. She'd been spiteful and vindictive, a toxic blend of grief and loneliness moulding her into someone she barely even recognized. How disingenuous it must seem to him to have her standing now at the foot of his bed with eyes full of concern.

She glanced back at the nurses' station – the nurse and the consultant were both still standing there, looking over and watching the encounter. She wasn't sure what it was they wanted her to do.

'So when will they let you go home?'

'When will my tent be gone from your garden, you mean?' he asked tersely. 'Don't worry, you can throw it. Throw everything that's in it. I apologize for the inconvenience,' he added bitterly.

'No, I . . . I didn't mean that. I don't care about the tent. It's fine.'

He glanced over her once, as though looking for clues this was some kind of sting. He relented a little. ' . . . They're saying I can be out of here by tomorrow lunchtime if I get up on my feet today.'

'Oh wow! That's amazing,' she exclaimed, genuinely shocked. She had assumed he'd be here at least a few weeks.

'Yeah.' He didn't sound amazed.

Her mind started buzzing. 'Well, have you got your flight arranged? Do you need a cab to the airport? I could call Seamus for you.' She felt desperate to be helpful, to atone in some way.

'No. I can't go home yet.' And when he saw her shocked expression, he added, 'Thrombosis risk.'

'Oh.' She felt another spasm of guilt. She'd done this to him. *She* had. 'And where's home?'

'New York.'

A transatlantic flight. There was no way the doctors would condone that a few days after surgery. 'So when can you fly?'

'Few weeks.'

'A few *weeks*?' She quickly calculated in her head. It was the tenth of December. 'Can you get back in time for Christmas?'

'They're saying there's a small chance, depending on my recovery. I'm going to have to have a lot of physio first.'

She placed her hand over her mouth, the earlier relief that she was off the hook beginning to fall away, the weights settling back onto her shoulders. 'God, that's awful.'

He gave a small shrug. 'It is what it is. They've been telling me it could have been a lot worse.'

He couldn't know it but his words were like a kick, a direct blow to her stomach. She forced a tight smile. 'So where will you go in the meantime?'

He shrugged. 'I can't stay here; they need the beds, so they're trying to get me into a rehab centre, I think.'

Ottie stared at him, remembering the consultant's directive at the desk. *Broad Oaks?* It was an old people's home – and not a reputable one, either. 'Surely there's another option?'

'Apparently there's not much of a rental market round here for recuperating invalids.' He looked at her. 'Unless you know a hotel where I could get a room?'

Hotel? No. There were rooms at the Hare but that was a rickety seventeenth-century building and the staircase up to them was narrow and perilously steep. She looked at his leg, suspended on the pulley, a bulky and frankly scary-looking brace with pins on his knee. There was no way he'd manage them.

Another thought came to her but she pushed it away again immediately. There was simply no way she could—

'Mr Gilmore—'

She jumped as a voice carried over her shoulder and she turned to find the nurse standing at the foot of his bed. 'We've spoken to Broad Oaks and they have a bed available for the dates you need. Shall I go ahead and confirm it for you? I'm sorry to press but as you might imagine, there's more demand than supply.'

He nodded bleakly. 'It's fine. Go ahead and confirm.'

Ottie looked at him, and then at the nurse. She knew Broad Oaks. It had views over the bins, and food that even Pip would think twice about eating. The girl in McGinty's, the grocer's, had worked there briefly as a care assistant and left after four months as a whistleblower to certain care practices.

'Okay,' the nurse said with a nod, turning to go again.

'Wait!' The word had left Ottie's lips before she even knew she was saying it.

The nurse and patient both looked at her quizzically.

'Uh . . .' She felt her voice falter. What was she doing? This man was a stranger and poor company. He made her nervous with his cold, taciturn manner. She didn't like being here visiting him; she certainly didn't want to share her home with him. 'He can stay with me.'

'What?' He didn't sound happy about it either.

'My place is all on one level – bedroom, bathroom, kitchen – he'll be able to move about easily. Plus there's a lot of natural light, which I imagine will make a difference when you're stuck cooped up like this.'

'How many bedrooms are there?' the nurse asked, looking between them both.

'Only one. But I . . .' Oh God, was she really going to say this? 'I can sleep on the sofa. It's not a problem. It's a big sofa, very comfy.'

'No, I'm sorry, I couldn't allow that,' Gilmore said firmly. 'It's very kind of you, Miss uh . . .' He'd forgotten her name again.

'Ottie. Ottie Lorne.'

'Right. It's *very* kind of you to offer but I can't accept.'

'Look, you don't know what that place is like. Trust me, you would not optimize your recovery there. And if you want to get home in time for Christmas . . .'

He shook his head. 'It's too much to ask.'

'But you're *not* asking. I'm offering.'

He frowned at her, looking at her with bafflement, as though her words – and proposed actions – made no sense to him.

'Besides, I'm only thirty minutes away from here if you need to come in for physio sessions. And I'm around in the day so I can help if you need to get to appointments. And things.'

The nurse looked back at her patient with a discreetly encouraging look. 'Mr Gilmore? It's your decision.'

But Gilmore was just staring at her. 'I don't understand why you would put yourself out like this. You don't know me.'

Was this it – the moment to come clean?

'It's the right thing to do, Mr Gilmore,' she shrugged instead, not quite able to meet his eyes. 'You were booked to stay at Lorne anyway. You'll just be indoors instead of out, that's all. And your stuff's already there, so . . .'

She felt he could see right through her, that her shows of kindness were a front for the guilt she felt and couldn't shake: that he had nearly lost his life because of her.

'It's a generous offer, Mr Gilmore,' the nurse prompted, and Ottie knew she knew the truth about the facilities at the care home too; it had been in all the local papers last summer. 'You may well be more comfortable in a private environment, rather than an institution.'

He was silent for another minute, regarding her critically as though waiting for her to suddenly turn round and say it was all a joke, a terrible mistake, a well-intentioned misunderstanding. 'I guess it would be churlish to say no, then.'

The nurse seemed to breathe a sigh of relief. 'Great. I'll call them and release the bed.'

Ottie looked back and met his gaze. She felt suddenly shy, awkward even. What had she done – inviting him to stay in her house?

'Well, I don't know how to thank you, Miss Lorne,' he said, even though the puzzled look remained on his face.

She smiled stiffly. 'No need.'

A little silence bloomed.

'– And please, call me Ottie,' she added.

'Ben.'

'Nice to meet you.' She gave another awkward smile. 'Again.'

'I'd shake your hand but . . .' He waggled his fingers from his cast.

'Ha, yes.' She looked back down at the bed again, at all the contraptions hanging from it and the way his broken body was firmly being held together. She was no nurse. She was no friend of his. She felt a burst of panic. What on earth had she done?

'Pick your leg up.' Pip patted at the foreleg impatiently. 'Come on, boy, pick it up.' She tapped it again but the horse stood stubbornly with his weight on all four legs.

She straightened up with a huff, her hands on her hips. 'Really?' she asked, looking into his deep chocolaty-brown eyes. 'How long are you going to keep this up for?'

Magnus didn't reply, just blinked slowly.

She sighed. 'Look, I miss her as much as you do but there's no point sulking with me. It's not *my* fault.'

He tossed his head, almost connecting with her cheek.

'Okay, yes, fine, you're right,' she groaned, reaching her hand up underneath his long head and resting her own against it. 'It *is* my fault. All of it. I'm a bloody eejit and there's no one for me to blame, no one at all, it's my own sorry mess.' She stroked the extraordinary curve of his cheek. 'If it makes you feel any better, I hate myself for it. I'd do anything to get her back,' she whispered.

She closed her eyes, feeling the smooth warmth of him. She had slept poorly again, tossing and turning all night, darkness and oblivion something her body was fighting against at the moment as it prompted memories and feelings she wanted to deny. And now Shalimar's absence in the stall beneath her bed was like a siren going off, making it impossible to rest.

His head nuzzled into her and she stepped closer into him, burrowing her face in his neck as the tears flowed again, unstoppable though thankfully silent. He never minded when she cried on him, plus he kept all her secrets. He seemed to understand just how tough everything had been recently, how losing her dad – work buddy, mentor – made the days lonely and long; how even taking a bath was suddenly a challenging proposition, the sight of a body of water now menacing in its stillness . . .

'You. My lovely boy,' she whispered after a while, pulling back and patting him lovingly, drying his muzzle that was now wet with her tears. She nuzzled his whiskery nose with the palm of her hand. 'Don't worry – I won't make the same mistake twice. *You're* staying with me whether you like it or not. We're going to spend the rest of our lives here, just trekking up and down these paths.' He whinnied, hot air blowing into her hand and she laughed. 'That's right. We are.'

She gave him a kiss above his eye and huddled forwards again, breaking into a coughing fit as she went upside down. 'Now, how about that leg?' She tapped at it again and this time he lifted it up, allowing her to clean out his hoof. 'Thank you,' she said in a sing-song voice, beginning to hum softly as she worked.

She had moved onto the back leg, hunched over and red in the face, when, through the open door, she heard the van pull up outside the stable block and saw a set of feet step out. She frowned as she looked between Magnus's legs – everything looked so different upside down. She saw the feet stop, turn in to face the van, then switch around and walk towards the building.

She scowled as she realized who it was: Taigh O'Mahoney, here on his latest mercy mission.

'Ssh,' she whispered to Magnus, stepping behind him in the stall and listening as she heard him climb the stairs to her flat.

'Hello!' he called out, his voice faint and sounding surprisingly distant through the stone walls. A pause, and then footsteps on the wooden boards overhead. 'Hello? . . . Pip?'

She cast a sly glance at Magnus, his giant eyeball already swivelled onto her, no doubt wondering what she was doing, sniggering into his mane. 'Ssh, don't rumble me,' she whispered to him.

'Pip . . . ? Anybody home?'

She closed her eyes as the giggles took hold upon hearing the confusion in his voice, the bewilderment that she might have dared to leave her own flat.

There was another silence, and then the sound of boots clomping back down the stairs.

Quickly, she ducked below the stall, trying to push Magnus's rubbery lips away from her head as he tried to nibble her hair. 'Get off,' she hissed, hearing Taigh walk into the stable block, the space filling up with the silence of incomprehension as he took in the sight of the horses, all nodding over their doors.

'Hello, Whiskey,' she heard him say, wandering over to her grey mare in the nearest stall and patting her hard on the neck. 'Not been put out yet? Where's she gone, hey? Where's that troublesome mistress of yours gone?'

Pip hitched up an eyebrow as he spoke to her horse. She was *not* troublesome, thanks very much. She was simply *not* a victim. And *not* his patient.

She listened as he rummaged in his pocket for a treat.

'. . . have to be a mint, I'm afraid. I'm all out of sugarbeet. Funny that.' He gave a low laugh and she knew Whiskey was tickling his palm with her bristly whiskers. It was something of a party trick of hers; she was the most terrible flirt.

Magnus moved jealously, pawing the ground as he saw Whiskey being given treats, and knocking Pip with his big belly, almost toppling her. She staggered forwards, one hand falling heavily against the stable door. She froze.

Shit! Had he heard? She couldn't see if he was looking across, or even walking over . . .

'I'm sorry, boy, that was my last one,' Taigh said. His voice still sounded like it was across the room.

As quietly as she could, she shuffled over to the side of the stall and held her breath, her thighs beginning to burn from her unnatural squatting pose. Her body wanted to straighten up and she was beginning to feel a tickle build in her throat, the urge rising to cough again, but she couldn't. She wouldn't.

She slapped her hand over her mouth and tried to control her breathing, to stay calm, her eyes beginning to water from the effort of containing the cough. She rolled her eyes as she heard him still talking to Whiskey, as though he knew she was there and was determined to simply flush her out by stalling. What was wrong with the man, anyway? Anyone walking in right now would take him for a fool, talking to the horses like this.

After what seemed an age – but had probably only been two minutes – she heard the sound of his bag being picked up off the floor again, the rustle of his postman's uniform. She listened to his footsteps on the cobbles becoming dull on the hard-standing of the drive, and she waited for his van to start up. Only when it had pulled away, did she straighten, lurching forwards almost immediately as the hacking coughs were finally released.

'Oh my *God*,' she wheezed, leaning against the wall, eyes streaming, as she recovered. 'That's what comes of hanging upside down for ten minutes. That was all your fault,' she said, pointing an accusing finger at Magnus. He whinnied in protest. 'Yes it was, don't give me your lip. And as for you,' she said, pinning a glare on Whiskey across the other side of the stables. 'Don't go giving me the big eyes act. We need to have words. You need to pick a side, lady. Pick. A. Side.'

Chapter Sixteen

'Willow, what are you doing?' her mother asked, coming tentatively down the stairs and finding her youngest daughter pacing across the great hall.

Willow stopped practising what she was going to say and opened her eyes, dropping down her hands which she realized she'd been wringing. 'Nothing.' She saw with some astonishment that her mother had put on a little make-up today, and that an attempt had been made to style her hair.

'I clearly saw you talking to yourself,' her mother said with a watery smile, walking straight over to the cloakroom and bringing out her navy coat. It was Max Mara, with a little grey faux-fur collar; she and her father had bought it in Florence during an anniversary week away several years ago now.

'Oh, *that*. I was just . . . doing a shopping list.'

'Excuse me?' her mother exclaimed in disbelief, doing up the buttons with fumbling hands.

'Yeah, Mrs Mac needs butter, an onion, kitchen roll and matches. Butter, onion, kitchen roll, matches,' she said, almost as a chant.

'Just write it down if you don't think you'll remember.'

'Yeah, maybe. Are you going out?' Willow asked, changing the subject instead. It was almost a source of amazement to her how easily she was able to draw the wool over her mother's eyes. Either that or her mother was wilfully blind.

'Yes, it's my first day back teaching the floristry class. Everyone wants to get on with their Christmas decorations.'

'Oh of course,' Willow said with practiced surprise, having not remotely forgotten at all; she had been anxiously waiting all morning for her mother to emerge from her room and go out. Connor would be arriving shortly and there was no question of them encountering one another again until this deal was decided one way or the other. Her conversation with Pip last night had left her cold and uneasy – learning he head undercut the deal by a million euros the day he and her father had been due to sign . . . How could she possibly trust him? And if she took the chance to do just that, how could she tell anyone until it was signed off? The sale could fall apart again at any moment, just as it had with her father.

'. . . It should all be okay,' her mother mumbled, more to herself than her daughter. 'Mrs Mac said she ordered the supplies for me.'

'It'll be fine. Everyone will be pleased to see you out and about again. A bit of normality will do you good.'

'Whatever that is, these days. It's been one thing after another lately,' her mother said, fumbling with the top button. 'Even getting dressed feels like an impossible task.' Her hands fell down from the coat in defeat, the top button still undone.

Willow felt a flicker of sympathy rise within her for the mother she wanted to hate. She seemed so broken. 'You're doing the best you can,' she said flatly, making no move to help. As the baby of the family, she knew her words or actions had never carried weight – she had no authority to change moods or lessen suffering.

They stood in spinning silence for a moment, eyes averted, arms hanging limply by their sides.

'Okay, well, it wouldn't do for the teacher to be late,' Willow said, drawing in her breath and trying to rally. She caught sight of the time on the grandfather clock. It was ten past. God forbid Connor should be early. She needed her mother out of here. Fast. 'Christmas wreaths are waiting to be made. Onwards!'

But, staring at the door, her mother made no move towards it.

'Onwards,' Willow repeated, this time taking her mother gently by the elbow and walking her quickly towards it. 'You can do this. It'll be good for you.'

'. . . Yes.'

She watched as her mother picked up the bag of supplies Mrs Mac had left by the door for her – gardening twine, cutters, scissors, wire – and walked slowly down the steps and over the drive to her trusty old Land Rover, affectionately known as Tinpot. It was air-force blue, a willow basket kept permanently on the back bench seat for shopping odds and picking up kindling on her walks with the dogs; whenever Willow saw it, she was reminded of her mother stopping by the roadside on their way home from school to pick wild garlic or elderflower, sprigs of magnolia blossom or ox-eye daisies. It was a totem of the mother she'd been *before*.

She waved as her mother reversed, spinning the car round in an easy arc – a few stray stones flying up from the compacted gravel – and disappeared through the hornbeam allée, up the drive. Willow waited with the smile fixed on her face until she was out of sight and almost at the gates, before she went inside again, sagging against the door with a sigh of relief. For a horrible moment, she'd thought her mother was going to bail and not go out at all.

She closed her eyes and tried to bring her mind back to the business at hand.

'I want a clause written in . . .' she murmured under her breath, hands wringing as she returned to pacing the hall. No, wait, did that sound too . . . amateurish? Was there a professional term for this?

She tried again. 'If you renege on this agreed amount—'

Mrs Mac, who had come in from the dining room and started dusting and polishing, glanced over. 'What are you up to, missy?'

'Nothing.'

'Doesn't look like nothing.'

'Really, I'm fine.'

'You've been like a cat on a hot tin roof all morning. I know you're up to something.'

Willow sighed. Much like with Pip, lying to Mrs Mac was always a futile exercise.

'It's a secret.'

'I can tell that,' Mrs Mac said as she rubbed hard on a section of the potboard where a candle had dripped.

'I can't tell anyone.'

Mrs Mac shot her an offended look. 'What is it?'

She blew out through her cheeks. 'I'm selling the castle.'

Mrs Mac fell still, straightening up slowly, her hands automatically falling to their default position on the back of her hips where she got backache. 'I see.'

Willow saw the disappointment flood her eyes and it was every bit as devastating to see as she'd feared. 'I have to. There's no other options, we all know that.'

'It just seems awful soon, that's all. It's not been two weeks since—'

'I know.' Willow felt her knees weaken. It felt like an

accusation: too soon. Unseemly rush. A rash decision made in haste, regretted at leisure. 'But another two months wouldn't make any difference, would it? Or two years? There's never going to be a right time for us to go.'

Mrs Mac nodded as though in agreement but she didn't speak. She didn't appear able to.

Willow felt the void widen, become deeper, her panic setting harder like concrete. 'I don't know why Dad's left it to me to be the fall guy, but I'm only doing what he would have had to do himself.' Her tone was defensive.

'Aye, well, that's true enough, I suppose,' Mrs Mac said after a moment, hearing the tremor in her voice. '. . . And does your mam know?'

'Not yet.' Willow swallowed. 'No one does. It's all happened so fast, I just need to . . . get my ducks in a row before I start telling people about it yet. It could all still fall apart.'

'Well, it did once before.' A warning note sounded in her voice.

'You knew about that?' Willow asked, surprised.

'Of course.'

Willow nodded. 'Of course.' There was no one her family trusted more than Mrs Mac. She wondered whether to reveal she was selling to the same buyer? She sensed it would be very poorly received.

'So I take it you're expecting them shortly then?'

'How did you know?'

'You mean, apart from the fact you're wearing grooves in the floor and almost threw your poor mother out the door?'

'Oh. Is it that obvious?' Willow bit her lip.

The housekeeper gave a snort. She always had been able to read them like books, ever since they'd been little. 'Well, you'd best hide the buckets before they get here. The leak's got worse in the ceiling above the back hall,' Mrs Mac said, fussing with the duster. 'That storm at the weekend didn't help. Another one like that and you'll end up with bits of the ceiling coming down, I shouldn't wonder. It's soaking to the touch. Ye should call Patrick.'

'I already tried. He's fully booked till after Christmas now.'

Mrs Mac tutted. 'I'm not sure it'll last till then.'

Willow felt the spike of anxiety that came every time she considered the reality of running a seven-hundred-year-old historic building and, in spite of her reservations and doubts, it only confirmed that she needed to make the sale as quickly as possible.

Mrs Mac pointedly looked at her blow-dried hair and best skinny jeans, mercifully included in the emergency bag Shaz had packed for her. 'Would I be right in thinking the buyer's that good-looking young man you were flirting with on the drive yesterday?'

Willow's jaw dropped down. 'Were you spying on me?'

'Hard not to, when your mother was flapping and squawking about in here like a headless chicken.'

'Yes, well, I was not *flirting*. That was business.'

'If you say so. But you'd best get to confession this week, all the same.'

'Mrs M!' Willow gasped as the older woman shot her a dark smile before turning back to polish the potboard again, seemingly not noticing that it was already gleaming.

In spite of the wisecrack, Willow felt sick as she watched the housekeeper work. Her response had hardly been a ringing endorsement that Willow was doing the right thing – and hers was probably the mildest reaction she was going to get from anyone: her mother, Pip, Ottie, the entire village . . .

'Hey, Willow, have you got a minute?'

She looked up to find Ferdy Hopwood standing in the doorway to the music room. He was the chief valuer leading the inventorying for the sale. He and three specialists (in Fine Art, Furniture and Decoratifs) had arrived yesterday lunchtime and were sweeping through the castle, photographing and documenting every objet in the house like forensic specialists in a crime scene. 'Tim wants to know if you're wanting to include the harp in the sale?'

'Oh, I—'

The knock at the door loudly echoed through the hall – as a little girl, it had always reminded her of the opening scene to *The Addams Family* – and she stared at it with her hands plastered over her mouth, unable to move, to think, to act. Connor was here again, right now, on the other side of that door. Oh God. She had a sudden urge to run, to pretend to be out. She needed more time. Everything was progressing too quickly. On the one hand, her head was telling her to do it – act decisively, make the deal, take the money, move on, go back to her life in Dublin. On the other, her father had gone to his grave hating this man; he hadn't been dead yet two weeks and already she was selling to his enemy?

For the first time, she realized it didn't matter how justified she felt – look what her father had done, burdening her with all this! She could sell to whom she pleased! – actually going through with this was going to take more nerve than anger.

Mrs Mac stopped her polishing and looked over at her quizzically as she stood rooted to the spot. 'Well, aren't ye going to open it then?'

'Yes, of course, I . . .' She felt flustered, turning a dizzy circle on the spot. She tried to focus. 'Ferdy, can I come and find you in a bit? Ottie might want the harp; she used to play it. I'll have to ask her.'

'Sure.' He nodded and disappeared from sight again, and with a deep intake of breath, she opened the door.

Her stomach somersaulted at the sight of him today. He was in a dark grey suit, no tie, his beautiful car gleaming on this dull day behind him.

'Miss Lorne.' No smile. A professional, even taciturn, demeanour.

'Mr Shaye.' She stepped back to let him in, hating the effect he had on her even though she now knew he was as ruthless as he was beautiful.

She saw Mrs Mac stand straight as he came in, his eyes instantly scanning up and around the great space before falling to her. The housekeeper had the polishing cloth thrown over one shoulder and a feather duster and can of Pledge in either hand, and yet she still somehow managed to look intimidating.

'This is Mrs Mac, our housekeeper,' Willow said. 'Mrs Mac, this is Connor Shaye.'

'Mrs Mac.'

'Mr Shaye,' the old housekeeper nodded, her signature warmth nowhere to be found as she briskly turned away and began spritzing a cut-crystal vase on the guéridon table in the centre of the room; it usually held extravagant sprays of flowers her mother had cut from the gardens, but there had been nothing in it since the calla lilies at the funeral. Clearly Mrs Mac wasn't hoping her job would pass on with the deeds to the new buyer.

Willow looked back at him with an embarrassed smile, finding his gaze back on her again and wishing they didn't have an audience. 'Uh, well . . . I imagine you'll want to re-acquaint yourself with the place. It's been a while since your last visit . . .'

At her words Mrs Mac straightened up abruptly and

looked at them both with a frown. *Reacquaint . . . a while since your last visit . . .* Willow realized too late she had already unmasked him as her father's rogue buyer.

'Shall we start in the yellow drawing room?' she asked, pointing the way with an outstretched arm and quickly leading him onwards. Anywhere where Mrs Mac wasn't seemed like a good idea.

'Sure.' He followed after her and she tried not to imagine his eyes were on her as they walked through. They stood in the opulent space in silence, his eyes roaming over the silk-lined walls, the old portraits hanging from thick wires, layered-up rugs and clusters of orange and blue chairs in chintzes and damasks arranged in groups around the enormous oak fireplace. Her eyes roamed the room too, trying to look at it with a stranger's perspective but she could only see the Christmas mornings spent unwrapping their stockings by the fire as children; Ella – Dot's mother – creeping in surreptitiously (or so she thought) to lie on the sofas and unwittingly leaving all her dog hairs on the mohair blankets; her eighteenth party when Tommy Callaghan, her crush at the time, had chased her in here and finally kissed her behind the door . . .

Willow risked a glance at him as he scanned the room impassively. It was impossible to tell what he was thinking and he revealed nothing at all when, finished, he looked back at her. He didn't say a word, just gave a nod, and – feeling her nerves grow – she led him into the dining room next door. The ground felt uneven beneath her feet. In spite of what they'd said yesterday about forgetting what had happened between them at the weekend, she had felt it pulse between them anyway – silent but ever-present. But today he was like a complete stranger again, the man on the phone.

Lined in claret linen with huge landscape oils on the walls

and ornately swagged curtains, the dining room was grand and stuffy. The only thing that had ever changed in it during Willow's lifetime were the napkin choices and flower arrangements; it had looked exactly this way when her grandmother had lived here, *her* own mother's gilt-edged wedding service still displayed in the dresser. The furniture in here had caused great excitement with the Christie's team when she'd given them the initial tour – the table sat twenty-six, the Chippendale chairs 'superb examples of their type', apparently. 'We've always used this as the dining room,' she said weakly.

Connor looked at her. 'So I see.' Her nerves grew again, their mutual surprise and push–pull rapprochement yesterday morning having settled into something more reserved. Formal. She had left him with a smile on his lips – *you went soft at my touch?* – but they had seemingly each retreated to new positions overnight. She knew now he was a man who had tried to undercut her father by a million euros. Had he learned something about her that changed his view? Or could he simply do what she could not and pretend this was just business? Had he dreamt of her last night as she had of him? Had he been nervous about seeing her as he stood on the other side of that door?

The questions in her head kept coming; the conversation did not. They walked from room to room, Willow feeling more anxious by the minute. They climbed the stairs – the beautiful split flying staircase she had had races on with her sisters – and looked in at the bedrooms and bathrooms. Having them fitted with en-suites had been the most significant change her parents had made; that was their thumbprint on the castle as they'd geared up to opening it as a luxury bed and breakfast business two decades ago. Willow remembered how well it had done in the beginning, her parents' excitement as the bookings had flooded in – everyone wanting to experience the romance of staying in a medieval Irish castle with drinks served by its very own living knight! The Celtic Tiger had been roaring back then, times were good: the Troubles were over, tourists were flocking in record numbers . . . But then the credit crunch had hit and the flood had slowed to a trickle, and then nothing at all.

She stood by the door of her parents' bedroom and watched as he walked in. She felt like Judas, allowing him into her father's inner sanctum. His clothes were still hanging in the wardrobes, her mother nowhere close to being able to go through them yet. The room was large but dated, painted a soft sage green, with swagged chintz curtains at the windows and a faded pink velvet sofa set at the end of the bed. Above the headboard were three large pastel portraits of the sisters set in pale-blue frames, and a large round table – covered with a crewelwork cloth – displayed family photographs, with a potted plant in the centre. Silk rugs were overlaid in a criss-cross mismatch over the camel carpet, some of them to hide old stains, and the several large handsome wardrobes had beribboned keys in the locks. One wall was entirely shelved with books, old 1980s paperbacks and cloth-bound volumes from the forties and fifties wedged in, but small towers of overflow titles were still beginning to rise from the floor.

Connor stood by the window and looked down into the gardens. Directly outside, looking west, the formal parterre led to a fountain and beyond that a walled garden with fanciful wrought-ironwork gates which opened onto the estuary, the open sea and their special curve of golden beach just around the promontory from here. From her position at the door, Willow could see the tide was coming in, a few moored clinkers nosing out to sea, curlews picking through the shallows.

'Great view,' was all he said when he eventually came away again, his eye casting over the bowing shelves and piles of books, and she saw suddenly what he saw: clutter. Dust. Old lives.

He looked in on all the other bedrooms from the doorways, seemingly assessing their proportions, dimensions, fireplaces, direction of light, and she said nothing, expecting – hoping – he would do the same at her room. Too late, she realized she hadn't thought this far ahead – in the rush to get the horses done and be back in time to do her hair, she'd forgotten to tidy up after herself: a wet towel, clothes strewn on the floor as she'd tried and discarded multiple options. There was no way of hiding her presence here.

'Another bedroom,' she said almost under her breath as she reluctantly pushed open the door. 'There are twenty-four in total.' Her point was: move along; nothing to see here. But her eyes instantly fell to the black silk blouse she'd been wearing on Saturday night, still thrown across the back of the chair. Did it still smell of him?

She saw him see it too. She moved away back into the hall, hoping he would follow her, but to her mortification, he stopped and stepped in instead. She clutched the door frame as she watched the walls close around him, as though spilling all her secrets. His expression didn't change but she saw him absorb every detail: a white china ballet slipper – a prize for top dancer in her class when she'd been eleven – hanging by its ribbons from a nail on the wall; her favourite teddy, Snowball, sitting in the armchair by the window; her collection of vinyl – most of them her parents', which she'd rescued from being taken to the dump. He clocked the book she was reading (a memoir of Hemingway), the empty tea mug and half-drunk glass of two-day-old water; hairbands, lip balm, phone charger . . . She swallowed. It all felt so horribly intimate; no glamour – just the minutiae of her daily routine suddenly laid bare before him.

His gaze skimmed over the dozens of framed photographs of her on the windowsills – high-jumping at an athletics meet, a hurling match, at college in her graduation gown, playing with Dot as a puppy, lying on the grass in a ballgown with her sisters, jumping off a boat in Ibiza . . . She saw him stop at the picture of her with Albie Mconaughie, a friend who'd become something more for a while, and then a friend again. The photo had been taken whilst they were an item, Willow sitting in his lap in the pub, her head thrown back in laughter at something he – or someone else – had said. She'd never thought to move it before. He was a friend, not an enemy; it simply made her happy to remember those times. But now, to a stranger's eyes, did it suggest more than was there?

He looked back at her and she found she couldn't hold his gaze – as though it had been her clothes he had been peeling back and now he saw everything about her. She was revealed.

He walked past her back into the hall but made no move to look at the other bedrooms. He seemed agitated suddenly. Restless.

'Look, Willow, there's no point going any further. There's something I have to tell you.'

Oh God. She'd known it. She'd felt it the second he'd walked in. He was pulling the deal.

'You don't want it.' She felt the weight of responsibility for this place settle straight back down on her shoulders again, pushing her earthwards. Escape denied.

'It's not that.'

'What then?'

'Look, you know what I do?' He shook his head as though the question was ridiculous. 'Of course you do, stupid question. *You* called me.'

She nodded. She did know – but not because she had asked the right questions about to whom exactly she was entrusting her family home. It had simply been enough for her that her father had dealt with him in the first place; it had been enough that her mother didn't like him. No, she only knew what he did because she had spent all last night googling him, poring over his profile on LinkedIn and reading interviews in newspaper articles, examining in microscopic detail the many photos of him at gala dinners, charity events and of course the races, checking out the invariably stunning women in shot with him. One, a blonde in dusty blue at Royal Ascot, had been holding on to him particularly tightly. But then he did rock a top hat.

'You're one of the founding partners of Home James,' she replied. It was a young but thriving and very exclusive private members' club franchise. Currently they boasted two classical, Grade 1-listed properties in England, townhouses in Dublin, Edinburgh, and several others scattered across Europe; one newspaper article in the summer had conjectured he was scouting for sites in New York when he was photographed with a top realtor at Sant Ambroeus.

'Yes.' He shifted his weight, looking uncomfortable. 'And right now I have two problems.'

Two? 'Go on.'

'The first is we have a liquidity issue.'

'Oh jeesht—' she said, turning away in disgust, already knowing what he was going to say next. He was a million short . . .

'No, hear me out. It's liquidity, cash flow. That is all. The money is good, it's just not . . . immediately accessible.'

'You're wasting my time, Connor, you're doing *exactly* what you did to my father!'

'No, I'm not.'

She shot him a disbelieving look.

'Okay, yes, I am, sort of, but—'

'I cannot believe you! I cannot believe you've got the nerve to behave in this way to us, all over again!'

'It's not what you think.'

'No? Can you buy my castle or not?'

He hesitated. 'Not yet. But I want to.'

'I *want* a black Chanel jacket and a foot massage every day for the rest of my life, but they're not going to happen either.'

'Look, I wasn't expecting your call last week, okay? Out of the blue, Lorne suddenly up for grabs again.' Stress inflected in his voice. 'A lot has changed since I was here last. We've just closed on a property in Copenhagen. We weren't banking on having to find another four-plus million out of thin air. I have to go back to our private equity team.'

'So then what was yesterday about – you talking numbers with me on the drive?'

'I needed to establish what number you'd accept. Now that I know, I can go back to our investors and get it from them.'

'And how long will that take?'

'Several weeks, a couple of months tops.'

'A couple of months?' she scoffed. 'I was only selling it to you at that price on assurance of a quick sale. A couple of months is not a quick sale.'

'It's not worth six, Willow.'

'In your opinion.'

'It needs a million spending on it.'

She bit her lip, staring at him, knowing that he was right. Knowing that even if it was another few months before he could buy, that would still, in all likelihood, be a lot quicker than any other sale. He was the bird in the hand. Hels – and Pip, that renowned real estate expert – had left her in no doubt as to the stagnation at the top end of the property market. 'You said there were two problems.'

He looked down at the ground for a moment, his hands on his hips. Slowly, he looked up at her again, locking onto her gaze. 'This is where I need you to trust me . . .'

She felt her stomach pitch at his words.

'Please. Just hear me out.'

'Said every conman ever,' she quipped.

He took a deep breath but there was guardedness in both their eyes now. 'Last night I received an unwelcome phone call regarding our Christmas pop-up. It's a loss-leader but vital for the brand USP of providing unique experiences.'

Willow frowned at the corporate jargon. She didn't know what any of that meant. 'I'm sorry, what's a Christmas pop-up?'

'Temporary clubhouse. We did one in Formentera in the summer and it was a massive hit so we decided to set one up for the festive period too: we take over a location for a weekend – or a week, as we did in the summer – and our members get to enjoy our signature hospitality, but with the novelty of being somewhere new: world-class DJs, food by Noma, black-tie ball, chartered plane from London.'

'So basically a glorified house party then.'

'Ye-e-e-s,' he said slowly. 'Although tickets were twenty grand a pop.'

'How much?'

'And we're completely sold out. We could have sold twice as many tickets but we were restricted by bedroom space at the venue.'

'Who would spend that kind of money on a party weekend?'

'To a lot of our members, that's a bargain. It costs more than that to take a table at most charity galas in Manhattan.'

'Well, if that floats their boat,' she spluttered, half amazed, half appalled. 'It all sounds grand but what's that got to do with me?'

He sighed heavily and she noticed for the first time the strain at the corners of his eyes. 'The venue hosts bailed on us last night – it was supposed to be held in a castle in Lichtenstein but with all the snow they've had this winter, half of the roof has caved and an avalanche of snow fallen in with it. Everything's flooded. Ruined. It's going to take months to sort out.'

'Oh.' And then her eyes widened, as she suddenly guessed what was coming next. ' . . . Oh!'

'If we have to cancel the pop-up and refund everyone, it'll be a PR disaster – we'll look incompetent – not to mention having to refund everyone will wipe out our cash flow for the house clubs over Christmas. The company's solubility is at stake.'

She stared at him, hardly able to believe what she was hearing. 'So you're saying you want to hold the thingy here?'

'I am.'

'Before Christmas?'

'The weekend after next.'

She laughed scornfully. 'You want to host a fancy shindig in my castle, the weekend after next, even though you haven't actually bought it yet and can't buy it for another few months?'

'I know it's a long-shot but we'd pay you a very generous hire fee.'

She frowned. 'How generous?'

'High six figures.'

Her frown cleared momentarily, before resettling again. 'No. This is bullshit Connor. You can't honestly expect me to go for this.'

'Believe me, I do not wanting to be standing here proposing this to you.' She saw the muscle ball at the edge of his jaw. He was tense, agitated, embarrassed. 'I wanted the deal to be clean and quick.'

'And instead it's the exact opposite,' she said drily.

'I'm not in the habit of explaining our company's cash flow issues to the people we do business with but . . . shit happens.' He gave a hopeless shrug. 'This is the only thing I can think of to keep all the balls in play: buy Lorne and keep the pop-up alive. It's an all-or-nothing punt. You either trust me and come all in. Or you walk away – and I wouldn't blame you if you do – and we sink.'

She stared at him, seeing the tension in his eyes. 'That's emotional blackmail.'

He stuffed his hands in his trouser pockets, looking more like a chastened schoolboy being told off for running in the corridors than a businessman closing a deal. 'No. That's all my cards on the table. No smoke and mirrors. It's where we are right at this moment.'

She didn't reply. Their gazes were locked, both of them searching for answers from the other. He was asking her not just to trust him, but to save him.

'What exactly is involved with this party?' she asked finally.

'Pop-up.'

'It's a house party, Connor. Doesn't matter what you call it.'

A tiny smile lit up in his eyes. 'Fine. It would mean a full-scale takeover, by which I mean we'd need to have complete control over the venue: decor, usage of space . . . It would have to fit in with our branding, and clearly –' he gestured to the lamps, vases, paperweights, photo-frames, little bronze sculptures that filled every nook – 'this is very much still your home.'

'You're saying we'd need to move out all our stuff?' Her eyes sparkled with amusement. Clearly he wasn't being serious. That alone would take weeks, if not months.

'Just for starters.' He turned round in a small circle, assessing, evaluating . . . 'Then we'd need to strip it back to exposed floors, neutral walls, bleached wood . . . Get the place breathing again. That would mean lifting the carpets, redecorating the bedrooms and bathrooms, getting the *centuries'* worth of varnish off all this woodwork on the stairs and the panelling.' He ran a hand over the squared oak newel post as he looked back at her. 'It would be a comprehensive overhaul.'

Comprehensive? It sounded invasive.

Willow blinked at him, open-mouthed with disbelief. 'Even if I did agree to it – and I'm *not* saying I am – there is no way on God's earth you could get all that done in two weeks.'

'Actually, I was up most of last night working out exactly that – and it could be done. *Just*. Our teams are in-house so we've got all the trades on standby: plumbers, sparkies, decorators. And our interiors department has a whole warehouse of things they find at auction and stockpile, ready to use in the next club. They're like SWAT teams – they come in, get the job done, bugger off again. But if you were to agree to this, we'd have to start immediately. I'd need to prep the teams today.'

'Today?' she laughed. It was so crazy as to be farcical.

'For the debrief. They'd be coming over from London, so they wouldn't get here till tomorrow now.'

'Oh well, then . . .' she drawled. 'Tomorrow's *fine.*'

He didn't smile, this wasn't funny to him. 'I realize it's a big ask, Willow.'

He had no idea. That this might be their last night in Lorne castle? Seven hundred years' unbroken ownership ended with a day's notice? How on earth would she *ever* talk her mother into it? 'But you're asking me anyway.'

'Look at it this way – what I'm proposing is to do work we would have done once we'd bought the property. Instead we'd be doing it before it's ours. That means the risk is all on our side. We could spend a small fortune getting it the way we want it, but the property is still yours – if you choose sell to someone else before we're in a position to move . . .' He shrugged. 'We lose.'

'On the other hand,' she countered, 'you're proposing overhauling my family's home, without making any meaningful financial commitment to buy at the other end.'

'My word is my bond.'

She arched an eyebrow. 'Did you say that to my father too?'

There was a silence as they hit the impasse. 'Well then, I guess it comes down to whether or not we think we can trust each other. Can you trust me?'

Willow stared at him, the question echoing through her body and vibrating in her heart. Could she?

Chapter Seventeen

'Here, take my arm.' Ottie held out her arm and braced to take his weight. Ben was hobbling around at a decent pace on the crutches, but any steps at all were problematic when he couldn't bend his knee.

She heard him wince as he tried to swing his leg over the step. Her house might be built on one level but that level still happened to be three steps higher than the garden path.

'You need to lean on me,' she said, stepping in closer and forcing him to put one arm over her shoulders. She felt his weight reluctantly bear downwards as together they struggled up the steps and into the house. She sensed he wasn't one for accepting help gladly.

'Well, here we are . . . home sweet home,' she said a few moments later, closing the door behind them, faintly embarrassed by the spartan Scandi-esque decor as he stopped to take in his new address for the next couple of weeks. Was it okay, she wondered, her gaze sweeping afresh over the black-stained elm floorboards and double-height plain white walls, the eighteenth-century calico chairs she had yet to upholster (she had done a course at the sixth form college in Gallaloe), the ill-advised white linen sofa she had bought in a sale and which had been permanently shrouded ever since with a black throw.

She didn't know what he was used to in New York – a

Manhattan penthouse bachelor pad? A rent-controlled brownstone? A picket-fenced cottage in the suburbs? An industrial loft in SoHo? She knew nothing about him at all. Not for the first time she wearied at the impulse that had propelled her into offering up her home to a complete stranger.

On the other hand, she reminded herself, he'd spent a night with a broken leg and arm on an exposed cliff edge in a storm thanks to her. She figured she owed him.

'That is one hell of a view,' he said, his eyes immediately fastening on the floor-to-ceiling glass wall that gave onto the crescent beach and the purple hills further down the coast. The sky was a heavy, moody blue today, the sea rolling into the beach in big froth-topped waves, a lone windsurfer in full neoprene-hooded body-kit cutting across the bay at speed.

'Thank you. I like it.'

Dropping his arm off her shoulder, he hobbled forwards, throwing a barely curious glance over the small all-white L-shaped open-plan kitchen on the right-hand side, heading for the picture window.

'The bedroom's just off to the right there,' she said as he passed by the bedroom door and he paused to look in from afar. The black metal frame of her contemporary four-poster could be seen through the doorway, the sheepskin rug on the floor straightened, all her worn clothes that usually spent three weeks draped over the calico chair before making it to the laundry now washed and pushed away again.

He twisted back to look at her. 'Look, Ottie, I know you said I could take your room, and I accepted purely to get the consultant off my back but I can't accept that. It's not right. I'll be perfectly fine on the sofa.'

But as he said it, he looked down at the snug two-seater. It was clear that even if its four-foot-wide frame could have accommodated his six-foot one, its squashy feather-filled cushions would never provide any support.

'I insist,' Ottie shrugged, seeing his expression. 'Miss Cunningham said you need to keep your leg straight and elevated for the next ten days and I'd rather not have to buy a new sofa just for that.' She gave a smile and made him think he was doing her the favour.

'God no.' He looked at her with his usual directness. 'I guess I still don't understand why you're doing this. It's not like we hit it off when we first met. I could just as easily have stayed at the rehabilitation home.'

She gave a wry smile. 'You really couldn't. The average age there is eighty-four and, besides, there have been . . . care issues recently. It's really not a problem having you staying here. I'll be out most of the time anyway.'

'Working in the campsite?'

'And on the estate.' She put down her bag and walked over to the kettle, but in truth, she wasn't sure if she even did work there any more. Legally, the estate was Willow's now and apart from at the hospital with Pip, they'd not seen each other or talked properly since their father's final wishes had been made known. The shift in responsibility – and power – was a boulder between them; they could talk over it but not step around it, and Ottie had no idea if Willow wanted her to continue with the projects she had been working on with their dad. 'Would you like a coffee?'

'Sure.'

She heard the dull tap of the crutches on the floor as he made his way over to the rocking chair near the window and awkwardly lowered himself down. It would have been hard enough for most people with just one mobile leg, but a strapped-up wrist too challenged even his strength and mobility.

'How's your pain? D'you need any more painkillers?' she asked, seeing how he struggled. 'You were due another dose half an hour ago.'

'No, I'm fine,' he said, wincing slightly as he used his good hand to pinch the fabric of his trousers to lift his leg into a better position.

'Sure? It's good for keeping the inflammation under control,' she said, reaching for the cups.

'I prefer not to use medicines if I can help it.'

Ottie arched an eyebrow. Post-surgical pain relief wasn't just any old medicine. Then again, the man clearly knew his own pain threshold. Most mortals couldn't run one and a half marathons per day for three days. 'How d'you like it?' And when he looked back at her quizzically, she held up the sugar pot. 'Sugar? Milk?'

'Black, no sugar.'

She felt him watch her as she poured. 'So how long have you lived here?'

'All my life. My parents own the estate.' Her hand stilled momentarily at the slip of tenses – when would it become . . . automatic? The new normal? 'We grew up in the castle but this was always my favourite spot. That view captivated me right when I was a little girl and it's never let me go.'

'You grew up in a *castle*?'

'Haven't you seen it?'

He shrugged. 'I just studied the course map.'

Of course he had. ' Well, you're on the Lorne Castle estate.' She gave a small smile. 'It's not that unusual here anyway; there's quite a lot of castles in Ireland.'

'So does that mean you're a princess?' His face remained impassive but she could hear the slightly sardonic tone in his voice. 'Should I bow?'

'Ha!' she scoffed, bringing the coffee over and handing him his. 'Only in my dreams. No, no airs or graces – although my father was the last living knight in Ireland.'

'That sounds very cool.'

'Thank you. It was.'

'What does a knight do, exactly, these days? I assume jousting requires safety permits?'

She laughed, appreciating his dry sense of humour. 'It's sadly just an honorary title now – a lot of charity work mainly, a few ceremonial dinners in funny clothes once in a while. We still have the suit of armour worn by the 1st Knight of Lorne. Rusty, we call it, for self-evident reasons. But there are no princesses to protect in towers any more.'

'Except you, surely? I'm sure he was very protective of you.'

She smiled. 'I have two sisters as well.'

'*Three* princesses for your knightly father to protect! Your teenage boyfriends must have been terrified.'

'Yes!' she laughed. 'They probably were, although more so of Pip, my middle sister, than Dad. He was a softie.'

He watched her curl up on the sofa, tucking her legs beneath her. 'And what was it like to be the daughter of the last living knight in Ireland?'

Jeesht, *there* was a question. 'Well, obviously it was nice for us to grow up here – these views, the grounds, the history of the place.'

'Why was he the *last* knight?'

'The title had to be passed down through the male line. It was rather bad luck that neither I nor my sisters deigned to be born as boys.' She shrugged her shoulders as carelessly as she could.

'Oh, I see . . . That's a tough gig .' A look she couldn't

explain lurked in the backs of his eyes, as though he found her faintly perplexing. 'That must be a pretty hard thing to live with.'

'For my father? Yes. I think he felt guilty, as though he'd failed.'

'I was thinking it must be hard for you too.'

She had never lived without it but she gave what she hoped was a careless smile, scuffing over the hollowness that came from knowing the moment of her birth was a devastating let-down, that no matter what she did in her life, it would never be enough to compensate for what she wasn't. She had always been the firstborn – and the first disappointment. A girl: bonny and bouncy, taller and faster than average, talking at ten months and walking by twelve – but no heir. That was the one thing she could never be. 'It was what it was. Our parents loved us. We knew that.'

He nodded, watching her interestedly. 'When did he die, your father?'

Ottie felt her expression freeze. '. . . A fortnight ago.'

Ben looked shocked. 'God, I'm sorry. I had no idea it was so recent.'

'Of course not, how could you?' she said lightly, forcing a smile. How had they wandered onto such intense – and private – ground so quickly? Shouldn't they still be discussing the weather and where she kept the towels?

An awkward silence bloomed and to cover it, she got up quickly again, grabbing the small footstool that also housed her sewing box and brought it over to him, lifting his foot and gently setting his leg up. She took a few scatter cushions from the sofa and elevated his leg higher still as he watched on, impassively. 'There.'

'Thanks.' His all-seeing eyes followed her, as though

knowing her fuss was simply distraction. 'So you were saying you live and work here?'

Back on safe ground again. 'That's right. I run the campsite when it's open but most of the time I help –' she corrected herself – 'helped Dad with the running of the estate.'

'It's very beautiful – well, what I saw of it, clinging to the cliff. Lovely . . . views.'

She gave a shocked laugh at his dark sense of humour. Her father would have liked him for sure.

He allowed a wry smile too and it softened his face inordinately. 'Have you ever *not* lived here?'

'Well, I nearly cut and ran five years ago. Almost escaped.' She grinned. 'I had a place at art school in London and rather fancied the idea of artistic destitution in a bedsit in Haringey.'

'But?'

'I got a better offer. Dad asked me to run this place with him, and as the eldest I felt it was my duty to do what I could here.'

He nodded, looking at her keenly. 'Not many people live by notions of "duty" these days.'

She shrugged. 'I can't pretend we Lornes are a typical bunch. What is it you do?' she asked politely, horribly aware all the conversation was about her.

'Well, I'm a pollster.'

She hesitated, not sure she'd heard correctly. *'Pollster?'*

'I know, it's close to mobster. But then I work for politicians so . . .'

She smiled.

'Yeah, I conduct surveys and polls for politicians, governments, think tanks, corporations . . .'

'It sounds very high-powered. Do you enjoy it?'

He thought for a moment. 'I'd say I like the unpredictability of it.'

'But isn't yours, by definition, the industry of predictability?'

'Ah.' He almost grinned. Almost. A slight light coming into his eyes. 'There's a difference between prediction and predictability, and I've found people never fail to surprise you.'

'Is that a good thing?'

He shrugged non-committally. 'It depends.'

'Who have you worked for? Anyone I'd have heard of?'

'We worked on Hillary Clinton's presidential campaign.'

'Oh my God! That is seriously big bananas!' she exclaimed.

'Big bananas?' he queried drily. 'Now, is that an Irish term I should be familiar with – or a Lorneism? "Seriously big bananas",' he repeated, his accent making it sound funnier. 'I'll try to utilize that in my next meeting.'

Ottie laughed. 'I wouldn't. Not unless you want them to think you're nuts.'

'They think that anyway.' He gestured vaguely to the surroundings but she knew he meant being here, racing in the Ultra.

'Is it going to be a problem, you being out of the country for so long?' she asked, sipping her coffee.

'It's definitely not ideal but hopefully they can patch me in on some conference calls. And things are slightly quieter now that the mid-terms are behind us.'

'Did you accurately predict the results for those?'

'We did.'

'Are your results always accurate?'

He hitched up an eyebrow slightly. 'You mean, did we predict Trump was going to beat Hillary to the presidency?' From his tone, she guessed this was a question he was asked a lot. She didn't suppose it was a good thing to be on the losing side of one of the biggest political upsets in the past century. 'No. Our surveys were accurate at a national level – we predicted she'd get the popular vote by three points; it was actually two. But at state level, our responding sample groups were proportionally too heavily weighted with college-educated voters; we didn't foresee the last-minute undecided voters' swing to Trump.' He shrugged. 'But we've learned from it.'

Ottie suspected he didn't take well to losing. 'So how did you get into the profession? Does anyone actually grow up wanting to be a pollster?'

Again, his almost-smile hovered on his lips. 'I started out in advertising initially. Worked with the big brands, had flashy lunches, accrued all the toys.'

She pulled a face. From his tone, it wasn't sounding like a good thing. 'But . . . ?'

He opened his mouth to reply, but for a moment, nothing came out. '. . . I had a wake-up call,' he said finally. 'Things that had once seemed to matter, didn't any more. I realized I was just part of a cycle of making people want things they didn't need; that all I was doing was just perpetuating the cult of *buying stuff*. We don't have experiences any more – we buy them. We watch people on Instagram journey to the places we'd like to go, we buy clothes only to wear them once . . .' He shrugged. 'I needed something that created and found connections between us and I found I liked that the data we collected for polls could directly affect a politician's policy or media strategy. Taken to its natural conclusion, it can alter the fate of an entire country.'

Ottie was impressed. The most she ever had to deal with was unblocking the loos and litter-picking the site, commissioning the masons to rebuild sections of old stone wall or getting the lake dredged. 'And ultra running. How did you get into that?'

'It was around the same time as my career switch. After my wake-up call, I decided to train for the New York marathon and on the day, I ran it six minutes faster than I'd hoped for. So then I ran the Boston one too and a similar thing happened. Then in Berlin. And London. Soon I was cruising them. Marathons just seemed to suit my body, so I needed another challenge. Something more.'

'That is nuts,' Ottie sighed. 'I can't imagine how anyone can be *suited* to running marathons.'

'I take it you don't run?'

'Only to the pub. Or to the loo in the middle of the night— Oh!' She gave a little gasp as she realized something.

'What is it?' he asked.

'Uh . . . nothing.'

'It doesn't look like nothing.'

She looked at him. Why hadn't she thought of this before? 'Well, it's just I remembered that the bathroom – the only bathroom – is off the bedroom through there.' She shook her head quickly. 'But it's fine. I can use the campsite facilities.'

'Out in the field? Now who's nuts?'

'It's important you rest properly. I don't want to disturb you.'

'Don't worry, you won't,' he said. 'I'm pretty sure the anaesthetist gave me a horse tranquillizer back there. I'm not so much sleeping as falling into complete oblivion at the moment.' He stretched his neck out, dropping his head down side to side. She realized suddenly how exhausted he looked. He was still freakishly pale, offset by a quickly growing fuzz of dark stubble. 'Speaking of which, I should probably—'

'Absolutely, you must rest,' she said, jumping up and setting down her cup. She'd kept him talking too long. In her rush to be hospitable, she'd forgotten he was a recuperating patient. 'Here, let me help you get up.'

She put one of his arms around her shoulders again and tried not to groan as his entire body weight had to be spread between his one good leg and her two, as she lifted him to standing. 'There.' She handed him the crutches. 'I've . . . put some fresh towels out for you and a blanket on the chair in case it's cold. It can get chilly here, but hopefully it won't be.'

He regarded her with his impenetrable gaze and nodded. 'You're very kind.'

'Do you need any help getting—'

'I can take it from here. But thanks.'

She watched as he hobbled into the bedroom, his gaze meeting hers for just a second as he closed the door behind him. She swallowed, feeling her nerves come down a little, and walked over to the window – the windsurfer was still out there, criss-crossing the bay in sharp angles.

That had gone well, she thought, crossing her arms over her chest and gripping them tightly. Conversation had been easy; he was clearly a driven and complicated man which, even if it didn't make him the most happy-go-lucky company, at least meant he was interesting.

She took the cups back into the kitchen and washed them up, something catching her eye in the corner of the window. She stared out at the little red tent, still flapping in the breeze at the back of the garden. It had been there for five days now and every sighting of it filled her with guilt and shame for how she'd behaved, her fit of pique for missing an opportunity with Bertie snowballing exponentially into near-tragedy.

She hurried into the garden and began unpacking the tent. There wasn't much to move anyway – a duffel bag with a fresh shirt and tie, clean boxers and socks, toiletries; his suit in the zipped-up suit bag and his sleeping bag. She rolled it up efficiently and brought everything into the house, returning a moment later to take down the tent; it wasn't raining for once; everything was dry. There was no better time to take it down and she couldn't cope with being reminded of how poorly she'd behaved every time she washed the dishes. She needed it gone.

She stuck her head in to check everything was cleared and went to zip down the door when she noticed something, a photograph, on the groundsheet; it must have been under the sleeping bag. Crawling in, she reached for it and stared at the image of the brunette. She was as glossy and scary-looking as Ottie expected a Manhattanite to be: perfectly blow-dried hair, lipsticked lips, gym-honed arms, direct gaze. It looked like a headshot for a fancy lawyer's website.

Wife? Fiancée? Girlfriend? Whatever, she looked right for him. Serious. High-flying. Ballsy. Tough. Seriously tough given she seemingly hadn't called him once since his accident, much less come over to see him.

Ottie slipped the photograph into her jeans pocket and backed out of the tent, zipping down the door and unhooking the guy ropes. She watched as the red tent collapsed in on itself like a lowered mainsail, pushing out the air and folding it in down in ever-decreasing squares. She had dismantled enough tents in her time to do it blindfolded – Pip had once commented she was like a soldier able to strip down a rifle – but as she hugged and folded the neat parcel to her chest, ready to go back inside again, she saw there was a yellow patch of grass left on the lawn now, like a little scar in her garden to remind her exactly of what she had done.

Chapter Eighteen

'Jeesht, what the *hell* is going on?' Pip exclaimed, jumping out of her Land Cruiser in such a hurry, she left the driver's door open.

Willow looked up from her conversation with a man in a navy boilersuit. They both had clipboards and were looking very officious. 'Oh, Pip, hi.'

'Hi, yourself. What's going on?' she asked, crossing the drive in short indignant strides, dried mud flying off her boots, as two men struggled past her carrying the pocketed pale-blue damask chaise from the breakfast room. There were five enormous lorries parked at matching angles, dozens of removal men hurrying to and from the castle, her family's treasures in their hands. 'I thought you said Christie's couldn't do the contents sale till after Christmas?'

'I'll come and find you in a bit, Harry,' Willow said to her companion before looking over at her. 'That's right. But everything's being put into storage until then.'

'Why?' Pip asked, coughing lightly into her fist and frowning as their grandmother's dressing table was carried past them.

'An opportunity came up that I couldn't turn down,' Willow replied, her eyes on the table as it was carried into the truck and fastened with ropes tied to the sides.

'What kind of opportunity?' Pip asked suspiciously.

She bit her lip. 'A private members' club has hired out the castle for their Christmas pop-up event.'

Pip stared at her in bewilderment. *'Huh?'*

'It's a big glorified Christmas house party basically. They're taking over the entire place the weekend before Christmas and installing all their own staff. All we've got to do is give them a blank canvas to work with.'

'All?' Pip laughed. 'Like that's no tall order!'

'Tell me about it,' Willow said with a groan as the kitchen table was carried past. 'Uh, Dower House for that, please!'

'But . . . a weekend hire? I thought you were selling the place. Does this mean you might be having second th—'

'No. We still need to sell,' she said quickly.

Pip stared at her.

'And don't look at me like that,' Willow said quietly, not returning her stare. 'You know there's nothing else I can do. We have to sell and that's all there is to it.'

Pip knew it *was* true. In spite of his best intentions, their father had left it to his youngest daughter to do what he could not – cut the cord and sever the link with his family's past. They both watched in silence as the grandfather clock was carried out feet first, its reassuring tick temporarily stilled. The sunlight glanced off the brass pendulum and it occurred to Pip that many of these items hadn't been moved, much less reacquainted with fresh air and the elements, for tens, if not hundreds, of years. It was a serene day today, the sun mild and low in the pale sky, winter birds pitching through the cold air. Blessedly, there was almost no wind at all, which was just as well seeing as she'd forgotten her jacket.

Pip shook her head, hardly able to believe her own eyes, as the contents kept on coming, their home being dismantled one piece at a time, like a woollen blanket being unravelled stitch by stitch, Willow pulling on a thread. Part of Pip had always felt like the place might fall down without the Lornes in it, like the ravens in London's Tower but she was the one who felt weak-kneed by the sight. 'How's Mam taking it?'

Willow cleared her throat, looking suddenly stiff. 'Much as you'd expect. She left before the first truck came this morning. She's gone to Shula's for the day.'

Pip rolled her eyes. That wasn't a surprise. 'Probably best. This is all going to be way too much too soon for her.'

Willow wheeled around to face her, a sudden flush spreading over her cheeks and down her neck. 'Look, Pip, you've got your place, okay?' she cried. 'You've got your land and your stables and your flat and your horses. You're sorted! Dad kept things easy for you! He wasn't quite as kind to me, *quelle surprise*! I didn't ask for this!'

Willow looked away as Pip stared at her in shock, seeing how her lips were pulled thin, angry tears shining at her eyes. It was clear she was right at the edge of her emotions. She never raised her voice. Chill Will they'd always called her as kids. 'Will—'

'Just forget it,' she snapped, folding her arms over her chest.

'Will,' Pip said more quietly, putting a hand on her arm and feeling how she trembled. 'Listen, I'm sorry. I didn't mean to make it worse for you. I know you're doing the best you can. And you're right, this *is* a shitstorm for you to sort out. I don't know why Dad left it all for you either. It mega sucks.'

Willow didn't reply but an eyebrow kinked slightly at the teenage language they had revelled in ten years earlier.

'. . . So where are you both going to stay while the party's on?' Pip asked more gently.

'The Dower House,' Willow replied after a moment. 'It's Mam's now, whether she acknowledges it or not; she's going to have to go there sooner or later. She point-blank refused to help so last night I went round putting red stickers on all the things I thought she'd definitely want to have with her there and then I started packing.'

'Jeesht. Fun night. '

'Got it in one,' Willow murmured, hugging her arms tightly around her torso.

Pip squinted at her sister, taking in her drawn pallor. 'Have you slept?'

'About three hours.'

'Will, that's not enough.'

'Says you. You look like the walking dead too.'

Pip cracked a relieved grin. Insults were always a good sign with the Lorne sisters. 'Thanks. Did a little *shading* under the cheekbones this morning. A bit of *contouring* under the eyes to really bring out the bags, you know?'

Willow gave a small chuckle in spite of herself. Pip had never knowingly worn make-up in her life; tinted lip balm at a cousin's wedding once was as good as it got. She sighed, relaxing again. 'I'll sleep at the weekend. Right now, I've just got to push on through. Soonest dealt with, soonest done. The first truck's already down at the Dower House unloading the first batch of furniture. I'm heading over later to unpack.'

'I'll help.'

'No. You need to rest.'

'Unpacking boxes is *not* arduous work. I'll sit down while I'm doing it if you like.'

'Ugh, fine,' Willow groaned. Pip knew it was easier for her to give in than argue.

'So how long is it going to take them to empty this place?'

'A few days, they reckon. They'll be done by Friday.'

'I don't understand how you got them all here so quickly,' Pip said, watching a sixteenth-century mahogany four-poster come out in various separate pieces.

'Christie's sorted it. They were here sorting through stuff for the estate sale anyway so I had a word with them and they're going to take it all back to their warehouses and just go through it there. They've got proper lights and humidity levels sorted so it's probably better for them anyway.'

Pip glanced at her sister. 'And does Ottie know about this?'

Willow hugged her arms around herself – a defensive gesture as much as a warming one. 'I rang and left a message for her the other day, asking whether she wanted the harp or any other bits but she hasn't returned my call. And she's not been up here for days. Apart from at the hospital, I've not seen her at all. She's still avoiding me.'

'Jeesht, you think everyone's avoiding you!' Pip replied.

'Because they are.'

'You're paranoid.'

Willow turned to face her. 'Am I? It should have been her who got this place, Pip, not me, and we all know it.'

Pip didn't reply immediately. What could she say? Her little sister was right. Things shouldn't have turned out this way. Their father had done more damage than he could have anticipated with that will. 'Yeah, well, I've only seen her 'cos I popped in on Monday – helped her with the post-race tidy-up. You should have seen it – protein bars, avocado nuts, thermal foils, lentils fricking everywhere.'

'Pip, you're *supposed* to be *resting*, not tidying up campsites!' Willow said exasperatedly. 'It's doctor's orders.'

Pip tutted. 'What else was I going to do? I can't sit on that sofa all day and I've no more bookings till after Christmas now; it's the dead zone for me. No one wants to trek when the Wild Atlantic Way's *really* wild.' Shalimar's magnificent image flashed in front of her eyes again, hitting her like a punch to the stomach. What was she doing now? Did she understand what had happened – that the days were passing and she wasn't going to go back to Lorne? Not ever?

'You are a nightmare,' Willow muttered.

Pip shrugged and looked around them, watching the men scurrying like ants. No one was standing around taking a break, drinking coffee, having a smoke . . . This was industry in action. 'So what happens when the place is empty? They putting up balloons?'

'Ha! Not before the club sends in its SWAT teams.'

'Its what now?'

'Tradesmen. Decorators . . . They're stripping back the place. Making it "breathe" again, apparently.'

'What? You're letting them change things?' Pip was scandalized.

'I'd let them cover it in feathers, what they're paying us for it.'

'Us?' Pip asked sardonically.

Willow tutted, ignoring the jibe. 'That's not the pertinent bit. It's all got to be up and running by next weekend.'

Pip looked at her sister as if she was febrile. 'There is *no* way that castle is going to be emptied, redecorated and refurb'd by a week Saturday!'

'I know, it's tight.'

'Tighter than Kim Kardashian's jeans!'

Willow shrugged, unperturbed. 'Well, apparently they've got all their own in-house people. They've got furniture stock in storage and can turn things around quickly.'

'. . . You seem very relaxed about it all.'

'Why wouldn't I be? It's not my problem – it's their deadline to make. We just need to ship out.'

Pip nibbled her lip as she watched her childhood home be dismantled bit by bit. 'Well, looking on the bright side, I guess it's two fingers up to that bloke too.'

'Which bloke?'

'The pretty one who tried to stiff Dad.'

Willow's mouth opened, but for a moment, nothing came out. 'The one who saved your life, you mean?' she said finally.

Pip gave a groan. 'Touché.' She looked across at Willow but her face was pinched and pale, the stresses clearly weighing on her. 'Hey, you okay?'

'Sure.' But she looked as stiff as a steel rod.

Pip jumped into action suddenly. 'Oh, wait, no, not that!' she cried running towards one of the men carrying a box and taking it off him, leaving the poor guy looking bewildered. She held up the kettle triumphantly. 'This doesn't leave until we do!' she cried. 'First in, last out!'

After a moment, Willow came to, realizing her point. 'I take it you'd like a coffee then?'

'Damn right I would. Hey, mister . . .' Pip cried, running after the removal man heading back into the castle. 'What did you do with the biscuits?'

It had been an exhausting day. Willow sat at the window seat on the landing and stared vacantly over the neglected garden, trying not to notice the thick spiders' webs in every corner. Somewhere down there was a moss-covered statue of Artemis, the goddess of wild animals, but it was almost impossible to see under the thick tangle of brambles that had grown steadily over her.

Absent-mindedly, she massaged the soles of her feet; they actually burned from all the running around she'd done. She figured she must have covered well over twenty miles today, haring up and down the stairs at the castle, directing the removals men on what went where, making cups of tea, going through final queries with Christie's, and then when everyone else had clocked off for the day, dashing over here to make a start on unpacking again.

Pip had come back here as promised after she'd nipped back to the stables to feed and rug-up the horses, and together they'd found the linen and made up two of the beds, decanted all the food into the larder and fridge, plumbed in the washing machine and somehow set the antenna to the right direction for the TV. Willow had even carefully set out her mother's travel clock and personal belongings on her bedside table, down to filling her water glass and leaving her book open on the correct page – giving the impression that she had merely stepped out of her bedroom momentarily, rather than it be moved half a mile away.

That would have to do for tonight. Dozens of boxes were still piled in high towers around the house but it would take days to go through them all and decide what would go where. There was no doubt they were also going to have to ruthlessly edit what stayed. It was going to be a big ask getting her mother to curate her lifetime belongings down to only what could fit here. Not that her mother was speaking to her right now. Willow had been obliged to tell her the new, very urgent plans when she had come in yesterday – buoyed up from her wreath-making course, it had been like taking the proverbial sweets from a child; she had retreated to her room again for the rest of the day, refusing entry even to Mrs Mac. Willow had red-dotted everything she thought her mother would want to have around her at the Dower House, but her heart had dived to see her father's clothes on their hangers here, the only thing her mother had stipulated herself before she'd left, ready to be put back out in the wardrobes again.

Mrs Mac had come over late afternoon, piling the contents of the freezer from the castle into the boot of her old Corsa and transferring everything to the box freezer the delivery men had brought down. She had thawed a casserole, ready for them to throw in the dismal little oven – she missed their sunny Aga already – but Willow wasn't sure she had the energy to eat and there was no one to insist upon it; after all her exertions, her mother had telephoned from the Flanagans' an hour ago, letting her know they'd 'insisted' she stay for the night. Willow supposed she really ought not have been surprised.

She closed her eyes, wondering if she could just sleep here in this nook, her legs tucked under, her head resting against the deep stone reveal. But there was a chill coming off the single-glazed windows and reluctantly she made herself stir. She should check the central heating system worked before she went to bed or she might freeze in the night. The temperatures were plunging – something about an Arctic front coming in, Pip had said, hence the need for double rugs on the horses.

She drifted through the house, feeling like an intruder. It wasn't a building she'd ever been familiar with, partly because of its position, set apart from the rest of the estate on the 'back' drive with no especial views and far out of sight of the castle. Partly too because it had been inhabited by lodgers since she was a little girl – a childless older couple, Mr and Mrs Wheeler, who'd moved here after he'd retired from his architect's practice in Limerick. They'd lived here till their deaths a few years back but they hadn't ever been friendly towards the estate's rather feral, wayward daughters, who were known for their pranks.

But that wasn't what had really kept Willow and her sisters away: it was their father's stories about the ghost that haunted here, rattling the doorknobs, he said, her skirts knocking over the fire irons as she drifted over the floors. Supposedly the ghost was Elizabeth Carr, the stepmother of the 15th Knight, otherwise known as Black Bess on account of her pure-black hair. Tradition said the 15th Knight had had the house built for her as punishment for the way she had treated him as a boy, and that when his father died and he inherited the title, the castle and all the lands, his revenge had been swift and sweet. Commissioning the building of the Dower House had been his first act upon becoming the Knight and it was built in the fashion of the day, Queen Anne style, with grey stone quoins, flush sash windows and a central triangular pediment set against the hipped roof. But, like Black Bess, its beauty was deceptive and only skin-deep, for beyond the stylish facade, the house was surprisingly small and mean. Most houses of this period boasted double-pile platforms, two rooms deep, but here was barely bigger inside than some of the estate cottages. The extravagant ceiling heights were a useless luxury and only served to highlight the meagre proportions of the rooms, rendering them higher than they were wide. As for the steep, narrow staircase, it would have been treacherous in long skirts and, indeed, it was how Black Bess had met her untimely end, two weeks short of the first anniversary of her husband's death. Legend had it, according to her father, that as she fell, the last words to ever leave her lips were a curse upon her stepson and the house of Lorne.

Of course, it may have been a downgrade for those used to

living with the proportions of a castle, but to the modern eye, the insults built into the walls of this house were slight. The smaller rooms were well suited for a couple or someone living here on their own and almost all the architectural features – windows and fireplaces – were original. If they did cut down some of the trees and tame the garden, redecorate the house . . . It could be a project, something to help occupy her mother as she adapted to widowhood—

'Hello!'

The unexpected voice made Willow jump, her knees buckling with the fright, and she stopped at the top of the stairs, looking down into the dark hall trepidatiously.

'Willow, are you there?' The voice sounded muffled coming through the thick wooden front door. 'It's me! Taigh!'

'Jeesht, Taigh,' she muttered, putting her hand to her chest to still her beating heart. She ran carefully down the stairs and opened the front door.

'So the doorbell doesn't work then?' he grinned, staring back at her.

'I don't think much works here, to be honest. Sorry, were you standing there a while?'

'Oh, there's nothing wrong with getting a bit of air.'

She noticed the tip of his nose was pink. He was wearing his paramedic's uniform, his bag by his feet. 'Quick, come in or you'll catch your death. It's freezing out there.'

'Brrr, it's freezing in *here,*' he said, stepping into the flagstoned hallway. He noticed the dark fireplace. 'Not got a fire going yet?'

'It was my next job,' she smiled, trying to hide her weariness. Going to bed and hiding under a blanket seemed the easier option. 'What's up?'

'I came over to see if Pip was here? She's not at home.'

'Really?' Willow frowned. 'Are you sure? She left here about an hour ago and said she was going straight back. She was pretty done in.'

'Well, she wasn't answering if she was there, although the lights were on.'

'Oh. That's odd. Why d'you need her? Is it something I can help with?'

'Sadly not. I just need to check up on her, listen to her chest again.'

'Oh, I see.'

'I know – fun times. But I keep missing her. Every time I go over to the stables she's not there and I can't seem to catch up with her. I swear to God, if I didn't know better, I'd say she was deliberately avoiding me.'

'Oh, I'm sure she's not,' Willow said unconvincingly. 'You know Pip – she's just incapable of sitting still.'

'That's the thing – she *really* should be resting. I'm not sure she understands the seriousness of it – she had a close shave at the weekend and the body needs to recover from something like that; the mind too. She can't be going around like nothing happened.'

Willow hesitated, because of course that was exactly what her wayward big sister had been doing. It had been business as usual for Pip as far as she'd been able to see. 'Well, I guess it has been an unusual time for us all lately; there's been so much going on it's been hard to stop. But if it makes you feel any better, she seemed perfectly fine when I saw her earlier, and we were working for hours. It's been mental, packing up the castle like this.'

'Yeah, I saw your note on the door up there, saying you'd moved down here. It's all happening really fast, isn't it?'

'Fast or slow, it's still got to happen one way or the other.'

She gave a careless shrug but, in truth, every comment on the matter felt like an accusation – of haste, lack of thought, sentiment, attachment. It made her feel exposed.

He looked around the hallway interestedly. 'I've not been down here before.'

'Nor us really. It was rented out for all our childhoods. The lodgers weren't particularly friendly.' She wrinkled her nose. 'Plus it's haunted, of course. We wouldn't come near the place.'

His eyes widened delightedly. 'You've got a ghost?'

'Oh yeah! Black Bess. Not a woman to be crossed, by all accounts. This is supposedly where she roams.'

He gave her a sceptical look. 'And you're going to be here *on your own*?'

'Well, only for tonight. Mam's supposed to be here too but she's staying over with the Flanagans tonight. Anything to get out of the unpacking, I reckon.'

'Will you be all right?'

'I don't believe in ghosts any more, Taigh,' she laughed.

He grinned. 'But you do fairies, though?'

'Of course!'

'And unicorns?'

'Ride them on the beach daily,' she nodded.

'Leprechauns?'

'Was just talking to one.'

He laughed. 'Knights in shining armour?'

She sucked in her teeth. 'Oh, nah, sorry. Never seen one of those.'

'I don't believe it! The knight's own daughter hasn't seen a knight in shining armour?'

'Knights' daughters don't need knights!'

'Pah, what's need got to do with it?' he chuckled, picking up his bag. 'You Lornes are hard women, so you are.' He walked back to the door. 'Listen, I've got to go, I'm on duty in twenty minutes. But tell that sister of yours I'm looking for her. If nothing else I just need to sign her off, that's all. Will you tell her that for me?'

'Sure.'

'I'll pop over to hers again tomorrow sometime.'

'You're a champ, Taigh. I'll ring her now and let her know.'

She closed the door behind him and took out her phone, checking for mobile coverage here. She watched as one bar of mobile reception flickered on and off the screen. To her surprise she saw that she'd missed a call and had a new message, even though her phone hadn't rung.

She listened to her voicemail.

'Willow, it's Connor.' His voice felt like velvet against her ear. 'I've got the scaffolders going over tomorrow to get the grid up for the roof. They're keen to get the lorries in and as close to the building as possible before the removals trucks arrive so they'll be with you early, around sevenish. Can you move any cars out the way before then? We don't want to risk anything falling on them.' There was a pause. 'Okay . . . bye.'

She hung up and pressed the phone to her chest. Didn't Taigh know? Knights didn't wear shining armour these days.

Chapter Nineteen

Friday, 13 December

The wind blew in playful gusts, snatching the bed sheets away from Ottie's grasping hands each time she reached for them, her rusty-blonde hair whirling around her head in vertical fronds. 'Mmnnff,' she spluttered, three wooden clothes pegs in her mouth as she grabbed the corner of a duvet cover and held on to it. She wrestled it into her body, hunching over and trying to fold it down before the wind caught hold again and sent it up like a sail into the blustery sky. Finally, with a groan of satisfaction, she pushed it down into the laundry basket and replaced the smooth rock on top, her laundry paperweight – no one ever said living by a beach was easy. The pillowcases and knickers were easier to catch and she piled the rest of the load into the basket before hoisting it under her arm and ploughing her way back into the house.

Safely inside again, she sagged against the door with a sigh.

'Blowy out there today, then.'

She looked up – through her mass of tangled hair – to see Ben standing by the kitchen counter. He was leaning on his crutches and although still in his tracksuit (for he had no other clothes), he looked better than he had in days. His colour had returned and the pinched, pained look had left his face.

'Good morning! You're up.'

'Thought it was about time.' He looked surprisingly sheepish. 'I can't keep sleeping.'

'On the contrary, it's obviously what your body needed.' She had brought through his meal trays to the bedroom for the past day and a half but though he had tried to rouse himself into consciousness each time she knocked and mumbled his thanks, he always immediately fell back asleep again and everything had been left untouched. Occasionally she heard him shuffle to the bathroom, faint groans coming through the walls as he grappled with the pain in his leg and his hampered mobility, but he hadn't otherwise left the room.

'I didn't think the anaesthetic would hit me quite so hard,' he frowned.

Ottie smiled as she walked over and set the laundry basket down on the small kitchen table. 'Anaesthetic?' she grinned. 'You don't think it had anything to do with the fact that you had also spent a sleepless night clinging to an exposed cliff in a storm, and before that, put your body through an ultramarathon?'

'But I only ran thirty miles. I'd barely started.'

'Yeah, you're right. Only thirty miles? It couldn't be that,' Ottie quipped, wrinkling her nose.

He arched an eyebrow. '. . . You're laughing at me.'

Ottie pulled out one of the pillowcases and started smoothing it flat. 'Yes, Mr Gilmore. I am.'

'Hmm.' His not-quite smile hovered over his lips again. 'Would you like a coffee?'

'I'll get it,' she said, instantly dropping the laundry. But he stopped her with a hand.

'No. I can manage. It's time I make myself useful – even if it's just boiling a kettle.'

'But you don't need to.'

'Nor do you,' he said, looking at her directly, before turning away again and beginning to hobble over to the kettle. 'Just tell me where to look.'

'Well . . . the coffee's in the narrow cabinet to the right, there. And the cups are in the wall cupboard on the left.'

It was awkward for him. The crutches meant he needed both hands and couldn't walk with the kettle once he'd filled it, having to set it down ahead of himself on the counter, then pick up his crutches to draw level with it, only to set it forwards again.

'Please let me,' she said, watching with a grimace. It was actually painful to watch.

'No.' He flashed a tight smile her way. 'Thank you.'

Biting her lip and deciding it was better not to watch, she picked up the laundry and began folding again. 'You seem to be moving better.'

'Yes. The swelling's beginning to go down a bit now. I'm going to start some of the physio exercises today.' He had reached the kettle now and set it down on its boiling base triumphantly.

'Really? It's not too soon?'

He reached for the cups, which were thankfully positioned dead ahead. No walking required. 'The consultant said to start as soon I felt up to it. And the sooner I start getting back to normal, the sooner I can get on that plane and be out of your way.'

'It's really not a problem,' she smiled.

'I can't believe you're not desperate to have your bed back.' He glanced over at the sofa, pristinely made up with plumped cushions and the throw smoothed of any wrinkles. No one would ever guess it was doubling as a bed.

'It's actually surprisingly comfortable,' she lied, absently folding up her knickers before realizing what she was holding and stuffing them back in the basket again.

His gaze flickered away discreetly too. 'Hmm,' he murmured again, picking up his crutches and making his way over to the fridge. Ottie blanched at the thought of the odyssey that would be involved in getting the milk across the kitchen again, but she didn't dare intervene. He'd made it clear he wanted his independence, that he wanted to give back in some way. She had to let him do that.

'You don't have any pictures on the walls,' he said, reaching into the fridge for the milk. It was said more as a statement than a question.

'No.' She stared at the double-height white walls. Most people didn't notice – their eye always drawn to the ever-changing view outside – but they did look very bare. She glanced at him, and down again. He was astute. An observer. '. . . I guess I'm waiting for the perfect picture.'

'What kind of thing are you looking for?'

She shrugged, walking over to the narrow coat cupboard by the front door and pulling out the ironing board. 'I don't know,' she said vaguely, even though she did know. She knew exactly what she wanted to put there. She gave a tight smile. 'I figure I'll know it when I see it. It's hard to find anything that can compete with that view, that's the problem.'

'It is a hell of a view,' he agreed.

A knock at the door made them both look up. 'Oh. That'll be one of my sisters, no doubt,' she said, pulling the board up to full height, the frame ratcheting through the notches. 'I apologize in advance for anything offensive or insulting they might say or do. Especially Pip.'

He looked bemused. The knock came again.

'Ugh, that's definitely Pip. She never brings her keys,' she muttered, walking over the floor in her socks. 'Pip—' she moaned, opening the door.

'Jeesht, I always forget how beautiful y'are—'

'Mr Flanagan,' she said primly, quickly stepping back as Bertie's arms reached for her, her heart suddenly sky-rocketing in panic, surprise.

Bertie stalled for a moment, his arms held out in mid-air like he'd just missed catching a ball, as he tried to get up to speed with the situation.

'I was just telling Mr Gilmore I thought you must be Pip forgetting her keys again.'

'Mr Gil – ?' Bertie started quizzically, straightening up and entering the cottage. 'Mr Gilmore! Ben! You're *here*!' The happy surprise in his voice didn't quite reach his eyes. 'I wondered where you'd gone. The hospital told me you'd been discharged when I rang but they couldn't tell me where you were staying, of course. I just assumed you'd have gone back to the States.'

Ben nodded. 'Ottie very kindly offered a roof above my head while I get through this phase. I can't fly for a couple of weeks.'

'A couple of weeks,' Bertie repeated, and Ottie knew that was his ploy for buying time, trying to think fast and assess the situation.

'Thrombosis risk,' Ottie said shortly, shutting the door behind him. Now that the shock of finding him on her doorstep was abating, her anger with him was growing. They hadn't spoken in days – not since Sunday night, in the panic to find Ben. He would have known about her house guest if he'd bothered to reply to her texts; she had even dared a call on his home line last night and to her utter astonishment –

and horror – Shula had picked up and put her on to her own *mother* who was supposedly staying there!

She knew Bertie had to have seen her messages. They always kept communications simple – no hidden and spare phones; she was simply saved in his Contacts as *Dave Bridges, Butcher.* Bertie supplied Dave his pheasants, so she was hiding in plain sight if Shula ever happened to check his messages. 'Ben was just making a coffee. Would you like one?' she asked snappishly.

'Well, I don't want to intrude.'

'Intrude on what?' She was intrigued to see how uncomfortable he looked. 'We're just chatting.' He picked up the edge in her voice and she saw the retraction in his eyes. He knew he was in trouble.

'That would be great, then. Black, no sugar.'

Ottie felt a ripple of relief that it at least simplified the job for Ben – no extra trips to the fridge. He made the drinks quickly, and Bertie walked over to take his from him. 'So how *are* you getting on? It looks like you're moving about well.'

'Beginning to,' Ben nodded.

'Sleeping all right?'

'Too much, actually. I'm trying to cut back.'

'Nonsense. That's the body's defence and repair mechanism,' Bertie said assuredly. 'Listen to what your body's telling you to do.'

Ben's eyes flickered her way briefly. He looked distinctly uncomfortable. 'Well, on that note, I'm going to take this into my room. My leg's beginning to throb. I need to elevate it again.'

'Oh, but . . .' He'd only just come out of the room. Surely his sanity if nothing else needed a change of scene. On the other hand, Bertie was here . . . 'Here, let me take the cup through for you,' she said instead, darting over and taking the cup from his hands before he could protest.

'Really—'

'I insist. Hot liquids and a limp aren't a happy match.'

She set it down on the bedside table, hurriedly straightening the duvet and replumping the pillows for him as he hobbled through. At the very least, it would feel better to lie on a made bed. She ran through to the bathroom and refreshed the carafe of water by his bedside too. 'Shall I open the curtains for you?' she asked as he came through, the tortoise to her hare.

He nodded, sinking onto the bed wearily as she drew them open as wide as they would go. The window, although nowhere near as dramatic as the full-height one next door, faced down to the sea so at least he would have a view from bed.

She looked at him. He seemed to have become tense, his body hunched and closed. Was it the pain? He was on less than a third of his prescribed dose. 'Have you taken your medication?'

'No. I don't need it.'

His body language suggested otherwise. She sighed, knowing better than to push him on it. 'Well, are you quite sure you want to be back in here again? You've only just resurfaced.'

'Yes.' His voice sounded tight. Was the pain ratcheting up?

'It's no problem to sit in the living room. Bertie and I are just going over—'

'Race details?'

Ottie flinched at the edge in his voice. What did that mean?

Ben looked away. 'I'm fine. Really.'

'Well, just let me know if you need anything,' she said quietly, retreating from the room, his gaze just catching hers as the door closed. It reminded him of the first night she'd met him, that undefinable look in his eyes, as though he had a secret.

Bertie was on her immediately. 'What is he *doing* here?' he whispered, eyes wide and looking furious at the unexpected development.

But Ottie pressed a finger to her lips and shook her head firmly, fire in her eyes. 'Not here.'

They braced against the wind, bodies hunched and coats held close as they walked along the wet sand. The tide was going out, striating the beach with narrow grooves and leaving behind the now-usual detritus of the Atlantic Ocean. Ottie had her reusable plastic bag with her and kept bending every few yards to stuff in old water bottles, drinks cans, twists of fishing net, plastic lids . . .

'You can't do this,' Bertie said furiously. 'He's a complete stranger. You can't have him sleeping in your house.'

'No! *You* don't get to have it both ways – you don't get to withdraw all contact and still think you have a right to say who I can or cannot have to stay in my house.' She gave a scornful laugh. 'Besides, the guy can't move, Bertie! What do you think he's going to do? Strangle me in my sleep? Trust me, he'd have to ask for my help getting out of bed to do it first.'

Bertie stopped walking. 'And where are you sleeping if he's got the bed?'

Her mouth fell open in disbelief. He couldn't seriously think . . . 'The sofa! Where d'you think?'

'Okay, I was just asking,' he said, holding his hands up in surrender as he saw her shock continue to bloom across her face.

But he wasn't *just asking*. There had been suspicion in his voice. 'Notwithstanding the fact he is bodily broken at the moment, do you really think I'd just fall into bed with the guy?' she cried.

He looked away, anguished. 'No, I . . . Jeesht, no, of course not. It's just – you don't see how beautiful y'are. Any guy would be a fool not to act on any opportunity he got with you.'

She stared at him in disbelief. 'We're not all like you, Bertie,' she snapped. 'We don't all sleep with people just because we can.' The words were out before she could stop them and she stopped walking abruptly as she saw the spasm of pain cross his face. '. . . I didn't mean that.'

'Sure you did,' he said quietly. 'Once a cheater, always a cheater, right?'

She stared at him, wanting to wind back time, unsay what she'd said. 'No. You're not like that. We fell in love, it's different.' But her words were stiff – it was an explanation, not a pardon – and as he reached to take her in his arms, she pulled away, stalking over the sand away from him. He didn't get to play the hurt puppy.

He hurried to keep up with her, his body still stiff from the weekend. They walked in silence for a few strides, Ottie bending down to collect the numerous bottles, straws . . .

'Ottie, look, I keep getting it wrong, I know that. I shoulda come over before now.'

'Yeah, you shoulda.'

'And I know I was "off"the other night – but I was stressed out of my mind. I thought we were going to find a body.'

'Yeah. We all did.'

'But it's my company — my responsibility. My fault.'

'No. You made it quite clear it was all mine. I was the one

who stopped you from putting out the signs, remember? I was the one who ducked out for a loo break. It was all on me.'

'Darling, that's not true,' he protested, looking aghast.

'That's what you said. As if I needed to be told it! Don't you think I felt bad enough?'

'Otts, I'm sorry if I made you feel that way. It was never my intention. I was just strung out. Please, forgive me?' His eyes searched hers but she looked away. She *couldn't* forgive him just like that. His accusations that night had hurt her not because they were true but because he was supposed to be her protector, not prosecutor. 'Of course I understand why you're doing this for Gilmore. You're too good-hearted—'

She wheeled around to face him again. 'I'm not doing this out of the kindness of my heart, Bertie. That man nearly died because of me! I couldn't just leave him. He's a continent away from home. No one's rung or come to see him. This is guilt, plain and simple – something you and I are both very well acquainted with.'

The unnamed mention of his wife made them both step back. Shula was always there between them, like a third shadow. For five years now, Ottie had lived with the duplicity and the lies that came with their affair because she loved this man. Being with him was the only time she could feel happy, herself, free: she went to bed at night wanting to dream of him and awoke hoping to see him. She scarcely dared leave the cottage in case she missed a visit from him and her every waking thought was dominated by wondering when she would see him next, when they could finally tell the world the truth and they could be free to live as they both wanted to. They had sneaked around trying not to hurt other people – Shula, her father, her mother – but how much longer could she go on waiting? Her heart ached for a normal life. She felt like a shell every time she had to see him in public – with Shula – and greet him as a family friend; it depleted her, having to pretend to everyone that she was happily single when all she wanted was to shout from the rooftops that she was radiantly in love with a man who felt the same. He was her drug and she couldn't pretend to be a victim when a man had almost died because of her blinkered, fevered need to get her next fix of him.

She turned to face him, the wind catching her hair and streaming it across her face yet again, but he caught and held it back with his fingers. 'We can't go on like this Bertie. People are getting hurt.'

He stared back at her, panic gathering in his eyes. 'Oh Christ, don't ask this of me Ottie. Don't ask me to give you up. If I was a stronger man, a better man—'

'No. I'm not saying that. I don't want anyone else. I want you.' She stepped in closer so that their bodies were touching, their coats flapping against each other and she closed her eyes as he clasped her head and kissed her finally. He tasted of coffee and marmalade. 'But I want us to be together – properly. I need it. I can't carry on like this. I'm tired of all the lies.'

'I know, so am I. And we will be, I promise.'

'When?'

'Soon.'

'When's soon?' she pressed. 'You always said we could never tell because of Dad; you said it would destroy him. But . . .' She couldn't say the words. She didn't need to.

'I know. I know,' he said quickly, rubbing her arms, the guilt curled up in his face like a fat cat.

'You have to tell Shula. It's the kindest thing to do. Your marriage may be dead, but she's an attractive woman; let her be free to find someone new, start over again. You owe her that. At least let her find the happiness we've found.'

He looked away, staring into the pounding waves. 'You have the conviction of youth, Ottie. Everything's easier when you have nothing to lose.'

'I have *everything* to lose,' she cried. 'You are my world. I base my entire life around you, waiting here for you, waiting for one night or twenty minutes with you – I never know what I'm going to get, or when.'

He ran his hands through his hair. 'I know, it's not fair on either of you. I'm in an impossible situation. I don't want to hurt her but I can't lose you.'

'You have to choose, you know that. We've been in this holding pattern for too long now. I want more. I want to be with you. To live with you. To wake up beside you every morning.'

He clasped her face and kissed her again, urgently. 'And I want that too,' he murmured, and she could feel his passion for her.

'So then do it. Tell Shula and make the break.' Her breath was hot upon his neck.

'I will, I promise.'

'Soon?'

'Yes.'

'By Christmas.'

His mouth parted in surprise. 'I—'

'I want us to wake up together on Christmas morning, Bertie. I can be your present to unwrap and you can be mine . . .' He moaned as she pressed herself closer to him and moved her hand inside his coat. 'Promise me. Tell me we'll be together by Christmas . . . Tell me . . .'

His eyes closed and he nodded as her hands moved to where he wanted them to be, her kisses covering his neck. 'I promise. We'll be together by Christmas.'

Chapter Twenty

'Same again, Joe,' Pip said, sliding her glass back across the counter to him.

'You're thirsty tonight,' the publican said mildly, glancing up at her as he pulled another pint.

'Aye, well, I've been working hard, haven't I?' It was Friday, but her first night back in the pub all week.

'Playing hard too, from what I heard . . . Glad you're okay.'

Glad you're okay. Code for 'glad you didn't die.' Pip rolled her eyes at the classic local understatement. Fuss wasn't tolerated well here. 'Ta.'

He pushed the pint back towards her but refused to take her cash, again. The first one had been on the house. 'Phil Meenahan,' he said, nodding towards the carpenter playing pool.

'Thanks, Phil!' she called over, holding up the pint.

'Aye-aye!' he called back with a cheery wave.

'Anyone would think you were liked around here,' Joe quipped, his eyes darting to the door as it opened and a couple of workmen came in. 'What'll it be, fellas?' he asked them, wandering up the bar.

Pip turned her head and looked over her shoulder, taking in the cosy scene in her local. It was especially busy in here tonight. It wasn't a fancy gastro place, nor did it have any of the twee decorations of some country pubs, with hops dangling from the rafters or rusted old threshers and harnesses pinned to the walls, although Joe and his mother had made a start on Christmas decorations – loops of tinsel held in place with Blu Tack and bunches of holly in pint glasses on the tables. The place was unpretentious: bright white walls that advertised the cleanliness of the place; rickety dark-wood tables that almost never stood flat on the flagged stone floor; an inglenook chimney with a couple of bench seats built in at the sides and a winder still visible up the stack from where they used to smoke the ham. There were never any specials and to her knowledge, an avocado or '*keenwah*' had never been on the menu. But there were punters at almost every table, most of them locals; the small size of the village meant pretty much everyone could walk – stagger – home.

She'd been invited by a couple of people to join them as she came in, but whilst she hadn't wanted to spend another night alone at home, she didn't particularly want to speak much to anyone either. She felt unlike herself, dislocated and rattled, as though on edge somehow. A little bit of low-key chat with the barman was all she really felt up to.

She shivered, wondering why she was cold. Someone had said snow was predicted but even so, the fire was roaring – Joe always made sure the embers were glowing before he even opened the doors in the morning; forget a dart board, don't bother with Sky access, he always said there was nothing that made people kick off their shoes and settle in for the night like a crackling fire.

The door opened again as more punters came in. It was approaching peak happy hour, six thirty on a Friday night. She stared down at the grain of the wood as they came to the bar and ordered. She was particularly well acquainted with this particular knot; it was her usual spot – out of the draught of the door, not so close to the fire as to make her beer warm.

'Pint, thanks.'

She looked up at the voice. Or rather, the accent. It wasn't local.

A guy in hobnailed boots and rip-stop workman trousers was standing there, drumming his fingers lightly on the bar like they were rhythm sticks. He had a thick dark beard that made his teeth look very white, shaggy dark hair and brown eyes, a tattoo peeking out of his cuffs.

Pip felt an interested smile grow on her lips.

'Hey,' he nodded, noticing her sidelong attention.

'Hey.'

He smiled, and hesitated. 'Would you . . . ?'

'Got one, thanks,' she said, tapping the pint glass between her clasped hands.

'Ah.' He looked back at the upturned spirit bottles on the bar but seemed to be holding his breath. There was a pregnant pause before he turned back again with another smile. '. . . I'm Jack, by the way.'

'Pip.'

'Pip? Cute name.'

Pip narrowed her eyes. No one had ever called her cute before. She decided she rather liked it and smiled. 'I heard your accent. Wicklow, was it?'

'That's right. We're just down for a few days. Got a big job on at the castle at the moment.'

'Oh?' She raised an eyebrow.

'D'you know it?'

Her smile grew as her amusement factor went up. She could see Joe was listening in on their conversation as he pulled

Jack's pint. 'Sure, everyone knows the castle round here. I hear they're doing a lot of work up there at the moment.'

Jack whistled through his white teeth. 'That's putting it lightly. They'd be better off pulling it down and rebuilding, if you ask me.'

'It's pretty old, though,' she frowned. 'Quite a historic building. It'd be a shame to lose it.'

He shrugged. 'Old is cold. No one lives like that any more, do they?'

Joe passed him his beer and threw an amused glance her way as Jack handed him the fiver.

'Cheers,' Jack said to her as he lifted his pint to his lips.

'Cheers,' Pip said, watching his eyes close as he took the first thirsty sip. Maybe this was what she was missing, she mused. It had been ages since she'd last fallen into bed with someone. Somehow, the guys she met seemed increasingly less worth the bother.

'So, Jack, what is it you're doing up at the castle?'

'I'm a tube monkey.'

'A what now?'

'Scaffolder,' he grinned.

'Ah.' His body was angling towards her now, solidifying the exchange from a chat into a conversation.

'Yeah, they're patching the roof.'

'I heard it was in pretty poor condition,' she said, wrinkling her nose conspiratorially.

'I don't know how it's still up,' he shrugged. 'Willpower?'

'Stubbornness, I should imagine. The owners are known for it.'

'Yeah? You've met them?'

'Loads of times,' she nodded, able to see Joe in the corner of her eye, chuckling away quietly to himself.

'Don't tell me – they're stuck-up, right?'

'Oh my God, the worst,' she breathed heavily, like he'd stumbled on to a grave secret.

'The gaffer sees it all the time –'

It took Pip a moment to understand what he meant. Boss?

'– These old families trading on past glories, but they've got no money, no nous, no idea how to live in the real world.'

'I can imagine.'

Joe, reaching for some glasses, threw his head back in silent laughter, but Jack had his back to him. Punters were coming in thick and fast now, driven in by the plummeting temperatures, but she scarcely noticed. The pub was filling up around them.

Jack took another sip of his drink, his gaze coming to rest on her interestedly. 'And what do you do?'

'Me? Oh –' She blew out through her cheeks. 'I run the local riding stables.'

'Ah-huh,' he nodded, leaning back slightly and taking in her filthy navy jodhpurs, boots, industrial fleece. 'A woman who's not afraid to get her hands dirty, I see.'

'I *love* getting my hands dirty,' she said flirtatiously.

'And so, what – do people keep their horses with you, or . . . how does it work?'

'No, the horses are all mine. I run trekking expeditions – full-week holidays down the coast, day trips, family excursions, Scouts and Guides, outward bound clubs, you name it . . .'

'Sounds like you're doing a lot of work with kids.'

'They're harder workers than their parents, I find.'

'Well, perhaps I'll get to see it before I go. I've always liked horses.'

'Yeah? Do they like you?'

He laughed. 'Usually.' His eyes were shining; they both knew what was going on here.

'So where are you staying?' she asked mildly, tapping her conspicuously bare ring finger lightly against her glass.

'Here actually. Upstairs.'

'Oh. I hear the rooms are nice.'

'They are. They are.' He looked down into his drink before looking at her again. 'You've never seen them?'

She shook her head. 'Nope.'

'Well, you should. They're . . .' His gaze fell to her lips. 'Nice—'

'Pip!'

The voice made her turn on her stool. What?

'Oh jeesht, you have *got* to be kidding me,' she muttered as she saw Taigh pushing his way through the crowd towards her.

'Everything okay?' Jack asked, seeing how she dropped her head into her hand, trying to hide her face.

'Pip, Jesus, where've you been?' Taigh demanded as he got to her.

'What do you mean?' she mumbled in her best bored voice.

'Didn't Willow tell you? I've been trying to track you down all week. You weren't at the flat, in the stables, at—'

'Yes, all right, I get the picture,' she said quickly, not wanting him to mention the castle. 'You've found me now. What is it?'

He looked taken aback by her abrupt tone, as he always did, as though her rudeness to him was something he forgot about between meetings. 'I just need to do that quick check-up on you. Don't you remember? We talked about it. That crackle—'

'Oh dear God, not the bloody crackle again,' she snapped.

'I am clearly fine, Taigh! Look at me – I'm out having a few drinks, with my friend Jack here—'

Taigh started, as though surprised to see the big man standing there.

'Hey,' Jack said, holding his pint and watching on interestedly.

'Hey,' Taigh muttered in reply, turning back to her. 'Look, I just need to sign you off, that's all.'

'Don't need it, I'm fine.'

But Taigh was scrutinizing her. 'Your eyes are bright.'

'Yeah, because I *was* having a nice time before you turned up.'

He put the back of his hand on her forehead. 'And you're burning up.'

'I am n— Jeesht!' She slapped his hand off her. 'Get your hands off me.'

Jack took a step in towards him. He said nothing but there was implicit threat in the move.

'I am trying to help you,' Taigh laughed in disbelief, stepping back nonetheless.

'And when will you get it through your thick skull that I don't want your help? I am fine.'

Taigh looked at Jack. 'She nearly drowned last weekend.'

'I did no— Pah!' she scoffed. 'Christ, you'd make a song and dance out of anything, Taigh O'Mahoney.'

'You nearly drowned and now you've got a chest infection. You need antibiotics.'

'If I'm feeling unwell I'll go to a proper doctor, thanks.'

Jack frowned. 'So you're *not* a doctor?' he asked Taigh.

'He's the postman!' Pip said scornfully.

'I'm a fully qualified paramedic,' Taigh said, looking angry now. 'It's postmaster duties that are part-time.'

'*And* he's a part-time fireman!' Pip said sarcastically. 'Just has to be helping people any way he can. Can't help himself.'

Taigh stared at her with a look she'd never seen in his eyes before. Gone was the happy-go-lucky, twinkly eyed lad everyone round here knew and loved. He looked furious. Pushed too far. 'Fine! Get pneumonia then. Get a collapsed lung.'

'I will!' she said defiantly, throwing back the rest of her drink and slamming down the glass on the bar. 'And seeing as I'm so damned lucky to be alive, I may as well start bloody celebrating it! Come on, Jack.'

Jack looked back at her in surprise. 'Huh?'

'You were going to show me your room?'

'Oh yes. Right.' And he downed his pint too.

She grabbed his hand and pushed past Taigh with a victorious look. 'Tell you what, Taigh – I'll let you know if he makes me wheeze, shall I?'

Willow stood at the bottom of the stairs and looked around the great hall, dumbstruck by the newly revealed space. Everyone had left for the day – even though it was a Saturday – bags of tools lying squat in every corner, dustsheets thrown over the floors. It was hard to believe how much had changed in just three days.

Every item of furniture, every memento that had been theirs, was now gone, either packed up in storage or relocated to the Dower House. All that remained were the bones of the place, and what bones they were: sculpted, fine, durable. She had never even noticed the carving on the corbels before or the ornate stone pediments. She had barely bothered to look up at the hammer-beam ceilings or to take a moment to admire the heraldic coat of arms painted on shields. Rusty, her father's beloved ancestral suit of armour, had seemed a part of the fabric of the house but he had been simply lifted up and carried out like a hoover, the floor and wall behind where he had stood faded from years of his stolid protection. Her home was like a soprano in her dressing room after the performance – make-up wiped off, clothes on the chair, hair pulled down round a pale face.

Was the castle breathing now? Was this what Connor had wanted to see – the Lornes' historic might stripped back to a naked beating heart?

She sighed, the mere thought of him distracting her from the moment and spinning her back into the past again – the heat in his eyes Saturday night, the shock on Monday, the guardedness as he'd come clean on Tuesday, the way he'd stopped talking to his workmen, gaze following her as she'd walked past with the last of the remaining boxes for the Dower House yesterday . . .

She dropped her head and stared at her feet. She wiggled her toes in her boots but couldn't see them beneath the thick leather. If a toe wiggles in a boot but no one can see it, did the toe really wiggle at all, she wondered? And if a woman kisses a stranger at a party but it turns out he's buying her castle, did the kiss really happen at all? Because in spite of the undercurrent that ran between them, entire conversations being spoken by eyes and not mouths, they'd been true to their word. *There is no us*. How could there be when there was four point three million at stake for her and the solubility of his company for him? Neither one of them could afford for this deal to go wrong.

Slowly, she began climbing the stairs, looking around in amazement at how the castle looked so dramatically different from every angle – high, low – its history as a fortification suddenly coming to the fore now that the soft comforts of domestic life had been stripped out.

From the galleried landing, she looked down. How many times had she stood here with her sisters, watching the shenanigans playing out below? Back then the parties had been frequent – every weekend, it had seemed to her – the three little girls swinging their legs through the bannisters and eating sweets as they watched the flirting and dancing, admired the beautiful dresses and jewels, the men sometimes in their dark kilts. How she had longed to grow up. Willow wondered if she was the only one of her sisters disappointed by the reality of being an adult. She went to enough parties herself these days, but the dazzling glitter and fuzzy edges that had seemed to frame her world view back then had gone, leaving only dull colours and hard shapes. Gilded moments such as she had known here were rare.

A sound at the front door made her look up. A carpenter forgetting something? One of the painters? She tutted irritably. She had deliberately come up to the castle late, waiting for everyone to have left before she saw for herself what her home had become. She didn't want an audience as she saw it gutted, for the first time certainly in her life, and she was glad to have had that moment to herself. Aside from being emptied and clad in scaffolding, half of the bedrooms had already been stripped of their country-house chintz and were being whitewashed. The teams weren't touching the silk wallpapers and jewel paint colours of the entertaining rooms downstairs; she had stipulated that at least. Not until the castle was officially sold to them.

Either way, coming in here this evening had been a shock. It wasn't that the castle didn't look better – it did. But already it didn't feel like home. The transition had begun and she didn't know how her mother was going to react when she saw it – apart from badly.

The sound of the lock turning and footsteps on the flags made her fall still and her elevated position meant she got to see him before he saw her; she got to see how he visibly retracted at the sight of her.

'Oh. I thought everyone had gone,' Connor said.

'Everyone has.'

'There were no cars outside so I assumed—'

'I walked up from the Dower House.'

He took his gaze off her like he was lifting a picture off a hook and scanned the space. 'So what do you think?'

'What do *you* think?' she countered.

'I think it looks a lot better.'

'I can't believe how much they've done already,' she shrugged.

'Yes. They're efficient.'

Efficient? He did like his understatement. 'I see what you mean now about SWAT team,' she said. 'I assumed you'd been exaggerating.'

He looked up at her, his body still and she had to force herself to stay standing on the spot, not to run down the stairs to him. 'I never exaggerate.'

'Still think you'll get it all done by next weekend?'

'We're on target, yes,' he nodded. 'Although I realize it may not look like it at the moment. Top coats tomorrow—'

'They're working on a *Sunday* too?'

'Needs must,' he shrugged. 'It means double pay but we've got to pull everything out of the bag to get it done on time. Woodwork's getting done Monday and Tuesday; scaffolding down and furniture in through Wednesday; caterers and staff in Thursday. Officially open first thing Friday, although the guests aren't due till late afternoon so we'll have an extra few hours for snagging.'

He looked up at her again, his focus seeming to shift, and she felt a small ball of tension gather in the pit of her stomach. She watched as he began walking up the staircase, the treads creaking underfoot because he didn't know – yet – which ones rubbed and which ones didn't. And maybe he never would; the problem might simply be fixed by one of his two hundred-strong army and fastened back into perfect silence. He would never know this place the way she did.

She realized she was holding her breath as he walked up to the landing; it was like getting closer to the sun, the heat building exponentially as he walked towards her . . .

Past her, his eyes grazing over her like a breeze.

'Where are you going?' she asked after him, feeling the cool chill of his wake.

'To see what the guys have done today.' He disappeared into the green room or, rather, what *used* to be the green room – crashing disappointment flooding her. He emerged again a minute later. 'Can you help with something?'

She walked over, stepping into the room that had always been her grandmother's when she had come to stay. She had liked getting the morning light as she always woke so early anyway – she said it made the nights feel shorter to see the dawn rays creeping up the wall. 'What is it?'

'What's this, do you know?' Connor was crouched down, pointing to a small perfectly round hole in the floor, set almost up to the outside wall. It had been hidden for years behind a rosewood armoire.

She squatted beside him, bemused. How could he not know this? 'That's a *meurtrière*. Or murder hole.'

'A mur—?' He looked down at it again.

'It was a secondary line of defence for when the castle was breached – which it only was four times in seven hundred years. They'd throw burning tar, oil, wax, you name it, on invaders downstairs.'

'A *murder* hole,' he repeated, looking back at her with a grin. She wished he wouldn't; he was so close.

She stood up, and he followed. 'This is a castle, remember.'

A light shone in his eyes from the discovery, boyish delight animating his usually aloof demeanour. 'Any other architectural peccadilloes I should know about?'

'Numerous. There are three of those across each wing. Then there's the sally port down by the postern—'

'The sally –' he echoed, watching her talk, his gaze blowing over her face like a feather dancing in the breeze.

'The priest's hole off the morning room. The secret tunnel from the library.'

He looked at her, intensity in his eyes, and for a moment, it was like he forgot to speak, a silence sitting where words were due. '. . . This place has a hell of a past.'

'And a bright future too,' she said simply, breaking the spell and moving away. How easy it would be to fall into him; the effort *not* to was making her sway.

He carried on looking at her and it was like he could rev up her heart, making it go faster and faster . . .

She took another step back. 'Anyway, look, I should go. I was just about to leave—'

'Willow, wait.'

'What?' she asked from the safety of the doorway.

He hesitated. 'I'm staying at the Hare tonight. If you're free we could . . . have a drink together? Get some dinner? Talk shop.'

She stared at him, wanting exactly that and nothing else: air with him. A drink with him. A meal with him. A night with him. The everyday and mundane became somehow vital with him. He was an alchemist, making the air shimmer, her skin tingle.

'Besides, it's our anniversary,' he added with a smile as her hesitation lengthened. 'A week today since we met.'

Was it really a week since she had first set eyes on him? A week since *those* kisses that saw her press her fingers to her lips every time she thought of them? A week since Pip had gone for a midnight swim? Almost three since her father had died? Life was changing faster than she could keep up. She had struck a notional deal on her home, stripped out in a few days a castle her family had occupied for seven centuries. All her anchors were gone. The ground felt like it had been whipped from beneath her feet and she wasn't sure if she was flying or falling.

He walked over to her and looked into her eyes.

It was both.

The Hare was heaving, locals jostling for a spot at the bar with the vast influx of workers drafted in to the castle works, Joe and Betty, his mother, working at full stretch to keep the orders coming.

'Perhaps this wasn't the best place to come to,' Connor said, as yet another workman passed by their table with his hands full of pints, tipping the boss a knowing wink as he passed.

'Actually, I think it's perfect,' she demurred, relieved to have an audience. They clearly couldn't trust themselves. The moment that had passed between them at the castle . . . it had been too close.

They were sitting at the table between the window and the fire. The windows were fogged up but the lights of the Christmas tree that had been erected on the village green shone through indistinctly. The festive fairies had been at work inside the pub too, bushy strands of red and green tinsel swagged along the beams and walls, bunches of holly and snowberries tacked to the mirrored bar, a slightly too large tree in the corner near the loos, the top having been hacked off and the angel bending forward at a precarious angle.

'What do you recommend?' he asked her, scanning the menu.

'The beef. Joe gets it from Paddy Mahoney, down the lane at Finnegan's.'

'Does he now? And if I ordered the lamb?'

'From Bob and Liz at Fairgreen Farm, the other side of the village.'

'Chicken?'

She pulled a face. 'That gets shipped in, I'm afraid.'

'Where from?'

'Cork.'

'All the way from there?' he teased.

'I know. Shocking.'

'How about the . . . pheasant?'

'Bertie Flanagan's estate. Always good.'

He put the menu down and studied her. 'It's a tight-knit place here then.'

'It is. Everyone knows everyone.'

'And everyone's business too?'

She shrugged. 'Of course.'

'So us having dinner here will be seen as . . . ?'

'A business meeting. With food. I'm simply telling you the local suppliers you need to tap if you want to run a restaurant in your new club.' She gave another casual shrug but the words felt funny to say. Her castle – her home – a clubhouse.

'I see.' His finger tapped lightly against his pint, condensation trickling down the side of it as the fire crackled and popped beside them.

'Oh, hey, Willow.'

She looked up to find Taigh shrugging off his coat as he came in. His cheeks were flushed and he wasn't in a uniform for once.

'Hi, Taigh. Off duty?'

'Thank *God*. There'd better be a beer barrel down here with my name on it.' His eyes glanced at Connor questioningly.

'Oh, this is Connor Shaye. He's . . . hiring the castle for a function next week. We're just discussing logistics.'

Taigh reached over to shake his hand. 'Hey.'

'Hey,' Connor replied.

'You've got a big team working for you,' he said, nodding his head towards the full bar.

'There's a lot to do. It makes for thirsty work.'

'Taigh, by the way, did you catch up with Pip?' she asked, taking a sip of her gin and tonic.

'No. Well, last night but –' His expression changed, his bright, open face darkening. 'I'm afraid I gave up there. She wasn't having any of it and I've got better things to do than try to convince her otherwise.'

Willow wrinkled her nose. 'Oh, I'm sorry. She's stubborn as a mule when she wants to be.'

'Aye . . .' He looked uncomfortable. 'Well, I'd best sharpen my elbows and go into battle for my pint. Jeesht, it's busy . . . See you anon.'

She turned her attention back to Connor. 'Pip's the most bloody-minded—' She stopped as she saw how he was looking at her. 'What?'

'Nothing. I was just wondering what you'll do when you've sold here. You seem pretty embedded into the place.'

'My family is, but I'll go back to Dublin. Frankly, it can't come soon enough.'

'You don't miss it here?'

'Nope,' she said quickly. 'Life is good for me in the big smoke. I work five minutes from where I live. Great bars. Good friends. it's a good set up. Work–life balance, all that stuff.'

'Where d'you work?'

'Pyro Tink.'

'Oh yeah, I've heard of that place. Got a lot of friends that go there. I hear things get pretty sweaty.'

'They can do.' She looked straight at him. 'You should try it some time.'

'Do you teach the classes?'

'God no!' she laughed. 'I'm just happy to survive them. The Rebel class saved my life.' That was no word of a lie. The intense and punishing sessions had been the only thing to help her vent her rage when she'd first turned up in the city – damaged and hell-bent on self-destruction.

'So then do you own it?'

'No. I'm the manager there.'

'Ah.'

He nodded but she sensed disappointment in the movement. 'We can't all be entrepreneurs,' she said defensively.

'Why not? You're clearly a fine businesswoman.'

'Hardly!'

'You've pinned me down to a deal that's several hundred thousand more than I wanted to pay. And a lot more than I was going to pay your father.'

She blinked. 'Really?'

He shrugged. 'You had me on the ropes. I wanted to buy and you caught me at a time when I was in no position to cut a hard bargain. I had to either agree to your terms or lose out altogether.' His finger tapped against his glass as he watched her.

'That's down to timing then, not any astute business sense on my part.'

'You're doing yourself down.'

She shrugged. 'I think it's best to know your limitations and accept them.'

He leaned in to her slightly. 'I'm not so good at accepting limits.' His eyes held her in a lock and she felt the tension between them thicken again. All the time they were sitting here, chatting, and what they *weren't* saying seemed to just get louder and louder.

'Hey, Willow.'

She looked up again to see the O'Finlan lad passing by. His family had managed the landscaping on the estate for three generations now. 'Hey, Tommy.'

Connor sat back with a smile, allowing her to breathe again. 'I'm really not sure that I believe you.'

'About what?'

'Leaving here without a backwards glance.'

'Mentally and emotionally, I've already left. I'm only here to get Dad's affairs wound up.'

'Don't you like it here?'

'Of course I do. It was my home.'

'Was?'

'And now Dublin is.' She stared into her drink, wishing he'd stop pushing.

No such luck. 'Why did you go?'

She looked back at him. 'Why does anyone leave a place like this?'

'Excitement and adventure. Chasing fortune.' He watched her. 'Or because they can't stay.'

'Well, there you go then. Take your pick.'

'You couldn't stay.' He looked at her thoughtfully. 'Let me guess. Bad break-up?'

'No, nothing like that.'

'So you don't have a boyfriend?'

Her eyes flashed up to his angrily. 'Do you think I would have kissed you if I did?'

Their gazes locked again and she felt the floor drop, just like that.

'Willow—'

She swallowed, cutting him off, knowing just from his tone, his look, what he wanted to say. 'We're talking shop, remember?'

There was a reluctant pause. 'Sure.' He took another sip of his drink. 'So then tell me about your sisters. There's Pip and . . . ?'

'That's not talking shop.'

'On the contrary, it's good practice to know who you're doing business with. First rule of entrepreneurialism.' He flashed her a smile that made her head spin.

She couldn't help but smile back. 'Well, you've met Pip. She's the middle one of us – two years older than me, pretty wild, as you saw. Does her own thing, doesn't understand the words "Stop" or "No". A real tomboy. Nuts about horses.'

'But not leather trousers.'

'No. Definitely not.' She grinned at the image, just as she noticed how many people were glancing over at them, seeming intrigued by their tête-à-tête. Why? Everyone knew he was hiring her castle.

'And your other sister?'

'Ottie?' She brought her attention back to him again. 'She's three years older than me. She's the one who should have inherited the estate, not me. She pretty much ran it with Dad.'

His brow furrowed. 'So why didn't she get it then?'

Willow gave a stiff shrug. They were back on dangerous territory again.

'Do you think your dad was trying to lure you back here, perhaps? Giving someone a castle estate is a hell of a way to tie them down to a place.'

'No. I think he just knew that I'd be able to do what had to be done and sell up. He knew I'm not as attached.' Her voice had grown hard. Flinty.

'So Ottie's more sentimental?'

'I guess. She's a creative type, ruled by her heart, not her head.'

'It sounds like I've got the toughest sister then.' His eyes flashed to hers. 'To negotiate with, I mean.' But the subtext crackled like an electric current across the table.

A man walked past the table. 'All right, Connor?' he asked cheerily, but there was a knowing tone in his voice. Innuendo.

Connor looked up and gave a wary nod.

'I'm afraid people are staring at us,' she murmured, taking another sip of her drink.

'Why?'

She rolled her eyes. 'Because it's a small village and everyone talks.'

'Would you rather go somewhere more private?'

She almost spat out her drink again. 'No!'

'Why not? My room's just upstairs. We could eat up there.'

She looked at him, feeling her heart pound. 'You know why.' They wouldn't eat up there and they both knew it.

'Willow . . . I'm not interested in idle gossip.'

She supposed not. There was plenty of society coverage of him with different women at different places, and never any sort of public comment as to who they were to him. 'That's because you're not from here but my family *is* this place. Nothing goes unrecorded.'

'So? Is it really so wrong for us to be sitting here together?'

'No. Not sitting here. Having a business meeting.'

'And what if it wasn't a business meeting? What if I really was trying to get you upstairs? Would they get a veto on that?'

'Are you?'

'Yes.'

The simplicity of his reply snatched the breath from her as his hand reached out, his fingertips touching hers. 'It's no one else's business what happens between us.'

She looked at him, shaken. 'There is no us.'

'You keep saying that.'

'Because we agreed.'

'Saying it doesn't make it true. We both know it's a lie. This had already started between us before we knew who each other was, and it's still there now . . . It's not going to go away, Willow. Frankly, it would be a lot *less* distracting if we could just stop fighting it.'

She stared at him, seeing how his gaze fell to her lips, feeling the heat coming from his hand, his thigh beside hers under the table. Was love at first sight real? Because her heart was telling her to run up the stairs with him. To submit to the inevitable. To surrender. But her head . . . 'Nothing can happen,' she said flatly. 'There's too much at stake. If things were to go wrong before the sale . . .'

She couldn't afford to be stuck here, saddled with a castle she couldn't sell and a mother she couldn't love. Her life was in Dublin now and she had to get back there, as soon as she possibly could. Before it left her behind.

'But why should they go wrong?'

'Because these things always go wrong,' she said stiffly.

He smiled with his eyes, so confident and persuasive. 'Unless they stay right.'

'They never do.' Her words here like a guillotine, final and sharp.

He frowned, staring at her quizzically. 'Wow, I wouldn't have taken you for such a cynic.'

'I'm just a realist,' she replied, her chest feeling tight as though ropes were trapped around it.

He tapped a finger against his glasses thoughtfully, his eyes roaming her face, as though considering her afresh. 'What was his name?'

'Who?'

'The guy who pulled the number on you.'

She felt the world tip on its side again, everything sliding, falling out of place. She wouldn't discuss this. It wasn't chit-chat. She grabbed her coat and went to shuffle off the bench. 'I've got to go,' she muttered.

'Willow, wait,' he said, startled, moving to stop her but she was already out of reach. 'I didn't mean to –' He gave a bewildered laugh but she felt her cheeks burning as she shrugged on her coat. It was no laughing matter to her – the lies, hollow vows, broken promises . . . 'Look, I'm sorry, I didn't realize you felt that way. Are you honestly telling me you don't believe in true love and happy endings?'

'Yes, Connor,' she said in a low, dark voice, her heart like a fireball, burning her up. 'That's exactly what I'm saying.'

Chapter Twenty-One

Wednesday, 18 December

The clapboarded door was open, pinned back against the stone walls, but there was little breeze today and with a thickly wound scarf at her neck, ribbed beanie and fingerless mittens, Ottie was warm enough to work in just her canvas tunic. The easel stood propped at an angle, giving her a view of the beach, the long sable brush held lightly between her fingers. Some days – the good days – painting was like a meditation, not a conscious *doing* but rather a gentle lapse into *being*; those were the days when the hours slipped by like melting ice cream, when even Bertie fell from her thoughts and she could access that quiet part of herself that was otherwise crushed by life. Everything else ceased to matter.

Usually at this time of year, due to the biting cold and often driving rain, she brought her supplies upstairs and into the house, painting by the window instead, but that wasn't an option with a house guest. It felt good, anyway, to throw open the boat-store door and get some air into the place; it quickly became musty without a proper blow.

She worked at the easel, feeling her body and mind harmonize; soothe. The canvas was to her what the mat was to Willow, and the saddle to Pip. When her mind was racing and her emotions felt too big to control, it always brought her back into herself – and right now, she needed that. She hadn't been down here since her father had died precisely because it had felt *too* dangerous to tap into her raw self; to acknowledge and feel those conflicting emotions of grief and anger that had threatened to overwhelm her since his death. If the past few weeks had taught her anything, it was that life was short, it was hard, and it could be cruel; it had shown her that she had to seize what happiness she had and grasp it with both hands, not hide it behind her back or ball it up into pockets. It had shown her that Bertie needed to leave his wife or Ottie needed to leave him. Either way, the next stage of her life had to begin.

She stepped back and looked at the canvas, tucking her hair behind her ear thoughtfully. For once, she liked what she saw – the vivid brushstrokes swept across in purposeful strides, thick layers and globules of oils building up on the canvas like Christmas cake icing. Her landscape felt intense, visceral, three-dimensional . . .

Her eyes grazed the painted curlicue beach again, thick tufts of colour-stripped grass in the foreground, the ancient mass of the distant hills sonorous in the background. Usually her palette was dominated by oxide of chromium, cobalt chromite, Prussian green, raw umber, Davy's grey, perylene black . . . 'Moody colours,' Bertie had said once, when she'd shown them to him. 'Like a nasty bruise.'

Today, though, she had reached for Cadmium Red Deep, dabbing a dot of it into the scene. Her eyes rose from the canvas to real life, at the walker crossing the sand wearing a red windcheater. It wasn't Ben – he was at the physio's, Seamus having picked him up half an hour ago and giving her a good hour to herself before he would be due back again – but he was so often out there, her eyes saw him anyway.

Whenever the tide was out, he would hobble down the track onto the wet sand. It was firmer underfoot than on the dry sand but still not the stable surface he should have been training on and every few steps his crutch would pierce and drop into the sand, like an arrow through ice, making him twist awkwardly. His knee brace would look bulky even from this distance, strapped on above his jogging bottoms, but he was down to using just one crutch already, his superior fitness and strength helping his body heal rapidly, his high pain threshold propelling him to push harder than most other patients in his position.

Some days, he would stand at the window, waiting for the tide to recede, like a dog sitting by the door, waiting for its walk. Although he was recovering fast, it still wasn't fast enough for his liking: he was a restless patient, irritated and almost unnerved by his uncharacteristic dependency. He was sleeping completely normal hours now, his body having finally recovered from the dual challenges of surgery and the extreme endurance test he had willingly put himself through. In fact, she suspected he was waking earlier than her now most mornings, but he stayed in the room until he heard her moving about, clearing away the bed sheets, and could be sure she was dressed.

She'd been surprised by what easy company he was to have around. The taciturn manner she had initially taken to be unfriendly she saw now was simply reserved; he wasn't given to unwarranted smiles or platitudes and he didn't go in for fuss or hyperbole. But he was interesting and rather funny, with a wry sense of humour, and they had fallen into something of a habit, spending the evenings chatting as they ate and cleared away the dishes, then playing cards – he was a decent poker player but, much to his respect, she was a fiend: her father had taught her and her sisters, saying no man would ever take money off his daughters. One evening, watching telly, she'd found a baseball game for him and he'd tried to explain its arcane rules, with hilarious results when the 'innings eater' came on. They had both got the giggles then and were still sporadically chuntering away over it thirty, forty minutes later.

The most surprising thing about having him as a house guest, though, hadn't been how easy he'd been to have around; it was that his company had made her realize how lonely her evenings usually were, and her grief for her father had been somewhat abated by his quiet, constant presence (not least because she didn't want him to hear her crying through the walls as she lay in the sofa bed). For her part, she had introduced him to the joys of soda bread, colcannon potatoes and Irish stew. It was nice having someone to cook for; there never seemed much point cooking up a big meal for just one and Bertie could never stay long enough for a home-cooked meal when he did come over – nor was it ever the hunger in his stomach that he yearned to satisfy, anyway.

He hadn't been over since he'd discovered Ben was recuperating here. 'It'll cause too much suspicion if I keep coming over,' he had said, somewhat resentfully and, for once, she had agreed. If they were to finally, imminently, be together, then for this last stretch, they had to be apart.

Curiously, the enforced absence didn't bother her, perhaps because the finish line was now in sight. Every morning she woke up to her heart fluttering like a tiny bird in a cage trying to get free. She had waited for this moment for so long – was her dream really about to come true? Like a child on Christmas Eve, the moment she had been waiting for was almost here and it felt impossible to believe after five years of patience, of silence, of tolerance.

Her phone rang but she ignored it. She only had it beside her for the 'chill-out' playlist playing quietly in the background and she let her hand move freely, disconnected from her conscious mind. Everything was coming together at last: she was going to be with Bertie; she had atoned for what she'd done to Ben. Even the raw grief for her father that had hollowed her out in the first shocking weeks was beginning to become . . . familiar. Less hostile.

The phone rang again, piercing her focus and she glanced at the screen with a tut. *Dave Bridges, Butcher.*

Oh! She scrambled to reach it. 'Bertie?'

'Otts, is he there?' He sounded out of breath – and on the top of a hill, the wind battering itself against the phone.

'Who?'

'Gilmore! Who else?'

She was taken aback by his snappishness. 'No,' she frowned. 'Why?'

'Has he told you what he's done?'

'. . . No,' she said cautiously. He sounded furious. Beside himself.

'He's bloody suing me!'

'What?'

'Says I'm liable for his accident. Reckless endangerment of life, he's saying! That the course wasn't clearly marked.'

She gasped, feeling her mellow buzz pop like a champagne bubble. 'But . . . that's not fair.'

'Fair? Of course it's not fair! He's just seen a bloody opportunity to screw me over and he's going for it! If he can't get the pot for the Triple – which he *can't* now because he won't recover in time to compete at Mont Blanc this year – then this is the next best thing! Except it's even better than that! He's after three times what he would have got for winning Mont Blanc.'

'He's suing you for three million?' she whispered, blankly watching the beachcomber on the beach. Ben was suing Bertie? She couldn't believe it. He'd said nothing to indicate it over breakfast – or during any of the time they'd spent together. He hadn't ranted about his injuries, he hadn't railed about the race conditions or set-up. He had seemed . . . accepting of what had happened, regarding it as one of those things. An accident, plain and simple.

'Otts, you've got to talk to him. Talk him out of this.'

'*Me?*'

'Yes, you! He's still staying with you, isn't he? He's still your guest?'

'Well, yes, but—'

'So then he's indebted to you. He owes you for the way you've gone out of your way to help him. It's more than reasonable for you to call in a favour from him in return.'

'Bertie, he's not going to call off a lawsuit for three million euros just because I've given him a bed and made him some meals . . . He won't listen to me.'

'Otts, baby,' he said, his voice changing, becoming softer. Cajoling. 'Surely you and he have become friendly now? He's living in your house. You're the closest thing he has to a friend over here. An ally. I know he'd listen to you if you just had a chat with him, made him see that this isn't *reasonable*. This isn't what the Ultra community is about. It goes against our *values*. We're about solidarity in the face of adversity. Team spirit. We don't *sue* one another. Risks are inherent in an event like this.'

Ottie bit her lip, remembering the sight of Ben out here every single day, limping across the sand, willing himself back to strength again with the same grim determination that enabled him to run ultramarathons in the first place. She couldn't see him being talked out of anything. 'He's his own man. I couldn't talk him out of a paper bag.'

'Not true. I've seen the way he looks at you.'

'Oh for Chrissakes, don't be ridiculous! He—'

'A man knows whenever another man is sniffing around his woman, Ottie.'

Her eyes closed at his words. She was his woman. 'Talking of which . . . Have you spoken to Shula?'

There was a pause, followed by a sigh. 'No, not yet.'

'Bertie—'

'How can I deal with telling Shula our marriage is over when Gilmore's going after my business, Otts, my *name*? I can only put out one fire at a time.'

She was quiet for a moment. 'Okay, look, I'll speak to Ben and try to bring him round. And *you* can focus on breaking the news to Shula.'

'Really?'

'Of course.'

She could hear the smile beaming down the line. 'Jeesht, you're a cracking girl, Ottie Lorne.'

'I know. When will I see you next?'

'I'm not sure. But soon, though – as soon as I can get away. Just keep your phone with you and I'll call when I can slip away.'

She inhaled shallowly, feeling the usual sensation of her heart being trussed with ropes. 'Okay.'

'I've got to go, but I love you, Ottie. Don't forget that. We'll be together soon.'

'Soon,' she echoed, putting the phone down and wondering why she never felt more alone than when she was with the man she loved.

*

She was just walking back round to the cottage when Ben limped up the garden path, forty-five minutes later. She had tried to lose herself in the process again, but she had been rattled by Bertie's news and she had lost her flow. She had only just closed up the boat store, rinsed out her brushes and pulled off her tunic, setting the easel a good way back from the door to protect it from any rain ingress, when she had heard Seamus's car and his hearty cheerios to his passenger.

'Hey!' she said brightly, noticing too late the paint still on her hands as he hobbled towards her. His cheeks were slapped pink – either by the wind or his own exertions – his eyes shining with an almost feverish brightness. 'God, that felt good,' he gasped as she opened the door for him and he came into the warm protection of the house, the moan of the wind shut out behind the closed door.

'You must be exhausted,' she said, watching how he winced a little as he walked to the kettle.

'No, it's all good.'

Ottie wasn't so sure. She was getting to know him – to read him – and she knew he was used to pushing past his pain barrier for his ultramarathons. Was that the best thing now, though? 'Here, let me do that. Have a rest,' she said, trying to take the kettle from him, her hand over his on the handle.

He looked back at her. 'Really, I'm fine. I can do it. You want a coffee too?'

She fell back, knowing better than to insist. He was always so determined to be independent, never to show vulnerability of any kind. 'Sure.' His limp was noticeably worse than when he'd left earlier. 'I really think you should have some painkillers after that session, though. It's bound to inflame the joint.'

'I'll be fine,' he said, putting his weight on his good leg as he leaned against the counter while the kettle boiled, his head tipped back with relief and exhaustion. 'I'll take the coffee into the bedroom and lie down for a bit. Elevating it should be enough to ease the pressure.'

'Want some ice?'

'Hmm, maybe. I'll see.'

'Ben.'

He glanced across at the tone in her voice.

'I'm worried about you. You're pushing yourself *so* hard.'

'And that's a bad thing because . . . ?'

'You're risking overdoing it and injuring yourself again.'

'Worried you'll be stuck with me?'

She groaned. *'You're* the one who can't get away fast enough.'

He shot her a funny look. 'I promise I know what I'm doing.'

She crossed her arms over her chest, feeling awkward somehow. 'I don't think you have the normal pain receptors of most people.'

He looked at her strangely. 'Sure I do.' He turned away as the kettle boiled and he reached for the cups, pouring their hot drinks. 'I just choose to ignore them.'

She gave a short laugh. 'You choose to ignore pain? I wasn't aware it was a choice.'

'Everything's a choice, Ottie,' he said simply, holding out her coffee. Even he had conceded it was still too difficult for him to walk on crutches and carry hot liquids at the same time.

She took it from him.

'– The trouble is, people assume pain should be avoided.'

'Because it should! That is precisely the point of it! It keeps us safe!'

'Yes. Pain tells us when something is wrong and must be avoided. But it's also the thing that tells us we're alive. It's a signal of our vitality. I'm far more afraid of the idea of *not* feeling things: apathy and numbness terrify me. They're more dangerous.'

'But do you never worry it'll be too much? More than you can handle?' she asked.

'No. I believe we're all infinitely more resilient than we know. It's only in the hard times that we get a chance to see what we're capable of.'

Ottie stared at him. If this 'dig in' attitude was his mindset, there was no chance he was going to climb down from this lawsuit against Bertie. She didn't have a hope of persuading him otherwise.

'Most people sleepwalk through their lives, Ottie. They stay in their comfort zones because it's easy, familiar, safe. But life is none of those things. It can turn on a switchblade. You can think you're happy, go off to work one day and in an instant—' He clicked his fingers. 'Everything can change. Nothing and no one is as you thought. We *need* pain. It tells us to move on, move away, it keeps us safe.'

She stared at him, suddenly hearing the hardness in his voice, seeing the tension in his mouth, the way his lips were pulled tight, his words becoming clipped . . . What had happened to him? *Something* had set him on this path to extreme experience: the need to face up to pain, to push through it. The 'wake-up call', he had said.

She realized he was staring at her but not seeing her. He was lost to another moment, another time.

'Ben?' His gaze switched back to her. 'Are you okay?'

He forced a smile and she knew even what he said next would be a lie. He never fake-smiled. 'Sure.'

She faltered, wondering where his mind had gone to, for in that moment of relapse, his body language – his energy – had changed, becoming slack. Weak even. She put her hand on his arm, feeling the sinew and muscle, the heat from his exhausted body. 'Ben, is there something you want to talk about?'

He looked down at her hand, as though startled by the touch, and then back up at her again. 'No.'

'I feel like . . . something happened to you.'

'It did. It's called life.'

Her hand dropped away and she turned to go. If he was going to be sarcastic—

'Ottie, wait, I'm sorry. I didn't mean –' He sighed. 'I'm tired. I know you're just being nice.'

Nice. Was that how he thought of her? For some reason, it felt like a jab in the ribs, a stamp on the foot. They stood in awkward silence again, somehow at odds with each other today, both clumsy, neither saying the right thing.

'Have you been painting?' he asked as she went to move past him.

'No,' she fibbed. It was her reflexive answer to that question these days. It was her secret, no one else's business how she chose to waste her time; she knew nothing could ever come of it; that she had a mediocre talent at best. But he picked up her right hand and turned it over. A streak of indigo paint had smudged along the outer edge of her hand.

Oh. She looked up at him. 'That's . . .' But she didn't know what to say, how to lie straight to his face. Standing so close, he suddenly felt different. All this time they'd spent together, she had been so focused on making amends that she'd somehow seen only the injury, not the man.

She felt the tenor of the room change. Did he know he was still holding her hand? She saw his gaze roam her face, as though he was seeing her differently too, and as he reached forward, her breath caught –

The tiny movement betrayed her and he paused, their eyes locking in a moment of searing, exposing honesty. He was going to kiss her. The moment pulsed . . . and faded away.

'You've got a little . . . I don't know what that is.' He dabbed her skin lightly and turned his finger to show her the dot of raw umber.

'Oh.' Her heart was beating at double time but not her mind. She couldn't think. 'That's . . . putty.'

'Putty?'

'Yes. There was a leak, one of the pipes in the shower block. I just . . . sealed it.'

'Huh.' He nodded but he had that look again in his eyes, the one she could never read but that she feared saw through her little white lies – and the big ones too. 'You're good at putting things back together again, aren't you? Leaky pipes. Broken runners. You'll be signing up for Humpty Dumpty next.'

She tried to smile. It was a decent quip – enough to break the ice again and rescue them both – but she was feeling unnerved by what had just passed between them. She pulled her hand from his and stepped away. 'Do you still want to go into town later and get some new clothes?' she asked, her eyes looking everywhere but him.

He paused, watching her, always seeing her. 'Sure.'

'I mean, do say if you'd rather not. We can always go tomorrow if you're tired after the physio –'

'I'll be fine after a short rest.'

She nodded. 'Shall we say two hours then?'

He watched her as she reached for her coat and headed for the door, forgetting all about her coffee. 'Sure. Two hours. Me and my leg will be looking forward to it.'

Chapter Twenty-Two

Thursday, 19 December

Pip stood at the door and tucked her chin into her chest like a roosting pigeon – but it wasn't warmth she was looking for. She needed courage and lots of it. Her hands balled into fists as she ran through the speech she had prepared on the way over and all last night as she had lain sleepless in bed, staring up at the ceiling. She had to do this. She couldn't *not*. She had tried taking her defeat on the chin, tried to be honourable about losing her beloved mare but the loss was like an ache in her side, keeping her awake at night and preoccupying her every waking thought. She had to get Shalimar back.

With a burst of bravado, she rapped quickly on the door and marched in before the occupant could even respond. She knew he was in here; one of the grooms had told her as she'd parked up, her eyes roaming enviously over the smart stables, the yellow horseboxes embossed with the black Cuneen logo.

'Hey,' she said breezily, disturbing Sean who was clearly watching something he shouldn't be watching on the desktop.

'Jeesht!' he cried, scrabbling to get his feet off the desk, hurriedly closing down the screen. 'Can't you knock?'

'I did,' she said with her sweetest smile. 'You must have been absorbed in your work.'

Sean had the grace, at least, to look sheepish and she watched with relish as he raked his hands through his hair and tried to look presentable. He was wearing jeans and a Cuneen funnel-neck fleece, his portly physique trying to escape in the middle like a squeezed tube of toothpaste. 'Pip,' he stammered. 'I've been thinking about you –'

Pip glanced at the black screen with a grimace. She sincerely hoped not.

'– I was wondering how you've been. I was going to call, check you were all back on track.'

Back on track – another euphemism for 'not dead'. She was tempted to start keeping a record of them. She shrugged. 'Of course, why wouldn't I be? You saw me the other day at the yard, after all. I'm right as rain.'

'Some people might . . . struggle after going through what you went through.'

Oh, she'd struggled all right, she thought to herself, but not on account of nearly drowning. It was the losses that were difficult to accept: her father, Lorne, Shalimar. 'I'm fine.'

He gave a nervous chuckle. 'You're a hard nut, Pip Lorne.'

'Well, *you* certainly haven't cracked me, Sean,' she said with a lopsided grin. 'Which is why I thought I'd drop in on my way past. I'm just on my way back from Cork.' That was a lie. She'd not left the estate all week, the dratted cold and cough she'd been trying to shake off laying her low.

'Oh yeah?' Sean's small dark eyes narrowed in his pale fleshy face, lending him a porcine look.

'Yeah. I've come to lay down a challenge.' Her wording was deliberate. Making an 'offer' would give him too much wriggle room to say no to her, but presenting him with a challenge spoke to his pride.

'What sort of challenge?' he asked, sounding as nervous as he was suspicious.

'I want the opportunity to win back Shalimar.'

He sat back in the swivel seat and clasped his hands behind his head. 'Oh no. No way,' he chuckled. 'I'm no fool. I know what I've got in her. *You* may have taken the punt for something better but she's steady and well bred, and exactly what I need here. I'm not risking losing her back to you.'

She sighed. 'Yeah. I told them you'd say that.'

'Who's they?'

'Just all the folks who think you came by her dishonourably.'

'I won her fair and square!'

Pip pursed her lips together in consideration. 'Hmm, I'd agree you won her in the legal definition, but I wouldn't say it was fair and square. That race was weighted against me from the start. Sheer BMI difference meant I never had a chance in those temperatures. Even if I could take on your extra height advantage and stride length, your extra muscular power . . .' She saw how his ego swelled at the veiled compliments. 'It didn't matter how fit or determined I was, surviving those water temperatures was a simple matter of physics and I didn't have the mass to make it. Of course, I'd have known that if I hadn't been so off my head. That was my bad. But a lot of people are saying you took advantage of my inebriated state.'

'*I* was wasted too,' he argued, swinging side to side in the chair, like a little boy allowed to sit in his dad's office. 'Plus the bet was your idea.'

'Yes, but put it all together: the inebriation, BMI difference, and the fact that I very nearly drowned . . .' She shrugged. 'I've had a lot of comments from folk saying it wasn't honourable of you to press for your prize under those circumstances.'

'Who? Who's been saying that?'

'Just lots of folk, round and about.'

He swung the chair again, looking at her intently, trying to think. 'Yeah, well, they can say what they like. A deal's a deal.'

'I know. That's exactly what I told them,' she shrugged, perching on the side of the desk. It was covered with papers – medical charts, event timetables, auction lists, old copies of the *Racing Post* – and a 2017 Emily Ratajkowski calendar was stuck on the wall.

'You did?'

'Sure. Christ, I don't care whether your behaviour was honourable or not. Who am I to take the moral high ground? I just told them that pride be damned, you'd take the win because you knew you couldn't beat me in a fair fight.'

'You're kidding?' Sean laughed, slapping his hand against the desk. 'You think I couldn't beat you?'

'You think you *could*?' she asked back in equal disbelief.

They stared at one another for a long moment, a small grin beginning to play on her lips. He was a sucker, reeled in by his own ego.

'What would this challenge be?' he asked finally.

'Just a straightforward, old-fashioned race. You on whichever horse you choose, me on mine, a straight drag along Lorne beach.'

'. . . When?'

She shrugged. 'Tomorrow afternoon? Unless you need more time to prepare?'

'Tomorrow's fine,' he said briskly. He stared at her suspiciously, clearly looking for a catch. 'So if you win, you get back Shalimar?'

She nodded, her heart fluttering at the prospect of having her beautiful mare back.

'And what about me? What do I get? No disrespect, Pip, but trek nags aren't any good to me and you don't have anything else I'd want.'

'Oh, I don't think that's true,' Pip smiled, crossing her legs and leaning towards him. 'I've got something money can't buy.'

He frowned but leaned in closer too, unable to stop himself. 'Oh yeah? Like what?'

'Sorry it's such a squeeze,' Willow said, shuffling her armchair a little further back so that at least their knees weren't touching.

'Not at all, I think it's cosy,' Ferdy smiled, his eyes doing a polite, interested sweep of the small parlour. 'You've made it look like a home already.'

'Oh, do you think so?' Willow asked, hopefully, looking around herself with objective eyes: she took in the faux-bamboo mirror above the fireplace, her father's favourite oil painting on the wall, a campaign chest that had belonged to his great-grandfather during the war, the grandest silk Oushak rug that had fitted in this room. As ever, the colours were riotous, prints clashing boldly against one another, with not a trace of beige to be seen anywhere. She had painted the walls apple green herself, wearing one of her father's old shirts. It wasn't like there hadn't been anything else to do. With her trying to keep away from Connor at the castle and her mother trying to keep away from her here – she was *still* at the Flanagans' – the days were long and lonely. 'It's been a real race against time to try and get the place set up for Mam. She didn't react well to being told that she had to move out of the castle with twenty-four hours' notice.'

'I can imagine not,' Ferdy grimaced. 'The castle was her home for how many years?'

'Thirty.'

'That's a big part of anyone's life.'

Willow nodded, looking into the fire and remembering her mother's stunned expression as she had detailed what she had agreed to, and the frenetic schedule it entailed. 'I know it's hard enough for her adapting to being a widow, without all this other change to deal with too. It's not so bad for my sisters – they've been living in their current homes on the estate for a while now – but when I wake up in the morning, in that moment right before I open my eyes, I can't actually remember which building I'm in, much less the room. It's the oddest feeling to be lying there, with absolutely no concept of where I am. I feel so displaced . . .'

'I get that when I travel,' he commiserated. 'I travel a lot for work and wake up in hotel rooms not knowing where I am either.'

'It's disconcerting.'

'Absolutely it is, but you should be proud of what you've achieved. You've done more to this estate in the past few weeks than anyone else has managed in at least five hundred years. You've done the hard part.'

'Actually I think *you're* doing the hard part,' she smiled. 'I don't know how you know where to start. We've so much *stuff*.'

'Beautiful stuff,' he clarified. 'I stopped in at the castle on my way over, just to make sure nothing was overlooked in the cellars and attics, and I couldn't even count the number of tradesmen they had on site.'

'Really?' she asked blandly, trying not to imagine it. *Him*. 'I've been trying to keep out of the way.'

'Very wise. There must have been thirty vans on the drive. It appears to be a slick machine they're running. Incredibly efficient.'

'Well, they're highly motivated,' she said with a tight smile.

She hadn't seen or heard from Connor since she'd left him in the pub at the weekend, the look of disbelief on his face as she ran out on him running in a loop through her head. 'Did you . . . see how it's looking?'

He thought for a moment. 'They've lifted the carpets and sanded the floors, and I think they're stripping the panelling at the moment. It's all much . . . softer looking. Still grand but with a contemporary feel, I suppose.'

'Right.' She felt a tremor of fear, not entirely sure what that meant. Not for the first time, she wondered what the hell she was doing, allowing this.

'I think you'll like it.' He looked at her. 'Although I must say I'm somewhat amazed you'd allow such comprehensive works for just a temporary hire.'

This was it, the moment to say out loud – tell someone it's all but sold. Lorne Castle is sold. Tell everyone. 'We needed to do the work anyway so it's something of a win-win for us,' she said instead, her courage failing.

He shrugged. 'Well, anyway, thanks for seeing me at short notice. I know you're busy.'

She looked down at her paint-splattered jeans, father's shirt, her dark hair tied back in an old Hermes scarf of her mother's. 'I'm grateful for the opportunity to stop, to be honest. I'm just sorry Mam's not here too. It's her sale after all.' Not that she'd been involved for a single step of it.

'Well, we're in good shape for moving to the next stage of the process. Everything's pretty much been listed in the warehouse now and so we'll move on to researching provenance and such before coming up with valuations and preparing a catalogue for the sale.'

'Let's hope we'll have a following wind on the day,' she said nervously.

'Don't worry on that score. I'm confident this sale will attract significant interest. Your father had a great eye. His military silverware collections and the continental oils especially are really going to attract some big bidders.'

'Here's hoping.' Willow took a sip of her tea.

'There was just one thing that I wanted to double-check with you.'

Willow arched an eyebrow. 'Oh yeah? What's that?'

'It's why I popped in to the castle for another look actually, in case it had been stored away somewhere and missed. It's not a small matter – we appear to be missing a Gainsborough.'

Willow groaned. 'Oh no, Mam didn't tell you about that, did she?' She sighed and gave an apologetic look. 'It's nothing more than family legend, I'm afraid. Wishful thinking on the part of some debt-addled gambling ancestor.'

'Well, that's the thing. It's not. We've found a reference to it in an old housekeeping book in one of the kitchen cupboards.'

Willow looked at him in astonishment. The kitchen? Had her father seen it then? Was that why he'd been so determined, so desperate to find it? 'What kind of reference?'

'There's all sorts in the log – details of building works and charges, rebuilding costs after a fire in 1749. Wages paid to the servants. Housekeeping costs. And according to an entry made on 3 February 1752, one of your great-great-greats paid a princely sum for a portrait – by Gainsborough. Ferdy looked at her. 'Willow, it would really make this sale an international event if we were able to find and include that painting.'

Willow stared at him, wishing she could offer some kind of hope. 'I just . . . don't think there's *any* chance. Dad scoured the castle over the years looking for it, but we thought it was wishful thinking. We never took it seriously. It was a running joke in the family about him putting on his headtorch and knee pads to crawl through rafters and pull up old insulation – which made him sneeze like a beggar! – hoping to find it. If anyone was going to find it, it would have been him. He was certain it'd be the answer to all our problems.' She smiled wistfully, falling back into an old memory. 'One time, we discovered a bricked-up fireplace in the old kitchen and he was so excited, thinking it must have been hidden up there. His face when all he found were old birds nests . . .' She looked back at Ferdy again; his disappointment was nothing to her father's. 'In the end, he concluded it had either been sold off to settle some debt, stolen by a vengeful servant or destroyed in one of the various fires over the years.'

Ferdy gave a regretful sigh. 'Well, it really would be a shame if it came to one of those ends. Although, if it had been sold off – either by an ancestor or servant – I think it would have surfaced by now in some private collection or other.'

'Yeah, probably,' Willow agreed. 'So most likely it succumbed to the flames then?'

He winced and nodded. 'In the absence of any confirmed sightings since . . . yes.' He set down his tea on the slender-legged George III card table and got up. 'What a shame.'

They walked to the front door together, standing in the narrow hallway. She had set a red poinsettia on a cherrywood console to bring a dab of colour to the otherwise gloomy space. It was a feeble first attempt to try to inject some festive spirit into the house but Willow suspected her mother would feel disloyal decorating any further for Christmas; as though she should apologize for continuing to live after her husband had died.

'I'm not going to ask you how much that painting would have been worth in today's market,' she said.

Ferdy turned and looked back at her with a wince. 'Probably best not.'

'Oh God!' she groaned. '*That* much?'

'You've just got to think of it this way – you can't mourn what you never had.' He shook her hand again and stepped out onto the overgrown path. 'I'll be in touch,' he called over his shoulder.

Willow closed the door, her gaze falling to Rusty now standing awkwardly – and somewhat menacingly – behind it. There had been no question of entering it into the sale but equally there was nowhere here for it to go either.

She remembered again her father wearing it at her mother's birthday party. It had clanked and squeaked with every movement, the bruises afterwards monstrous. It had been brought back to life that night, as vital again as it once had been on the battlefield, but now it stood stiff and silent, just a shell. A reminder of past glories, and past happiness. A reminder that her father, the last knight in Ireland, was gone. A reminder that there was no one to protect her now.

For all her supposed family, she was on her own.

Chapter Twenty-Three

The same day

'Is that snow?'

Ottie looked up, turning a circle slowly, one hand upturned to the sky. Soft flakes fell into her palm like sifted icing sugar, disappearing on contact. She gave a small shiver and pulled the zip on her coat higher under her chin. 'They said it was coming.'

'I'd better buy a coat then too,' Ben said.

'I think so,' she smiled, hitching the shopping bags higher on her shoulder, the strings beginning to dig in through her jacket. 'Although it must be annoying having to buy all this stuff when you'll be home in a few days or so anyway.'

'As long as the physio gives me the sign-off later,' he said cautiously.

'Of course she will. You said she indicated as much at your last appointment.'

He looked dead ahead as he swung on his crutches. 'Yes, but there are no guarantees.'

That wasn't true. He'd worked tirelessly on his exercises, eliminating all possible risk of failure. He would be on that plane come Sunday, he'd made sure of it. 'How could she not let you go? You've worked so hard. This place will be a distant memory a week from now.'

'Hardly,' he said, glancing over. 'Besides, everything I buy today can be a souvenir of my time here.'

'Ah, well, that's nice to know you'll think of us every time you pull on your new stripy socks,' she laughed with an ease she didn't feel. Something had changed between them since the moment in the kitchen yesterday, though she couldn't say what exactly. It was barely there, like a trick of the light, visible only at certain times.

They walked slowly. She felt protective of him in the crowds, wanting to hold a stick out and wave it in circles around them, keeping people away. Bags swinging in their hands, concentration on shopping lists, they didn't tend to see his stick or the brace on his leg – much less the cast on his wrist – until the very last moment and several times this afternoon she had had to launch herself forward as a barrier between him and some distracted shopper about to barrel straight into him.

Pools of light fell from the shop windows, mannequins frozen in position with jazz hands and kicked-up heels, draped in sequins, plush velvets and chunky knits. Overhead, Christmas lights were strung up between lamp-posts, giant stars and icicles twinkling as if magically suspended. An enormous Christmas tree draped with gold baubles stood proudly in the pedestrianized square, stalls selling hot chocolate, waffles, crepes and toasted hazelnuts set up around it.

'I suppose you must be very used to snow in New York,' she said. 'You get proper snow there.'

'Oh yeah. It doesn't play at it. When it snows, it's serious.'

'Is it snowing there at the moment?'

'Yep.'

'I bet you can't wait to get back. Are you excited? This time Sunday you'll be in the air.'

'I'm not sure how I feel. It's been an intense couple of weeks,' he said, looking at the ground as he swung over a puddle.

'Have you missed home?' she asked. The only times the phone had rung for him, it had been work calls – brisk hurried voices asking if he was 'contactable'.

'I guess,' he shrugged. 'Although New York's just where I live. It's not where I consider to be home.'

'Oh? Where's that then?'

'Nantucket, a few hours further north of Manhattan. Not dissimilar to here really – rugged Atlantic coastline, small communities. Pretty rural. You'd like it, I think.'

'Well, maybe I'll come visit some day then.'

He said nothing and she felt a rebuke in the silence. No? Didn't he want to stay in touch?

She looked sidelong at him, seeing how he winced with each step. They hadn't been able to make this trip yesterday after all. In spite of his protestations to the contrary, she had seen the pain he was in as he'd emerged from the bedroom after a rest and she had point-blank refused to drive him. It was just about the only power she had over him. He wouldn't allow her to even make tea at all now, and the promise she'd made to Bertie about convincing him to drop the lawsuit seemed an ever more impossible task. Several times she had opened her mouth to ask him, steeled herself to use their friendship to manoeuvre him into a position from which he couldn't refuse her, but each time her courage – and voice – had failed; for reasons she didn't understand, it felt like a betrayal to him, not Bertie.

She gave a small groan. 'Ugh, my feet are killing me,' she said, pulling a grimace. 'I don't suppose you fancy stopping for a drink? I could really do with a sit-down.'

The look came into his eyes. The one where he knew she was lying.

'What?' she asked, feeling herself blush.

'I am fine. And you are an *atrocious* liar, for the record!'

She bit her lip. Busted. 'You're wincing.'

'Yes. But it's manageable.'

'It shouldn't have to be manageable. You're pushing yourself too hard.'

'I need to recover and get out of your way.'

'But you're not *in* my way. As far as I'm concerned take all the time you want. I'm enjoying the company.'

'Ottie, you're very kind, but we both know you can't . . .' He seemed to struggle for the right words. 'You can't live your life properly with me in your house.' He looked at her and she felt sure he was avoiding saying something, that sleight of light flashing between them, uncatchable, indefinable.

'Ben, that's absolute poppycock.'

'Poppycock. Huh. Another new word.' He began walking again. 'I'll file it with Big Bananas.'

She laughed. He liked teasing her for her creative language and she had realized she liked him teasing her.

He stopped outside the window of the fanciest designer boutique in town – she'd never been in for that reason; she couldn't afford a pair of tights in there – and looked at the male mannequin wearing a slate-grey Canada Goose parka.

'A coat. Great. Done,' he said resignedly, limping in.

Done? Just like that? It was a four-figure purchase!

She hurried in after him.

'– take the coat in the window in a medium, please,' he was saying to the assistant.

Ottie stood in the middle of the store, biting her lip as they waited, her eyes raking over the rails of expensive dresses and cashmere jumpers, vertiginous shoes and studded handbags.

Her gaze fell on a mid-length red silk dress. It had long bell sleeves and a drawstring waist, a deep notched neckline with ties. She wandered over as the assistant hurried back to Ben and he slipped the coat on for size.

She let the fabric slide through her fingers. It was fluid and light, the skirt full and flowy, a delicate gold thread spun through at intervals.

'Try it on.'

She turned. Ben was standing behind her, the coat already off again and being carted to the till by an overjoyed assistant. His easiest ever sale, surely.

'What?'

'The dress. You should try it on.'

'Oh jeesht, no,' she pooh-poohed, immediately letting the sleeve drop from her fingers.

'Why not?'

'You mean apart from the fact it costs more than my car?'

'Apart from that.'

She rolled her eyes. 'I'd never have anywhere to wear something like that, for one thing. I don't live a Red Dress kind of life.'

He stared at her. 'I think that might be the saddest thing I've ever heard.' But there was a wry glint in his eyes and she laughed.

'I know,' she chuckled. '*Tell* me about it.'

He wandered over to the till to pay for the coat and wore it out of the store. She had to resist the urge to stroke its furry trim.

'Well timed,' she said, looking up at the flakes falling harder now. It was beginning to settle. 'Was there anything else you wanted to get?' So far they'd bought him new jeans, boxers, socks, some T-shirts, two casual shirts, a jumper, a pair of loafers and now this coat. And she was carrying it all – something which clearly bothered him as he winced every time he looked at her, as well as every time he took a step.

'No, that should do me now till I get home. You won't have any more washing to do for me.'

'Yes. Hurray,' she said limply, her eyes briefly meeting his again. It was beginning to feel odd, wrong even, the idea of him going home. Living in such close proximity, the relationship – *friendship*, she supposed – had accelerated quickly. She'd come to think of him as a housemate; she'd never had one of those before – and wouldn't again. It was Christmas in five days' time and in spite of her airy offer to stay as long as he needed, Bertie would be moving in to the cottage with her; she had been adamant she wouldn't have Shula leaving her own home. 'Well, let's head off then. It'll no doubt surprise you to hear I don't have winter tyres on my car.'

He pretended to be shocked. 'No!'

They limped slowly back through the town, towards the car park. 'You know there is one thing I'd like to do before I go back to New York,' he said in a thoughtful voice.

'Oh yes? What's that?'

'Have a pint of Guinness.'

She was amazed. 'You've never had one?'

He shook his head. 'Any time I've come over here, I've been competing. Alcohol was always off the table.' He shrugged. 'It just seems like now's the time, don't you think?'

'Damn straight it is! And if it's a pint of the black stuff you're after, I know just the place,' she smiled, swinging his shopping bags in her hands. 'Come on. Let's head home.'

*

They took the booth in the corner, between the Christmas tree and the window. The pub was busier than Ottie had ever seen it.

'Who *are* all these people?' she asked Joe as he pulled slowly on the tap.

'Your fellas,' he smiled, bemused, watching the black stout flow.

'My . . . ?'

'Up at the castle. They're just finishing doing the renovations.'

Ottie blinked. What renovations?

'Haven't you heard?' Joe asked in amazement as he saw her expression setting down the first pint. 'Jeesht, you really do need to get over here more often, Ottie. There's some fancy private members' club taken over the place for the weekend. It's a house party really but what did they call it? A blow-up . . . oh yes, a *pop-up* club.'

'I have no idea what that is.'

'Nor's any of us. But apparently we're all invited to the big do Saturday night – the entire village. Black tie. Proper fancy.'

'Black tie?' Ottie repeated in disbelief. 'At the castle this weekend?'

What the hell had Willow been up to, Ottie wondered? She'd only seen her . . . Christ, when had she seen her last? The past few weeks had gone by in a blur what with looking after Ben, looking out for Bertie . . . She realized it had been around ten days ago, when Pip had been in hospital. Bertie had texted her to say her mother was *still* staying at theirs – he had sounded pretty annoyed about it – so she hadn't had any particular imperative to go over to the castle in the meantime.

'Thanks, Joe,' she murmured, handing over the money and picking up the pints, a bag of nuts clamped between her teeth.

'What's up?' Ben asked her with a quizzical look as she came back, reaching up to take the nuts from her. His leg was propped up rather comically on a high bar stool to raise his foot higher than his heart; she had been able to tell from the pinch at his eyes that it had begun to throb after their shopping trip.

'I'm not sure. My little sister appears to have arranged some sort of . . . civic event at the castle in the space of a fortnight.' She sat down beside him and handed him the pint. He admired it for a long moment, the black velvet body, the narrow froth of foam across the top.

Ottie watched as he took a mouthful, his eyes closing. He'd shaved this morning, the first time since he'd come to stay, and it had come as a shock as he'd debuted the look at breakfast. It suited him, revealing his finely angled face that had been steadily obscured by encroaching stubbly fuzz, but it also made him look more 'corporate' again, one step closer to being the man who had stood on her doorstep in the rain that Friday night. He looked ready for his suit now, ready for home.

'Oh . . . yeah,' he breathed, looking at the pint again before looking at her nodding appreciatively. '*Well* worth the wait.'

She grinned. Him saying he hadn't liked it would have been tantamount to saying he didn't like Ireland. Or the Irish. Or her.

He took another mouthful, before setting the pint back down again. 'So, you were saying . . . *civic* event?'

'She's apparently hired the castle out to a private members' club and they're holding a big black-tie party on Saturday, to which the entire village is invited.'

'Would the entire village *want* to go to a black-tie party?'

Ben asked, looking around the pub. Anyone not in work trousers either had a white beard or bald head.

'Probably not,' she chuckled. 'But maybe they knew that when they extended the invitation: friendly gesture, low uptake.'

Ben sucked in his teeth. 'Such cynicism for one so young, Miss Lorne.'

'Listen, the only black ties around here are worn at funerals.'

It was his turn to laugh. 'So, will *you* go?'

'Jeesht, no.' She took a sip of Guinness herself, quickly dabbing off the white moustache with her index finger.

He watched her with a bemused expression. 'Why not?'

'I'm not a black-tie-party kind of person.'

'Because you don't have a Red Dress life you mean?'

She grinned. 'Exactly.'

'Got it,' he nodded, that signature wry tone making the corners of her mouth turn up.

The pub door opened and they glanced over to see an older couple walking in – followed by the Flanagans.

Ottie immediately shrank back in her chair, as though trying to push herself through and behind it. She let her hair fall forwards, screening her profile, as Shula and her companions went straight to the table by the fire, a Reserved sign on it. Bertie went to the bar.

Ben looked at them, not saying anything, before glancing across at her, noticing her newly huddled posture. 'You okay?'

She gave an innocent nod. 'Sure.' Actually, she wanted to get the hell out of there now but they had only just started on their drinks and she couldn't think of any reason why they should suddenly leave.

She flipped her hair across her head and rested her cheek in her right hand. 'So . . .' But she could still see Bertie's reflection in the old pewter tankard on the table which held the cutlery. He was standing at the bar, one foot up on the rail. He was wearing jeans and a twill shirt, a moss-green Schoffel fleece gilet.

A hint of a frown puckered Ben's brow but he passed no comment on her suddenly defensive behaviour and took another sip of his pint. 'This might have to become my new vice.'

'*New* vice? You mean you have other ones?' she asked, her interest piqued and drawn off Bertie momentarily. 'I was under the impression your body is a temple.'

'If by temple you mean a crumbling Aztec ruin.'

She laughed.

It was the wrong thing to have done. In the reflection of the tankard, she saw Bertie – knowing the sound well – turn. He went still for a moment as he took in the sight of them here, sharing a pint together.

Then he was walking over.

Ottie felt herself tense, knowing she had let him down, for she still hadn't mentioned the issue of the lawsuit yet. It wasn't that there hadn't been plenty of opportunities since yesterday – they had been together almost all the time but it had just never seemed the right time. Chatting as Ben did his physio and she ironed, or walking slowly together along the beach this morning whilst she did the daily litter clear-up . . . How was she supposed to just drop into the conversation the small matter of letting three million euros go?

But Bertie had needed her to do it, no matter how hard. She realized she had unwittingly made a choice and it hadn't been him she'd chosen.

'Mr Gilmore.' Bertie's voice was as hard and sharp as flint.

'Mr Flanagan,' Ben said coolly.

'I had expected you'd have seen sense by now.' Bertie's eyes slid over to her. 'Ottie?'

She stared back at him, feeling her heart pound, adrenaline tearing through her veins like a spring flood. 'Hey,' was all she could say.

His eyebrow arched at the reply, understanding perfectly that she had failed him. She saw his disappointment with her in the pull of his lips. He looked back at Ben.

'My barrister assures me you don't have a leg to stand on.'

Ben wiggled the foot of his up-ended leg. 'Not quite true. I do have *one* to stand on.'

To Ottie's horror, a bubble of shocked laughter escaped her, her father's legacy rearing its head at all the wrong moments. She slapped her hand over her mouth and looked up at Bertie almost with fear. 'I didn't mean that,' she whispered. 'It's not funny.'

Bertie glowered at her, his anger and disappointment in her palpable. Slowly he leaned down, his palms flat on the table and astride either side of Ben's leg. Should he choose, Ben could kick straight up and hit him square in the jaw, but they all knew he wouldn't do that. Bertie knew it.

'Let me make this very plain to you, Gilmore. I will not have my brand sullied by your baseless and unwarranted accusations. I have spent many years developing Ultra and I take the security and safety of the course every bit as seriously as you would hope I would.'

'So then, how did I end up, in broad daylight, clinging to a rock for thirty-four hours in a storm, with multiple fractures? There were no signs at that junction, Flanagan.'

'Yes, there were.'

Ottie felt her heart constrict at the outright lie, as she stared at Bertie. Ben could have died because of them. How could he deny such an important truth? But Bertie wasn't looking at her. His eyes were locked on Ben – and vice versa – in mutual antipathy.

'I'm going to counter-sue for defamation of character,' Bertie growled. '*Five* million from you.'

'Oh, I wouldn't go anywhere near the realms of character if I were you,' Ben said placidly, looking not at all ruffled. 'People in glass houses and all that.'

There was a long silence.

'. . . What does that mean?' Bertie asked in a quiet voice.

'What do *you* think it means?'

Ottie didn't move. She scarcely dared to breathe. What *did* it mean? What did Ben know?

She became aware that the pub was growing quieter, people beginning to notice their 'conversation', Bertie's body language overtly hostile and intriguing.

He straightened up slowly, his face redder than when he ran. 'This isn't over.'

Ben arched an eyebrow but made no reply and after another tense stare-off, Bertie turned and left, making his way back to the bar. Heads followed him, gazes shooting back and forth between their two parties, a buzz of gossip beginning to lift up like a swarm of hoverflies.

Ottie stared at her pint, not sure what to say.

Ben took another sip of his Guinness. 'Mmm, so good,' he said appreciatively. 'Not sure I'd want two though.'

Chapter Twenty-Four

Friday, 20 December

Willow picked her way uncertainly over the rough ground. The snow had come in hard all yesterday afternoon and overnight, and it was difficult to make out which was firm ground and which bog. Ahead of her Mabel and Dot trotted with their noses down, making it look easy, their Prussian-blue rope leads straddled across her body like lassos.

She crested the hill with a sigh of relief and, pushing her windswept hair back from her face, looked down the sweep of fields to the deserted campsite and the beach beyond. Snow lapped up to the very fringes of the sand, the long fronds of tufted grass like frozen wands pointing into the air. The sea was a stormy battleship grey today, white horses tussling in the bay, towering clouds rolling overhead. She squinted slightly as she saw an unusual number of people on the beach.

Being privately owned and part of the Lorne estate, it was always quiet – not that her family had ever stopped the villagers from using it: 'mi castle es tu castle', her father used to joke in the pub, although most of them went to Dingle's Cove anyway which was longer and closer to the village. The campers were allowed to use the Lorne private beach but there wasn't one tent pitched there now; Ottie always closed up shop after the Ultra, in the run-up to Christmas.

A light was shining in the cottage, even though it was after midday, and she started making her way, falteringly, over there again. She hadn't seen her sister in well over a week and had realized with a start, as she was dropping off to sleep last night, that she wouldn't yet know about the 'occupation' this weekend. If she were to just drop in to the castle, she'd get a hell of a fright. They had to talk – and not just about this weekend.

She walked on over the fields, the little pink door in the gable end getting bigger, along with the crowd on the beach, a steady stream of people filing down the lane, puffa jackets on, dogs on leads. She knocked at the door, Mabel and Dot sitting on the mat beside her feet, as she watched hatted heads bobbing past the hedge, her curiosity piqued. Something was definitely going on.

'Willow!' Ottie looked surprised. Her strawberry-blonde hair was tied up in a loose topknot, wispy tendrils falling down at the sides, a basket of laundry on her hip.

Willow felt her smile freeze at the welcome. Or rather, unwelcome, the tension as thick as clotted cream. '. . . Hey, stranger. Thought I'd pop over for a coffee.'

Ottie nodded but there was hesitation in the movement. 'Great! Come in.'

She and the dogs stepped into the cottage, Willow pulling off her wellies, noticing a cluster of shopping bags piled by the coat cupboard and reminding her she really must start with her Christmas shopping. The cottage smelled of roses and . . . something else. She couldn't place it. 'What's happening on the beach, do you know?'

'I've got absolutely *no* idea,' Ottie shrugged, going over

and standing at the big window. 'I've just been watching from here. At first I thought it was just a coincidence – a few dog-walkers deciding to come out this way today. But this?' She sighed. 'It's crazy. This is private land, after all. I was about to go down and check.'

'Oh. Well, I'll come with you then,' Willow said, pulling her boots straight back on again. 'We can have that coffee afterwards.'

Ottie's smile became fixed. 'Yes.'

They stepped outside together.

'So, what've you been up to?' Ottie asked lightly, pulling on her jacket and fiddling with the zip. 'I've not seen you.'

The statement sounded innocuous enough but they both knew there were fast-running waters beneath this bridge. Willow was the usurper to Ottie's status as heir apparent and nothing either of them did or said could change it. 'No. Sorry. I've been concentrating on getting Mam moved in to the Dower House. It was pretty depressing in there. The decor hadn't been touched in years so I've been painting all the rooms.'

'*All* of them?'

'Most of them. The ones she'll be using most. Just to get her settled in.'

'Yes, I heard she was at Shula's—'

'Did you? Who told you?' Willow asked, feeling defensive. Did the whole village know her mother had moved out of her own home? Did they think she'd been pushed out?

'Bertie mentioned it,' Ottie mumbled. 'I ran into him the other day.'

'Oh.' Willow glanced at her sister, trying not to react to his name.

They were walking down the tiny lane that narrowed to

just a path onto the beach. There were people ahead of them, behind . . .

They both frowned at the spectacle.

'And I hear we've got houseguests at the castle this weekend,' Ottie said lightly.

Oh God. Who had told her? Willow's mouth opened but it was another moment before she could push the words out. This was harder than she'd feared. 'That's right,' she said, trying to sound bright. 'Weekend hire to a private members' club. It's for their Christmas party.'

'Right,' Ottie said mildly.

'They're hosting a black-tie party tomorrow night. Everyone's welcome. You should definitely go.'

'Are you?' Ottie asked.

The thought of seeing Connor again, after the way she'd run out on him . . . 'Oh . . . no. No, I think I'll have a quiet one.'

'But it's your castle, Will. Don't you think you should be there?' There was a definite edge to Ottie's voice.

Willow bit her lip, knowing this was her moment to tell her sister the whole truth: to admit that the hosts were the soon-to-be new owners. It had to come out sooner or later. People would have to know: the Lornes' long reign was officially at an end.

'Look, Otts, there's something I have to tell you,' she said as they stepped onto the sand, the crashing sound of the sea suddenly amplified as they came around the shallow dunes.

'What the bloody hell . . . ?' Ottie frowned. They both stopped short. There had to be at least a hundred people down here. 'This is not on.'

Willow scanned the scene, trying to make sense of it too. The plastic bunting that had been strung up through the village for the Ultra the other week, was now being threaded between metal poles stuck in dual lanes in the sand, almost down the entire length of the beach. The brightly coloured plastic flags fluttered and flapped noisily in the wind.

'Is this a sports day for the Sunday school or something?' Willow asked her.

'In *December*?'

'Some sort of parade then?'

'No one's mentioned anything to m—'

The sound of music suddenly being played from a speaker – 'Eye of the Tiger', no less – made them both turn, just as a loud cheer went up.

'You have *got* to be joking!' Ottie cried as an overweight man on a bay horse suddenly trotted onto the sand, holding the reins for another horse – that looked strangely familiar – trotting beside him. Bringing up the rear was Pip and she had that look on her face that they had both seen before, too many times. Her jaw was held forwards as though locked in position, her eyes simmering with a fierce intensity and almost glowing brightness.

'Oh God,' Willow groaned as their wayward sister trotted past without even seeing them. 'What the hell is she up to now?'

Fergus whinnied, tossing his head back and giving a little rear as Shalimar was cantered out of range, down to the far end of the beach.

'Ssh, it's okay, boy,' Pip said soothingly, reaching down to stroke his neck. 'She's coming back. We're going to get her back, I promise.' He shivered in reply, his skin already prickled with sweat, the damp humid sea air mixing with the slippery trot down from the campsite car park, the excitement of being reunited with his old stable mate again.

She never took her eyes off her beloved mare, being led

down the beach to the finish line by one of Sean's grooms. It made her feel sick to see it, her proprietorial instincts bridled by the very sight of someone else casually taking away her prize horse, but she knew she had to be calm. Clear-headed. That thing she could never normally be: patient.

Just ahead of her, Sean was playing to the crowd, spinning his stallion – Galway Pride – in circles. At 16.2 hands and with a lineage to make her weep, she knew she was the underdog, by a country mile. Fergus was 15.1 hands and no looker, but he had heart, and a long memory – and like her, he wasn't taking his eyes off the prize.

He took a few steps back and whinnied again, eager to get going, as though he knew what was expected of him. Which he did. But he didn't know what was at stake. What they would lose if Sean was first to cross the line drawn in the sand.

She knew it was gamesmanship, Sean rallying the troops like this, whipping up what was supposed to have been a private race into a local event. Ottie was going to be furious when she—

'Pip!'

She looked down. Talk of the devil. Ottie and Willow were staring up at her with accusing eyes, their cheeks pink from the biting sea wind. Pip was shivering too, even though she couldn't feel the cold.

'What the hell is going on?' Ottie asked her crossly. 'Why are all these people here?'

'Don't blame me. Sean told them. We've got a race.'

'No! *Really?*' Ottie asked sarcastically, indicating the demarcated course. 'What do you mean, you've got a race?'

Pip's eyes slid over to Willow's guiltily.

Willow understood immediately. 'Oh, Pip, no! It's not another bet?'

'I had to,' she said quickly. 'You don't understand.'

'We do! We understand you almost died last time!'

'Yes, well, that's not going to happen this time. I'm not drunk, for one thing. I've given it a lot of thought. This is balanced this time. Equal.'

'Pip, it's not equal. His horse is huge!' Ottie cried, waving towards Sean with a sweep of her arm.

'I can take him,' Pip said determinedly, coughing. 'I know I can.'

'You thought that last time too,' Willow said bitterly.

Pip stared down at both her sisters. 'Look, I just have to do this. I have to win back Shalimar. I know you don't understand what she is to me but . . .' Her voice trailed away.

'And what if you don't win her back, huh? What are you losing this time?' Willow asked. 'What will *he* get out of it?'

It was a long time before she replied, the words refusing to form. 'The Lorne Cup.'

It was an even longer time before they answered.

'Tell me that was a joke,' Ottie said in a quiet voice.

'Otts, I'm *not* going to lose it—'

'That was Dad's most prized possession.'

She nodded. 'I know. It was the only thing I could offer as inducement.'

'You're not doing this.'

'Otts, I won't lose.'

'No. You're not doing this,' Ottie said more firmly.

'It's my cup,' Pip said obstinately. 'Dad left it to me.'

'And this is *my* beach! I'm calling this whole thing off right now!'

Pip sat straighter in the saddle at her words, pulling back on the reins and lifting Fergus's head up. Readying him. He pawed the sand, taking a few steps on the spot before she squeezed her knees in on his sides. 'I'm sorry.' And she trotted over to where Sean was parading near the start line.

'Pip!' Ottie cried, but her shout flew headlong into the wind, dousing back over her like a bucket of water. The crowd rushed forward seeing the two riders get ready, an expectant hush coming down like a veil so that all could be heard was the sea and the wind and the horses snorting.

Another of the grooms from Sean's yard had brought a starter's gun along with them and he raised his arm in the air. Fergus had never raced competitively before; frolicking in the field was as close as he got to gallops, but his shock from the forthcoming gunshot might just give him an edge to begin with. That or he'd go completely berserk and cart her backwards instead.

'Come on, boy,' she murmured. 'Don't let me down. Let's go get her.'

'Good luck, Pip,' Sean smirked from on-high, on her right-hand side.

'You're going to need it!' someone shouted from the crowd.

She'd have liked to flick them the bird but the reins were already threaded through her fingers and she looked dead ahead, down the straight towards the distant chestnut-brown blob by the cliffs.

The gun fired and as she had hoped and prayed, Fergus shot into action as fast as the bullet, tearing across the sand in fright before he even knew what he was doing. An almighty cheer erupted as they were off and Pip dipped down low, feeling her eyes instantly start to stream as they ripped through the wind. Out of her peripheral vision, she saw sea and sky, but no stallion, and she knew her instinct had been right, that the initial element of shock had been to her advantage. But Galway Pride was a seasoned racer; his head would be down, his rhythm balancing out and she knew his top speed would outgun theirs, and he would edge into her frame of sight, sooner rather than later.

She squeezed her knees harder around Fergus's stocky body, her knees almost up to her shoulders as she tried to bring her face down between his ears. 'Come on, boy, come on,' she urged him as they covered the beach in galloping strides, eating up the distance. Already Shalimar's shape could be seen more clearly, prancing friskily and causing the groom some problems as she watched the horses advancing rapidly towards her.

They weren't even at the halfway mark when Galway Pride edged into view, his dark muzzle gaining inches with every stride. Panic shot through Pip but she tightened her body deeper into the fold, reducing wind resistance. She could hear Fergus's breathing – heavy, rhythmic, desperate – and she spoke to him as they raced. 'That's my boy . . . Let's get her . . . Come on, boy.'

It was neck and neck. There was a hundred metres left to go and Shalimar was having to be trotted in figures of eight to keep calm. The roar of the crowd could have parted the clouds but it was dim to Pip's ear as she trained all her focus – her entire being – onto the finish line. Galway Pride had extra stride length, propulsion, horse power, conditioning on his side. But she and Fergus – they had heart. Ottie and Willow didn't understand that she wasn't doing this for glory or money, spectacle or even pride. It was for love, plain and simple, and sometimes that meant risking everything.

She saw the simple line ahead in the sand, drawn with a stick and ready to be washed away by the next tide – but it heralded everything for her. Fergus was sweating heavily, his nostrils flared for extra breath, his head dipping as Galway's rose, out of time with one another and yet nothing between them.

She could see the 'judges' either side of the line, their mouths parted in concentration as they filmed on their phones but would that be enough? Without slow-mo technology, would it detect the margin between them? This would be a photo finish, open to conjecture . . . Even if she edged it, could she make the verdict stick?

But then Shalimar, seeing them so close now, gave a loud whinny of recognition. It was the sound that she used to greet her with every morning when Pip would come down the stairs from her flat and wander straight into the stables, eyes still half closed, her hair wild . . . With a gesture of delight, she jumped high into the air, kicking her back legs out like a Lipizzaner. It had been her party trick whenever she was let out into the field and Fergus added a lunge to his gallop in reply, clearing the line by a neck's length and haring beyond it, almost sliding to a stop and nuzzling his old companion.

Pip heard a scream and realized it was hers, her fist punching into the sky as she slipped her feet out of the stirrups and jumped down onto the sand, laughing and crying so hard she triggered a coughing fit that saw her eyes stream. But she was crying anyway as she bent double, trying to believe it, her whole body shaking with adrenaline. As soon as she could breathe, she threw her arms around Shalimar's beautiful head, kissing her cheek and Fergus's too, patting his flank and telling him through her sobs how well he'd done, how proud she was, how much she loved them.

It was no accident she had suggested Shalimar be positioned at the finish post. Sean had readily agreed, considering it almost a taunt – so near, yet . . . Certain in his belief that she had no chance against his superior stables. But she knew better. It was a lure. The only being who had needed to act with any passion here was Fergus. He'd make sure he got to her first.

'Good race, Pip.'

She turned to see Sean slumped on his horse, Galway breathing heavily, his hide shiny with sweat.

'Yeah, good race,' she managed, still unable to stem the tears. She was crying like a lunatic but she didn't care. She didn't care.

'That was close. I thought I had you at the end.'

'Yeah,' she sobbed as Shalimar and Fergus nuzzled her neck, making her laugh again.

His eyes narrowed as he looked down at her, seeing the sweat matting her hair, her too-bright eyes as she coughed and laughed and cried. 'Was it worth it, all this? You've risked everything, including your own life – only to end up with exactly what you had in the first place.'

He was absolutely right. And yet, everything had changed too. She didn't know how to explain it. She laughed again, trying to control her tears. 'D'you remember that fable about the old woman who complained her house was too small, so the wise man told her to put a cow in it?'

Sean squinted in confusion.

'And then a goat. And a pig. And a dog and a cat and so on . . .' She repeatedly wiped her cheeks dry but the tears kept on coming, an unstoppable force. 'And just as she was beginning to lose her mind because they were all tearing around the tiny house, he told her to take them all out again – and suddenly her empty house felt huge . . . ?' She shrugged. 'That's kind of how I feel.'

'Right.' From the blank look on his face, she suspected he wasn't big on allegory. He gave a weary shrug. 'Look, I think you're nuts but good luck to you, Pip. I reckon you'll get what you want somehow.'

'Somehow,' she whispered back, watching him pull on Galway's reins and turn him round, slowly walking back the way they'd come. The crowd at the far end of the beach was advancing towards them in a jubilant mass, but Pip didn't need to do a celebratory lap or receive their plaudits. She took Shalimar's reins from the groom and pulled her horses in closer. She knew the value of what she had now and it was everything she wanted, all that she needed. From now on, treading water (in every sense), would be enough for her.

Chapter Twenty-Five

'See you tonight then?' Pip said, throwing the bolt on the horsebox.

'I'm up for that. Sounds fun,' Ottie shrugged. 'Will?'

'Uh . . . maybe,' Willow replied evasively, Mabel and Dot back on their leads and waiting patiently to be walked home and to the comforts of an afternoon sleep in front of the fire.

'There's no maybe about it,' Pip said staunchly. 'It's not Christmas till I've sung "Silent Night". Just look at this, we've got snow, we'll have carols, mince pies . . .' She winked and gave a cheesy smile. 'It's beginning to feel a lot like Christmas—' she sang.

'Oh God. Winning's put someone in a good mood,' Ottie grinned. 'Seven on the green, yes?'

'Yep. See you there,' Pip said, pulling the collar of her jacket closer as she shivered.' Both of you.'

'As long as you wear a thicker coat,' Ottie chided. 'You're chattering like a monkey.'

'Only because I'm sweaty now and that wind's a bastard. Laters.' She blew them both a kiss and climbed into the truck.

'Well . . . ' Ottie sighed, watching as she pulled away before turning back to Willow again. 'D'you still want that coffee?' she asked as they began to trudge up the lane too.

'Oh . . . another time,' Willow smiled weakly. 'I'm feeling pretty windswept now. I'd better get the dogs back.'

'Sure?'

'Yeah. Thanks though.'

Ottie frowned as her sister turned to leave. She seemed distracted, flat. Flattened?

' Listen, Pip's right – for once,' she called after her. Willow looked back. 'Try and make it to the carols tonight if you can. You've clearly been hard at it recently. It'd be good for you to get out. For all of us, I think. It's been so long since we did anything all together.'

Willow hesitated, the wind catching her dark hair and making it stream like ragged black silk. 'Okay then.'

'Okay,' Ottie said, watching her go, her apprehension only growing. Willow looked like she had the weight of the world on her shoulders and she felt a sudden pang of guilt that in all her shock, anger and disappointment, she'd effectively abandoned her baby sister to her new fate. Finding out she hadn't inherited had been a shock for her, but for Willow to find out she *had* . . . might that have been worse?

She walked carefully over the grass towards the cottage – the snow made it hard to see the rabbit holes so she kept her gaze firmly downward, not wanting to risk a twisted ankle – when she suddenly remembered her sister had been on the brink of telling her something, just as they'd stepped onto the beach. She turned and made to call out to her but Willow was already halfway across the field, Dot and Mabel trotting contentedly beside her. She dropped back, watching her slight silhouette become smaller and smaller. It would have to wait, whatever it was.

Ottie opened the gate at the bottom of the garden and stepped onto the smooth lawn – that was safe underfoot at least – when she noticed the boat-store doors downstairs were open. She hesitated. Burglars? It wouldn't be the first time she'd had opportunistic passers-by from the Way, looking for a spare bike or kayak. But as the door rattled against the stone wall, she realized it was the wind that was her culprit. She couldn't have closed the bolts properly when she'd been here the other day; she'd been in such a rush to get back upstairs before Ben had come back . . .

She went to fasten the door shut, when she heard a movement inside.

Tentatively, she peered round.

'Hey!' Ben grinned back at her, looking more animated than she had ever seen him. 'Are these *yours*?' he asked, indicating the dense racks of canvases propped up on rails off the ground.

She felt the floor drop away from her feet. 'What are you doing here?' she asked.

'We got back early from my appointment. I've been given the all-clear.' He looked like he was expecting a cheer, but then he saw her expression. 'Oh you mean, *here*? I saw the crowd on the beach and when you weren't here, I figured I'd walk down and join you. I noticed the door banging in the wind, so I came to shut it and—'

'And then just decided to have a nose around?' She stared at him, emotions rushing at her all at once – anger, embarrassment, shame.

'What? No—'

'How dare you? You can't be in here.'

'I'm sorry.' He looked perplexed. '. . . what am I missing here? These are incredible, Ottie' he said, holding up one of the smaller canvases. It was a vignette painted at the foot of the Morran hills. She had taken the boat out across the bay last summer and spent the day painting *en plein air*, scarcely able to stop herself. It was her favourite. She had dared to be so pleased with it. He looked back at her again. 'You have real talent, Ottie. Why did you never say you were an artist?'

'Because I'm not.'

He cocked a half-grin, as though he thought she was pulling a prank. 'Uh, *yes* you are. A blind man could see it. I mean, I know you mentioned having a place at art school, but I never realized . . . And why are none of these upstairs? You've got those huge blank walls and nothing on them?'

'Because they're not good enough.'

'Ottie,' he laughed, but the smile faded as he saw, finally, the expression on her face. This wasn't false modesty. It was fact. 'Ottie, are you serious? You honestly think that?'

'I know that. They're childish, self-indulgent, melancholic, over-dramatic.' She rushed across and grabbed the canvas from him, tossing it into the corner of the space. It caught on one of the hooks of the rack, tearing across the upper corner. She gave a horrified gasp, tears instantly springing to her eyes.

He looked down at it in disbelief. 'Ott—'

'Just get out! You have no right to be in here!' she cried, feeling herself begin to fall apart.

He stared at her, shocked by the wildness in her eyes, not understanding that this was her most private space. Her secret. The part of herself no one was allowed to see, not anymore.

'Ottie, I'm sorry, I had no idea.' He reached an arm out to her but she dodged away easily, knowing he couldn't move fast, running out with a sob. She ran into the cottage, slamming the pink door behind her, but there was nowhere for her to go, not even her own bedroom. He was everywhere. She hurried over to her bag by the front door, looking for her car keys but they weren't there. Where are they? she thought frantically, running from the sofa to the bathroom to the kitchen counter . . .

He limped through the front door a few later, looking ashen, and for a moment they just stared at one another, her sobs still high in her chest.

He closed the front door softly as she turned away, unable to bear his clear-sighted gaze.

'Did he say those things to you?'

'Who?'

'You know who.'

'No. I don't.'

He gave a weary sigh. 'Bertie.'

She shot him her most withering look but her pulse had spiked. 'Why would *Bertie* say those things to me?'

He shrugged. 'To keep you here, I imagine. To keep you small.'

She felt herself begin to tremble; after the shock in the boat shed, her emotions already felt dangerously out of control. 'That makes no sense,' she said with scorn.

'Sure it does. He wants to keep you here, waiting for him. He doesn't want you out in the world, being free, doing what you're supposed to be doing, following your talent. He'll lose you that way and he knows it.'

She blinked, staring at him on and on. This was a bluff. He couldn't know about them. *How* could he know? They'd been so careful. Discreet. '*Lose* me? Look, I don't know what you think is—'

'Just stop, Ottie.' His voice was quiet but firm and she saw in the stillness of his eyes that he did know. That he'd always known. 'I knew it the first time I saw you together – when he came over to discuss the *race details*. And the other day on the beach – you opened the curtains, remember?'

She stared at him, hardly able to believe he had guessed, that he had seen what no one else could. Hot, angry tears stung her eyes, knowing she was cornered. '. . . And what business is it of yours?'

'None,' he shrugged. 'But I know that affairs destroy lives. And I know he's not good enough for you. That what he's doing is *wrong*. Surely you can see that? He's old enough to be your father, for Chrissakes.'

'So? Age is just a number.' It was a pithy, Hallmark-card thing to say and she saw it spark his anger.

'Is it? How old were you when it started?'

'Nineteen,' she snapped back. 'Old enough to make my own decisions.'

'And how did it start?'

'That's none of your business.'

'Tell me.'

'No.'

'Tell me.'

'No.'

'Tell me.' His eyes searched hers, not letting go. He collected data for a living; he knew which questions to ask to alter the courses of entire countries. He knew how to get to the truth.

She felt something in her slacken. Give up. They'd all know in a few days anyway, and as for Ben – he'd be gone, anyway, far from here. 'He was helping me move in here, all right?' she said finally, more quietly, her eyes casting around the room, unable to meet his. 'I was about to go to art school but I wanted my own space for when I came back in the holidays. Dad knew I loved painting down here so he said I could do up this place and have it for my own, as a studio.'

'And?'

'And so that was what I was doing. Bertie happened to be

out riding on the beach one day and he looked in and offered to help.'

'And what – one thing led to another? Just like that?' Anger flashed in his eyes again, a rare peak of emotion breaking through his controlled veneer.

'No, not just like that. It happened over time.

'How much time?'

She swallowed. '. . . About a week.'

'Oh, well,' he scoffed. 'It must have been incredibly romantic.'

'It happened by accident, okay? I hadn't – I hadn't thought –' she stammered, feeling her cheeks burn. 'But he was funny. And clever. He knew about stuff.'

Ben stared at her, his mouth set in a grim line. For every one comment he did make, she could see there were ten he didn't. 'So that's why you jacked in art school. For him.'

'No.' She was vehement. 'He asked me to stay, but I said no.'

'Until your dad asked you?'

'That was different. He was my father. He needed help. I had responsibilities here.'

'And you don't think it was a coincidence that your father should do that, when he'd been helping set you up for art school – giving you the studio here? It wasn't odd to you, that he'd suddenly ask you to stay instead? Give up on your dreams just as you were packing your bags?'

'No . . .' But her voice wavered. 'Look, I don't know what you're trying to imply. Bertie couldn't have had anything to do with that.'

'Couldn't he? He was your father's best friend – a casual suggestion on the golf course to him, a few snide, crushing comments about your talent to you . . . Suddenly you're not motivated to leave and your father wants you to stay. And

Bertie gets to keep you as his pretty little secret on the private beach – right here, whenever he wants you.'

She stared at him, hardly able to believe the cruelty in his words. 'You bastard,' she whispered. 'He wouldn't do that.'

'Ottie, you need to hear the truth – he's manipulated you and he's using you.'

'He's leaving his wife for me!'

'No. He won't. They never do.'

'We're in love.'

'That isn't love. It's obvious why you're with him.'

'Oh really?' Sarcasm spiked every word. 'Could you enlighten me then? Tell me what I'm doing with my own life and why?'

He stared at her, looking almost sad. 'You've never felt good enough for your father.'

'Bullshit!' The word tore from her like a bullet.

'Is it? You're the first child and eldest daughter of the last knight of Ireland. I saw it on your face when you first told me about him – just by virtue of being born female you felt you had already failed him. It's why you were so prepared to drop your own dreams the moment he asked. You thought it would compensate at last for not being a boy. His heir.'

'Take that back,' she said in a quiet, shaky voice, her eyes burning.

Instead he stepped closer to her and, for the first time, she noticed he was walking without a crutch. 'In your heart, you've always feared he didn't really want you, so you attached yourself to the closest thing to him: his best friend. And now you think that getting Bertie to give up everything for you will finally prove you're enough, that you're worthy. But you deserve better than this, Ottie,' he said, waving his hand around the small, bare cottage. 'You should be out in the world, not kept a virtual prisoner in a field on your parents' estate.'

'Why are you doing this?' she asked, her voice cracking tears shining in her eyes, his words like hot pokers.

He stared at her for a long moment, seeing her tears. He stepped closer and swept them away with his thumb. 'Because you are throwing your life away with him.'

His voice was low. Sad. She looked up at him, seeing the care he took over her, like she was delicate. Precious. 'And what? You think I could have a better one with someone else?'

'Yes.' His eyes locked onto her and she felt it again, that change between them. The sob caught in her throat like silk on a thorn as they stood there, inches apart.

'Why do you care who makes me happy?' she asked in a voice so low it was almost a whisper.

'I just do.'

'You care about me?'

He didn't respond for a moment, but then nodded. 'Yes.'

Their faces were so close, she could have kissed him with a single pout of her lips. 'You think you could make me happy?'

He swallowed. Suddenly it was his turn to be quiet, on the back foot. '. . . Yes.'

There was a long silence. She raised a hand and traced it lightly over his newly shaven cheek, feeling his hand hover, and then settle, onto her hip, his head begin to dip towards her –

'Then drop the lawsuit.'

There was a moment of stillness as her words settled. Neither one of them moved but the air between them became solid. Dense. 'What?'

'If you care about my happiness, as you say you do, then drop the lawsuit.'

He jerked his hand away, backing off from her. 'Are you serious?' Anger inflected in his voice again.

'Bertie was with me when he was supposed to be putting the signs out; he only came over here instead because he was worried about me: my father had just died and I was distraught. Lonely. But if you carry on with this action, it'll all come out about me and Bertie and the people who'll be hurt most will be Shula and my mother.'

He had gone pale.

'Why d'you think I brought you here in the first place, Ben?' she cried. 'It wasn't out of the goodness of my heart. It wasn't because I'm a good person. It was guilt because it was *my* fault you were injured in the first place. All of this is on me. If you sue Bertie . . . then you hurt me.' She stared at him with bright, desperate, beautifully green eyes. 'Is that really what you want?'

It was her favourite day of the year. Not Christmas Day itself, with the presents and the turkey and the television specials, but this one, when anticipation beat revelation. Just the spectacle of it made Pip's skin prickle: two hundred faces lit up by flickering tea lights held in home-decorated jam jars, carols sung with white breath that hung in the night air, the church choir warm in heavy cassocks, children running between adults' legs, everyone clustered around the Christmas tree like some ancient village elder, the welcoming lights of the Hare shining in the background . . . None of the villagers ever missed this and Pip knew she wasn't alone in treasuring this annual tradition.

Ottie came back with their glasses of mulled wine, seemingly on a mission to get them all drunk – this was their third in twenty minutes. Pip hated the stuff but was drinking it nonetheless; it was the only fitting drink for tonight.

'Thanks,' Willow murmured, taking hers obediently, even though she was far from being in the party spirit. In fact, she'd barely said a word since getting here, falling back into her signature silence again.

'Thanks, Otts,' Pip said, taking hers too. 'And you can have that back.'

'What is it?' Ottie frowned, peering closer at the photograph.

'Fell out of your pocket when you took your card out to get the drinks.'

'Oh.' Ottie stared at it intently.

'Who is she?' Pip asked. 'Cheers.'

'Cheers,' Willow murmured again, casting her gaze almost nervously around the green.

'Oh, uh . . . just a camper,' Ottie replied distractedly. She had been in an odd mood all evening too, surprising Pip by turning up to hers early for a 'quick snifter' as she'd put it and making no reference at all to her red bleary eyes. Pip didn't need to ask – the bad days over Dad came and went without warning and there was never any telling when the tears would hit. 'I found it in one of the pitches when I was cleaning up the other day.'

'*She* does not look like a camper,' Pip guffawed, checking out the corporate-looking image again as she sipped on the wine. Despite both her sisters' low moods, she was in better spirits than she'd felt in weeks. Winning back Shalimar had felt karmic somehow, the universe giving her something back after the thorough kicking it had inflicted on her lately. Ottie slipped the photo back in her coat pocket. She seemed distracted too, looking around the crowd constantly, as though searching for someone in particular.

Pip coughed into her fist and pulled her collar up as high as it would go. She had put on her heaviest jacket as promised but the cold night air wasn't helping her chest and she felt wheezy. It was trying to snow again, occasional flake flurries dancing above their heads in dervishes, and she'd got chilled back at the stables after the race, trying to rug-up the horses for the night without having a moment to shower and warm herself up first.

'Brrr,' she said, stamping her feet and bringing the glass to her face to allow the steam from the wine to provide a little warmth. She wasn't sure if she was freezing cold or burning up. 'Why don't they start already? It's freezing. God, I hope Joe can hold my stool at the bar for me. I feel like a block of ice.'

'Really?' Willow said, looking at her closely for a moment, before pulling off a mitten and pressing the back of her hand to her forehead.

'You spend far too much time in that pub,' Ottie murmured.

'You don't spend enough time in it, if you ask me,' Pip quipped.

'Jeesht, you're burning up, Pip!' Willow said, removing her hand as though it was scorched.

'Or your hands are freezing and I just feel hot in comparison?'

'No. You are very definitely hot. Feel her, Otts.'

'Oh jeesht,' Pip groaned, trying to lean away and duck as Ottie leaned in too, giving a similar scowl.

'Yeah. You are. How are you feeling?'

'Same as you. Frozen. It's trying to snow out here, in case you hadn't noticed.'

'I don't think you're shivering because of the weather, Pip. You've got a nasty cough and a temperature.'

'Fine. Big deal. I'll take a paracetamol when I get in then. But please, please can we get on and sing "Away in a Manger"?' she asked pleadingly, her hands pressed together in prayer. '—Ooh.'

'Sausages, girls?' Betty, Joe's mother, asked. She was going around with a deep oven dish full of hot honey-glazed sausages.

'Your timing couldn't *be* more perfect,' Pip beamed, taking two, coughing again.

'Pip—' Willow frowned, just as Fred Malone, the choirmaster at St Agnes' church, picked up his conducting stick – or 'wand', as they'd insisted on calling it as kids – and a hush fell over the buzzy crowd. A small boy with side-combed dark hair that was trying to remain neat stepped forward, a hymn sheet in his hand.

'Once in royal David's city . . .'

His voice, as pure and crystalline as a raindrop, soared into the air so that even the babies were stilled and Pip felt a moment of peace descend. Suddenly the world felt beautiful again. Innocent and hopeful as though perhaps love really could save them all.

Her gaze fell across the faces of the gathered village residents – most of them she had known her whole life – a quiet happiness shining from them; none of them had much but her father had always said 'enough is as good as a feast' and they had what they needed. What struck her most was how *contented* they seemed and tonight, with her equine family reunited in their stables, she felt like one of their number too. She had enough.

The sound of a car door softly clunking shut made her look up and through the halo of a street light she saw her mother stepping down from the Flanagans' black Range Rover, wearing the old fox fur hat that she had bought in

Moscow with their father twenty-five years ago and which still looked chic.

'Mam's here,' she whispered to the others, nudging Ottie's arm to get her attention and sipping on her wine as she felt yet another bracket of coughs begin to tickle her throat. It was getting beyond tedious.

Ottie looked over and saw them too, her eyes fastening intently on the party of three as they tiptoed over the snow into the Hare, all eager for a warming aperitif first, before joining in.

'So at last, our hearts shall see him . . .' The village's collective voice swooped around the green as one: young and old, deep and high, tuneful and tone deaf. Pip felt herself lifted up. She smiled as she sang, her gaze swinging over the crowd gratefully and eyes met hers in silent communion, feeling it too.

But one face . . . She couldn't quite place it, her mind reaching back through the day, the week, the . . .

'Oh my God,' she whispered urgently to Willow, grabbing her sister's coat sleeve and shaking it excitedly as she remembered those movie star looks beneath a crystal chandelier. 'There's that fella from the party, the one you liked. He's here! What's he doing *here*?'

But as the question left her lips, she remembered the other things Willow had told her about him too: how he was the one who'd pulled her from the water, her hero (to be honest, he looked like a hero). But not only that – he was the one who'd wanted to buy the castle from her father, who'd undercut him in the deal. Anti-hero too then.

She fell still. Why was he here? The Lorne carol concert was of no interest to anyone but locals. It was just a small village event, not flashy enough for the likes of him. Unless . . .

Unless he planned on becoming a local too.

She looked across at her little sister with alarm, but Willow's eyes had already found him, and his her, the two of them locked in a sort of silent tussle. They were communicating without words across the crowd, their faces lit by candlelight, but what were they saying? Pip felt locked out of their conversation.

She felt a swell of coughs begin to roll through her lungs again. It always came in waves and she knew the night air was making it so much worse tonight. She pressed a fist to her mouth and tried to cough quietly, discreetly into it, but it only triggered the attack further and it took off, leaving her struggling for breath as she hacked and spluttered.

Several people took a step away from her, Ottie slapping her firmly on the back. 'You okay?'

Unable to speak, Pip nodded and gestured with her thumb that she was going to the back of the crowd, to cough away from everyone. Ottie nodded in understanding, watching with concerned eyes as she turned and dipped through the carol-singing throng, staggering over the green towards the bright lights of the pub.

Her lungs felt like they were on fire, the pain in her chest which she'd pointedly ignored on the beach and at the stables, insisting on her full attention now. Her breathing felt laboured and shallow, as though it was difficult to pull oxygen from this vaulted black star-studded sky. She looked upwards, trying to breathe and calm down, but instead she felt dizzier, like the world was tipping onto its side.

And then suddenly it did – tilting over, bringing the ground out from under her feet and pressing her cheek against the snow.

'– Pip.' The voice was urgent in her ear.

She opened her eyes, feeling the cold. She saw the Hare, perpendicular in her field of sight.

She scrabbled her feet in and tried to stand.

'Whoa!'

A hand pressed on her shoulder, trying to keep her still and she looked to see Taigh O'Mahoney crouched beside her. 'You passed out, Pip. What happened?'

'N-nothing, I slipped.' She tried to get to her feet again but she felt shaky and weak.

His eyes roamed her face. 'Your lips are blue.' The back of his hand pressed against her forehead. 'And you've got a fever. Have you had any pains in your chest?'

She pushed him away. 'No. Go away.' She stood up but her balance felt precarious, her legs like a new-born foal's, about to give way.

'Pip, you're sick. You've got pneumonia.'

'Get over yourself, Taigh,' she muttered, beginning to stagger forwards. She just needed to get into the pub and beside that fire. Once she'd warmed up she'd be fine.

'You need help.'

'I don't need any help from *you*, Taigh O'Mahoney,' she said, batting him away with a dismissive hand. 'You're not a feckin' *hero*. You don't get to *save* me.'

'I've already done it once.'

She whirled around to face him. 'No. You didn't save me, Willow did. She pulled me from the water – her and the handsome fella – so don't act like you were the saviour that night.' She narrowed her eyes, his image blurry in the brightness.

'Jesus Christ, you like to hold a grudge, don't you?' he yelled as she staggered away from him.

A grudge? She pivoted straight back towards him again

like a drunk. 'What is it with you, huh? It's like you *want* me to be indebted to you in some way. What's that about?'

He stared at her, looking at a loss, and somewhere deep inside her befuddled mind, she realized she'd hit upon a truth. 'Okay yeah, maybe you're right – I do want to save you. I do want to do something that makes you indebted to me for once.'

'Why?' she scowled.

'Because I'm forever on the back foot with you, aren't I? Doesn't matter what I do, you won't let me forget what I did all that while back, kissing that damned girl the day I finished with you. Christ, I don't even remember her name.'

'Lizzie Galloway,' she spat.

He looked surprised. 'Oh yeah. Lizzie. But you won't let me make it up to you.'

'That's right. . .' she sneered, but she was feeling so dizzy again, the cold air swirling inside her chest.

'Can't you just let it go and let bygones be bygones? I was sixteen years old, for Chrissakes!'

'I'm not interested,' she said but her voice was almost a whisper, her stare fixed on the cone of light on the ground spilling from the Hare's windows as she tried to place one foot in front of the other.

He was walking beside her, determined to have his say. 'Let's face it, it's not like it was ever going to go anywhere anyway. The likes of you don't end up with fellas like me, I knew that. I saw the writing on the wall, that was all.'

A small, sour smile played on her lips as she tried to reach the light. 'I never took you for a snob, Taigh O'Mahoney.' But as her knees buckled and she felt herself go down again, she heard his words, distinct in the dark.

'I'm just a realist, Pip.'

Chapter Twenty-Six

The blue lights whirled out of sight, the ambulance making careful progress on the snowy road. The gritters never came out here, the lanes too narrow and supposedly 'not enough' people in this little knot of land to justify the expense; it usually fell to the farmers to get their tractors out and do what they could.

'She'll be all right, won't she?' Willow asked in a scared voice as Shula tightened her arm around her.

'Of course she will. Your mam's with her and Taigh was sure it's pneumonia. He says she'll make a swift recovery just as soon as they get the antibiotics into her.'

'Poor Taigh, he looked so upset. He kept saying it was his fault.'

'That's nonsense,' Shula hushed. 'He wasn't to know.'

'But he did, that's the thing. He kept running around after her, trying to check up on her after she was discharged from hospital. He told her – and *me* – she had to rest, that we had to take it seriously. But we didn't, none of us did! She helped me move out, she helped Ottie clear up the campsite after the Ultra race, the day after she was let out of hospital. And then she was racing on the beach this morning! She's not stopped for a minute, Shula, and we *let* her just carry on. All of us.'

Shula sighed, seeing the self-condemnation in her face. 'Willow, you know your sister is a tour de force. Nothing and no one can stop her if she decides she doesn't want to stop. But at some point, she is going to have to confront the fact that she isn't superhuman. Underneath it all, she's as vulnerable as the rest of us.'

Pip, vulnerable? There was an oxymoron if ever she'd heard one.

'Hey.'

She looked up. Connor was standing just off to the side of them, clearly not wanting to intrude. Shula's arm slid off her shoulder as she saw the way they looked at each other. 'Make sure you come in for a drink and warm up.'

'I will.'

She watched Shula walk into the pub. Bertie had gone ahead to order some drinks and Ottie – well, she didn't know where Ottie was now. Talking to someone probably.

'How is she?' he asked, forcing her attention – her gaze – back onto him. This was getting to be a habit: them, Pip and a medical emergency.

'We're hoping she'll be fine. Suspected pneumonia.'

'A complication from the other weekend?'

She nodded.

'But treatable?'

'In most cases.' She stared back at him. He was wearing jeans and a navy padded Prada jacket that looked like it should be worn in the streets of Milan, not a Christmas carol concert in some tiny village in the south-western corner of Ireland. 'I didn't expect to see you here tonight. Haven't your guests arrived?'

'Yes, we've kicked off. I can't stay long.'

She swallowed. It felt violently odd, the thought of all these people . . . strangers . . . staying in her home. 'Did you get it all done in time?'

'Just. There's a few bits left to do but nothing they'd notice particularly. I hope.'

She realized he looked exhausted. She shrugged her eyebrows, desperately curious to see it on the one hand, desperate not to on the other.

'I had thought I'd see you there this week actually. If nothing else, I thought you'd want to . . . just see what we've done.'

'There's been a lot to do at the Dower House, so . . .' They both knew she'd been avoiding him but how could she tell him she felt mortified by the way she had left things between them at the pub? Reacting the way she did to what had just been an off-hand comment, a tease – her emotions had been all over the place, her response too revealing.

'Right.' There was a small pause as she looked away, refusing to connect. 'Well anyway, I thought you'd want to know as soon as possible – the finance is ready.'

Her head jerked back. 'What?'

'We managed to move fast. Our investors agreed that we can't lose Lorne twice. So the contracts are ready and being couriered over from Dublin tomorrow.'

She felt her stomach swoop like a hunting eagle. 'Right.'

He frowned. 'That's okay, isn't it? You said you wanted a quick deal.'

She stared into the distance, feeling her heart race. This was it? She'd got what she wanted? 'Of course.'

'So if you can come over tomorrow, we can sign it off and get this deal done.'

'Fine. Right. Yes.' An overdraft of 784 euros tonight. Four point three million euros in credit tomorrow.

'And then that will be our *business* together concluded.' Her eyes flashed up to his, catching the undercurrent to his words. He hadn't given up on her? 'Shall we sign at the party?'

'If you like,' she shrugged, desperately wishing she wasn't wearing a hand-knitted bobble hat. Mrs Mac had made it for her years ago and it was still her favourite, but that didn't mean she wanted to be caught wearing it by Handsome.

'Were you planning on coming to the party anyway?' he asked, jamming his hands deeper into his jeans pockets, trying to stay warm.

'No.'

He frowned. 'Why not? You *should* be there. It's your castle.'

'It'll be yours tomorrow,' she countered, quickly looking around to check whether anyone had overheard. It felt like treason just saying the words.

'It just feels wrong to have an event like that and the Lornes not be a part of it.'

'But we're *not* part of it any more. We're the past and everything's already moved on.'

'Fine then. *I'd* like you to be there.' He stared at her with the uncomplicated longing that had made everything complicated from the start. 'I want to see you, Willow. I know why you steered clear this week and you were right – it *was* better not to confuse business with pleasure. But the second that contract's signed . . .' He shrugged. 'Can't we just see where we end up?' He blinked, looking at her with eyes that made anything seem possible. Even happy endings. 'Say you'll stay.'

Ottie paced in the ladies' toilet, listening for the distinct knock on the door that elicited a Pavlovian response in her these days – dilated pupils, shortness of breath, warm flush across her chest – the sign that he was here. Finally.

It came and she unlocked the door, stepping back quickly so that he could hurry in without being seen.

'Did anyone see you?' she whispered, as he squeezed in

with her in the small space. They had met in here various times in the past – clandestine encounters gathered up on the hoof on the few occasions they had both inadvertently come here with other people; eyes following the other as they got up from their table across the pub, walking casually past with not so much as a glance . . . But that hadn't been possible on their last visit when she'd come here with Ben and it appeared his resentment with her then still lingered.

'I can't stay.' His eyes were cold and he looked older. Tired. The stress of the lawsuit was getting to him.

'I've got good news,' she smiled, undeterred. She was determined to get a happy ending out of today; her fight with Ben, Pip's collapse – there had to be some edge of silver lining.

He looked at her, hesitation in his eyes.

'He's dropping the case.'

'What?' He looked astounded. 'Gilmore's—?'

She nodded excitedly, seeing how the light came back into his eyes, making him younger again, revitalized. Her smile grew. She did that for him. *She* did. Not Shula.

His hands reached for her. 'But how did you get him to agree?'

'I just asked him to drop it,' she shrugged, tapping the buttons on his shirt like they were musical notes, fiddling with agitation.

'That was it?'

'Yeah.'

He stared at her. Could he tell she was tipsy? Upset? 'You just asked him to drop a three-million-euro lawsuit and he agreed?'

'Exactly.'

'But he must have wanted something in return?'

'Like what?'

'I don't know, Ottie. You tell me.'

She looked up at him quizzically, a confused smile on her lips. 'Bertie, I just *asked* him and he said yes. That was all.'

He held her hands, stilling them, calming her down and staring at her as though trying to read her for what she wasn't saying. But there was nothing to tell. 'Did he say anything about us?'

She swallowed, feeling her mouth dry up and her heart twist, remembering how she'd played him. Used him. 'Nope,' she lied.

Bertie looked thoughtful. 'Interesting. I thought he knew. I thought that was what he was alluding to the other night. It's his Achilles heel so I thought it was exactly the place he'd try to strike out.'

'What are you talking about?' she asked. 'What Achilles heel?'

'Huh?' He looked back at her distractedly. 'Oh, his wife left him for his best friend.'

'*What?*' Her hands dropped down from his shirt.

'Yeah. She was shagging him for years before he discovered them. Hasn't he told you?'

'No!'

Bertie looked pleased. 'Huh. No, I guess he wouldn't. No man wants to play the cuckold.'

She felt winded. 'How do *you* know all this?' she asked, appalled.

He shrugged. 'I employed an investigator to look into his life. If he was so determined to ruin my life, I'd ruin his first.' He looked back at her. 'But he definitely said to you he was calling off the suit?'

She nodded, staring past him into the reflection of the mirror. Was the woman in that photo his ex-wife? And did he still love her? Why else would he be carrying her photo around with him?

Bertie pulled his phone out. 'Listen, I'd better call my lawyer, call off the dogs. We'll pick this up later, okay?' He dipped down and pecked her on the lips, but she didn't kiss him back, too distracted by the story she'd been told – remembering how Ben had drifted away from her when he'd talked about the 'wake-up call' in his life. *Affairs destroy lives, Ottie.* His wife had betrayed him with his best friend. *That* was why he ran for days and nights, through storms and up mountains. *That* was why he hated Bertie. And she . . . she had sensed his desire for her and used it against him, she had manipulated him to get what she wanted for her lover's sake. She was no better than that woman in the photo – she had betrayed him too.

'Check the coast's clear for me, will you?' he asked, stepping back from the door so that she could peer round. 'Ottie?'

'Huh? Oh . . .' She slid back the bolt and looked out. The narrow corridor was empty, just a potted geranium on the small console table and some chunks of melting snow from someone's boots on the red and black floral-patterned carpet. Noddy Holder was yelling from the speakers in the bar.

'All clear,' she murmured.

'Great. I'll call you,' he said, slipping past and pushing open the door to the gents' as he passed so that it would be swinging back slowly on its fire-door hinges if anyone should come round the corner.

But he didn't say when he'd call.

And for once, she didn't ask.

Ottie stared at the wall with owlish eyes – the large, white, blank wall, spotted with the dark shadows of snowflakes spinning outside the window. She couldn't sleep. It wasn't that the sofa wasn't comfortable – she had slept on it every night for nearly two weeks now – nor was there any noise to distract her. If anything, it was too quiet, even the sea tonight just a gentle shush behind the glass.

Ben had been in the bedroom – still – when she had got back from the carols. They were doing a good job of managing to avoid one another: he had been in there when she'd left for Pip's earlier too, unable to stay in the house a moment longer, with him on one side of the door, her on the other.

She'd heard his voice, low on the phone to someone or several people perhaps, as he'd spoken for a while, the bass of his voice coming under the door. But she knew he'd left the room whilst she'd been out – the food she had left covered for him in the fridge had been eaten, the plate washed and put away when she'd returned. Had he been waiting for the sight of her headlights to come down the lane before disappearing into the bedroom again, avoiding her as much as she'd avoided him? She didn't blame him. But his flight was still two days from now and that felt unbearably long to suffer if it was going to be like this, the two of them like wooden figures in a Swiss cuckoo clock, one in while the other was out.

It was an odd sensation to feel displaced in her own home, unable to move freely about her own bedroom, or even go to the toilet. Talking of which, too many mulled wines . . . It only served to highlight how easy the past fortnight had been when they'd still been friends.

She turned over to take the pressure off her bladder – it was far too cold to go out to the shower block tonight – trying to get comfortable and bunching the duvet up around her neck to keep the warmth in. She stared through the window of the woodburner – a few flames still flickered weakly through the glass, embers glowing orange.

She closed her eyes and tried to sleep, willing it to come over her like a rain. But it was no good – her mind was racing, her heart too. She felt agitated and restless, her legs kicking, her fingers twiddling.

After another half hour of tossing and turning, she was no closer to sleeping and her bladder felt ready to burst. She threw the duvet off and got up, stuffing her socked feet into the muck boots by the door. Grabbing her jacket from the hook and the master set of keys, she quietly slipped outside.

'Jeesht!' she gasped, any relief at moving counterbalanced by the shock of the cold. Clouds skidded past the moon and stars, throwing intermittent shadows on the ground as she ran carefully down the garden path, through the gate, over the lane and into the snowy field to the wash block. The biting temperatures immediately snapped at her bare legs, her oversized T-shirt nowhere near oversized enough to afford any meaningful thermal protection, and she gave a prayer of thanks that the campsite was closed.

Cold fingers meant she fumbled with the locks and she went to the loo in the dark, her eyes nervously watching all the shadows, before locking up again and running back to the cottage. She may have been outside for less than three minutes but her core temperature felt like it had plummeted by half and as she let herself back in, she gasped with relief as the warm temperatures folded around her like pillows.

'Ahhh,' she shivered, shrugging off her jacket and going to pull off her boot with the opposite foot. '—Oh!'

She almost shot into the air as she suddenly saw Ben standing by the bedroom door.

'Sorry,' he said, half retreating in shock himself. 'I heard something. I thought someone was . . .' His words faded out and she realized how ridiculous she must look in a sloppy T-shirt, old socks and one boot. Her hands automatically tugged down on the hem of her T-shirt. 'But you're fine, so . . .'

He made to leave.

'Ben!'

He turned back. He was wearing his new pyjama bottoms, the ones they'd bought together – navy-and-grey striped cotton ones – no T-shirt. She tried not to stare at the outline of his abs. '. . . Yeah?'

Her mouth opened and she realized she had no idea what she wanted to say. '. . . I'm sorry.' That, but not that too.

He stared at her, giving her that inscrutable look that she would never, ever understand. 'I'm sorry too,' he said quietly.

And he went back to bed.

She stared at the closed door, words rushing through her now, too late. She wanted to tell him she was sorry about what she'd done, she was sorry about his wife – but she couldn't, not without revealing who had told her, and how he'd come by it. She wanted to tell him they should have an adventure together tomorrow – go somewhere in the car, have lunch out, a final day as friends before he crossed the ocean and went back to his own life. She wanted to tell him that she was going to miss him.

Instead, she pulled the photograph of the brunette out of her jacket pocket and set it down on the worktop, ready to secretly slide back into his bag in the morning when she heard him go into the bathroom. Had he missed it? Noticed it was gone? She climbed back into the bed, shivering from her midnight dash and tucking the duvet in tightly.

He'd said only three words but they had told her enough – that he didn't hate her, in spite of the way she'd played him.

That they were still, just about, friends. She would make it up to him tomorrow she determined, closing her eyes as the firelight flickered on her face, and this time falling straight to sleep.

It was early when she awoke. Earlier than she usually rose. Blearily, she hoisted herself up on her elbows and checked the time on her phone. Not yet six.

She frowned. Why was she awake? She'd been fast asleep, dreaming, she was sure: something about Pip, riding a dragon. A *dragon*? And it had blue eyes that flashed and—

Pip.

In an instant, she remembered last night, the terrible fuss and cries as her sister had collapsed in the snow, Taigh O'Mahoney carrying her into the Hare, an ambulance being called.

How was Pip? She needed to ring, she thought, looking up and reaching for the landline. She could never get mobile coverage down h—

The bedroom door was ajar.

The sight of it made her go perfectly still. She remembered Ben too – their fight yesterday afternoon, the tentative rapprochement in the middle of the night. 'Ben?' she called softly, wanting him to answer but not wanting to wake him either.

Nothing. She felt her heart rate accelerating like a sledge down a hill. She pushed the duvet back and swung her legs onto the floor. She walked over slowly, staring through the crack and seeing the red glow from her alarm clock casting a faint haze in the dim light. The curtains were drawn in there. He was still sleeping.

With a wave of relief, she realized he couldn't have closed it properly behind him last night, when she'd disturbed him coming back in. Closing her hand around the knob, she shut the door as quietly as she could. She breathed out one long, slow breath: waking early was bad enough, without waking to a scare too.

Wandering over to the sink for a glass of water, she wondered if it was too early to ring her mother to find out how Pip was doing. They'd travelled together in the ambulance so they'd need collecting from the hospital, *if* Pip was well enough to come home today – unless Willow was going to do it? Perhaps she would be doing it if Mam was going back to the Dower House? That would probably make more sense. She should ring her first then and find ou—

She put her glass down and stared at the counter, not understanding at first why the sight of it made her freeze. There was a scald stain in the wood from where she'd once placed a pan when Bertie's knock had come at the door unexpectedly. But it wasn't what was there that was so shocking. It was what wasn't.

The photograph was missing – and that meant only one thing.

She tore into the bedroom, flinging the door open so hard it bounced against the back wall. The curtains were still drawn but the bed was made and the bathroom was empty: towels folded, pillows plumped . . .

'No!' she cried, tears springing to her eyes as she took in the scene of desertion. Not a sign of him remained. Ben Gilmore had gone.

Chapter Twenty-Seven

'Yes, I promise, I won't move,' Pip said as her mother tucked the blanket tightly around her and pulled the curtains so that the glare of sunshine wasn't hitting her straight in the face.

Pip looked around the small bedroom, feeling like a child again: hot Ribena on the bedside table, a book beside her, the TV set up on a small table at the end of the bed.

'You really did all this?' she asked Willow, who was arranging a milk bottle with cut stems of eucalyptus and holly berries, the closest thing she'd been able to find to flowers in the garden.

Willow straightened up, looking proudly at the canary-yellow walls, the pale-pink bedroom chair, the red eiderdown. It had the same chaotic, thrown-together, mismatched vibe of the castle, only with less *stuff*. 'Well, I had nothing else to do. I was trying to make it homely.'

Pip noticed their mother's head lift up at her words and her gaze slid between the two of them, seeing how they never quite made eye contact, talking across – rather than to – each other. She had never understood what had happened between them – Willow wouldn't be drawn and her mother simply acted as though nothing had changed. But it had. Somehow she knew something terrible lived between them now, a sleeping monster.

'Now, your next antibiotic is due in an hour and a half. I'll bring some lunch up for you then as you shouldn't have it on an empty stomach.'

'Thanks, Mam.'

Her mother reached over and kissed her forehead tenderly. She looked down at her with still-frightened eyes. 'Rest,' she said firmly.

'I will. I promise.'

Her mother squinted at her through slitted eyes. 'I never trust it when you're being obedient.'

'Even I recognize I've hit the wall, Mam.' Pip sank her head back into the pillow. 'I'll stop this time, I promise.'

'Good.'

Pip watched as her mother left the room carrying out the dirty clothes ready to put in the wash, tutting at the way she'd thrown off her boots – and for a moment she had a sense of déjà vu, remembering, glimpsing, the mother she'd been before their worlds had slid into gentle ruin, fussing over them all, lovingly despairing.

Willow came to sit at the end of the bed, her back leaning against the wicker Bergère footboard, her feet tucked under the eiderdown. 'Well, it may have almost killed you – *again* – but at least you've got Shalimar back. You can relax now.'

'She'll be wondering where I am though. She was only in the stable a couple of hours before I went out again – and didn't return.' Pip felt a twinge of anxiety spike through her again.

'She was absolutely fine when I looked in this morning. Fergus kept dropping his head over her side of the stall. I think they probably slept like that, nuzzling each other's necks all night. I don't think they missed *you* at all.'

'Aww.' Pip grinned, soothed.

'And I spoke to Kirsty on the way over. She's going to deal with everything for the next few days – turn them out, poo-pick, give them fresh bedding, soak the oats and whatnot.'

'You're a good sister, you know that?'

'Hmm, you won't say that when you hear what I've got to tell you,' Willow said, staring suddenly at her hands and looking like she was about to throw up. She took a deep breath, looking ashen.

'You're selling up,' Pip said for her.

Willow's mouth dropped open. 'Today. How did you know?'

Pip looked back at her, trying to hide how her heart suddenly felt like a heavy thing. Losing Lorne, today. She'd known it was coming; Willow had warned her – in general terms, at least. But the reality of it. The finality of it. It was as though their father was dying a second time: the knighthood had gone with the knight, and now the castle too . . . 'Because I saw the buyer at the carols last night – my Hunky Hero no less. Why else would he have been there, unless he was trying to ingratiate himself with the locals?'

Willow didn't reply.

'When are you going to tell Mam?'

Willow visibly deflated. 'Christ knows. She's not been around all week. Ever since I said we had to move down here, she's been avoiding me by staying at the Flanagans' – and don't say that's me being paranoid. She's totally avoiding me.'

'Of course she is,' Pip agreed, seeing how her sister's face fell. 'It strikes me you and she are long overdue a frank conversation. And not just about the castle.'

Willow kept her gaze firmly on the eiderdown. 'Nah. As soon as the paperwork's signed, I'm out of here, Pip. I need to get back to Dublin.'

Pip frowned. 'What would you do a thing like that for?'

'Because it's where my life is now.'

'Could have fooled me,' Pip scoffed. 'You've done a fine impression of someone enjoying country life – bracing walks with the dogs every day, decorating houses, arranging flowers, flirting with handsome strangers at Daniel O'Donnell parties . . .'

They stared at one another from opposite ends of the bed, their legs overlapping the other's like an apple-pie lattice, and for a moment Pip thought she'd get her to admit it, that actually she did love it here, she did belong—

'Knock knock.'

They both turned to see Ottie's fair silky head peering round the door.

'Jeesht, you look worse than me,' Pip said as their biggest sister wandered in with a bag of jammy doughnuts from the bakery and *Horse & Hound* magazine. She tossed them down on the bed and leaned over to give her a kiss on the cheek.

'How you feeling?'

'Better than you, by the looks of things.'

'One bad night's sleep. One,' Ottie muttered, climbing into the other side of the end of the bed and tucking her feet under the eiderdown too. 'Chilly out there today.'

'Still snowing?' Pip craned her neck to see better but from her semi-recumbent position she could only see a white sky and twiggy treetops.

'Not at the moment. Brief hiatus, thank God.' Ottie looked around the room interestedly, becoming aware of her surroundings. 'Huh. It's sweet in here, isn't it?'

'It is now Willow bust a gut making it nice,' Pip said, her eyes sliding between the two of them, noticing how they didn't talk to each other directly either, the tension between them set hard.

'*You* did all this, Will?'

'I told you that yesterday,' Willow said flathy.

'Yes, but . . . I didn't realize you meant you'd done it like *this*.' Ottie appraised her through a fresh filter. 'You've got a good eye for colour.'

'Guess you're not the only painter in the family,' Pip teased, but Ottie gave only a stiff smile in return. Pip rolled her eyes. Were her two sisters trying to out-misery each other? It was like sitting with The Glums.

From downstairs, they heard a knock echo through the house; the bronze lion's-head knocker rapped against the front door.

'Ugh, please not more visitors,' Pip groaned. 'The bed's not big enough.'

That raised a smile at least, and Pip reached into the bag and handed them each a doughnut.

'So, anyway, Will's got some news,' Pip said, taking a bite of hers and instantly hitting the jammy spot, a river of red oozing down her chin.

'Oh yeah?' Ottie asked, looking across at Willow as she picked a portion of doughnut with her fingertips, like it was a croissant.

'Pip!' Willow chastised, looking panicked. Pip knew her little sister had been dreading telling Ottie as much as she was their mother. But it was like ripping off a plaster – it had to be done fast.

'What? You can't keep it from her. If it's happening today, you're going to have to come clean about it.'

'Clean about what? What's dirty?' Ottie asked.

Willow took a deep breath, her shoulders rising up to her ears. 'I'm selling the castle. Well, the estate. Tonight. The contracts are ready to be signed.'

There was another long pause, both of them looking at Ottie, waiting for . . . something. '. . . Oh. Right.'

'. . . Right?'

'Okay then.' Ottie shrugged.

Willow looked across at Pip, in case it was some kind of trick. 'This was *not* how I envisaged this going,' she cried. 'I've been bracing for tears, hysterics, thrown shoes. What is wrong with you both?'

'Half dead,' Pip shrugged, taking another bite of doughnut, almost finishing it.

'Me too,' Ottie agreed flatly and Pip frowned that she didn't even appear to be joking; her big sister really did look like she'd been steamrollered.

'Ask her who she's selling to,' Pip prompted helpfully.

'Pip!' Willow cried again, still holding her doughnut like it was a ball.

'Who are you selling to?' Ottie asked obediently, but she didn't look like she cared about the answer; she didn't look like she cared about much right now – not Lorne, not even the doughnut.

Willow bit her lip nervously. 'It's an English fella called Connor Shaye. He's got a private members' club chain: Home James.'

'Hmm . . . I think I might've heard of him.' Ottie frowned slightly, sounding vague, still disengaged. Disinterested. Distant.

'I've seen him,' Pip grinned, pretending to singe her fingers and blow on them. 'Ooh, *smokin'*!'

Even Ottie cracked a half grin at that. 'Yeah?'

'Yeah. No good though for either one of us,' Pip pouted. 'Willow got there first.'

'I did not!'

'Sure you did. You were snogging the face off him when I decided to go for my midnight swim the other week.'

'That was before I knew who he was!' Willow said hotly.

'*That* guy?' Ottie asked in surprise. 'The one whose number you didn't get?'

'Nothing's happened between us since we . . . since I decided to sell to him.'

'Yeah. 'Cos it looked strictly platonic between the two of you last night,' Pip said with her best sardonic tone. She looked at Ottie. 'You shoulda seen him, mooning over her from the other side of the green, everyone wassailing all around and her, here, bloody oblivious.'

'I'm amazed you noticed anything, given you were in the process of coughing up a lung,' Willow quipped.

'Eww!' Ottie and Pip both protested, laughing.

Ottie readjusted her legs over Willow's, looking like she'd woken up a little. 'Well, aren't you the dark horse, little Will,' she said. 'I had no idea there was all this action going on in your life.'

Willow opened her mouth to protest again but there was another quick rap at the door and their mother walked in.

'Honestly, I could hear you girls shrieking from downstairs,' she said, coming in with a large brown-paper-wrapped box. 'I thought there was a riot happening.'

'Just discussing Will's lov—'

'Pip!' Willow shrieked.

Pip chuckled tiredly with delight, her eyes widening at the sight of the parcel. 'Ooh, what's this? Pour moi?' She reached for it.

'No, not for you, I'm afraid, darling. Your sister.' And she held it out to Ottie.

Pip looked scandalized.

'For *me*?' Ottie asked in amazement. 'But . . . how did the courier know I was even here?'

'It was Taigh and he didn't. He's doing the delivery round and was about to go to yours next when he heard the racket and I said you were all up here.'

'Taigh?' Pip looked over towards the door expectantly. 'Well, isn't he coming up?'

'No. He said he had to get on.'

'Oh.' Pip blinked. 'Right.'

'Oh, girls, really, what are you . . . have you untucked the covers?' their mother tutted. 'I was trying to make Pip *cosy*.'

'She is cosy,' Ottie shrugged, finally taking a bite of doughnut. 'Although she could do with shaving her bloody legs. Ugh, they're *prickling* me!'

Pip rubbed her leg up and down for good measure, making both of them squeal.

'And what are you all doing eating doughnuts in bed?' their mother despaired. 'You'll get sugar in the sheets and Pip'll never sleep tonight with sugary sheets.'

Their mother untucked the offending sheets at the side of the bed and began sweeping out non-existent sugar granules – they were all on top of the bed – before tucking her (them all) back in again.

But Pip and Willow didn't care about sugary beds; they were watching as Ottie slowly opened the box, trying not to rip the paper. 'I just don't know what this could be . . .' she murmured. 'I haven't bought anything recently. Have I?'

'How would we know?' Pip asked, throwing her hands out to the side questioningly and spraying sugar all over the pillows.

'Christmas present?' her mother suggested.

'Fat chance.'

'Paints?' Willow tried.

'No.'

'Oh jeesht, just hurry up and open it already,' Pip muttered, losing patience as Ottie began folding down the Sellotape strip in order to reuse the packaging paper.

Ottie pushed the paper to one side and lifted out a large matt-black box tied with an ivory satin ribbon. She pulled on the ties and opened it, peeling back the dense layers of tissue like they were the petals of a rose, her mouth falling into a perfect 'o' as she saw the bundle of red silk folded inside.

'Wow!' Willow cried.

'Jeesht!' Pip spluttered.

'Oh no!' Ottie whispered, her fingers tearing at the small envelope of the notecard that lay on top.

'For a Red Dress life, you first need a red dress. Thanks for everything, Ben.'

'A red dress life?' Willow asked in bewilderment, as Ottie read the words over and over, her fingers threading the smooth silk.

'Ben?' Pip lay back in the pillows and smiled. 'Who's the dark horse now?'

'Mam?

Willow stood on the landing at the bottom of the ladder.

'Up here.' Her mother's voice sounded distant – in every sense.

Willow climbed the rungs and peered into the cavity of the attic. It was an entirely different beast to the roof rooms of the castle, where they could stand and play and do star jumps if they so chose. Here, the low roof meant passage across the rafters was on hands and knees only.

She peered into the dimly lit space, a hand-held torch providing only a narrow cone of light in which to see. 'What are you doing up here?' she asked, watching her mother rifle through a large chest.

'I thought I'd see what was up here – there's never going to be enough storage in the rooms to take all our things. Just look at this.' And she sat back on her heels, holding up what looked – in silhouette – to be a fringed shawl. 'My goodness, the quality.'

'Whose is that? The Wheelers'?'

'No, it's all ours. They never had the key to get up here. Your dad only found it a few years ago by accident, but he didn't want to disturb the Wheelers. They weren't the easiest people to deal with. He said it could wait till they left.'

'What else is there?' Willow asked, turning her head left and right to see the size of the attic. The entire roof cavity was one space with just the stone chimney stacks interrupting the flow. She could make out dark, irregular lumps and bumps all over the place.

'An old pram. Victorian, I think, although sadly it looks like the mice have got to it. And there's a box of what looks like old wallpapers and a—' She gasped, pulling out something large and rather . . . rustly. 'Oh my goodness, Willow, just look at *this*!'

Reaching for the torch, she shone the beam on an emerald-green satin dress. It looked Edwardian, with puffs at the shoulder slimming into tight sleeves, a tiny waist and a long skirt. 'It's immaculate,' she whispered, her hands skimming over the fabric, looking for tears, holes, stains, any blemishes at all. 'Whoever packed this trousseau knew what they were doing – there's layers and layers of acid-free tissue paper. Everything's just perfectly preserved. Oh, *what* I would have done to have worn a dress like this. I wonder whose it was . . . ?'

Willow watched her mother rummage like a child in a

sweet shop through the long-forgotten family treasures. Was it a good omen that she should be delving so physically into their past like this, on the very day they let go of their ownership of Lorne? Was it a sign they weren't losing everything after all, but just acreage and stones? That what remained of the lives of the people who'd lived here, they'd still have: the castle's contents, this house, everything up here . . . She balled up her courage, knowing the moment was upon her. She couldn't put it off any longer. 'Mam, there's something I need to talk to you about.'

'Uh-huh?' She reached into the chest again and gave another gasp as she pulled out a cotton chemise.

'It's important.'

'Darling, can't it wait? Can't you see how *thrilling* this is for me? I always longed for a moment like this back home but there was nothing left to find. All your ancestors had already raided the castle's secrets long before we ever got there. Oh, Daddy would have loved this so much. Just so much.' She clasped the chemise to her chest, her voice wavering slightly as she lost herself in some old memory, cutting out the present. Willow herself.

Always that.

'Sure. We can talk about it when you come down,' Willow said quietly, going to climb back down the ladder.

'Oh, but take this, darling.' She looked up to find her mother carefully rolling the green dress into a ball and throwing it to her. 'Now that the chest has been opened, I don't want any dust getting into it. The colour is just sublime. Put it on my bed, would you?'

'Sure.' She descended the ladder with the dress draped over her shoulder, turning to find Ottie coming out of Pip's room with the red dress over hers.

'She's sleeping,' Ottie whispered, closing the door quietly behind her. 'Pretty much dropped off mid-sentence.'

'Oh.' They stood together on the small landing for a moment, still somehow distant and apart, divided by secrets. Willow's gaze fell to the red dress. '. . . So who *is* Ben?'

Ottie gave a careless shrug. 'Just a guy I've been helping out. He was the runner in the Ultra who got injured.'

'That one who got lost?'

'Yes. He was supposed to be camping but he clearly couldn't stay in a tent with a torn cruciate ligament, so I said he could . . .' She shrugged.

Willow's eyes widened as she remembered suddenly the other smell in the cottage when she had stopped by yesterday: it had been . . . male. 'You let him stay in your house? A complete stranger?'

'He was a nice guy – mellow. Professional. *Injured*.'

Willow stared at the dress again. 'And he bought you a red dress?'

'. . . Yeah. To say thanks, I guess.'

'Yes. Because people often say thanks with exquisite red dresses.'

Ottie arched an eyebrow, not appreciating her sarcasm. 'That isn't what this is.'

'No?'

'No. It's in response to a conversation we had about Red Dress lives.'

Willow blinked. 'Okay, you've lost me. What's a Red Dress life?'

Ottie stared at her with exasperation, as though she was willingly being obtuse and Willow saw suddenly how truly upset her sister looked. 'It's a life that's bigger and bolder and better than this one. It's a life where you get to travel and meet new people and do exciting things and go to glamorous parties and wear—'

'Red dresses,' Willow finished for her, seeing the tears shining in her sister's eyes.

Ottie swallowed, staring down at her own feet. 'You get that, right? You left and found yourself a Red Dress life in Dublin.'

'I guess so,' she said in a quiet voice. It just wasn't *why* she'd left. 'Ottie . . . are you okay?'

There was a long pause before she responded. 'Yeah,' Ottie nodded, pushing her lips together and composing herself, but it was a lie – her movements seemed unnatural. Forced. She gave a small sniff and looked back at her. 'What's that you've got, anyway?' she asked, reaching out to take the green dress from her. '– Oh my god!'

'I know. Beautiful, isn't it?'

'It's sensational.'

'Mam's up in the loft on a treasure hunt, looking for more.' Willow rolled her eyes. 'I just went to find her to tell her about . . . tonight. But she's too wrapped up in rummaging through old boxes to even listen.'

As if on cue, they heard another small shriek from the rafters.

'Well, another few hours won't make any difference, I guess. There's no turning this tanker around now. And if it means she's happy a little while longer . . .' Ottie shrugged.

Willow sighed. 'D'you want a cup of tea then?'

'Could do,' Ottie shrugged, walking a few steps before stopping and turning back to her. 'Unless . . .'

'Unless what?'

A conspiratorial smile crept onto Ottie's face. 'Unless you want to try on these dresses.'

Chapter Twenty-Eight

Ottie stared at her reflection. The dress didn't say thank you. It said 'Hello!', 'Wahay!', 'Come closer', 'Take me off . . .'

The colour was a scarlet bloom against her skin, a blood-drop in the snow, the dress cinching her waist, skimming her hips, the low front making a discreet show of her décolletage. She'd never worn a red dress before for precisely this reason. It made a statement. It was a dress with intent. She couldn't blend in in this, nor hide away.

But wasn't that exactly what she wanted? Wasn't that what Ben was saying to her in giving her this? It wasn't an encouragement for her with Bertie, of course, but no more hiding in plain sight was what he meant. It was time to step out of the shadows. To be noticed. To be claimed. She had given everything to Bertie and done all that he'd asked. She had exacted her pound of flesh from Ben – excrutiating though it had been. Now it was his turn to act.

She had waited long enough. It was time to take matters into her own hands.

She stared at herself in the mirror and understood that the time had come: tonight was the night she was claiming her man.

Willow blinked, giving a little twist this way and then that. The green satin rustled like an autumn morning, her silhouette whittled and moulded as if carved from clay. She had never seen herself look like this before: womanly and sophisticated, and she'd certainly never foreseen a puff sleeve in her sartorial future.

The colour made her hair look even more raven-black and, for once, that didn't seem like a bad thing. Beside her, Ottie was looking dumbstruck in red silk, and she sensed both of them were changelings, moving from what – or rather who – they had been, to someone new.

Ottie turned to face her with not so much as a glint of jokiness in her eyes. 'I want to go to the party.'

'. . . Okay. You make that sound like a scary thing.'

'It is. Which means you're coming with me.'

'What? N—'

'In that.' She gestured towards Willow's dress.

'No! No way!' Willow laughed.

But Ottie's eyes were burning with the intensity that Willow knew only too well from her other sister, now placidly sleeping in the next room. She swallowed, knowing what it meant . . .

'Okay, look, I need to go over there to sign the paperwork anyway so I'll go with you but . . .' She swallowed, thinking of Connor's words last night, the promises in his eyes. The deal was almost done. There was nothing to stop them now. How easy it would be to fall for him, to let herself believe in love at first sight and Happy Endings . . . No. She shook the thought away. 'I just need to do what has to be done and leave again. I can't hang around.'

'Exactly. Me neither.' Ottie clutched her arm desperately. 'Just say you'll wait for me.'

'What is it you've got to do?'

'I . . . I can't tell you yet. I will, I promise, but there's something I have to do first. *Please* – safety in numbers?' She held out her little finger in a crook. Pinky promise. Their girlhood game. 'Sisters before misters.'

Willow stared at it. She could do with a back-up option too. Someone to make her go through with what had to be done. Someone to make her leave. She crooked her little finger too and linked the two of them together. 'Sisters before misters,' she smiled.

Pip lay in bed, listening to the murmur of her sisters' voices coming up through the floorboards. It sounded like they were preparing to go out, shouts of 'Come on!' and 'What now?' drifting up the stairs.

From the crack between the curtains, she saw it was dark outside. Were they off to the party at the castle? She hoped not. There was something perverse, in her mind, to be visiting your own home as a guest.

Still, there had been enough damned buzz about it. Perhaps curiosity had got the better of them? It was all anyone had been talking about in the Hare for the past week: should they go? Why go? What would they wear anyway . . . ?

She didn't know how long she had been asleep, only that she had slept deeply. Her limbs felt shot through with lead, the blankets heavy upon her; someone had tucked her in again, she saw. The copy of *Horse & Hound* was now set on the bedside table and the empty doughnut bag carefully folded and placed in the waste-paper basket. Ottie, then.

Suddenly the front door slammed, the reverberations shaking the windows in their frames, her sisters' voices just about audible as they walked down the overgrown path towards the car.

Alone again, Pip looked around the room – her room –

with pensive eyes. She would never live here, of course; her home was at the stables now. But her mother had been at pains to get her to 'choose her room' as they'd come in from the hospital this morning, as though this detail of ownership would make all the difference. Willow had done a terrific job in cleaning everything up and getting a coat of paint on the ceiling and walls, but the room was still pretty bare – in fact, Pip had never seen such a dearth of 'stuff'. It was a typical 'spare' room with a lamp on a table, a chair by the window, one or two books pulled from a box and set on the windowsill but which no one would ever read. It paid lip service to the idea of the life that would be lived in this room but the reality was, her mother would be alone in this house. A widow in her new home.

She thought back to Willow's confession, the fear in her face as she'd revealed the sale was happening today. Or was it tonight? Perhaps it had already happened. Oh God, had she slept through it? Was Lorne lost to them already?

The thought of it was like a cold hand around her heart. She tried to turn under the covers but she was so tightly held down, like a moth on a pin, she fell back into the same position again, too feeble to argue for once.

She tried to submit to the inevitability of it all, to summon the laissez-faire vibe she had passed off to Willow as she'd looked into her scared eyes. The castle had to be sold, they all knew that – this was an inevitable reality that had had to be faced and she couldn't continue trying to be like her father, fighting unwinnable battles. In her desire to have everything, she'd very nearly lost everything. She had to remember that.

Tread water, that was what she'd told herself when she'd won Shalimar back. Everything was simply back to how it had been to begin with and that was enough. *Enough is as good as a feast*. She had Shalimar and Fergus, her name on the deeds for the stables . . . So why, then, did she feel like something was still missing? She had a feeling she couldn't shake, that something vital had changed. But what?

A sudden scream made her jump, loosening the blankets enough that she could scramble out of bed, but her blood pressure needed another moment or two to catch up with her and she stood, feeling woozy for a second, before staggering to the bedroom door just as the cry came again.

'Mam! Mam! I'm here,' she called, lurching into the hall and trying not to pass out as she reached for the ladder. 'What is it?'

Chapter Twenty-Nine

'Oh my *God!*' Ottie hollered as they turned onto the castle drive from the Dower House and abruptly stopped, their headlights facing directly into those of the trail of cars coming nose-to-tail through the main gates opposite. But it wasn't the cars they were looking at.

'It's . . . pink,' Willow replied, in case that fact had been missed by her sister.

They looked at each other in mutual shock horror.

'The castle's *pink*?' Ottie spluttered, giggling, before throwing her head back against the headrest and beginning to laugh. Hard.

'The castle's pink,' Willow echoed, joining in and belly-laughing too, convulsing ever harder as she thought of her father's face had he ever seen his ancient, rugged, stoic castle draped in pink light. 'B-b-bad enough he had three daughters,' she gasped, having to clutch her sides. 'But to have a pink castle too . . .'

'It's not . . . it's not funny,' Ottie howled, beginning to slide down the seat, only her seat belt keeping her up.

'I'm not laughing,' Willow roared, slumping in the driver's seat too.

They hadn't laughed like this since they'd been kids and Ottie had wet herself when Pip – in a riding lesson at Halloween

– had dressed as a scarecrow and her horse had spent the class trying to snatch at the straw stuffed into her shirt and trousers.

A sharp rap at the window made them both jump and instantly stop laughing.

Slowly, Willow rolled down the window. 'Yes, officer?' she asked, setting Ottie off into another fit of hysterics. Willow had to dab her eyes to keep from following suit.

'I'm afraid you can't stop here,' a young guy in a black Nehru jacket said to them, a torch in his hand.

'I'm afraid we can. This is our castle.'

'Our *pink* castle,' Ottie blustered, completely unable to stop from laughing. She had lost the plot.

'It is. It's our pink castle,' Willow giggled, turning her head to her sister. 'Oh my God, I feel drunk and we're not even in there yet!' Her shoulders shook. 'I've got paperwork to sign! I've got a pink castle to sell!'

'And I've got a marriage to break up!' Ottie wheezed.

The laughter died in Willow's throat. *'Huh?'*

Ottie stared at her, not blinking, seeing the horror in her sister's eyes. 'Just kidding!' she laughed, bursting into hysterics again.

'Oh my God!' Willow screeched, slapping her hand over her chest as if to still her heart. 'I thought you were serious!'

The young guy looked between them both, completely baffled by their behaviour. 'Um . . . well, if I could just ask you to park the car somewhere over there. We need to keep this access clear in the event of an emergency.'

'Absolutely, officer,' Willow agreed, still giggling, wiping her eyes dry and certain she must have rubbed all her make-up off. 'Oh jeesht, Ottie, am I all streaky now?'

'What? Streaky like bacon?' Ottie asked, craning her neck to examine Willow's face as she drove. 'No, you're not streaky like bacon,' she chuckled, little pockets of laughter still making her shoulders shake as they drove up to the front and parked overlooking the lawn. The grandest of the specimen trees had been picked out with spotlights, fairy lights draped over new, perfectly half-domed bay trees that had been positioned around the edge of the parking area in smart black-painted containers.

They climbed out of the car together, seeing how the taxis kept on coming, extravagantly dressed guests spilling out in frothy dresses and smart tuxes.

'Right . . .' Willow sighed, feeling her laughter finally fade as she looked back at the castle she was about to sign away. Nerves had a funny way of showing themselves sometimes. 'So then I guess this is it.'

'Yeah,' Ottie murmured, looking significantly less amused herself now. 'You ready?'

'. . . As I'll ever be.'

They walked side by side – so close their hands brushed each other – along the drive, up the steps and into the great hall.

'Oh my God,' Ottie gasped in amazement again.

Was this still Lorne, Willow asked herself? Unlike Ottie, she had at least seen some of the transition from what it had been to this: she had seen the tatty stair carpet lifted, the million and one rugs rolled away, the stern ancestors no longer bearing down from the walls. She had helped pack away all the photos and vases, jugs and trinkets, shields and heraldic memorabilia, the hall tables and chairs, Rusty, their entire lives, so that all that remained was this basic framework – the imposing split staircase, coffered panelling, galleried landing . . .

But where once the wooden walls and floor had been a

rich, polished, almost burgundy oak, now it was pale and stripped back to a raw, texturized blonde. And she had certainly never anticipated seeing, hanging from the centre of the ceiling, almost filling the gallery space, four metres tall and *upside down,* a Christmas tree! There wasn't a bauble or swag of tinsel to be seen on it, instead its bushy branches splayed floorwards as though reaching for the guests as they passed underneath, its lush verdancy so tactile she wanted to reach out and brush her palm against it. There was a purity to the bold design statement that felt modern but also timeless, putting a stress on the natural, the raw, the crafted – and not the grand, as she had expected.

'That thing's not going to fall on us, is it?' Ottie muttered under her breath, as they heard the gasps of the other guests coming in behind them.

'This place!'

'Ohmigod, how did they get that tree up there?'

'Imagine living here . . .'

Ottie and Willow shared a knowing look. The delights of this place were as much about what couldn't be seen as what could. Little did anyone here know – and would never know – that beneath the floor was a narrow staircase that led down to a small room which flooded when the water table was high and had been used in the past as a cell for trespassers, enemies and unfortunate tax collectors. Nor would they ever know what speeds you could get up to whizzing down the bannisters. Or that there were listening holes in some of the walls, allowing conversations to be overheard several rooms away.

A waiter came over with drinks and they automatically took one each, eavesdropping on the awestruck comments as they walked slowly with the line that had formed, making its way into the ballroom.

'Do I look okay?' Ottie hissed under her breath as a model-type drifted past in a tiny sequinned Balmain number.

'Incredible. Although I still can't believe your lodger bought you that dress,' Willow remarked, glancing over at her again as they both took hurried, nervous sips.

'Yeah, well, you know how poor the flower selection is in Tesco.'

Willow chuckled.

'Besides, I can't believe Mam found *that*. It fits you like a dream.'

'Hmm, I'm not sure,' Willow murmured, feeling self-conscious in it and not just on account of the bright colour and sweeping neckline. Most of the women were in Net-a-Porter's latest and by comparison this dress looked like what it was: a very old hand-me-down.

'What are you not sure about? You look the bomb. I already caught some fellas checking you out over there.'

'Ugh, that's the last thing I need. I've got to keep my focus – do what I need to do, you can do your thing, and with any luck we can be out of here and in front of the telly before *Strictly* finishes.'

'You do realize that's the most tragic thing you've ever said, right?' Ottie asked as they stepped through into the ball-room.

'Totally— Whoa!'

Again their eyes rose up as they were forced to scan the sight of the room in silence: a giant six-metre cloud of tiny white flowers and feathers seemed to hover just off the ceiling, the monolithic pillars wrapped with thick garlands of ivy and white Christmas roses. 'Who *are* these people?' Ottie shouted as they shuffled in, the volume levels quadrupling immediately. 'Is this normal in their world?'

'They might say the same of us? We're the ones who lived here, remember.'

Her use of the past tense made them both flinch.

'Yeah, well, not like this we didn't.' Ottie bit her lip. 'And I still don't know how the hell they did all this in a couple of weeks.'

'Manpower. Joe said they put two hundred people onto it apparently.'

'Jeesht, no wonder he's been in such a good mood lately. His Christmas has certainly come early.'

At the far end of the room was a ten-metre-long onyx bar, a DJ playing on a purpose-built stage, the vibrations thrumming through her chest, and for a moment, Willow felt her worlds collide: Dublin and Lorne, freedom and familiarity, present and past. She swayed a little.

'You know this song?' Ottie asked her, having to shout in her ear to be heard.

'Sure. They're playing it in all the clubs.'

'That makes me feel old. I can't remember the last time I went to a club,' Ottie said.

'I don't know why. You're twenty-six, not fifty. You should be going out and meeting hot guys.'

'Like you, you mean?'

'Exactly. Have some fun.' Willow tossed her dark mane back, feeling the party mood begin to twist around her in spite of her nerves – or perhaps because of them.

'And what if I want more than "fun"?'

Willow shot her a warning look, stepping into the bigger sister's shoes again. 'Don't buy into that trap, Ottie. There are no happy endings.'

'Well, clearly that's not true. Look at Mam and—'

'No!' Willow's tone stopped her in her tracks. 'Don't perpetuate that lie.'

'Willow!' Ottie said, baffled. 'What on earth –?'

But Willow was looking around the crowd with a studied determination. 'I don't recognize anyone. Do you?'

Ottie blinked, disconcerted, by what had just passed between them. 'Not so far.'

'Looks like the local uptake is low.'

'Course it is. That invitation was just a PR stunt. Everyone saw through it. They're having their own party in the Hare instead.' Ottie suddenly clutched her arm gratefully. 'Just thank God *you're* here. I don't think I could go through with this on my own.'

'Through with what? You still haven't told me what's going on and you promised you would.'

'And I will.' She sipped her champagne nervously, scanning the crowd. 'I definitely will. I just don't want to jinx it. I just need to see him first.'

'*Him?* Okay. Well, that's some sort of clue, I guess.'

Ottie looked back at her nervously. 'You are not Poirot so don't even try.'

Willow groaned. 'Oh jeesht, the Flanagans are here,' she said with a roll of her eyes.

'Where?'

Willow pointed them out across the room, standing by the bar. 'Might've known *they'd* make it. They're always so terrified of missing out on anything. It's sort of sad really.'

'I blame Shula. Just look at her,' Ottie muttered, staring over from the top of her glass. 'That dress is way too young for her. She's so desperate to be noticed.'

'Yeah – by her husband probably.'

Ottie's head whipped round. 'What does that mean?'

Willow hesitated, then leaned in. 'Keep this to yourself – but Shula's convinced he's having an affair.'

'. . . *What?*'

'It doesn't surprise me,' Willow said witheringly. 'He's absolutely the type: egoistic, vain, desperate to stay young . . .You know what they say – once a cheater, always a cheater.' She took a vicious swig of her drink.

'How do you know all this?'

'What – the type? Jeesht, there's guys like that all over the place in Dublin. So fucking tragic, they really are.'

'No, I mean . . .' Ottie looked flustered. 'How do you know Shula thinks this?'

'Shula told Mam, who told Pip, who told me at the hospital this morning. Apparently, that's why Mam's stayed with them so long – not just because of her crisis with moving out, but Shula's! Mam's been trying to get her to leave him.'

Ottie's eyes were wide. 'And is she going to?'

Willow shrugged. 'Who knows? Easier said than done, I guess.'

'I guess.' Ottie bit her lip. 'Does Bertie know she knows?'

'Don't think so. Apparently she's playing her cards close to her chest till she's consulted a lawyer and decided what to do.'

'Does Shula know who the other woman is?'

'Yes, but Mam said she wouldn't say who.' Willow sighed. 'Not that it'll stay secret for long. If there is some huge expensive divorce, all the gory details will end up in the papers anyway. Grim. Absolutely grim.' She tipped her head towards her big sister, eyes blazing. 'One more reason why never to get marri . . .' Her voice faded out as she caught sight of Connor coming into the room.

Every time.

The sight of him floored her every time.

He had entered via the hidden door in the panelling that

led to a passage between here and the kitchen – were the castle's nooks and crannies becoming known to him already, the old lady of Lorne giving up her secrets so soon? He was wearing black tie – no novelty print or tricksy details, just a classic bespoke suit that didn't need to shout for attention. But then with that face and that physique, he didn't need gimmicks . . .

He looked uptight and distracted, very much on duty as his gaze swept over the crowd, checking all the details were correct. He had worked around the clock to make this party happen: employing a small army, throwing money at every problem, all to give his guests a wild time and consolidate his brand. Was he happy? Relieved? Was this how he'd imagined tonight – this weekend – playing out?

It was an unmitigated success, without question. She looked at his guests – almost all of them young, beautiful and rich, in spite of the 'open house' invitation that had gone out to the village. They all looked like they *ought* to be dancing in a ballroom in an Irish castle the weekend before Christmas, as though their lives were filled with these gilded moments.

She turned away sharply, feeling the reality of the moment fall upon her as she realized this was 'it', the moment of transition when Lorne stepped into the future.

'Christ, I need another drink. *Now,*' Ottie muttered agitatedly, looking around for a waiter. At some point in the past minute she had drained hers.

Willow watched as Connor chatted to one of his staff, saying something in his ear and oblivious to the interested glances landing on him like arrows. He hadn't seen her yet and she was keen for it to stay that way a little longer. Their interactions were invariably weighted down by invisible forces that tipped them both off balance. One of them always seemed to say or do the wrong thing and the urge to avoid him was as powerful as the need to run to him – an unwinnable push-pull that kept her rooted to the spot. 'Yeah, me too. Let's go to the bar.'

'Oh, no, but . . .' Ottie lagged back. 'Can't we just find a waiter?'

'Don't worry. I've got a technique that gets me served at any bar in under a minute flat,' Willow said assuredly, just as a waiter suddenly stepped in front of her.

'Miss Lorne,' he said, taking her by surprise.

'Perfect,' Ottie gasped, looking relieved and taking two glasses for herself, half downing one in a single gulp.

'Yes?'

'Mr Shaye has asked if you can meet him in the library in a few minutes.'

Willow blinked at the messenger. Connor had seen her? When? She'd barely lifted her eyes off him. '. . . Sure.'

'Would you care for a fresh drink first?' the waiter asked, seeing her empty glass and nervous expression.

'Better had,' Ottie said with a knowing look and seeming slightly more relaxed herself now as she downed her other glass too.

The waiter glided off.

'So then it's finally time to let this old lady go,' Willow murmured, her eyes casting around the room as if for the last time, coming to rest on her sister.

'And you're absolutely sure about this?' Ottie asked her. 'No second thoughts?'

Willow hesitated, then shook her head – it was all done anyway. Her signature wasn't going to make it any more real; the handover had already happened – the lives she and her sisters and her parents had lived here were already part of the past. They had moved out, the castle patched up, stripped back and brought back to life with this glamorous party crowd . . . It was more painful than she had imagined it would be; sitting in the study that day, staring at Connor's telephone number, this revenge had tasted sweet. But it was bitter now. She swallowed hard. 'No. You?'

Ottie sighed and looked at her with apprehensive eyes. She looked terrified too, yet her voice was firm. 'No.'

'Okay then. Well, you go do whatever it is you've got to do and I'll do what I've got to do and I'll see you back in the hall in ten minutes.'

Ottie grabbed her hand and squeezed it hard. 'Ten minutes and it'll all be done, Will. And then the rest of our lives can begin.'

Red Dress life. It was an easy concept to define; grabbing hold of it, though, was another matter. In her head, it had all seemed so clear: they loved each other. This was what she'd always wanted, the opportunity to live their lives freely. Together. But standing here now, alone, preparing to grab it . . . She felt overwhelmed and unsure. Was this *really* the right time? If Shula suspected, who else did too? She already knew what the gossips would say – like Ben, they wouldn't see love, only the age difference, the betrayal, the *scandal*—

'Hey, Ottie, I didn't expect to see you here,' a voice called out of the music.

Ottie looked in surprise to see Lorna Delaney making her way over to her. Ottie didn't know her well, other than that she lived in the next village, Ballymorgan, and worked at the Stores for her parents. She was wearing a second-skin python-print dress, her hair dramatically blown-out and far too much make-up. Ottie guessed that she was feeling intimidated by the sophisticated party crowd and was grabbing for any familiar face. 'Hey. How are you? I've not seen you for ages.'

'Been keeping myself busy,' Lorna shrugged. 'You?'

Ottie wondered whether it had passed Lorna by that her father had recently died, or whether she just didn't give a damn. 'Oh . . . yeah. Things have been . . . hectic . . . Quiet season now though, thank God. It's nice to have a few weeks of peace before everything kicks off again in the New Year.' Ottie forced a smile but she didn't want to be making small talk with this girl; she wanted Bertie to look over and see her here. She needed to tell him that Shula knew, the pretence was over. His marriage was dead one way or the other.

She could see him from here, still at the bar, engaging in polite chit-chat with a man to his right, his glass held loosely in one hand, the other stuffed casually in his trouser pocket. He looked infinitely at ease, and clearly oblivious to his own impending disaster. For Shula, beside him, was looking miserable, lost even, as she scanned the crowd with blank eyes. She looked pale beneath the lights and seemed to have lost weight too . . . Was he really so blind to his wife's evident distress?

Ottie swallowed, feeling a pang of self-doubt at the sight of her rival looking defeated already. Though she was her mother's best friend, Ottie actually rarely saw her; she and her mother always having long lunches in Waterford or spa trips away together, dinners at the Flanagan estate or else evenings at Lorne when Ottie was ensconced in her beach cottage. She had become almost theoretical in Ottie's mind, someone who neglected her husband and was more interested in her social life and status than a fulfilling personal relationship.

She saw Bertie's head turn in her direction, saw him startle at the sight of her in the red dress. Here to be seen; she would no longer hide nor be hidden. His mouth opened, as though to say something to her? Or his companion? She couldn't be sure.

Their eyes were locked, two hundred people between them when she needed, more than ever, to see him alone. But –

It was already too late.

Shula had seen her too, as though feeling the flow of her husband's focus across the room, and now she was hurrying towards her, pushing through the crowd with an anguished expression that told her everything: that this was going to happen right here. Right now.

Everyone was going to see. Everyone was going to know. Be careful what you wish for, right? Wasn't it what she'd wanted?

Beside her, Lorna was saying something, rabbiting on between sipping her drink through a straw and scanning the crowd for the next vaguely familiar person to latch on to.

Ottie couldn't move. Her feet like tree roots, fastening her to the ground, helpless as Shula advanced with all the righteous fury of the betrayed. She swallowed and took a few deep breaths, aiming for a dignity that was going to be scattered in the next twenty seconds. Ten seconds . . . Five . . . And then she was there, less than two metres away, the crowd that had separated them like a school of fish now reduced to just the predator and the last remaining prey.

She saw Shula's arm reach back as if in slow-motion, saw the way her mouth twisted and her eyes narrowed to slits, the flat of her hand slicing through the air and—

Ottie staggered back in stunned horror. The world shattered into a million crystal pieces.

Lorna's hand flew to her cheek, the handprint immediately livid and raised.

'Stay away from my husband, you little bitch!' Shula screamed at her. 'You hear me?'

Willow walked down the hallway, past the dozens of strangers carousing in her home. Small groups stood clustered against the walls, nibbling on canapés and chatting casually beneath the flower clouds, scattered couples getting close in deep doorways; one pair, arms slung around each other, seemingly already retiring for the night, a magnum in one hand as they staggered up the stairs.

She walked past, feeling like a ghost in her own castle, wearing the dress of one of her ancestors – Black Bess escaped on last night out . . .

'Hey, Willow!'

She looked up to find Joe coming out of the back hall that led to the boot room and downstairs toilets. 'Joe! You're here,' she said with relief as he jogged over and gave her a hug. It was so comforting to see a familiar face. 'I'm not sure I've ever seen your legs before. I thought you had wheels, not feet.'

He laughed. 'I decided they could let me out from behind the bar for the night. We've been that busy recently and I wasn't going to miss this. What a party!'

'You're having fun then?'

'Are you kidding? This is the best shindig I've ever seen. There's a fella in the bogs saying he can fly us to Marrakech on Monday if we want to keep the party going.'

Her mouth parted in surprise. 'Oh.'

'And someone said they've got fireworks planned for later. What next – hot-air balloon rides to watch the sun come up?'

'I've no idea, Joe.' She shrugged. 'This isn't my party.'

'Your pad, though. What a party palace it is! You shoulda done this years ago!

Her smile faltered. The thought of missing out on a single one of their memories as a family here . . . 'Yeah. Listen, I'm just meeting someone. But I'll catch up with you in a bit, okay?'

'Sure thing. I'll be in the mosh pit.'

Willow stared at him. There was a mosh pit? Please god not in her grandmother's rose garden.

'Oh and your mam's looking for ya!' Joe called over his shoulder.

She stopped. What? 'Mam's *here?*' she called back.

'Aye. And she's desperate to find you. Tearing all about the place, she was.'

She knew exactly why. Pip must have told her about the sale, presuming Willow would have told her by now.

She stood for a moment in the hallway, staring at the library door. Her mother had come here to stop her, she knew. She wanted to delay, yet again, the moment her entire marriage had been heading towards. But it was too late. Even if Willow had wanted to change her mind, she couldn't. Too much had changed already, surely she would see that now she was here? The stone was rolling down the hill.

The library had a *Private No Entry* sign hanging from the doorknob and she turned it, but not before she automatically knocked – the habit of her lifetime.

It was empty, Connor not yet here.

She walked in, feeling a surge of emotion trammel through her at the sight of this room left almost untouched. The only one, bar the kitchen. Her father's desk and chair had been moved to the Dower House, his rugs rolled up and taken to the Christie's depository, but the shelving was still stacked with his books, his clock still ticked on the limestone mantel. A couple of sofas had been positioned there, possibly as a quiet space to retreat to?

Her hand trailed lightly over the oak shelves, her eyes picking up the gleam of the gilt-edged spines. It had been a source of great pride that her father had read every book in here, methodically working his way through them over the years. He had always said to her and her sisters that there was no point in having them simply as *decorations*. They had to have a purpose. It had been something of a sore point for the three of them, the irony lost somewhat on him.

She walked to the fireplace, staring down at the coal husks still in the grate from the last fire, a few paper twists pre-prepared in the kindling basket, a foible of Mrs Mac's to 'speed up' setting the next fire.

'. . . in here and calm down. You'll make yourself ill.' The voice – female, faint – came to her ear, making her stop in her tracks. It was Ottie's, she knew that immediately.

'Get your hands off me!' Another woman's. Willow frowned. She sounded hysterical, sobbing, wretched. And then a man's voice, his words too quiet and indistinct to make out, simply the low timbre travelling down the listening tunnel.

They were in the kitchen. Many was the time her father had hollered down it for another slice of fruit cake or to have a dog bring his slippers, a trick they'd all been taught as puppies.

What exactly was happening in there?

'No I don't want to listen to you! I hate you! Did you think I wouldn't find out?'

The man's voice again issuing urgent murmurings, platitudes, she supposed, falling on deaf ears.

'You've made me look a fool! How could you do this to me? After everything I've given up for you?'

Willow frowned. The voice was vaguely familiar and yet it was so hard to be specific – the tunnel distorting sound as well as transporting it.

'Have some water.' Ottie again. 'It'll help.'

Silence. More murmurings, the man's voice. And then the

sound of glass shattering. It made Willow jump, even three rooms away.

'Don't you dare try to put this on me! . . . No, I won't accept that!—' There was an anguished cry. 'Serena!' Willow stiffened. Her mother was in there? 'He brought her here! Here, right under my nose!'

'Who?'

'His little whore!' Immediately, Willow walked over to the wall and put her ear to the air block.

'That is *not*—' The male voice was firmer now. Distinct. Bertie! Willow stiffened like a rod, feeling her hatred rise. Was his secret out then? *One* of them anyway?

The woman began screaming. Shula. 'Stop lying to me! Stop lying! I won't take it any more, do you understand?'

The sound of hushing.

'– best if she comes with me. This isn't the time or place . . . much better once she's had time to calm down.' Her mother, cool, calm, serene, taking control.

'You're a lying, cheating bastard! . . . going to take you for everything you've . . . Do you hear me?' Her voice was growing more distant. Quieter.

A door slammed shut.

There was a silence and then –

'Fuck!' The man's voice again. Angry. Stressed. 'Fuckfuck-fuck! She's fucking mental! Did you see how she just went for me? Look at that! She's drawn blood! She's a maniac!'

There was another long silence. Then a loud, stinging slap.

'Fuck!' He hollered again. 'What the hell was that for?'

'You dare to ask me that?' Ottie, her voice an ominous growl.

Another long silence, the sound of . . . footsteps. Chairs scraping along the floor.

'Stay away from me.' Ottie again.

'She meant nothing.'

'She's your wife!'

What? Willow frowned, feeling confused, an unsettling feeling beginning to descend.

'No, not Shula. I . . . I meant Lorna.' There was panic in his voice.

Disembodied voices, half-snatched conversation, an explanation that made no sense . . . couldn't be . . . no . . .

'How *could* you? You said you loved me!' The floor dropped away. Willow stepped back, feeling her breath hitch.

'I did! I do!'

'I believed in you! I trusted you!'

She felt her stomach drop, horror pooling, the full truth dawning, undeniable – and then her feet beginning to move, carrying her over the floor and back to the door, flinging it open and seeing Connor there, papers in his hand.

'Willow . . .' Shock on his face, a furrow in his brow. 'What's happened?'

But her legs kept moving, carrying her down the hall towards the kitchen, her sister's words alone reverberating through her head. *I've got a marriage to break up.*

Chapter Thirty

Pip sat on the bottom step of the stairs, not caring how incongruous she looked in her pyjamas and slippers. She'd have preferred to be wearing them to any of these dresses anyhow – boobs out, tummy in. No thanks.

She watched as the revellers staggered, lurched and skittered past on their way to the bar, the loos, the bedrooms, the ballroom, but her eyes kept coming back to the inverted Christmas tree hanging from the ceiling. She couldn't decide if it was insanely cool or ridiculously daft. It was as though her childhood home was on acid – bright pink on the outside, all the colours bleached out, inside, adults running around like kids, everything 'back-to-front' somehow.

She was waiting for the happy scream, wondering if she'd hear it over all the noise. There'd been some sort of to-do in the ballroom a short while ago but someone had said it was just a lovers' tiff. What would Willow do, she wondered? Or were they too late anyway, the scurry over here a wasted exercise?

She coughed lightly into her fist, hoping to God not. She hadn't dragged herself out of bed without good reason. The antibiotics were kicking in but she still felt utterly depleted, like a wrung-out rag and for once she wanted to get back into bed and do as she was told – follow doctors' orders.

Taigh. Was he here? She looked around the great hall at all the convivial groups and heated couples. He hadn't come by all day, nor to the hospital either. Was *he* finally doing as he was told, and following her advice to stay away? It didn't bother her if he was – he'd been a nuisance, forever on her tail. It had just been a surprise, that was all; she supposed she'd become rather used to his pestering do-gooding.

'Willow!'

Pip's head turned sharply at the sound of her sister's name being shouted and she stood up in time to see her running from the library, a romantic heroine in green satin, her dark hair streaming behind her.

'Willow, come back!' the man yelled, and Pip caught sight of her very own anti-hero, the good-looking bloke from the party and the carols, the buyer, calling after her, looking alarmed.

But it was nothing to the expression on Willow's face. Pip felt her heart skip a beat. Jesus, what *had* happened? She hadn't expected to see her react like that!

'Will!' she cried, rushing forward – or trying to – to catch up with her.

Willow's head turned as she ran, as though her brain was telling her one thing but her body was following another. 'Pip!' Willow faltered, looking confused to see her there. Confused and alarmed. She looked desperate. 'Where's Mam?'

Now it was Pip's turn to look bewildered. 'You mean she wasn't in with you?'

'She just left with Shula. I need you to keep her out of the kitchen for me.'

'Why?'

'I . . . I can't explain.' But she looked frantic, scanning the hall every which way, looking like a spy on the run.

'Will, you have to tell me what's going on here. Is the world coming to an end?'

'Yes.' Willow blinked, trying to get her breath back. 'It's Ottie. She's in the kitchen with Bertie.'

'So?'

'They're together.'

Pip rolled her eyes. 'Yeah, you said. So what?'

'No. I mean they're *together*.' She swallowed hard, as though the words were rocks to climb over.

Pip's own words wouldn't come. Thoughts wouldn't form. The statement – the *fact* – hung suspended, spinning and directionless, like a beach ball in space. No, it simply wasn't possible. There was absolutely no way . . . But then she felt a tug on her sleeve, her feet propelled into forward motion as Will dragged her along and Pip found herself stumbling past the people, away from the bizarre hanging tree, down the corridor. They burst through the kitchen door, eyes meeting first with Mabel lying under the table, the cheery yellow Aga as reassuring as the sun in the sky. But there was no happiness here. No bright optimism.

Ottie was alabaster-pale in the red dress, slumped on a chair and tears streaming down her cheeks, her gaze far beyond the perimeters of the room. Bertie was on one knee beside her, like a chivalrous suitor. A knight, even.

He froze at the sight of the Lorne cavalry arriving, before rising slowly to his feet again. He didn't dare speak and Pip knew he was stalling, wanting to see what they knew first; he wouldn't incriminate himself, he was too skilled a manipulator for that.

Willow rushed over to Ottie, throwing her arms around her shoulders and drawing her close. 'Otts, you bloody idiot. What have you done?'

'Whatever you think is going on here, you need to know

this is not how it looks,' Bertie said, daring to take a step closer, to take charge and direct the show.

But Willow looked up at him with an expression Pip had never seen before. Contempt oozed from her, hard-baked hatred setting her to stone. 'No, you're quite right, Bertie,' she said in a dangerously cold voice. 'How this *looks* is entirely innocent – an old family friend comforting his best friend's daughter. How it sounded on the other hand, from the listening hole in the library, was a disgusting, lecherous, deluded, conniving old man manipulating and seducing his best friend's daughter!'

There was a fragile silence, the air filled with pauses, hesitations, falters. Every word was crucial. Entire futures were now relying on them.

'Okay. I realize it might have sounded bad—'

'Oh, it sounded worse than bad,' she snarled. 'It sounded to me like a reputation being smashed, a business being discredited, a marriage destroyed . . . Bad doesn't begin to cut it.' The threats dripped like blood.

He held his hands up and Pip saw that they were shaking. He was cornered. 'I never intended for this to happen, you have to believe that.'

'You were having it off with Lorna Delaney!' Ottie screamed. 'Of course you meant for it to happen. This is what you *do*! It's who you *are*! How many others are there, huh?' She motioned to the door. 'Are there any more of them out there too? Right now?'

'Don't be ridiculous!'

'Me ridiculous? You were just standing in a ballroom with your wife and two mistresses!'

Pip couldn't believe what she was hearing. Bertie and Ottie – together? Her brain couldn't accept it. Wouldn't. How long had it been going on for? *Why?*

'Ottie, you were special to me—'

Were? Pip heard the past tense – they all did – and that specifically non-specific word: special. Could be avuncular, paternal . . .

'– But at the end of the day, if this gets out, there'll be no winners. I'll deny everything. It's your word against mine, darling.'

His voice was cool, collected. Ottie – they all – looked back at him in shock.

'But I've got photos,' she stammered. 'Gifts you gave me—'

He shrugged. 'I won't deny the affair. But I'll say you came on to me. You're a beautiful young woman. How could I say no? What man would?'

Ottie's expression changed, her mouth falling open in disbelief.

'You bastard . . .' Willow whispered.

But Bertie's eyes never left Ottie. His body language was changing, becoming more powerful. Dominant. 'This can't go any further than this room, Ottie. It won't,' he said, never taking his eyes off her. 'I'm sorry you've been hurt, but I won't let my entire life be torn down by a silly little girl with a daddy complex. Shula can never know about this. No one can.'

'Do you think I'd *want* anyone to know?' Ottie screamed, standing up from the chair so quickly it fell backwards. 'I feel sick just at the thought of it! I can't believe . . . I can't believe . . . Oh my God, what have I done?' She began sobbing, her shoulders heaving as she hid her face in her hands.

He stood watching her for a few moments, seeing how Willow positioned herself between them, like an attack dog. 'Ottie, you may not believe it now, but you'll move on from this, I assure you. You'll forget about me.'

She shook her head frantically. 'Stop talking!' she screamed, her face puce. 'Just stop talking! I can't even look at you.'

'I want us to part as friends,' he said, growing calmer in the face of her hysteria, taking his time. 'There must be something I can do to make it up to you. Let me do that.'

'There's nothing! I want nothing from you apart from you to fuck off!' she yelled, her voice hoarse from her screams.

He stared at Ottie, at Willow, at Pip – a bemused look crossing his face as he processed the sight of her there in her father's old pyjamas – and then shrugged. Lackadaisical. Bored even. 'Okay then.'

He crossed the kitchen, a smirk on his face that made Pip's heart catch. She felt the breath swell in her lungs, puffing her up as he went to pass by.

'Actually there is something—' Pip said, stepping into his path. She saw the shock in his eyes as her fist connected with his face, his every reaction one second too late: eyes shut tight, his grimace of pain – when it was already done.

He staggered backwards, tripping over Mabel, who had come out from her spot under the table, and sprawling heavily on the floor. 'You broke my fucking nose!' he yelled, one hand to his face as blood saturated his shirt.

'And you broke my sister's heart,' she shrugged coolly, but she felt the white-heat in her stare. A pyjama-clad assassin was still an assassin. 'Not to mention my father's trust. My mother's trust. Your wife's trust.'

He scrabbled to get to standing but she kicked his feet away again before he could find purchase. 'No. You can stay down there,' she sneered. 'We're not done with you yet.'

Her hand swirled over the table top, making shapes that she didn't see, Mabel's head heavy upon her foot. Outside the ancient door, the party whirled on like a tornado, the shrieks and laughs of strangers punctuated by silences as they kissed under extravagant mistletoe clouds.

Willow was grateful the kitchen – like the library – had remained untouched; even with Connor's small army on the ground, there hadn't been enough time to strip out and remodel a room of this size in the time they'd had, so the caterers had set up a working kitchen in the old scullery instead, wheeling in hired stainless-steel work benches and steam ovens. It meant she could be alone in here with just her thoughts and the dogs, the revelations settling in her mind like a shipwreck to the sea bed.

The truth was like a joker at every turn, laughing in her face, mocking her. How could her sister and . . . *him* . . . ? Of all the people. Every single other person in the world – why him? Why always him?

She looked down at her green silk lap, the yellow Aga, the slumbering dogs . . . The vignette seemed to encapsulate, somehow, both the soul of the castle and everything that was wrong in her life: there was a party pounding just metres away and she was in here, like Miss Havisham, locked away from it all. Always on the wrong side of the glass.

The doorknob turned and she looked up, stiffening automatically as she saw her mother coming in. She looked drawn, the agonies of the evening etched into her face, she, for once, under-dressed in her jeans and cashmere jumper.

'Where are the others?' her mother asked, pulling out a chair as though it was made of lead.

'They've gone home. Pip was tired,' Willow replied obliquely, not wanting to reveal it was Ottie who had needed the chaperone – or why. 'How's Shula?'

Her mother gave a heavy sigh and didn't answer for a moment. '. . . Devastated.'

Willow nodded. Of course she was.

'And ashamed.'

Willow arched an eyebrow. What did Shula have to be ashamed of? It was her husband who was the cheating bastard.

Her mother tapped a single fingernail on the table top. 'But more than anything, I think she's relieved.'

'Relieved?'

'Relieved that her suspicions have been confirmed. Bertie had convinced her she was going mad, imagining things.'

Bastard! Willow felt another spike of fury. She could hardly contain her contempt. Her rage. She was trembling from the sheer effort it took *not* to stand there, screaming until her lungs bled. 'She's better off without him,' she sneered.

'Yes. She is.'

'He's a cheating bastard.'

'Yes. He is.'

'Once a cheat. Always a cheat.'

Her words, deliberately provocative, hung in the air as Willow stared at her mother, waiting for a reaction. It would be now, surely . . . ? The conversation they had spent three years avoiding was now in the room and pulsing like a light, unable to be ignored a moment longer. Lives were falling apart around their feet. *How* was her mother ignoring it?

Willow felt her anger flare again as the silence lengthened.

'He obviously never loved her if he could run around cheating on her like that. No one would do that to someone they loved.' Every word was a hot prodding iron. 'It's despicable.'

Her mother looked up, hearing her finally – understanding

her tone, recognizing her subtext, facing her challenge. 'It's not always that straightforward.'

Willow felt her heart somersault, anger and fear eddying through her. 'Isn't it?'

'No . . .' She heard the catch in her mother's voice. 'Sometimes people cheat *because* they love their partner.'

Willow gave a mocking laugh. Was that it? Was that actually her defence? 'No, Mam. They don't.'

'Willow—'

She couldn't do this after all. She wouldn't listen to the excuse that love had made her do it. 'I've got to go find someone,' she said, pushing her chair back abruptly. 'I'm tired. I just want to go home.'

'You are home—'

The simplicity of the words stopped her in her tracks. Willow stared at her mother, aware their words were a dance tracing the shape of the subject they had avoided for so long now.

'This has always been your home.'

Willow shook her head. 'No – not mine. I never belonged here. And words in a will don't make it true.'

Her mother's eyes instantly filled with tears, overcome with emotions she usually buried so well. '. . . I never . . .' Her voice was tremulous. 'I never knew he knew, Willow. You must believe that. I only realized when the will was read.' Her voice cracked on the words, like shells being dashed against rocks, and she pressed a finger to her lips, as though the emotions could simply be pushed back in like knickers in a drawer. 'The shock of it . . . I felt so ashamed. So horrified. I couldn't bring myself to look at you. I thought you must hate me. I thought he must have d-died hating me.'

'Maybe he did,' Willow said coldly, though her blood was rushing like a flood. '. . . How did he find out?'

'I don't know.' Her mother shook her head and swallowed. 'He took your leaving here very badly, your silence . . . He tried to hide it from us but he felt sure you'd been driven from here. He must have . . . worked it out somehow.'

'The fact that I'm dark and the others are fair, perhaps? That they've got green eyes and I've got blue?' she asked sarcastically. It was so obvious once you saw it.

'No – lots of siblings have different hair and eye colourings. It's not so unusual.' Her mother's lips were stretched thin.

'So maybe he found the letter too then.'

Too? Her mother's eyes flashed up to hers, seeing the anger, the hardness that had formed at the very heart of her, freezing her from the inside out. She didn't – couldn't – speak for several moments. '. . . Perhaps,' she nodded finally. 'I never knew what became of it. I had to hide the letter in a rush, I didn't see which book . . .' She squeezed her eyes shut, tears bleeding through her lashes. 'I should have burnt it.'

'Yes. You should have,' Willow said coldly. But perhaps, she thought to herself, so should she – she shouldn't have slipped it back in the covers of the book in the library where her father was making his way through every single one . . . But she had thought he'd already known.

'I was never sure if you knew.' Her mother stared back at her, broken, still beautiful. 'I feared it – the thought that you knew terrified me. The suspicion that was why you'd gone haunted me. I was crippled by terror that I'd hurt you and yet I could never say, never ask, in case I was wrong.' Her voice wavered. 'And then to discover that your father knew too . . . It breaks my heart that he never gave me the chance to explain it to him.'

Willow's eyebrows shot up. 'So you're angry with him for

robbing you of the chance to justify what you did?' she said scornfully.

'I did it *for* him, Willow.'

'How?' Willow cried. 'How was cheating on your husband *for* him?'

Her mother flinched, shaking her head. 'The odds of having another girl were going up with every daughter. I was trying to break the pattern—'

'Pattern? Or curse?' Willow sneered, remembering the famous family legend, Black Bess's curse.

'He *needed* a son. I needed to give him that.'

'And so you decided the way to achieve that was by sleeping with someone else?'

Her mother recoiled, but the words hung in the air, solid and true.

They stared at one another across the table.

'Not a great plan, huh, Mam? You ended up with not just another bloody daughter but an illegitimate one to boot!' She gave a bitter laugh that made tears fall from her eyes. 'Jeesht, I bet you couldn't believe it when I popped out! It was bad enough with Ottie and Pip but with me? What more did you have to do, right?' Willow threw her arms out.' You couldn't *ever* have been more disappointed in your life! Either one of you!'

Her mother jumped up, her palms pressed flat on the table. 'No! *I* was the failure, Willow, not you! Your father never blamed you, never.'

'He wasn't my father!' Willow sobbed.

'Yes, he was. In every single way that counted! He loved and adored you! You were his little bird.'

'Yes! The cuckoo in the nest!'

'Willow!' Her mother stared at her with imploring eyes. 'Your leaving here broke his heart. It was all my fault and I knew it. And now I can never make it up to him.' A sob broke up her words and she collapsed down into the chair again, hiding her face in her hands as the sobs wracked through her. Willow watched, frozen; it was as though the little boy had removed his finger from the dam, the tears like a flood.

Willow sank back into her chair too, feeling depleted. She had thought that with confession would come peace. Closure. Instead there was only more sorrow and more regret.

The minutes ticked past, both of them lost in their own pain. Talking would change nothing.

Her mother looked up finally, her face swollen and blotched. '. . .Let me make it up to you, Willow.'

'How?' Her voice was toneless. 'How exactly can you undo all the damage you've done?'

'The same way your father did – by letting you have the final word. Everything that came before, it was done to you, chosen *for* you. Now you get to choose what happens next.'

Willow shook her head. 'I don't understand.'

'I came here tonight to try to stop you; Pip told me about the sale. And when she told me you were selling to Connor Shaye again, I knew you were doing it to punish me. But that's your right. It's precisely why your father left the estate to you.'

'No – he left it to me because he knew I was the only one who could sell it without the burden of guilt. I'm not a Lorne by blood. I'm an interloper, not really supposed to be here. And when he realized I knew that, he knew I could be rid of it without a backwards glance – fuck it! Take the money! His legacy, this birthright, none of it was ever mine to begin with, so what do I care, right?'

Her mother shook her head sadly. 'You're wrong, darling. That's not why he left it to you.'

'Yes it is.'

'No. He left it to you because he wanted to give you the freedom to be rid of it – *if* that's what you wanted. Don't you see? By giving you Lorne and the choice to decide what to do next, he was saying you mattered more to him than any son, any title, any castle. Nothing else was important. He chose *you* above all else. You were his little bird, his youngest daughter, his b-baby girl . . .'

Willow turned away, but the tears were sliding down her cheeks too. Was that true? These past three years of thinking she'd been a mistake, a failure, an impostor. A stranger in her own family . . .

'I'm not asking you to forgive what I did. It was unforgiveable, I know that. And it was the biggest mistake of my life – there's not been a day when I haven't hated myself for it – but on one point alone, I will never ever regret it.' Her voice became choked. 'And that is because it gave me *you.* And if I had the chance to do my life over, I would do it again because I would always choose you.'

Her mother rose and came over, pale and trembling but there was a fire in her eyes that hadn't been there since before her father had died. 'I came here tonight to give you that, because I thought it would stop you.' She pointed to a large Tesco carrier bag propped up against the side of the larder, tufts of newspaper sticking out of the top. 'But I'm not going to try to stop you. Take it anyway. Sell Lorne. None of that matters. Daddy gave you a choice in order to show you how loved you are and I'm doing the same. I'm giving you a choice too.'

'What is it?' Willow hiccuped, looking over at the bag.

'The freedom to decide your future. Your whole life has been dominated by the past and my and your father's feelings of obligations to it. But no more. We won't look back. You get to choose what happens next and whatever it is, it will be the right thing because you are loved, no matter what.' Her mother clasped her wet face between her warm hands, kissing her on her forehead and the tip of her nose, as she'd always done as a little girl. Their eyes locked for the first time in three years. 'No matter what. Okay?'

Willow nodded as she kissed her forehead again: tender, motherly. '. . . I'll see you back at home.'

Willow watched as her mother walked across the kitchen. 'Mam,' she called weakly, as she reached the door. Her mother turned back.

'. . . Does Shula know?'

Her mother looked down at the ground, two spots of shame staining her cheeks, before she looked back at her again. 'No. I believe it's a kindness to keep some secrets.'

Willow nodded, thinking of Ottie's.

Yes, perhaps sometimes it was.

Chapter Thirty-One

'I know! I'm in my bloody pyjamas! Get over it!' Pip snapped at an aghast-looking couple on their way in to the castle, as she and Ottie staggered out. They looked more like a Hallow-een pair than Christmas revellers, with their pale faces and streaked cheeks. 'Have you got the keys?' Pip asked her, one hand held out as they got to the car.

'Willow drove,' Ottie replied flatly. She seemed to be hear-ing everything five seconds later.

'Oh great. And Mam's got my keys.' Pip sighed with her hands on her hips. 'Okay, fine. I'll go back in. You just wait here.'

'No, I'll go.'

'You're not fit for walking anywhere in the state you're in. Just sit here.' And Pip perched her against the car bonnet like she was a doll that needed propping up.

'Hey, Pip!'

They both looked over to see Joe lurching down the steps, arms waving wildly.

'You're looking a little worse for wear there, Joe!' Pip called back brightly, disguising the shock and devastation that was still reverberating from the events in the kitchen. None of them was okay right now.

Ottie frowned as she noticed her sister shivering in the cold temperatures. Even in her stunned state, she knew Pip couldn't afford to get cold.

'Aye! Sign of a great party! Oh, hey Ottie!' he called over, noticing her, sitting motionless and silent.

'Hey, Joe.' She sounded like a shadow – dark and flat. Flattened.

'You're not leaving already, are ya?' he asked, almost weaving straight into a potted bay tree.

'Joe, it may surprise you to learn this but I am in fact at the party of the century in my feckin' pyjamas,' Pip hollered. 'I've also nearly died twice in the past couple of weeks so I'm thinking I'll head back to bed soonest if it's all the same.'

Joe laughed. 'Shame. I was going to invite you back to the Hare for a lock-in.' He pressed a finger to his lips. 'VIPs only. I reckon tonight's the night to open a rather special bottle of Teeling Vintage Reserve I've been saving.'

Pip's eyes narrowed interestedly. 'Teeling, you say?'

'Aye, the thirty–year-old platinum.'

'Pip, you need to get back to bed,' Ottie said, rousing herself as she saw that look come into her sister's eyes.

'Tsht,' Pip hushed her. 'I'm not due my next antibiotics for another . . .' She checked her phone. 'Two hours.'

'You can't drink whiskey on antibiotics.'

'Maybe not, but I can *smell* it.'

'You'd go to a lock-in just to smell the whiskey?' Ottie asked in disbelief.

'Only for two hours, mind. I'm *recuperating*.' Pip looked back at Joe as he staggered over to a waiting car they all knew well. 'How you getting into town, Joe?'

'Seamus here. Why? D'you need a lift?'

'Well, we've not got any bloody car keys so . . . yeah.' Pip looked back at her. 'It's that or freeze to death. I'll text Willow when we get there. She can pick us up.'

Ottie groaned but her sister had a point and it was more important to keep Pip out of the cold right now. At least the Hare was guaranteed warmth.

Reluctantly, she allowed Pip to link arms and lead her over. Joe opened the back door for them and they slid in. 'Hey, Seamus!' Pip said brightly.

'Hey, Seamus,' Ottie said, but she was distracted by something she'd noticed as her little sister had climbed into the car – she was holding her hand strangely. And now that she was sitting down, she saw it was curled up in her lap like a wounded bird. 'Pip, let me see your hand,' she whispered.

'No, it's fine,' Pip said quickly, sliding it away, out of reach, as the taxi lurched into throaty life.

Ottie said nothing but it was clear she wasn't the only one hurt tonight. Pip was injured and not just physically. Ottie knew her devil-may-care attitude was just a cover for her dismay at what Ottie had done, the shocking secret she had kept from her sisters and her family for all these years. At heart, her fiesty little sister was a far more fragile creature than she let on.

Joe started singing along to the radio, Pip joining in with him, and as they pulled away Ottie turned to look back through the window at the pink castle and its not-so-pretty surprises. She had gone in tonight wanting to grab her Red Dress life, and instead she was leaving as a scarlet woman.

But all the while, Lorne Castle just kept on standing.

Joe locked the door behind them, a low cheer going up amongst the small group of regulars still in there. 'Lock-in!' he cried, prompting another cheer.

Ottie saw Taigh O'Mahoney come back in from the toilets, taking in the sight with a look of surprise – the look turning into a scowl as he saw Pip making her way over to the bar.

Ottie gave him a little wave and he came over. 'She shouldn't be out of bed!' he said firmly.

'I know. But we've had a bit of a night,' Ottie said quietly. 'I think she needs to come down a little first.'

Immediately he frowned, looking concerned. 'Everything okay?'

'It will be,' Ottie nodded, hoping she sounded more certain than she felt. 'You didn't go to the party then?'

He gave an apologetic shrug. 'Sorry, no. I should've been more supportive, I know, but it's not really my scene, all that dressin' up.'

'Hey, you don't need to apologize to me, Taigh. It wasn't our party.'

'Was it any good? I heard there was some big scandal.'

She instantly stiffened. 'Scandal?'

'That Lorna Delaney's been having it off with Bertie Flanagan and Shula's kicked him out.'

She felt sick to her stomach every time she heard the words, every time she thought of it. And to think she had left home tonight *wanting* the world to know . . . 'Oh. Yes.'

'Did you hear about it too then?'

She swallowed, managing a nod. 'Mmmhmm.'

Taigh wrinkled his nose. 'I can't say I'm surprised.'

'No?' For years she had wanted the truth about them to come out, to have everyone know about their love, admire them for it, but now the scales had fallen away and she saw their relationship for what it was, she couldn't think of anything more horrifying. She felt ashamed. Appalled by what she had done.

'No. I mean, it's no secret I was seeing Lorna for a while back there. She said a few things which, looking back, I should've seen were red flags . . .' He shrugged. 'But I just wasn't looking for it, you know?'

'Of course not. How were you to know?' she mumbled, knowing her own cheeks were flaming.

'Well, the American fella called it,' he shrugged. 'He saw what the rest of us were blind to.'

Ottie fell completely still. '*American?*'

'Yeah. Ben. The runner guy who got injured. Did his ACL, broke his arm . . . Old Paddy made some comment at the bar about him dropping his big lawsuit, and Ben said Flanagan was a cheat in more ways than one.' He shrugged. 'It was lost on us at the time, we thought it was sour grapes 'cos Bertie's lawyers had him on the run, but not a half hour ago, in comes Fergal Sheehan with the gossip about Lorna and he was proved right.'

'When were you talking to him?' Ottie asked in astonishment. She had only brought him in here the one time, after their shopping trip.

'Ben? Just a short while ago.'

'What does that mean, Taigh – two days? Last week?' she prompted, urgency in her voice.

Taigh laughed. 'No, about twenty minutes ago.'

'He's still *here*?'

Taigh looked bemused by her response. '. . . Yeah. He's got a room upstairs.'

Ben was here-here? Ottie looked up at the ceiling in disbelief. She'd thought he'd gone straight back to Dublin, ready for his flight tomorrow afternoon. There were more places to stay there – hotels with lifts . . . How the hell had he managed these stairs? She'd been up gentler ladders.

'Is everything okay, Ottie?'

'Yes, I . . .' But she felt like she was underwater, everything muffled and slow.

'D'you want a drink? You look a wee bit pale. I think Joe's gone to the cellar to get this fabled bottle of Teeling he's forever preaching about. I personally will believe it when I see it.'

'Uh . . . no. No.' She bit her lip. 'There's something I've got to do first.'

He looked back at her in puzzlement. 'Okay then.'

'I'll not be long.' She went to walk away but remembered something. 'Oh, but Taigh . . .'

'Uh-huh?'

'Pip's hurt her hand.'

His shoulders slumped. 'Look, Ottie, I'm sorry but I'll pass, if it's all the same. I've learned—'

'Please. I think she might have broken it but she's trying to hide it from me. You know what she's like. And if she doesn't get it seen to fast, like—'

He frowned. 'What did she do to bust her hand up?'

'She uh . . . uh . . .' Oh God, what could she say? 'Someone accidentally walked into it.'

Taigh stared at her, his ready-smile already bouncing in his eyes. 'Someone . . . ?'

'Someone deserving.'

Taigh laughed. 'Oh jeesht,' he cried, shaking his head, his eyes alighting on her little sister sitting by the bar. He frowned. 'Is she in her *pyjamas*?'

'Another long story.'

'It always is with her,' he said, pulling his hands down over his face before giving a resigned sigh and walking over to her. 'Honestly, what's that crazy-arse girl done now?'

Ottie watched him go up to Pip and tap her on the shoulder.

She saw how Pip jumped at the sight of him, then her head tilted to the side slightly as she saw her little sister swallow and deny and resist and protest, the way she always did when she felt vulnerable. Her eyes widened in amazement as she saw the way Pip looked at him as he examined her hand.

Taigh? . . . Really?

Ottie knocked at the door, stepping back into the hallway as though she might change her mind at any moment and need to run in one direction or the other. But as the door opened and those penetrating eyes fastened upon her, she knew she wouldn't be running anywhere.

'Ottie.'

She wet her lips, feeling nervous and suddenly realizing she had no idea whatsoever what to say. '. . . Hi.'

He stared at her, his eyes sweeping over her and taking in the details of her pale face and limp hair that told an entirely different story to the red dress. Instantly, she knew he knew. He stepped back, holding the door wider. 'You'd better come in.'

She walked hesitantly into the bedroom. It was pleasingly decorated – a blue-green tweed chair by the window, a double bed made up with sheets and covered with a wool blanket. Antique lamps, some oils of Dingle Bay that she recognized as the work of Molly McCabe, another local amateur artist. In the corner was his North Face duffel bag, stuffed full, the parka they'd bought together draped over it. Ready to go.

'This is nice,' she mumbled, turning to face him, seeing how he still limped, but already less noticeably than when she'd seen him last.

Had that really only been last night? When she'd run in from the wash block in the middle of the night and made the wrong call, their argument still festering between them, feelings hurt and brittle? It felt like her world had ended between now and then.

She knew there was no point in making small talk. She sank onto the end of the bed, noticing how he kept a distance between them. 'I thought you'd left for Dublin.'

'You were supposed to.'

She looked back at him, caught short by his bluntness. 'And that's okay? You just left without saying goodbye?'

'I felt we'd said everything there was to be said between us.'

She frowned. 'Did you?'

The air thickened between them and it was his turn to look away. 'I don't want you to think I wasn't grateful for everything you did for me.'

'Grateful,' she echoed.

'Sure.' She watched as he walked over to the window and drew the curtains closed. He was wearing the jeans they'd bought together, one of the T-shirts too.

She gave a bitter laugh. 'Well, don't be grateful to me, Ben. You know I'm the reason you ended up in that position in the first place.'

'No. Bertie should have put the signs out, whatever else he was doing. He should never have let you shoulder the blame.'

'Look, I am no longer his greatest fan – as you might have heard,' she said lightly, not quite able to meet his eyes. 'But it really wasn't entirely his fault. You would never have gone down that path if I'd been at my post.'

'You weren't on your post?' He frowned.

She swallowed, mortified she had to keep admitting to this. '. . . I needed to pee. Really badly. So I had gone further around the headland to hide.'

He was quiet for a long moment. 'So – just to be clear – you're telling me that I incurred a ruptured ACL, broken arm, three broken ribs and a concussion – all so you wouldn't get caught pulling a *moony*?'

She inhaled – and held the breath, not quite sure whether he was about to shout at her or— 'Why are you smiling?' she asked.

'Because it's funny.'

'You could have died.'

He gave a shrug. 'That would have been a lot less funny.'

God, that dry humour; she'd missed it even in the space of a day. She cracked a small grin. 'So you don't hate me then?'

'No,' he sighed, his smile fading, looking away again. 'Already tried that.'

'When I asked you to drop the case?'

'Yeah.'

'You *should* hate me for asking that.'

'I know.'

She watched him, seeing now the invisible wall that surrounded him. 'If it's any consolation, I hate myself.'

He shook his head. 'Don't do that. If there's one thing I do know it's that people will do anything for the one they love, and you're in love with him.' He shrugged, but she saw how his Adam's apple bobbed in his throat, his shoulders inching imperceptibly higher.

'Except . . .' Her throat felt dry. 'I'm not.'

Ben gave a small snort of disbelief. 'Oh, you are.'

'No.'

She let the word hang between them like a full stop, forcing him to look back at her.

'I thought I was. I went to that party tonight to tell everyone about us. I was tired of waiting. I wanted my Red Dress life,' she faltered, pinching at the fabric of the beautiful dress and seeing how his eyes skimmed over her, his breath catching.

'I know. And then you found out he'd cheated on you too,' he finished for her. 'It was around the pub in minutes. "The Bertie Flanagan scandal".'

'Exactly. And you know what?'

He tipped his head, questioningly.

'It was precisely what I wanted to hear. It was a huge shock, I won't deny it, but it was also the most curious thing: it woke me up. Suddenly it was as if I could see myself from the outside – as if I'd climbed out of my own skin and all these confused feelings I had – and I could just see the whole sad, sorry mess of it. Like you did.'

His jaw clenched, as he remembered their argument.

'And I felt sick. With myself, with what I'd done to others – to Shula, to my parents, my family.' She looked directly at him. 'And most of all, to you.'

'Ottie—'

She got up and took a step towards him. 'There's that saying, isn't there. Be careful what you wish for; you might just get it. Well, that was me tonight. Even before it came out about Lorna, as I was standing in there, I was realizing that I *didn't* want him. I was trying to make myself do it, but I couldn't. And it was so confusing, because he was all I'd thought I wanted for so long.' She stared into space, remembering the crowded room, the sight of Shula coming through the crowd and the feeling of panic that she might actually leave her husband and let her have him. 'And when it did all come out, what I mostly felt was relief. And what probably should have been this devastating loss wasn't that at all – because that was what I'd felt when *you'd* gone.'

He looked up from staring at the patch on the carpet to find her walking over to him, and she saw all the vulnerability in his face that he always hid so well. His wife had broken his heart and he'd channelled his suffering into sport, made a virtue out of tolerating pain. 'Ottie, I'm flying out tomorrow.'

It was supposed to be a defence. A reason to stop something before it began. There was no point. There was no time. But she stopped in front of him, toe-to-toe, knowing her Red Dress life when she saw it. She snaked a hand up his neck and into his hair.

'Tell me that after you've kissed me.'

Chapter Thirty-Two

Willow stood at the window, staring down at the sparkling silver ribbon of sea, the moon dancing over the water like a swan on a lake. The bench symmetrically positioned in the parterre immediately in front of here had always been her father's favourite spot in the garden: set between the ancient yew hedges planted in four lover's knots, the castle at his back, he had loved to watch the sailing boats glide past.

He had probably never envisioned a night when his beloved castle was pink, though. Or Christmas trees hung upside down from the rafters. Had she brought 'teen spirit' to Lorne? Had she given the grand old lady of the mount a facelift, or was this a travesty of her dignity? The party was still thumping away, various lovers walking the grounds, enjoying the moonlight.

She turned away from the window and walked around the library, the way he had done whenever he had something to 'mull over'. It was one of the smallest rooms in the castle, and yet somehow the most important. It was the nerve centre of all Lorne operations. It was where her life had changed – and his too, for she had left the letter there knowing – sensing – he would find it one day; she had wanted him to suffer the way she did, for him to punish her mother when she couldn't.

She stood in front of the volume of Silas Marner where her life had uncoiled. It had been an accidental happening, or perhaps a sleight of fate, for of all the books to have opened in this library, what had made her choose that one? It didn't have any of the fancy lettering or ornate gilding of many others; it wasn't the biggest, or the smallest, the rarest or most valuable. It had been an innocuous thing, plain and yet also deadly.

If she closed her eyes she could still see the bold, looping script – black ink, vellum paper – fragments of phrases indelibly scratched into her mind: '*My darling Serena . . . everything I ever wanted . . . have longed for you . . . sick with love . . . give me another night . . . let me give you another life . . . deserve more than he can give you . . . I'll leave Shula . . .* ' It was the date written on it, nine months before her birth, that had revealed the whole truth.

What must her father have felt when he saw that letter? And painful though it must invariably have been, had it remotely compared to what its contents had meant for her – robbing her of her family, her identity, her legitimacy, in one fell swoop?

She pulled the book out by its spine, feeling the weight of it in her hands again. She tipped it forwards, her breath catching as she saw the envelope fall. Still there. Still bleeding poison between those pages . . . She picked up the letter – and stopped.

Her father's handwriting. Blue paper. Her name.

She swallowed hard as she opened it, feeling a tremor through her hands, the past reaching into the present as though the wind was carrying a breath onto her neck.

May 13th, 2019

My little bird,

If you are reading this, then you are not only home, but you are here, back in the study, holding the book where you first learned the secret that made you run. That has been my hypothesis, anyway: that something happened to make you turn away from us. And I never knew what it was till I found the letter here too. Am I right?

If I am, let me start by saying I am sorry and I will be forever sorry, for I am to blame in all this, not your mother. She made a choice, forced upon her by my terrible guilt; the burden I placed upon her for a son was insufferable and it is a wonder that she ever stayed with me at all.

All my life, from the moment of my birth, I was told how lucky I was to be the 29th Knight of Lorne, how worthy, how privileged – and, of course, I was constantly told that it was my duty to provide a son to continue the line. For too many years, I believed that and I felt I had failed, for it is a terrible thing to know you shall be the break in the chain. But far worse than any of that was the shame that came over me when I learned what my selfish suffering had done: forcing my beautiful wife, your beloved mother, into an unthinkable situation; my cherished daughters growing up believing you weren't enough, or worthy – when the truth is, I was the unworthy one.

I have loved you with every fibre of my being from the very moment you were born and the letter you and I both found here didn't change that, not one bit. You are my daughter, not his, not ever, and I will fight to the death defending that. Because I have realized a very simple truth: the desire for a son, to produce another knight, is back-to-front thinking, for what use is a knight without his queen and princesses to serve and protect? Why would you even have knights if you didn't have them?

You are why Lorne was built and you are why Lorne still

stands and I hope, as you are reading this, that I am in the next room and that you will come to me – and forgive me.

But if I am too late – and I know I am sick – then take away this: that I may be the last knight, but I shall eternally be your father and my love for you will endure longer than any castle.

Always and forever,

Daddy.

The letter trembled in her shaking hand, tears falling onto the page and splashing onto the ink, making it bleed like her heart. Because he was too late. They both were.

'Willow?'

She turned with a gasp, finding Connor standing across the room, the door closed. How long had he been there?

She hurriedly wiped the tears away with the flats of her hands, trying to gather herself back into a cohesive shape again, but she felt undone. This night had unravelled her, stitch by stitch.

Without a word, he walked over to her and pulled a handkerchief from his suit pocket.

'Thank you,' she murmured, patting her eyes dry and taking a moment to hide her face in the cotton square.

When she finally drew back to look at him, she saw the reservation in his face as his eyes roamed over her, pouring light into her darkest corners, finding her secrets.

'What's—?' He took a step back, as if she'd slapped him. '. . . You're not going to sell to me.'

She inhaled sharply and held the breath for a moment, as though weighing the answer in her body, but she already knew: 'No. I'm sorry.'

He rolled his lips together, looking angry but not surprised. '. . . Can I ask why?'

'Because this is my home. It's where I belong.' She folded the letter back into thirds again, closing her eyes as she pressed it to her lips. 'I'm home again.'

He stared at her, seeing the wetness of her lashes, understanding that the letter in her hands had somehow changed things. Everything. 'But how are you going to afford to keep it? The capital you need to reinvest in it—'

'I know. It's huge. But we've had a little luck – for once,' she gasped, a little sob of happiness and disbelief bursting from her again. Could it really be true?

She pointed to the Tesco bag on the desk.

With a puzzled look, Connor walked over to it, pulling out a package loosely wrapped in newspaper. He pushed back the sheets, revealing an ornate gilt-carved frame, and within it, the luminous portrait. He held it up.

'She was my great-great-great-great-great-step-grandmother – I think. Elizabeth Carr, but she was known as Black Bess.'

Connor's eyes fell to the signature in the corner before he looked back at her in astonishment. 'It's a Gainsborough.'

'Yes,' she said, the delight fizzing like bubbles in her throat. 'He painted her in 1752. We assumed it had been lost in a fire but she must have stolen it from the castle when her stepson, the 15th knight, evicted her after his father's death. She was notoriously vain and must have wanted to keep it with her.'

'It's stunning,' he said flatly.

'She hid it in the roof of the Dower House, in the furthest corner. We can't believe it's survived but she'd put it in a small wooden crate. She was no fool, I guess.'

'Like her great-great-great-great-great-granddaughter.' He put the painting back down again, carefully, staring at it for a long moment, seeing everything clearly now. 'And so you're going to sell this.' His voice was tense. Brittle.

'Yes.'

He paced slowly, glancing over at her. 'Sell it, do up this place, live happily ever after. Oh no, wait, I forgot – you don't believe in happy ever after.'

Didn't she? She felt the letter between her fingertips: her father's understanding and forgiveness for what his wife had done, her mother's sacrifice and remorse. Their love had endured in spite of the worst betrayal. They had remained happy together even after her father had learned the truth. How *had* her father stomached seeing Bertie, she wondered? Had they come to blows, had it out? Or had it simply been enough for him to know he had the one thing Bertie's riches could never buy: her mother's love?

'Obviously I'll reimburse you whatever you've spent on renovations to date. You won't be out of pocket.'

'Oh. Good of you. Thanks.' A cold sarcasm chilled his words. 'And what about the time and effort I've invested in this place? I've lived and breathed Lorne since I saw it. I fell for it.'

She looked at him, feeling him receding from her, their chemical charge winding down in the face of his freeze. 'If you remember, you said I was under no obligation to sell to you because of the pop-up. You knew you were taking a risk.'

'But I got the money together anyway. In the same time as if we'd shaken on it.'

'But we didn't shake on it.' She bit her lip. 'I am so sorry, Connor, I never planned for any of this. A lot's happened in the past few days.'

'Clearly. You've *conveniently* found an old master just lying around. How helpful. That should get you out of the bind.'

She tipped her head to the side, hating the bitterness in his voice, unable to blame him for it. 'I promise I came here tonight in good faith, intending to sign the papers.'

'And I came here tonight intending to kiss you.' His eyes blazed. 'I guess we were never on the same page.'

'Connor—'

'Don't. At least I've got the answer now to whether I could trust you.'

She frowned. 'This wasn't deliberate.'

'Wasn't it? Or have you actually been playing me all along? Was it revenge for your father?'

'No!'

'Really? I told you what happened with your father was never personal. We're leveraged to the hilt, that's not a state secret – it's written into our business model for the first eight years: invest in assets, consolidate the brand – but that week our bank had just called in a loan. I had no choice but to slash the offer price or walk away. It was just business and we were the losers, not him.' He inhaled sharply. 'And now it looks like I'm the loser all over again.'

'Connor—' Her voice broke. She didn't know what to say.

He looked at her coldly.

'I didn't want it to be like this.'

'Neither did I. Believe me,' he snapped, picking up the contracts and turning to leave.

'Please don't hate me,' she blurted to his back.

He stopped and turned. 'Hating you wouldn't be a problem, Willow. Trust me, I would bloody love to be able to hate you.'

'Can't we . . . ?' She stepped towards him but he stopped her with a stare.

'No. This thing is done now. For good.' And he walked out, slamming the door shut behind him.

Willow stared into the space where he'd been, her heart pounding wildly – the letter in her hands, the Gainsborough on the floor. She was home at last. But this was no happy ending.

Chapter Thirty-Three

Sunday, 22 December

'Good boy, down you come,' Pip said soothingly, as the ramp was lowered onto the cobbles. 'Come and see your new pals.'

Carefully, leading him by the harness with her good hand, she led the young stallion out of the truck and into the yard. Kirsty had done a good job of keeping it swept clear of snow whilst she'd been laid up in bed, all the horses' bedding fresh and clean.

He gave a small snort as the cold temperatures hit his nostrils, a shiver rippling down the length of his black velvety flank. 'Come in here, this way, you'll like it, I promise,' she murmured, leading him in to his new stall. It was opposite Shalimar's but the ones either side had been left clear deliberately, in case he turned out to be a kicker.

Slinki was keeping watch over proceedings from her favoured position in the cross-beam, looking down from on high. Fergus and the other horses nodded over their doors, watching curiously as she led him in and turned him around. He nosed at the hanging ball of hay, sniffed the sugar lick. She'd put a mirror on the wall too, and Pip laughed as he admired the handsome reflection, nosing it interestedly.

'No, it's not *you* I want you to love – but her,' Pip said, positioning him so that he was facing Shalimar. She stepped out of the stall, throwing over the bolt on his door and stood in the passage between them both. 'This is Shalimar, your new girlfriend. Shalimar, this is Dark Star. And it is *very* important that you two love each other.'

'I'm not sure it works that way, Pip.' The sudden voice made her jump. 'In my experience, it'll happen whether you want it to or not—'

'Jeesht!' she cried, almost collapsing at the knees as she turned round. 'What the hell, Taigh? You almost gave me a heart attack.'

'A heart attack? Hmm, okay, sure, why not . . .'

'Huh?'

'Let's add it to the list of things you'll do to get me to check up on you: near-drowning, pneumonia, busted hand. Heart attack.' He was walking straight over to her, not slowing down . . . kissing her.

She pulled away in shock. 'What are you doing?'

'Kissing you.'

She blinked. Then blinked again. *'Why?'*

'Well, your big sister collared me last night, asking me exactly what my intentions were towards you.'

She frowned, bewildered by what was going on. 'And what did you say?'

'Survival, chiefly.'

She stared at him for a moment, a laugh caught in her throat as she scanned his face for clues of a trick or joke . . . But as ever, his eyes were already laughing.

'Why . . . would she ask what your intentions were? I don't understand.'

'According to Ottie, no one despises someone as much as you despise me, without actually, perversely, being nuts about them too.' He grinned. 'You're crazy about me, Pip, you just don't know it.'

'I am not!'

His grin widened, eyes dancing. 'That's not what your kiss just told me.'

'I didn't kiss you. You kissed me.'

'No, not that one. This one.' And he stepped in and kissed her again. And this time, as she felt his lips against hers, the taste of him, his hands clasping her head . . . she kissed him back.

'. . . O-*kay*,' she murmured when he finally drew back, trying to hide how fast he was making her heart beat; no doubt he'd get his stethoscope out. 'So maybe you're not all bad.'

He gave a lopsided grin. 'Progress!'

'But you don't like me,' she scowled. 'You've never once done anything to indicate—'

'Jeesht, woman, are you blind as well as accident-prone? I've been nuts about you since we first went out. I only dumped you to save meself the pain of getting dumped – it was inevitable as far as I could see.'

'Well, you did a good job of hiding your heartbreak!' she scoffed, remembering Lorna Delaney by his side only a few weeks ago.

'Only because I've spent far too long listening to you and keeping well clear, when you've got absolutely no idea at all of what's good for you.'

'Oh.'

He looked down at her tenderly as he ran a hand through her hair. 'So let me tell you how this is going to be. First we're going to get this horse settled. Then I'm going to take you upstairs and do what I've been dying to do to you for eight long years. Then you're going to put your pyjamas on.'

She looked back at him, delighted. 'Why will I put my pyjamas on?' she asked.

'I thought we'd go for a drink at the Hare and tell everyone we're together finally.'

'Finally?'

'Apparently Joe's had a book running these last eight years.'

Pip threw her head back and laughed. 'He has not!' she cried, covering her cheeks – and blushes – with her hands.

'He most certainly has,' he grinned. 'Does that sound like a plan you can live with, Pip Lorne?'

She laced her arms around his neck. 'Taigh O'Mahoney, for once you're talking some sense. It sounds just grand to me.'

Chapter Thirty-Four

Monday, 23 December

Kirsty MacColl was singing to Shane MacGowan, telling him he was a scumbag and maggot, as Taigh came back to the table with another round. 'No "Fairytale of New York" for you this year, mate,' he grinned, handing Ben his pint of black.

'Well, not yet, anyway,' Ben said, one arm slung around Ottie's shoulder. 'What's the phrase? Manhattan can wait.'

Not for long though. Willow still couldn't believe Ottie was going to leave here with him in the New Year and try to make it as an artist in New York. On the one hand, it seemed too soon, too fast. On the other, after the way Bertie had kept her isolated, wasn't a life change like this long overdue? She watched as Ben kissed the top of her sister's head as she leaned in to him. They were already as tight as a knot, forever talking in low voices, eyes locked on one another as though no one else existed.

Taigh and Pip were no better, hyperactive puppies the both of them, laughing at every joke, reaching over for kisses every few minutes. They were already talking about him moving in with her above the stables.

Willow looked away. She was happy for her sisters, she really was. It wasn't like she was going to have time to worry about her love life – or lack thereof – with the amount of work she was going to have with the castle anyway. She'd resigned from Pyro Tink that morning, finally giving up the pretence that the splashy, angry life she'd plastered over her social media pages was the one she wanted. She didn't need Dublin to workout, and she'd resolved to have a word with Al Brody in the Lorne Stores about stocking matcha and extra celery. There were roads from here to the cities, weren't there?

Caz had cried when she'd called to say she wasn't coming back and that she should start looking for a new flatmate. Willow had promised to go up for New Year for 'one last blowout' and to empty her room but, other than that, extricating herself from the city's grip was as simple as snipping the string on a balloon and just floating free. This was her home and she was with her blood, her tribe, here.

She looked around her at the familiar bustling scene. The pub was full – not the crazy bursting-at-the-seams level it had been at for the past few weeks as Connor's SWAT teams had moved in to get the castle ready for the pop-up, but almost every family in the village was represented by at least one member here. The Big Christmas Eve Eve Quiz was happening in half an hour, and everyone wanted to get a table. Pip always took it very seriously, on account of having a problem with losing, and was already drilling Taigh on Eighties pop hits.

Across the room she saw Seamus sitting at a table with his wife Mary reading through the menus, even though everyone knew they'd both order Betty's Christmas Eve special coronation chicken, Paddy Mahoney filling in the crossword as he waited for the quiz to begin, Mrs Mac with poor beleaguered Mr Mac, who rarely got to see his own wife such was her devotion to Willow's family, Joe pulling yet another pint with a slow hand and that contented smile on his lips he always had, standing behind his bar. Conn—

She froze as she saw Connor through the window. He was climbing out of his car, that innocuously beautiful E-type which had always been too perfect for here. She watched as he closed the car door behind him and then turned – immediately catching sight of her too, alone at the busy table. He always seemed to find her in a crowd.

Time paused, just for a beat, their eyes holding the moment as she tried not to outwardly react. It was a shock to see him here; she had assumed he had left already and she'd spent the past couple of days and nights in a new kind of mourning, trying to absorb the fact that it was finally finished between them – over before it had ever begun, the love affair that wasn't perpetually caught in a state of abeyance, something else always having to come first. What was it Ferdy had said to her – you can't mourn something you never had? But she had so nearly had him – fleeting touches, glimpses, tantalizing tastes . . . And it was a physical ache to let him go.

Slowly he raised his arm and she saw the giant set of keys dangle from his fingers – the castle keys – and she understood why he was here. *Now* he was leaving.

The knowledge felt like a fresh blade across her skin, drawing blood easily.

She looked away, feeling her chest constrict. 'I'm just going out to make a call,' she said to the others, her voice strange.

'Who are you calling?' Pip asked nosily.

But Willow was already walking across the floor, towards the door. She stepped out into the chill, his E-type looking so dark and shiny against the snow. It had started snowing again overnight and the farmers had been clearing the local roads with their tractors all day. She hoped they wouldn't go past, gritting, whilst Connor's car was still here.

'So everything's locked up,' he said stiffly, no preamble, holding out the castle keys.

There was something exaggerated in the gesture and as she held out her hand to take them from him, he glanced through the pub window – sixty faces immediately turned away. Of course they had an audience. Everyone knew who he was now: the guy who'd nearly knocked the Lornes from their perch.

'Thanks,' she murmured.

'You'll find it's been cleaned and everything that was brought in, removed.'

'Okay,' she said again, feeling a weight on her chest. It was hard to look at him, impossible not to.

'Basically, it's left as we found it – repairs notwithstanding.'

'Thanks. And I'll get all the money we owe over to you within the calendar month. With interest.' Ferdy had received the news of the Gainsborough's discovery with rapture; in a very short space of time she was going to be a rich woman.

'Fine.' He exhaled, as though that was all there was to say. 'Right then.'

Not sure what else to do, she held out her hand, her gaze meeting his dartingly, like a dragonfly skimming the surface of a pond. 'Thank you for everything . . . I'm sorry things . . . didn't work out the way we hoped,' she faltered. 'I wish it could have been different.'

'. . . Yeah.' He shook her hand, holding it for a fraction longer than necessary as he always did, never quite able to let go easily. 'Me too.'

Their eyes locked for the last time, both knowing there was nothing more to be said. He was going back to London and she was staying here. They were back in their own lives and even chemistry couldn't compete with the tide of events rushing against them.

His mouth parted and, for a moment, she felt sure he was going to say something else, something more – but then he turned and she watched as he walked over to the kerb.

She didn't think anything of it when she heard the pub door open behind her, nor did she at first clock the auburn streak flying past her. But she jumped to attention as she heard the words: 'Hey, fella!'

Connor turned to find Pip haring up behind him. She slipped on a bit of ice and almost slid straight into him. He caught her just in time.

'Hey!' she smiled, getting her balance back.

'Pip, what are you doing?' Willow demanded, feeling panic set in. Pip on 'a mission' was never a good thing.

'Hi, I'm Pip,' Pip said, ignoring her completely and holding her hand out.

Bewildered, Connor shook it. 'Hi, Pip.'

'You might not remember me but you hauled me out of a lake just a few weeks ago?'

A bemused smile hovered at the very corners of his mouth. 'I remember.'

'Good, I'm glad you remember that,' she panted, still not up to full strength after the pneumonia. 'Because the thing is, we have a problem.'

His eyes narrowed. 'We do?'

'Yes. Technically you saved me that night – although don't tell my boyfriend that; he likes to think he was the one saving my life in the ambulance and whatnot.' She waved her hands around her face. 'But you did it. You saved me, and that means I am obliged to save you back.'

Connor stared at her. 'Excuse me?'

'Yes,' she nodded solemnly. 'I'm afraid it's Chinese law.'

'It's a Chinese *proverb*, Pip,' Willow said desperately, not knowing where this was leading and not wanting to know either. 'Connor, I have no idea what she's—'

'Law. Proverb. Same difference. Either way, I'm indebted to you so if you could just kindly kiss my sister here, then I'll have saved your life back and we'll be even-stevens.'

Connor looked between Pip and her, as though Willow might have some sort of clue as to what she was going on about.

Willow felt her cheeks burn with indignation. 'Pip! What the actual hell . . . ?'

'Why would . . . kissing your sister save my life?' he asked, bewildered.

'Kiss her and find out,' Pip said firmly.

'Pip, no!' Willow said crossly. 'This is ridiculous. You're embarrassing me!'

'Wilhelmina—'

'Oh my God, *don't* call me that! Seriously? This isn't enough for you?' Willow groaned, turning away.

Behind her, she heard Connor give a low chuckle at their sisterly spat.

'Look, all I need is for him to kiss you so that I am released from this otherwise eternal bond of debt.'

'Oh my God! You are not held in some eternal bond of debt!' Willow cried, throwing her arms out in frustration.

Pip looked back at Connor. 'Would you tell her, please? She never listens to me.'

Connor was still for a long moment, his eyes flickering between the two of them as he struggled – and failed – to comprehend what was actually happening here. 'Well, actually – technically speaking, I think Pip is . . .' He walked forwards and took Willow by the wrist, pulling her slowly in to him. 'Yes, I think Pip's right. It is the law.' He looked over at Pip. 'It's the law?'

'Totally the law,' Pip nodded sombrely, sounding like a judge passing sentence.

Connor looked down at her, making her stomach flip. 'So then I'll just kiss you once,' he murmured, his gaze already on her lips. 'And then she'll have saved my life back and she'll be freed from . . .'

'The eternal bond of debt,' Pip supplied for him.

But neither one of them heard her, because his lips were already on hers, his arms gathering her close. And Willow felt the world swirl faster around her as he held her tight. She was straight back to that first night in his arms – before Pip had dived into a lake, before he'd driven up to her castle – back when it had just been the two of them, subject to the twin mercies of chemistry and fate.

He pulled back, looking down at her, both of them breathless with longing.

'See? You're not getting in that car now, are you?' Pip asked, her cheeky smile intruding on their private moment.

'No,' Connor said, not taking his eyes off Willow.

'Good. Because those icy roads are a death-trap in a rear-wheel drive like that. Boom! *Totally* just saved your life,' Pip chuckled. 'And by the way, Will, if you want to make a call, you need a thing called a phone?'

Willow felt the weight of her mobile being stuffed into her back jeans pocket and groaned as she realized she had left it on the table. Pip laughed, enjoying herself immensely, as she went back into the pub, earning herself a rousing cheer

Connor grinned. 'Interesting, your family.'

Willow laughed as he drew her back into him. 'You don't know the half of it!'

Epilogue

Christmas Day 2019

The fire crackled drowsily, spitting out occasional embers that curled and blackened on the old stone hearth, mere inches from the cold wet noses of Mabel and Dot snoozing in their prime spots on the rugs. The tray of breakfast Mrs Mac had left prepared was already demolished – her overnight porridge and Bircher muesli long gone, toast crumbs everywhere – and the four Lorne women were looking at the neat pile of presents beneath the tree with something approaching amazement. Had fairies been in in the night? No one had had much appetite for Christmas shopping this year; it had felt *de trop* against the backdrop of so much loss, and if the truckloads of Christie's lorries carting away their worldly goods had proved anything, it was that they didn't need any more 'stuff'. Still, someone had been a busy Christmas elf, because a pile of boxes skirted the base of the tree.

Willow could feel the memories beginning to accrue at the Dower House already, all three sisters sleeping in their new bedrooms last night – Connor had flown back to London on the last flight and Ben had stayed with Taigh, before they descended here for lunch later, both men understanding the Lorne women's needs for a quiet family affair. The Christmas tree itself had been 'rescued' from the garden, a small fir that had been growing slowly under the canopy of a beech and had been earmarked for chopping up as the garden was cleared to bring sunlight in. They had spent Christmas Eve decorating it using old silk ribbons found in the trousseau from the attic and some long ropes of their great-grandmother's 1920s pearls (their usual decorations currently sitting in a box in a Christie's warehouse somewhere). Pip had put her beloved old, tiny teddy Mr Bunts on the top of the tree – the best they could do for a fairy this year – and along the windowsills and ledges, they had lit all but one box of the tiny tea lights, which they always kept stocked from the village shop in case of power cuts. Someone – Pip – had even supplied Rusty with a purple paper crown.

The Gainsborough had temporary pride of place over the mantelpiece for the festive period. It would be boxed up and shipped off first thing in the New Year but they had all wanted to enjoy the portrait for a little while at least; and it had seemed only fitting that Black Bess – whose deviousness had brought them such luck – should finally have her moment in the spotlight, her fierce dark eyes watching over them imperiously as they sat curled up in the armchairs in their pyjamas. But in art as in life, her reign would be short-lived, for they had other hidden masterpieces that needed to be displayed now that – thanks to Ben – Ottie's dramatic canvases had been rescued from her hiding place, and she and their mother and Pip had all 'dibbed' their favourites.

'Who wants to go first?' their mother asked. But it was a rhetorical question.

'I will!' Pip said eagerly, scooting off her chair and reaching for the first present with her name on. 'Does it go glug?' she grinned as she brought the long narrow box to her ear and rattled it. The contents shook inside, rattling slightly. 'Hmm,' she said, sounding perplexed as she pulled on the ribbon and tore off the paper.

'What is it?' Ottie asked, just as curious, as Pip lifted the lid, her mouth dropping open.

She drew out a red leather bridle. 'Oh my God,' she whispered, her fingers pinching the padded cheek-pieces, brushing the cool brass hardware for the bit, tenderly plucking the intricate black stitching. She looked back at them all. 'Who . . . ?'

Willow looked at her mother and Ottie, for it certainly wasn't from her, but they looked just as blank as she did. 'Is there a card?' she asked.

Pip peered into the box, under the tissue paper, checked the wrapping. 'No. Nothing.' She looked back at the bridle. 'It's got a black star embroidered across the browband . . .' She looked back at them again in amazement. 'It's for Dark Star!'

Willow smiled. 'It must be from Taigh then. He knows where your heart *truly* lies.'

'Those three jobs of his must be paying well,' Ottie quipped, warming her hands around her mug of tea.

'I'll kill him,' Pip said softly, kissing the noseband. 'We agreed no presents this year. There was no time . . . Oh, I can't wait to put this on him.'

'Who? Taigh?' Ottie quipped, giving a little shrug. 'Well, if kinky's your thing—'

'Dark Star!' Pip protested, blushing furiously.

Their mother smiled at their teases. 'Ottie, why don't you open yours next?' she asked, handing over the box with her name on it.

'It's suspiciously light!' Ottie said, shaking it as her sister had done.

Everyone waited expectantly and very patiently – even Pip

– as she pulled off the ribbon and carefully rolled it up, before managing to open the paper without ripping it. Willow watched her face as she opened the box, seeing how her expression fell.

'It's an envelope.'

'Oh, I love envelopes!' Pip trilled, getting her own back, the bridle draped lovingly over one bent knee as she sat with her back against their mother's armchair and allowed her to absently play with her hair.

'It'll be tickets to New York, I bet,' Willow said. 'Ben can't get you there fast enough. Am I right?'

Ottie pulled out the tickets from the envelope. 'Yes and no.' She looked back at them all, astonished. 'He's taking me to Florence.'

'Oh, darling!' their mother laughed, clapping her hands together happily. 'You've always wanted to go there. The art capital of the world!'

'I can't believe it. We said no presents too.'

'Well, those boys have clearly been plotting behind your backs then,' Willow said, sipping her tea.

'So maybe behind yours too?' her mother asked, handing over the box with her name on it. But she and Connor had already given each other their gifts, yesterday afternoon before he'd left to catch his flight to London – from her, a diecast model of an E-type that Dave Nolan, the mechanic, had had sitting on a shelf in his garage for the past twenty years from a long-ago promotion; from him, a tiny bronze elephant he had picked up on a recent trip to India for his niece and which was still in his case. He had said she was to keep it in her room as a reminder of the attraction between them which they had tried to ignore – and would never deny again. She smiled at the memory of the kisses that had come with the gift; he would be flying back to Dublin to be with her and Caz and all their friends for New Year's Eve and already she was counting the hours.

She handled the present, intrigued. It felt weighty. Substantial. 'Heavy,' she murmured. 'Paperweight?'

'You'll need one of those with all the bills you've got coming your way,' Pip guffawed.

Willow shot her a 'ha-ha' grin but couldn't help chuckling as she pulled on the ribbon. As usual, Pip had a point. Her fledgling notion of setting up the castle as a luxury spa and yoga retreat was going to take vision, organization and a lot of cash. But Connor had contacts he was going to introduce her to and he had already, loosely, mooted the idea of Lorne becoming somehow 'affiliated' with the Home James group, perhaps as a partner venue . . . ?

She lifted the lid and pushed back the tissue paper. Inside was a frosted crystal sculpture of a bird, its feathers exquisitely rendered, even the downy plumage beautifully conveyed as the bird nestled its beak downwards, its eyes contentedly shut into slits.

'Is that Lalique?' her mother gasped, holding a hand out. Willow passed it over and watched as her mother examined it, a small frown puckering her brow. '. . . I could swear I've seen this before,' she murmured, turning it over. 'It's an antique . . .'

Her voice failed suddenly, but Willow already knew what she was going to say. Because, caught forever in a single moment, she realized that little bird was roosting. It was a little bird that had come home.

'It can't be,' Willow murmured, feeling her heart rate suddenly bolt as she reached for the wrapping paper by her knees and checked the handwriting on the gift tag. She looked up at her mother, both of them pale. '. . . Mrs Mac wrote these.'

'These pressies are from Mrs Mac?' Pip spluttered, still stroking her bridle, her bent knee doubling as a horse's head.

'No,' Willow whispered, feeling the tears press against the backs of her eyes. 'But she must have found them . . . They're from Dad.'

Silence erupted into the room, all of them looking at their gifts afresh: Pip's bridle – commissioned for the horse he'd been on the brink of buying for her; Ottie's flights to Florence – tickets back to the world she had forsaken for him; Willow, his little bird who had flown away, come home again.

'We saw this little thing at the Lapada Antiques Fair in London in September,' her mother murmured, cupping it in her hands, feeling the reassuring weight of it. 'He just loved it on sight; he kept coming back and back to it, even though I told him we didn't need another trinket . . . I had no idea he went and bought it.'

Pip and Ottie had their hands pressed over their mouths, silent tears beginning to fall as they felt his presence and his absence all at once.

'But Dad never bought us presents,' Ottie murmured eventually. 'It was always you, Mam.'

But it didn't need to be said: by September, their father had known he was a marked man – that any minute might be his last, that a ticking time-bomb in his head was waiting to go off.

'You're forgetting the time he was left in charge of Willow's fifth birthday and he got her a photo frame,' Pip said. 'Don't you remember?'

Their mother giggled at the memory, her teary eyes suddenly mixed with flushed cheeks. 'I do. I thought I'd never forgive him for that. He was abysmal at buying presents!'

'Well, he's redeemed himself this year,' Pip said, pressing the bridle to her cheeks, cherishing it even more than before; Willow fully expected her to slip it over her own head any moment and she wondered how pleased her father would have been to have learned that Bertie had been called to account at long, long last – sprawled on the floor in the kitchen, for Pip's silence he had readily agreed to simply give Dark Star to her; for Ottie's silence, he had agreed to accede to Shula's demands for an uncontested divorce; and for Willow's silence – and the secret only she and her mother now carried – he had agreed to make a significant donation to the Headway charity in memory of Declan Lorne by his youngest daughter. But he hadn't thought to negotiate Ben Gilmore's silence and in the Christmas period, as lawyers' offices were closed around the country, his lawsuit remained live, with rumblings of further claimants coming forward with other allegations of negligence. Ultra was fast becoming toxic.

'So then . . . what's he got you, Mam?' Willow asked, looking down at the last remaining present beneath the tree.

Pip reached over to pass it up to her and they all straightened up, waiting expectantly. She pulled on the ribbon and lifted out a flat blue Tiffany box. No one breathed as she slid off the lid and tearily stared down at her husband's final gift. His final words on a thirty-year marriage.

'Oh, Mam!' Ottie sighed, clambering out of her chair. 'I've never seen this photo of you and Dad before.'

Pip got up on her knees and walked around to the side of the armchair. It was a black and white image enlarged, her mother's head thrown back in laughter at something, her father standing just behind her and gazing on with a look of rapt adoration.

It took her mother a moment to place it. 'That was taken the night I met your father – at Archie O'Malley's twenty-first birthday.' She squinted, smiling, falling back into the memories. 'I think we had this on a slide somewhere. He must have had it printed up.'

'Can't be many places left with the technology for doing that, can there?' Ottie asked.

'What does it say at the bottom?' Pip murmured, turning her head at an awkward angle to get a better look. '. . . Eternally.'

He would love her eternally.

Her mother's gaze rose to meet Willow's, neither of them having to say a thing. Because in that promise, nestled another one: that she was forgiven. He had died loving her as fiercely on his last day as he so clearly had on their first. The last knight in Ireland may be dead. But his legacy was his love.

And that was enough.

Acknowledgements

This story is set in a fictitious village in south-west Ireland but the original idea for it came from reading a magazine article about a mother and her grown-up daughters trying to make their ancestral seat a going concern. There are many castles in Ireland so it wasn't that which particularly caught my attention, but the single line referring to the woman's late husband as having been the last surviving knight in Ireland. My mother is from Cork and I knew we were – incredibly distantly – related to an ancient king of Munster, but I hadn't realized the Irish peerage had continued into modern times. It made me think though – what must it be like to know you are the last of a line? The break in a chain? And what does that pressure do to a family? How do you take those first steps forward when a seven-hundred-year-old legacy has been suddenly stopped and life needs to start again?

This was not an easy book to write – that's just how it goes sometimes – and I really must thank my agent Amanda Preston, and the entire team at Pan for not completely freaking out when the first draft was submitted. I was freaking out, but they kept calm and carried on, devising beautiful marketing and advertising campaigns, getting the books onto all the most important bookshelves and making sure those who needed to know about it, knew about it.

There's a big team behind every one of these stories and I'm so hugely grateful to everyone involved in the journey, but I'd like to make special mention of a few people in particular: Louise Davies, my editor on this book. She really held her nerve when this story was just a collection of bones and calmly helped me flesh it out and shape it; I really needed that clear-sightedness, so thank you! Also Natalie Young, my desk editor, for her patience and for coping with my abysmal handwritten notes on the page proofs. And to Mel Four for conjuring that most beautiful cover! It was actually so strong I felt under pressure to deliver a story that could live up to the promise of that image, but I hope I've delivered and that you, my lovely readers, feel all the girls end up with their differing Red Dress lives by the end. I hope we all get that!